Romantic Suspense

Danger. Passion. Drama.

Tracing A Killer
Sharon Dunn

Montana Hidden Deception
Amity Steffen

MILLS & BOON

Sharon Dunn is acknowledged as the author of this work
TRACING A KILLER
© 2024 by Harlequin Enterprises ULC
Philippine Copyright 2024
Australian Copyright 2024
New Zealand Copyright 2024

First Published 2024
First Australian Paperback Edition 2024
ISBN 978 1 038 92173 4

MONTANA HIDDEN DECEPTION
© 2024 by Amity Steffen
Philippine Copyright 2024
Australian Copyright 2024
New Zealand Copyright 2024

First Published 2024
First Australian Paperback Edition 2024
ISBN 978 1 038 92173 4

MIX
Paper | Supporting
responsible forestry
FSC® C001695

Published by
Harlequin Mills & Boon
An imprint of Harlequin Enterprises (Australia) Pty Limited
(ABN 47 001 180 918), a subsidiary of HarperCollins
Publishers Australia Pty Limited
(ABN 36 009 913 517)
Level 19, 201 Elizabeth Street
SYDNEY NSW 2000 AUSTRALIA

Cover art used by arrangement with Harlequin Books S.A.. All rights reserved.

Printed and bound in Australia by McPherson's Printing Group

Tracing A Killer
Sharon Dunn

MILLS & BOON

Ever since she found the Nancy Drew books with the pink covers in the country school library, **Sharon Dunn** has loved mystery and suspense. In 2014, she lost her beloved husband of nearly twenty-seven years to cancer. She has three grown children. When she is not writing, she enjoys reading, sewing and walks. She loves to hear from readers. You can contact her via her website at www.sharondunnbooks.net.

Behold, I will do a new thing; now it shall
spring forth; shall ye not know it? I will even make a
way in the wilderness, and rivers in the desert.
—*Isaiah* 43:19

DEDICATION

For my beloved dog, Bart the nervous border collie,
who was my best friend for over thirteen years.
I'm so glad you were a part of my life.
I miss you every day.

Chapter One

From the moment she turned onto the causeway that led to the island where Antelope State Park was, a feeling of unease settled around Utah highway-patrol officer Hannah Scott. As if sensing the drop in mood, her K-9, a male Newfoundland named Captain, groaned from the back seat of the patrol car.

This anxiety wasn't about the job she'd come here to do as a member of the Mountain Country K-9 team. This was about the past, the tragedy that had happened when she was ten. Her stomach clenched as flat land, straight road and expansive sky stretched before her. Images of the mountains and trees were reflected in the lake on either side of the seven-mile causeway. Such beautiful scenery normally would have created a feeling of serenity in her.

Instead, she was having a hard time shaking the sense of dread.

The sun was low on the horizon. She'd already put in a full day with the highway patrol.

She gripped the steering wheel tighter and spoke out loud. "Come on, Hannah, focus on the assignment that brought you back here."

Captain let out a muted yip of support.

Saying a silent prayer that God would help her do the job she'd been given with the Mountain Country K-9 unit, she concentrated on her driving. The task force had been formed with members of law enforcement from across the Rocky Mountain states to catch a serial killer, dubbed the Rocky Mountain Killer. Ten years ago, three young men under the age of twenty, all members of the now disbanded Young Rancher's Club, had been killed in Elk Valley, Wyoming, on Valentine's Day.

The case had gone cold until recently. Three new victims, all from Elk Valley but now living in other states, had been murdered with the same MO—shot at close range in a barn. The new shootings had started on Valentine's Day, less than seven months ago. The murder weapon had never been found, but matching 9mm slugs had been located at all the crime scenes. The task force had narrowed down the suspects to two men who had motive. Ryan

York's sister Shelly had committed suicide after being dumped by Seth Jenkins, one of the initial victims. It could be that Ryan saw Seth's friends as equally culpable. Because of the young men's reputations for using women and dumping them, Ryan's desire to right an injustice had spilled over to targeting other members of the club. Ryan owned a Glock 17, which could have been used in the shootings.

The second suspect was Evan Carr. His sister, Naomi, who had recently married one of the K-9 team members, had been the butt of a cruel joke ten years ago. When one of the members of the YRC, Trevor Gage, had asked her to a formal dance the club sponsored, Trevor's friends had ridiculed her saying she'd been invited as a prank. In interviews, Trevor had sworn that he actually had liked Naomi and hadn't intended it as a joke.

Hannah had read the transcript of the interviews the team had done with Trevor. She had no idea if he was telling the truth or not. Ten years ago, the members of the club were known for being troublemakers and having a love-'em-and-leave-'em reputation with the young women in Elk Valley. Why should

Trevor be any different than the young men he'd run with?

She'd met her share of that type of guy. Her sympathy was with Naomi. In high school, a boy had invited Hannah to a dance, but he'd never shown up. The utter humiliation of having taken the time to get dressed up only to stand alone in a corner of the gym still hurt after all these years. The memory of the group of boys who sneered and pointed at her from across the dance floor was seared into her psyche. She'd been hurt by men in other deeper ways including being cheated on.

Her assignment seemed straightforward—convince Trevor, who now lived in Salt Lake City, to agree to go into a safe house since he was the most likely next victim. As if to confirm the team's suspicions, the Rocky Mountain Killer—or the RMK—a tall man with blond hair, had been spotted in Salt Lake recently. Most of the team were in Salt Lake, including the task-force leader, Chase Rawlston.

Trevor appeared to be working against his own self-preservation, though. He'd left his home in Salt Lake for a remote campsite on the island, causing him to be even more exposed. Members of the team had tried via phone to talk him into going into a safe house until he stopped answering their calls. Now, it was up to her to try some face-to-face persuasion.

She clenched her teeth. Men could be so obstinate about accepting help sometimes.

She shook her head. Some people were just hard to understand. She had Trevor's dossier with her. Transcripts of the interviews the team had done, background information and a photograph. Intense green eyes framed by blond hair peeking out from beneath a silver Stetson seemed to look right at her from the picture. Trevor was handsome, she would admit, but the story of his meanness to Naomi lingered in her mind. Knowing how men were, she didn't believe that he had really liked Naomi, and she doubted he'd changed. Once a scoundrel always a scoundrel. Wasn't that what her own dating history had taught her? After so much pain, she'd given up on the possibility of finding love. Better to focus on her job and being the best auntie she could be to her nephew and niece.

As the miles clipped by, a new feeling invaded her awareness. The fluttering heart and shallow breathing indicated fear. Glancing off to the side where the Great Salt Lake was, she found herself struggling to take a deep breath.

There was a reason she'd not come back to the island for eighteen years, though she lived less than an hour away. Only work and wanting to prove herself to the rest of the team had compelled her to overcome the mental barriers that had kept her away. The island was where her best friend, Jodie, had been murdered, drowned in the lake, when Hannah was ten years old.

Her mind fogged, and her heartbeat thrummed in her ears. As if she was wearing headphones, all outside sound was muffled. She felt lightheaded as the sensation of floating overtook her.

She passed through the park entrance showing her badge to the woman in the kiosk.

Almost involuntarily, she found herself taking the turnoff that led to the remote stretch of beach where the murder had occurred. As the tires rolled over gravel, unclear images flashed at the corners of her mind. The memory of the sound of waves lapping on the shore made her breath catch. She was back at the place that had marked her life in a way that she could not overcome even after all these years. Only her sense of professionalism had eclipsed her fear about the past and the memories she'd locked into a dark closet. Maybe this was God telling her she needed to confront the event that had defined her life for so long.

Hannah pushed open the door and then let Captain out. He looked up at her with his teddy-bear face. She reached out to stroke his squarish, furry head. As always, it was a comfort to have her partner close. She was sure she saw empathy in his brown eyes. There was a reason the dogs in this breed were called gentle giants.

A chill September wind whipped around her when she made her way past a rocky outcropping and onto the white sand beach. As always, the lake had a faint rotten-egg smell. While she stood on the shore, she heard a boat in the distance.

For years she hadn't wanted to think about what had happened here. Only fragments of memory punctuated by black spots came into her mind. She wondered, too, if she had just adopted the newspaper accounts as her own memories because guilt and trauma made it impossible to recall the tragedy in any detail.

Jodie had gone out for a swim while Hannah had chosen to stay on shore to look for pretty rocks. Though she could remember the moments before the murder, she could not quite bring anything else into focus. The police told her that she must have seen the man who had drowned her friend. Yes, she had noticed a man approaching the beach, but she could not remember his face or what he was wearing. Had she turned away before he'd gotten close or was her mind blocking it out?

She shuddered as she walked closer to the water, shielding her eyes from the setting sun. Wind rippled her uniform. The boat that she'd heard earlier came into view, a small motorized craft with only one man in it.

Turning her attention back to the shore, she thought about the years of therapy to try to get past the tragedy and yet, it still held her prisoner. She'd even chosen to have a K-9 whose specialty was water rescue, thinking that she could prevent another child from suffering Jodie's fate.

Captain licked her hand, bringing her back to reality.

Time to get back to work. Convincing Trevor Gage he needed to accept the unit's offer of protection would be a challenge.

The man in the boat pulled it up on the beach and got out. He was far enough away that she could not see his face, but she recognized the park service uniform. He pulled a trash bag and poker stick from the boat and stabbed at a wrapper as he worked his way up the shore toward her.

Hannah turned sideways and watched the man when he leaned over to pick up a soda can. His baseball hat with the park logo on it partially shielded his face from view.

Why was her heart beating so fast?

The man kept working his way up the shore while she remained frozen in place. As he drew closer, he lifted his head and made eye contact.

A wave of terror engulfed her. She knew this man. The curly brown hair and close-set eyes. No, it couldn't be. Was this the man who had killed her friend? Her heart pounded when the long-buried image of a face escaped the cage she'd locked it in.

She took a step back. Maybe she was mistaken. It had been eighteen years. What were the chances he would come back to this spot? She shook her head as her heart raged against her rib cage.

The man continued to work his way up the shore. She couldn't look away. Was her mind playing tricks on her?

He must have sensed her staring. Now only

fifteen feet from her, he looked right at her. His eyes grew wide.

As if to confirm her suspicions, a sort of brightness, like a light switch being thrown, came across the man's features.

Her stomach twisted.

He recognized her.

Even after all these years, Hannah's distinctive red hair would make her memorable.

The man tossed his bag and stick and darted toward her. With Captain close at her heels, Hannah turned to sprint back to her car, where she'd left her gun belt. The man closed in on her. She stumbled on the rocks, scraping her arm. Pain shot through her.

He grabbed the back of her jacket and yanked hard. The collar of her uniform dug into her neck.

Captain barked and leaped around them as they struggled.

Before she could cry out a command to her K-9, the man wrapped his arm around her neck and dragged her backward. The tight grip of his elbow cut off her breathing. Black dots filled her vision as she felt herself being dragged across the sand toward the water.

She tried to twist her body to break free. The

man's other hand suctioned around her stomach. Hannah fought to remain conscious as it became harder to breath. Her vision was reduced to a pinhole. She managed to kick her assailant's shins. The move caused him to loosen his grip around her waist. Grabbing his forearm to pry it loose, she angled her body and twisted free. The momentum of her move propelled her forward, where she fell to the ground on all fours.

Captain's frantic barking pummeled her eardrums, as did the waves crashing against the shoreline. They were so close to the water's edge.

She pushed herself to her feet and turned to disable her attacker, landing a blow to his stomach. He groaned in response. A fist collided with the side of her head, disorienting her. He grabbed her hair, which had worked free of the bun she kept it in.

Water soaked through her shoes as he dragged her deeper into the lake. His hat had fallen off. She saw his face—just the flash of an image but crystal clear. The arched eyebrows and redness of his skin. His features were contorted into an expression of rage.

She clutched at his shirt. He pushed her into the water and was on top of her before she could react. As she flailed, his hand was full on her face, forcing her under.

Dear God, no, this can't be happening.

After all these years, she knew what Jodie's killer looked like, but she would not live to see justice.

The water enveloped her as she fought to stay conscious.

The noise of a barking dog caused Trevor Gage to draw his attention to the shore. Diverting from the trail where he'd been walking, he ran toward the lake. A large black wooly-looking dog paced the shore. He narrowed his eyes, trying to discern what he was seeing. The setting sun hitting the water made images murky. He saw the back of a man in a park employee uniform as he bent over in the waist-deep water. What had the dog so upset?

He drew closer, running past a patrol car with the Mountain Country K-9 insignia on it. He'd had more than one encounter with that multistate task force since the recent murders of men he had known when he lived in Elk Valley, Wyoming. The Mountain Country K-9 task force believed that he was the next target for the serial killer and that he should accept the unit's offer of a safe house. The loss of three of his friends ten years ago had been hard enough and now, it was starting all over again with three new victims.

The man in the water angled sideways.

Trevor's heart pounded when he saw a woman's head bob to the surface and then the man turned and pushed her under again. The woman thrashed in the water, her arms and legs flailing while the man held her down. The buoyancy of the salt water probably required extra effort to keep her head under, but she was still being drowned.

Still some distance away, Trevor broke into a run as he shouted, "Hey, you. Stop."

The man's head shot up. He glanced in Trevor's direction and then rushed toward a nearby boat, jumped in and yanked the rip cord. As the boat lurched forward, the man reached out and grabbed the floating woman, dragging her into deeper water.

Trevor slowed when he reached the rocky shore as terror surged through him. He hurried as fast as he could. His feet sank into the sandy beach, but he kept running.

It looked as though the woman had raised her head and shouted something.

The dog lunged into the water and swam toward the boat. The man in the uniform tried to push the woman back under from his position in the boat. As the dog drew closer, he let go of the woman and sped away.

The dog reached the woman and grabbed hold of her collar, then pulled her toward shallower water. Trevor ran into the lake up to his knees. Still holding the woman by her collar, the dog swam with a ferocious energy toward the shore.

The woman said something to the dog, who let go of her. She stood up in the waist-deep water, blinking and shaking her head.

Trevor stepped toward her through the water. "Are you all right?" he shouted. It seemed a ridiculous question to ask considering he had just witnessed an attempted drowning. The man in the park uniform was now a tiny dot in the distance. The engine noise had become a low-level hum almost drowned out by the waves hitting the shore. The culprit was long gone.

The redheaded woman caught sight of Trevor. Water dripped off her face and long hair. Her hand reached out for the back of the dog as they pushed through the water and got closer to him. Her slack jaw and wide unfocused eyes told him she was in shock. She shook her head in disbelief.

He hurried toward her.

When she drew close, he reached out and guided her to the shore, putting an arm across her back. "I gotcha." The dog followed dutifully beside her. Still supporting her, Trevor led her across the sand and up the rocky shore. She was dressed in a uniform with the MCK9 logo on the pocket and back of her gray jacket. The car he'd run past must be hers. No doubt, she had come here looking for him.

She gripped his arm. "I just need a moment." She sat down and stared at the ground. There was a cut on her arm.

"You're hurt. Can I look in your car for a first aid kit?"

She nodded without looking up.

He searched the car, finding a first aid kit under the front seat and a blanket. When he returned, the dog shook the water off his substantial fur coat far enough away not to spray her and then settled down beside the woman. Trevor wrapped the blanket around her, squeezing her shoulders before sitting beside her.

He flipped open the first aid kit. "Give me your arm. It's scraped up."

She twisted her arm toward her face. Her forehead furrowed as she examined the injury. "I fell on the rocks when he chased me." Her voice sounded faraway and disconnected. She was still in shock.

Cupping his hand under hers, he squeezed out some disinfectant from a tube, then placed a bandage over the cut and patted her forearm gently. "Better?"

Hannah drew the arm closer to her body, holding it at the wrist. "Thank you."

She stared at the ground. "I should call this in and make sure a report is filed. I need to catch the man who attacked me."

He wondered about the use of the word *I*, as if it was her sole responsibility to arrest the man who had tried to kill her.

"What happened out there? It looked like that guy was trying to drown you."

She nodded her head. "Yes, he was." She folded her arms over her chest and rocked. Her eyes glazed over.

"Who was he?"

"It's a long story." She lifted her head and stared off into the distance. Her response indicated it was not a story she was ready to share.

The dog pressed closer to her, making a sympathetic noise.

She clearly needed more time to recover from such a traumatic event. "Maybe you should take a second to catch your breath," he said.

She ran trembling fingers through her wet hair and let out a heavy breath. "First, I need to call this in." She rose to her feet. "I'm going to radio the park police. Maybe they can catch him. He works for the park. They might even know who he is."

With the dog trailing behind her, she walked to her vehicle. She opened the driver's side door, leaned in and retrieved the radio.

Trevor followed her. He listened as she gave the details of the attack, the kind of boat the man was in and what he looked like.

She put the radio back then looked directly at him for the first time. Light came into her eyes as recognition spread across her face. "You're Trevor Gage."

He nodded and then pointed toward the patrol vehicle. "I'm assuming you're here to talk me into going into a safe house since the phone calls didn't work." His tone was more defensive than he'd expected. The truth was the guilt he felt over his friends dying ten years ago—and all over again more recently—had never left him.

From the phone interviews he'd had with members of the unit, he knew they suspected that the murders might be connected to an incident he had been a part of ten years ago. All the victims, the first three and now three more recent ones, had been members of the Young Rancher's Club in Elk Valley. Trevor had asked a girl to a formal dance the club put on. He had really liked Naomi, but his friends had told her that she'd been invited as a joke. Maybe if he had been more forthright in coming to her defense none of the murders would have happened.

She crossed her arms. "I'm supposed to be protecting you, not the other way around."

"I'm just glad I showed up when I did," he said. "If I hadn't heard your dog barking, I wouldn't have known something was amiss."

The woman brushed her fingers over the dog's head. "We look out for each other."

The dog licked her hand.

"What's his name?"

"Captain." She held her hand out to him. "And I'm Officer Hannah Scott."

Hannah's grip was firm. The softness of her

skin sent an electric pulse up his arm. Her hair must have been in a bun at some point, as part of it was secured and hanging off to the side. Even in her bedraggled state, she was a striking woman. Perhaps it was the green eyes. "You didn't call and say you were coming?"

"You stopped answering our calls. Besides, I thought you would be more likely to agree to be taken in if you didn't have time to think about it."

He pressed is teeth together. "So that's the new tactic. An ambush from the Mountain Country K-9 team. I already said I could take care of myself."

"We're only trying to protect you, Trevor." Her words took on a biting quality that matched his tone of voice.

He shook his head but restrained himself from saying anything more.

He stared off toward the lake. He wasn't going to a safe house. Hadn't he made that clear?

When he turned in her direction, he noticed that her hand still trembled a little when she brought it up to her neck. Was she still upset from the attack or was this about his refusal to cooperate with her plans for him?

She was clearly shaken. He couldn't just leave her here.

"Why don't we drive back to my RV so you and I can get dried off? You can have a moment to catch your breath."

She turned in his direction. "Did you walk here?"

"Yes, I was out trying to clear my head." The truth was, he had been thinking about the RMK and what he could do to catch him. Trevor could handle himself, and he'd grown up shooting guns. Coming to the island had been partly to get away from the busyness of Salt Lake, but he wondered if his being in the open would draw out the killer and end this whole nightmare. From the questions he was asked in interviews, he'd deduced who the main suspects were. Even if the RMK was Ryan York and not Naomi Carr's brother, Evan, Trevor felt a responsibility for the killings. If he had called out the other young men on their behavior all those years ago, even if he'd never acted that way toward a young woman, maybe no one would be dead. "What do you say? Do you want to go back to the RV to get dried off?"

She glanced down at her soaked uniform. "I

guess that's what we should do. Plus, you really shouldn't be out in the open by yourself."

After Hannah loaded her dog in the back of the vehicle, she got behind the wheel. He directed her to where his campsite was.

They drove past a herd of buffalo. The island was famous for its wildlife, including the antelope it was named for, as well as bighorn sheep, foxes and an abundance of birds. The land around them was flat but mountains were visible in the distance. When he glanced through the back window, the silvery lake had just slipped out of view.

"So that guy who came after you. Do you know who he was, or was it a random attack?"

She shook her head and stared through the windshield. "It's a long story." Her voice had taken on that flat disconnected quality again.

He longed to know the reason behind such a violent attack, but it was clear she wasn't ready to share. If the attempted murder was for personal reasons and hadn't been random, he wondered if the guy would come after Hannah again. Probably, if he wasn't caught soon.

The prediction the MCK9 unit had made was that he would be the RMK's next victim and that had been the plan from the beginning. That meant that both he and Hannah had targets on their backs.

Chapter Two

Hannah tried to quell her irritation at herself as she drove toward where Trevor had indicated.

Things had really gotten off on the wrong foot. How was she going to convince him that it was in his best interest for the team to protect him when his first impression of her was that she couldn't even keep herself from being attacked?

Her clothes, still wet from the lake, felt like they weighed an extra ten pounds. Her skin itched from the saltiness of the water.

Hannah looked over at Trevor just as he leaned toward her and pointed. Their heads nearly banged into each other. His soft hair brushed her cheek. She sat up straighter as her heart fluttered at his proximity.

The photo in his file really didn't do him justice. The shaggy blond hair and clear green eyes made him a very handsome man.

"Oh, sorry," he said, settling back into his seat rubbing his head. "I was just going to point out that the RV is just around that bend behind that blue camper."

"Got it." Her mind reeled with everything that had happened. If she was going to do her job, she knew she had to put the attack on the back burner. Maybe the park police would catch the man who had tried to drown her—the man who had probably killed Jodie. The thought caused a chill to run down her spine.

"You okay?"

"Yes, fine." She wasn't sure what to think about Trevor. He'd shown a great deal of courage and compassion in rescuing her.

The RV, along with other tents and campers, came into view. The campsites were fairly far apart. The sky had turned a soft shade of pink as the sun hung low in the sky.

"Breathtaking view, isn't it?"

She nodded.

"It's worth it to come out here just for the sunsets." His voice filled with appreciation as he leaned closer to the windshield. "The night sky is something else, too, with so little artificial light to obstruct the view."

"Yes, I know. My family used to come out

here all the time," she said. "I just don't think it's a good time for you to take a vacation. You're in more danger by being out here alone."

"Of course, I'm aware of the threat on my life. I've had several phone calls with your boss...what's his name? Chase Rawlston." A defensive tone had invaded his words. "I'm also a grown man who can make his own decisions."

She let out a breath and glanced at the roof of the car. Tension settled around her like a lead blanket. As if things could not get worse. Out of the frying pan and into the fire. How was she going to get this whole mission back on track?

Convincing Trevor to accept protection was her first big assignment with the Mountain Country team. Although she'd done some training and helped out in Elk Valley last month, including interviewing Evan's ex-girlfriend, Paulina Potter, she still felt like she needed to prove herself.

Hannah pulled up to the RV, where a blue truck was parked. The logo for Trevor's ranch consulting business was on the driver's-side door.

Both of them stared out their side windows for a long moment.

"Look, I appreciate what you and your team are trying to do," said Trevor.

How could he be so obstinate? She met his gaze. Afraid of saying the wrong thing, she simply nodded. She worried that her coming out to convince him in person had set things back rather than moved them forward. She grabbed her gunbelt and pushed open the door. Once they both got out of the patrol car, she opened the back door and spoke to Captain. "Dismount." The dog lunged to the ground with an easy agility.

Trevor reached into his pocket and withdrew a key. He stared off into the distance. "I still can't get over that sunset." His voice softened.

She was drawn to a man who could appreciate sunsets and night skies. "How can you get any work done out here?"

"Most of my ranch consulting work is remote right now. I wouldn't want to put any of my clients in danger." He swung open the door and gestured that she could go ahead of him up the two metal stairs. Captain trailed behind her.

The inside of the RV, which looked to be over thirty feet long, was quite spacious, with a table, seating area and kitchen. He pointed toward a pocket door. "Bathroom is back that way. I'm sure you want to wash the saltwater off."

His comment made her itch her forearm. The lake had a higher salt content than the ocean.

"I can loan you one of my shirts and sweats while I get your uniform washed up."

"You have a washer and dryer in here?"

"No, not quite enough space for that. The campground has a community room with washers and dryers."

He opened the pocket door, revealing a queen-size bed and a door off to the side. He pulled out some clothes for her in the drawers beneath the bed. "The bathroom is behind that door."

She showered and changed quickly. When she stepped out into the main living area, Captain was sitting at Trevor's feet. The dog thumped his tail when he saw her.

She handed Trevor her wet clothes. He excused himself and headed out the door. Hannah took a seat at the table, where she could see him through the window as he walked with an easy gait toward a concrete building painted white.

Once he went inside the building, she stared around the small space. The signature silver Stetson he wore in the photo she'd seen rested on a hook. She rose to examine the books on a short shelf above the couch. A lot could be revealed about a person by what he read. And she was curious about who Trevor Gage was beyond what the file had told her.

There were several paperback westerns, a guidebook for Antelope Island, a book about prayer and one about apologetics that she'd read.

Trevor cleared his throat. She hadn't realized he was standing on the threshold of the RV.

Heat rose up in her cheeks. "Sorry, you caught me snooping."

Shrugging his shoulders, he took a step inside the RV. "I do the same thing when I'm at someone's house. You can learn a lot about a person by the books on their shelf."

"Exactly." She was a little stunned to hear her thoughts coming out of his mouth.

"And what would I find on your shelf if I got a chance to look?"

She liked that he was curious about who she was as a person. She pointed to his book on apologetics. "This. Some mysteries, a book about watercolor painting for beginners." She wanted to tell him that there was a whole section on her bookshelf about how repressed memories and recovery from trauma worked, but she held back that information, knowing that she didn't want to fall apart in front of him. She had been enough of a hot mess after the attack. If she was going to achieve her mission, she needed to repair the impression he had of her as a law-enforcement professional.

But the look in his dancing green eyes was so inviting, she wanted to share more.

He raised an eyebrow. "Watercolor painting?"

"I dabble. I'd like to take some classes someday."

He nodded and then stepped toward the kitchen counter. "Gonna be a while before your uniform is washed and dried. Can I get you something to drink, a soda or flavored water?"

"Water would be nice." She took a seat at the table.

He opened the tiny fridge, pulled out a plastic bottle and set in front of her. He grabbed a soda for himself and sat opposite her.

She took a sip of water and glanced out the window at the now dark sky. Was the man in the park uniform still out there searching for her? The thought made her shudder.

She'd come to visit Trevor with a goal in mind, but what could she say that wouldn't cause him to become defensive? It seemed he'd dug in his heels.

Trevor traced the water stain his soda can made on the table as a tense silence enveloped them.

Captain huffed and whined.

Her sentiments exactly. Her partner's verbal response captured the level of frustration she felt.

She was at an impasse as to what her next move should be. "You know, I think I better call my boss on the task force and let him know what happened."

"You can go in the other room if you want some privacy."

She moved to the end of the RV and closed the pocket door behind her before she dialed Chase Rawlston's number.

Chase picked up after two rings. "Hannah, good to hear from you. Any progress on getting Trevor Gage to take up our offer of a safe house?"

"Not really, and things have just gotten more complicated." After a deep breath, she relayed to him about being attacked and nearly drowning, explaining that she was pretty sure it was the same man who had killed her friend all those years ago.

"That sounds like a lot to go through. Are you okay?"

She sucked in a breath through her teeth. "I have to be okay, right? I have a job to do."

Chase did not answer right away. When he did, his response was slow and measured. "Do you think this man will come after you again?"

Her throat constricted and she squeezed the phone. "Yes. I think the only thing that protected me all these years is that I couldn't identify him. This is my first time back to the island since Jodie died. Seeing him and being on the island must have jarred the memory I had repressed because of the trauma."

"Sounds like you could use some protection yourself," he said.

"I need to see this thing to the end. I want this guy in prison for what he did to my friend. If I'm out in the open, he's more likely to make an appearance, and I'll be ready for him next time."

"All the same, the team will offer you some protection."

She didn't want to be the one who needed protecting. She wanted Chase to see she could do her job. "Trevor has some distrust toward the task force. I'm not sure why. I would like a little time alone to convince him to go into a safe house."

"Okay, you have a night. In the morning, part of the team will come over there to provide both you and Trevor with some protection."

"I appreciate that. There is a chance the RMK could follow Trevor here."

"The last sighting was in Salt Lake. We will assume he's still here until more evidence comes in. That's why some of the team will stay here." He paused. "Hannah, are you sure you don't want to take a sabbatical from the task force and the RMK case until the guy who came after you is brought in?"

She closed her eyes and pressed her lips together. This was the question she'd dreaded. Being part of the Mountain Country Task Force was a real feather in her cap, but not if she was sidelined. Plus, she had grown fond of the other members of the team and their K-9 partners. "I'm the only one based out of Salt Lake, so I think I should be the one to handle this. Besides, Trevor saw the guy, too. I think we can help each other." If Trevor would accept the help.

"If the guy is a park employee, it shouldn't take that long to track him down."

"That's what I was thinking. The park police already have a description of him. This could be over quickly for me, and I would hate to miss out on helping the team bring in the RMK."

"Maybe I can help persuade Trevor. Can you put him on speaker?"

"Sure." She pushed open the pocket door. Trevor was holding his soda and staring out the window. With the phone in her hand, she stretched out her arm after pushing the speaker button. "My boss wants to talk to you."

Trevor stepped toward her. The *W* that formed between his eyebrows and his narrowed eyes suggested he wasn't happy about being put on the spot to talk to Chase.

Choosing to ignore the shift in mood, she spoke into the phone. "He's here."

Trevor moved closer to the phone.

"Trevor, you understand the risk you're taking by choosing to remain out in the open." Chase adopted a neutral tone of voice.

"Yes, it's my decision," he said.

"I wonder if you would be open to accepting Officer Scott's protection at least for tonight."

"You mean like she's my bodyguard." He locked her into his gaze as his mouth formed a tight line, communicating disapproval. "I'll think about it."

Her heart sank. He wasn't showing much confidence in her abilities.

"Do that," said Chase. "Some of the team will be coming over there tomorrow early. We'll talk some more." He said goodbye to Hannah and disconnected.

They stood only a foot apart. Her eyes searched his. "Why are you doing this, Trevor? Putting yourself in danger? You're not a trained law-enforcement officer."

He turned away, running his hands through his blond hair, then massaging the back of his neck. "What happened ten years ago wrecked me. Yes, my friends were immature, but why didn't I speak up with more force before it got out of hand?" His voice faltered. "And now, it's happening again, the murders of people I cared about. All because of me."

"We don't know for sure if it was because of the incident at the dance. All we know is that members of the YRC are being targeted. There are two suspects who have reason for going after the men who were in that club." Though they had interviewed Evan Carr early on, both he and Ryan York had fallen off the radar and been impossible to contact, making them both look suspicious. Plus, when she and Chase had interviewed Evan's ex, she'd finally confessed that she had lied about Evan being with her at the time of the murders. There was an unaccounted-for hour when he would have had time to shoot the first three victims.

"No matter who the killer is," Trevor said, "this is about the caliber of bad behavior that the members of the club fostered. I should have said something about the way they were treating women. I should've stopped it. I have to do something to make this right." His face contorted with anguish. He retreated to the table, where he'd left his soda. He took a long swig, then crushed the can in his hand and tossed it in a tiny trash can.

"I can appreciate how you feel." The emotion in his voice tore through her and caused a tightening in her own stomach. "You should let law enforcement take care of this though."

He turned to face her, shaking his head. "Really, it doesn't matter if it was about the dance or not. Yes, many of my friends in the club were immature, but that doesn't excuse their behavior. I wasn't a Christian back then. But common decency should have made me call the guys out on some of the things they chose to do."

"You can't undo the past." No one knew that better than she did.

"I get that. I thought I had forgiven myself for the self-absorbed way I was back then. But these new murders made me realize there is a whole other layer I have to deal with."

"Self-forgiveness is hard." She knew she was speaking about herself as much as him. She felt a level of responsibility for Jodie's death. Why hadn't she stayed closer to her friend?

"Tell me about it," he said.

She realized they were both choosing to make themselves bait for a killer to see that justice was done. "I think I understand. We have more in common than you realize."

What are you talking about?"

Taking breaths between phrases to calm her nerves, she relayed to him what had happened to Jodie all those years ago.

Trevor remained attentive and silent while she told the whole story of how her best friend had died. When her voice faltered or she choked up, she found warmth and caring in his eyes. "All these years I keep thinking that I could have prevented her death, or at least been more helpful in catching the killer."

"You were just a kid," he said. He rested his hand on her forearm. "That's a lot for a ten-year-old to deal with." His fingers warmed her skin as his voice filled with compassion.

His response to her story had been so gentle, she found her attitude toward him softening. She finished with a final comment. "I think that man we both saw is the one who killed Jodie. Why else would he attack me?"

He nodded. "That means you have a whole new set of complications to deal with. It's a lot for anyone to handle."

Though she was drawn to his kindness and the intense warmth she saw in his eyes, she caught herself, pulling back her head. She reminded herself that she was here to do a job. He already didn't think she was competent enough to protect him. Had opening up to him been a mistake? Best to keep this on a professional level.

He excused himself, saying that he would put her uniform in the dryer.

He returned a few minutes later. "Look, are you hungry? You might as well eat something while you wait for your clothes to dry." His voice had taken on a businesslike quality.

Did he think she was leaving after her uniform was washed?

She hadn't had time for dinner before she came out to the island. "Sure, that sounds nice."

He opened his dorm-size fridge. "Burgers all right?"

"That would be delicious. Can I help?"

"The cooking area is only big enough for one. Why don't you sit and relax?"

She took a seat at the table while Captain settled on the floor beside her. The burgers sizzled in the pan.

Trevor turned to face her. "This is getting real, isn't it?"

It wasn't fear she saw in his face. The hardness of his jawline and his steady gaze suggested resolve.

"It was never a game." She nodded, shaking off the fear that invaded her awareness. To protect Trevor and deal with the man who attacked her, she needed to remain clearheaded.

As he lifted the burgers from the pan and placed them on the buns he'd pulled out, Trevor wrestled with a sense of anticipation and fear. If he could help catch the RMK, there would be some justice for the friends he'd lost. If all this was because of what had happened with Naomi, he was the catalyst that had set this violence into motion. Hiding in the safe house was not the answer. Staying out in the open meant he could draw the killer out and end this once and for all.

He placed a jar of pickles, and bottles of ketchup and mustard on the table and then set a paper plate with the burger on it in front of Hannah. He took a seat on the other side of the table.

Captain raised his head and sniffed the air.

Despite his size, the dog seemed to have a sweet, mellow temperament.

Hannah reached down and ruffled Captain's head. "He does make people smile."

From where he sat, Trevor stretched his arm the short distance to the counter, opened a drawer and grabbed a fork, which he set on the table. "For the pickles," he said.

She grabbed the jar and put pickles on her burger. She looked at him with a piercing gaze. "I'm on guard duty for the night whether you like it or not until the rest of the team can get here."

The pleasantries of sharing a meal vaporized with her strong words.

Hannah had initially shown such a vulnerable demeanor, the force of her words took him by surprise. "Fair enough. I have a gun, too. I go to the range every week." Then again, his first encounter with her had been right after she'd nearly lost her life.

"Let me do my job," she said.

He nodded and squeezed some mustard onto his burger. Despite the attack, she seemed to be getting her spunk back. Maybe he was seeing the real Hannah now, assertive and direct.

They both ate their meal in silence. Like him, she was probably lost in her thoughts about the gravity of the situation.

Captain rose to his feet and licked his chops. As the minutes passed, two lines of drool formed on his jowls.

Trevor chuckled. "He's pretty convincing."

"Yeah, I know, you'd think he was starving to death, but I fed him earlier. He won't take food from you, though, even if you offered it. He's trained to only accept it from me."

"Why is that?"

"To prevent him being poisoned." She lifted the burger. "This is really good. Cooked to perfection."

Focusing on Captain seemed to make them more relaxed around each other.

"Thank you."

After the meal was cleaned up, Trevor moved toward the door. "Your uniform should be dry by now."

Hannah rose to her feet. "I'll go get it."

"There are only three washers in there. Your uniform is in the one on the south-facing wall."

She commanded Captain to follow her and stepped outside.

From the small window, he watched as she headed toward the laundry room. He could see light from a few other campsites. Though the weather was nice in the fall and there were fewer bugs, most of the campers came in the summer.

He studied the darkness beyond the campsites.

Hannah and Captain returned. After pulling the gun from her utility belt, she placed the belt on the counter. She put the gun on a shelf, within easy reach. She retreated into the bedroom and returned to the main area of the RV wearing her uniform. Her hair had been pulled back into a bun.

Trevor retrieved his laptop. "I need to get

some work done." Focusing on his job might take his mind off the looming threat. He sat down on the couch.

"Don't let me bother you. I have a book on my phone I can read." Captain positioned himself by the door.

The minutes ticked by as Trevor only half paid attention to the emails he needed to send and the financial statements he looked over. He found himself sneaking looks at Hannah as she read her book.

When she glanced over at him, he turned away as heat rose in his cheeks. Trevor drew his attention to the big shaggy dog whose mouth was hanging open. "Glad you're watching out for me, buddy." He yawned and stretched. "Think I'll get some sleep. You're staying up, are you?"

"Yes. That is what guard duty entails." She raised her eyebrows. "Like I said before. That's the plan."

He wasn't about to argue with her.

He nodded. "Okey dokey."

He put his laptop away in a drawer. She settled in on the narrow couch. Trevor excused himself and retired to the sleeping area, closing the pocket door behind him. He pulled his own gun out of a drawer and set it under the unused pillow.

Sleep was slow in coming, but he eventually drifted off. Somewhere between dreaming and alertness, he heard a banging noise.

Startled, he sat up in the darkness. He had the sensation the RV had been shaken, but he couldn't discern if it was real or he had simply dreamed it.

"Hannah?"

When he heard no reply, he pulled back the covers and placed his feet on the floor. Grabbing his gun, he reached for the pocket door and slid it open.

His heart pounded. The door to the RV swung on its hinges. Both Hannah and Captain were gone.

Chapter Three

Captain kept pace with Hannah as she raced through the campground. In the darkness, she could hear the man who had tried to break into Trevor's trailer, though she could not see him clearly. She followed the sound of pounding footsteps past several RVs and a tent.

The air around her fell silent. She stopped and listened, still gripping the gun she'd grabbed earlier. Her heart pulsed in her ears as Captain brushed against her leg. The air around her felt electrified.

She could see the outlines of several more RVs and campers, before the area opened up to flat desert-like brush. Only a few exterior lights above RV doors were on at this hour.

She turned slightly just as a force like a brick wall hit her. She fell to the ground on her back. Hands suctioned around her wrist, holding her in place. In the darkness, she could not see the face of the man who loomed above her. She could hear him gasping for breath.

He released one of her wrists. Fingers pressed on the sides of her throat. The collision had caused her to drop her gun. She reached a hand out for where she thought it had fallen, patting the dirt.

Captain barked and circled around her.

Giving up on the gun, she sought to free herself from the clutches of the attacker. With her free hand, she punched him hard on the side of the face. The man groaned in pain, but the blow only caused him to clamp his fingers tighter around her neck.

Struggling to breathe as black dots formed in her field of vision, she knew she had only moments before she passed out.

Captain's barking intensified. He moved in closer and growled.

"Go away," said the attacker.

The distraction Captain created caused the man to loosen his grip, and she managed to punch his solar plexus. The man gasped. Twisting her body so she was on her stomach, she crawled out from beneath him.

Before she could get to her feet, he grabbed her leg. She flipped over but only managed to kick at air as he dragged her across the dirt. Sharp pebbles pressed into her skin.

Captain moved in, lunging at the man.

The man cried out. "Outta here."

Captain growled in response.

Again, he reached for her neck. She thrashed back and forth and gripped the man's wrist, seeking to keep him from tightening his hold as she struggled to breathe.

A thudding noise caused the man to let go of her. Her assailant bolted to his feet. From the ground, she saw the silhouette of two men fighting—no doubt one was Trevor—and heard blows being landed. Both men grunted and cried out in pain.

One of the men broke free and sprinted away. She heard footsteps coming toward her.

"You all right?" The voice was Trevor's, though he was no more than shadow in the darkness.

She pushed herself to her feet. "We have to catch him." She bolted into a sprint, searching and listening for any sign of the man who'd attacked her.

With Trevor and Captain at her heels, she headed across the flat open country in the direction she thought her assailant had gone. Her feet pounded the hard earth until she was out of breath.

All three of them stopped. She could hear Trevor gasping for air.

"I think we lost him," he said between breaths.

She didn't want to give up so easily. She had not seen the man's face. Was this the man who had come after her at the lake, or had the RMK changed his MO to get to Trevor and needed her out of the way? The man was the same build as the one who'd attacked her.

Only the sound of a car starting up in the distance made her realize Trevor was right. She ran a short distance toward the noise seeing only the faint red glow of taillights far away. The assailant had gotten away. Her shoulders slumped.

Trevor patted her back. "Let's head back to the RV and notify the park police about what happened."

She fought off the sense of despair that dragged on her spirit. "What would we tell them? I didn't see his face. I don't know what he was driving." Despite the lack of information, she knew a report would still need to be filed. The park police might provide additional protection until the team could get here.

In less than half a day, a suspect had gotten away from her twice. The situation felt a little hopeless. And she worried that this made her look less than competent to Trevor. "I need to find my gun. I dropped it."

They trudged back toward the RV park until they came to the area where the fight had taken place. With so little light, they both bent over and walked around. If she'd had time to grab her phone, she could have used the flashlight on it.

Once again, Trevor had come to her rescue. She had to give credit where it was due. "Thanks for helping me out."

"I wouldn't have known where to go if it wasn't for Captain's barking," he said.

"He's a good partner. Always has my back." Her foot came up against a solid object. She bent down, touching cold metal. "I found it."

Walking side by side, they headed back toward the RV.

"Thanks for looking out for me and going after that guy," said Trevor.

"Just part of my job." She did not hear in Trevor's voice the condemnation she directed at herself. "I wish I'd gotten a look at his face. I may have been his target."

Once back at the RV, Hannah phoned the park police and offered the scant details about the attack.

She ended by saying, "It would be good if you ran a patrol through here." She gave him the number of the spot the RV was parked in.

"We can assist with that," said the officer.

"It might be worth it to dust for fingerprints as well," she said. "He must have touched the door handle."

"We can do that when we have some daylight. Do you think this is related to the earlier attack on you?"

"It could be. It also might be that a man I've been assigned to protect was the target this time." She glanced in Trevor's direction.

Trevor, who was sitting on the couch, cleared his throat.

She looked directly at him. His expression suggested distress or even irritation. She wasn't sure which. She feared her frustration over losing the suspect had made her overstep a boundary in saying she was protecting him when he hadn't agreed to that. Was he upset with her or at the situation?

She turned her attention back to the phone call. She said goodbye to the officer and disconnected.

Trevor rose to his feet. "I'm going to try to get some sleep."

She took two steps toward him. "I meant what I said about protecting you. The whole team will. But we need a level of cooperation from you."

He studied her for a long moment. "None of this would be happening if I had just been more assertive ten years ago. No one would be dead. I want to do everything I can to catch this guy and make it right. If that means being bait, then so be it."

She shuddered from the force of his words and the steely look in his eyes. "I understand about guilt, but you don't need to risk your own life."

"Maybe I do." His words were saturated with intense emotion. "Good night." He turned without saying anything more to her, disappearing behind the pocket door.

Hannah plopped down on the couch. Captain sat at her feet. She reached out to touch his soft fur, then stroked his head and neck while her thoughts reeled. The voices of Jodie's parents filled her mind. Though they had not come right out and blamed Hannah, they had implied that she should have been watching out for their daughter. They wanted to know why she and Jodie hadn't gone out swimming together.

The image of the anguished expression on Jodie's mom's face floated in her mind as the words the distraught woman said echoed in Hannah's brain. *Why can't you remember what happened more clearly? You were there.*

But now that she'd seen the man's face, she did remember. Yet, none of that would bring back Jodie.

Yes, she knew all about guilt.

Hannah stared out the window at the darkness. Would the attacker come back and try a second time? She shifted in her seat, knowing that she could not stay awake all night.

Within twenty minutes, she saw headlights of a vehicle. She stood up and stared through the blinds to see the park police vehicle roll by slowly. The tightness in her chest eased a little.

It was a comfort to her that if there was any noise outside, Captain would let her know. She needed to be ready for another attack, no matter what.

★ ★ ★

The next day, Trevor woke up as the sun slanted through the blinds of his sleeping quarters. He dressed, washed his face and combed his hair before sliding open the pocket door. The aroma of coffee greeted him, but Hannah was not in the RV.

He swung open the door to find her standing not far from the RV with a steaming mug while Captain sniffed around and did his business.

She turned toward him and smiled. "I hope you don't mind. I made coffee."

With her red hair and emerald-green eyes, she really was quite beautiful. The spray of freckles across her round cheeks added a girl-next-door quality to her appearance. If he'd met her under different circumstances, he might've acted on his attraction. "Thanks for making the coffee."

"I heard from Chase. They're on their way. We need to get an early start today."

His stomach clenched. The use of the word *we* upset him. She was assuming so much. Just like she had done last night when she'd told the other officer she was protecting him. After a night's sleep, he'd realized why he was so resistant toward the unit's offer of protection.

It was his lack of faith in what he thought the police could do. Law enforcement had let down Elk Valley ten years ago. A cloud still hung over the town. Like his family, so many people had been wrecked by the murders and the lack of closure that they moved away. His father had sold a prosperous ranch in Elk Valley.

On some level, Trevor felt like it was all up to him to see that justice prevailed.

He took a step toward her. "What are you talking about?"

She sipped her coffee before answering. "Chase has secured the team a place to stay at the Fielding Garr Ranch here on the southeast side of the island. There are no permanent residences on the island, but the bunkhouse has been turned into sleeping quarters for park employees when they have a big project, and there's a meeting room close by where we can set up temporary headquarters while we wait to see if the RMK shows up."

He was familiar with the ranch she was talking about. It had not been a working ranch since the 1980s and now was a living museum and site where tourists could picnic, hike or take horseback rides. "I'm glad you were able to find a place to stay, but that doesn't mean I'm coming with you."

If his point in staying out in the open was to lure the RMK out, he wasn't sure that would happen if he was surrounded by cops.

Her eye twitched in response to his assertion. "Please hear me out. Some of the team that came down here will stay on the island and the other officers will be in Salt Lake in case the RMK makes another appearance in the city. You'll have a lot of protection, not just me." Her expression filled with earnestness as she stepped toward him. "You can't actually think you can catch this guy all by yourself and not be killed?"

She had a point. He didn't need to be foolhardy. His default position seemed to be to oppose her. She brought out his stubborn nature.

His thoughts raced as he looked into her green eyes. Twice now, she'd almost met her death at the hands of an assailant. Perhaps *she* needed *his* protection. Not that he would tell her that. "All right, I'll go, but I'm taking my gun."

"Is it legal?"

"Of course it is," he said. "I even have a conceal carry permit."

He picked up on the note of challenge in her

voice and the defensiveness in his response as they stood face-to-face.

"If that's the way it's got to be…for now, but leave the gun here until I can clear it with Chase."

"Look, I have never been one to sit on the sidelines. That is just not my style. I'll go with you under one condition—you have to allow me to help catch this guy."

She lifted her chin as the muscles around her mouth tightened. "That's the only way you will agree to accept our protection?"

He put his hands on his hips. "That's the only way."

She folded her arms across her chest. "I'll have to clear that with Chase too. Please, just come with me for now."

The note of vulnerability in her voice made him cave. "All right then, let me get us some breakfast before we go." He saw that she was just trying to do her job.

After Captain was done, they stepped inside to finish their coffee. Trevor prepared a quick breakfast of cold cereal for both of them.

Hannah consumed the last few spoons full of cereal. "I think you should leave your truck here and ride with me in my vehicle."

His first instinct was to protest. He didn't want to be stranded without his truck. Then again, he could protect her more easily if they were in the same vehicle. "Sure, I'm taking my laptop, so I can get some work done."

"No problem," she said.

While she stepped outside, he grabbed his laptop and his gun, which he slipped into the laptop case. If he was going to protect himself and Hannah, he would need it.

Within a few minutes, they were sitting in Hannah's vehicle with Captain loaded in his kennel in the back.

They drove on the road that led to the ranch from the north part of the island. At this early hour, not many other cars were on the two-lane road.

Hannah glanced in the rearview mirror.

"Something wrong?"

"I just don't know why that other car is following us so closely," she said.

He glanced over his shoulder at a white compact car. He couldn't see the driver due to the angle of the sun and the visor being down.

The turn off for the ranch was up ahead but still out of view. Hannah pulled over and the white car rolled by.

"Guess he wasn't following us. Can't take any chances of leading someone to headquarters." She pulled back out onto the road and drove.

She hit the blinker and turned where a sign indicated the ranch was. Silos, a sheep-shearing shed and a white stucco house came into view. Hannah drove along a dirt road past a brick building, several outbuildings and a display of farm equipment that probably went back to before the invention of the car.

She seemed to know where she was going. Chase must have given her directions.

She drove a little farther, past a crumbling brick structure parking in front of a long narrow building with several doors. A tall muscular man with brown hair and wearing the same uniform as Hannah stood outside the building talking on his phone. A German shepherd sat erect not too far from him. The officer waved at Hannah.

Hannah got out of her vehicle at the same time that Trevor did. The other officer walked over to them.

"Trevor, this is Officer Ian Carpenter. He just joined the team in July."

Trevor shook the man's hand.

"And that's his partner, Lola." She pointed toward the German shepherd.

Ian turned toward Hannah. "Chase told me what happened to you…about the attack. For your sake and Trevor's, we'll make sure someone is standing guard around the sleeping quarters and our meeting room." He bent his head toward the dog, who had not moved. "Since Lola's trained to protect and catch suspects, you'll be in good hands."

"Why don't you show us around?" Hannah turned toward Trevor. "You can meet the rest of the team."

"Sure, let me show you where you'll be sleeping first," said Ian.

Trevor glanced back at the way they'd come. On the drive to the bunkhouse, he had noticed several barns. He knew from the newspaper accounts of the other murders that all of the other victims had been shot in barns.

Antelope Island had few options for the team to stay if they were to have a presence. The only other building was the visitors' center and the only other place for lodging were the campgrounds.

Still, as his gaze rested on one of the barns, he wondered if they were giving the RMK ample opportunity to repeat the pattern of the other murders.

Chapter Four

After being shown to her sleeping quarters, where she would be rooming with the task force's tech expert, Isla Jiminez, and a sheriff's deputy, Selena Smith, Hannah followed Ian and Trevor one door down to a room with two bunk beds.

"You'll be rooming with Rocco and me," said Ian. "And the K-9s, so lots of protection." There was one other door to the bunkhouse. Chase and his K-9 partner, Dash, must be occupying that room.

Hannah still had her overnight bag from her trip up to Elk Valley in her patrol car. She retrieved it and put it in her sleeping quarters.

She and Trevor were ushered to the meeting room, a short walk from the bunkhouse. The meeting room looked like it may have served as mess hall for the cowboys who had once occupied the bunkhouse, or maybe it had been used by the family that had owned the farm for social gatherings. It had a functional kitchen and a large seating area with several couches, a fireplace and a long dining table.

Isla pulled computer screens and laptops from a box, then arranged them on a large fold-out table. She glanced up from a keyboard. Petite features and long brown hair enhanced her welcoming smile. "Hannah, good to see you."

Hannah stepped toward her colleague and hugged her. "Isla, this is Trevor Gage."

Isla held out her hand to Trevor. "Pleased to meet you. You're in safe hands with Officer Scott."

Trevor's response was simply to nod and say, "Oh?" Not exactly the vote of confidence Isla had given her.

Isla picked up an electrical cord and plugged it into the back of one of the computer screens. "We'll all be working hard to take in the RMK before he can get to you."

"I'm sure Chase has a game plan if he does show up here," said Hannah.

After finding an outlet for the electrical cord, Isla returned to the table. She stared at one of the screens while she tapped the keyboard. "In the meantime, I am going to familiarize myself with the island and make contact with some key people."

Trevor wandered off with his laptop and found a spot on one of the couches.

Hannah came around the table and stood beside Isla, who had already pulled up several maps of the island.

"I heard about what happened to you yesterday." Isla touched her dark brown hair at the temple, face filled with concern. "Chase informed the team."

"The man who came after me was wearing a park uniform. I was wondering if you might be able to pull up all the employees who work in this area that match his age and description. We might be able to figure out who he is."

"Sure, I can do that as soon as I get set up." Isla pushed back her chair and stood up.

"I know the RMK case needs to be your priority," said Hannah.

Isla wrapped an arm around Hannah's back, squeezed her shoulder and pulled her close. "I'm a major multitasker, Hannah, so no worries. And I just wanted you to know, I appreciate your courage in choosing to stay on the case."

"I didn't want to let the team down. I feel like I can make a substantial contribution since

I'm from Salt Lake and know the area." Isla had had her own share of similar turmoil. Someone was trying to sabotage her efforts at becoming a foster mom, and it had escalated to her house being set on fire last month.

The rest of the team members slowly filed into the room—Rocco Manelli and his chocolate Lab, Cocoa, along with Selena Smith and her Malinois, Scout.

Chase entered and gathered the officers on one side of the room. Rocco and Selena took a seat on the couch, while Hannah and Ian remained standing. Isla rolled her office chair closer to the group.

Trevor closed his laptop and moved to a nearby chair, so he could hear the conversation.

Chase paced the floor with his hands behind his back. He was a tall man with brown curly hair cut close to his head. In her time working at HQ in Elk Valley, Hannah had found him to be reserved but a good leader, always concerned for the members of the team. Perhaps some of his quiet nature was due to the tragedy in his life. A supervisory special agent with the FBI, Chase had come back to Elk Valley from DC after his wife and child had died in a revenge bombing.

Chase stopped and addressed the other members of the team. "Hannah informed me that someone tried to break into Trevor's RV last night. But the intruder may have been the man who came after Hannah when she got to the island. You all have been briefed on what happened to her at the lake."

Everyone nodded.

Hannah felt her cheeks flush. It was humbling to have become the victim of a crime instead of the one catching the law breaker. "I didn't intend to complicate this case."

"Could have happened to any of us," said Rocco. The rest of the team mumbled in agreement.

"We got your back," Selena insisted.

The show of support made her lower lip quiver. What a privilege that she'd been chosen to work with such a great group of officers.

Chase squared his shoulders. "Now for the big news. As you know the park police and employees have been informed about the RMK case. For now, we're not informing the public. We don't believe he's a threat to anyone but YRC members and we don't want to scare him off." Chase let out a heavy breath. "I just got a call. A man matching the description of the

RMK was spotted walking a dog that looks like Cowgirl along the shore of the lake."

A tense hush settled in the room.

Hannah heartbeat revved up a notch. "So he's here on the island, and he still has Cowgirl."

Cowgirl was MCK9's missing therapy dog. Seemingly as a way of taunting the team's attempts to catch him, the killer had kidnapped the Labradoodle. She'd been brought in as a compassion K-9 for the residents of Elk Valley who'd been wrecked all over again by the recent killings. Cowgirl had been in the RMK's care for months now and was believed to have gotten pregnant. By now, she would have given birth. She had a distinct dark splotch on her right ear, making the RMK easy to spot when he was out in public with her. Despite sightings of a tall blond man with the dog in Idaho months back and the recent one in Salt Lake City, he'd so far evaded police.

Chase continued. "What we don't know is if the RMK is staying on this island or returning to Salt Lake. Some of the team members are still in Salt Lake, questioning witnesses and being ready in case there is another sighting reported. It's also possible the RMK could be staying in Syracuse, the town closest to the island. Lodging is limited here on the island, but he could be staked out in one of the campgrounds. Since it's clear he knows Trevor is here, this island is where we are most likely to catch him. Our job today will be to conduct a search of the island to see if anyone has spotted our man."

"We still don't know what he's driving?" Rocco asked.

Chase shook his head. "It's possible he would have changed vehicles by now, anyway, or even rented an RV."

Isla folded her arms over her chest. "I can call the RV rental places in the area and see if anyone matching the RMK's description made an appearance. He may have had Cowgirl with him, so he'll be memorable. The team members in Salt Lake can visit the RV rental places there. Sometimes you get better results with an in-person interview."

"Those puppies must have been born by now. I wonder where he's keeping them," said Selena as she played with a strand of her red hair.

"*If* he's keeping them." Ian's voice had become solemn.

So far, it appeared that the RMK had taken good care of Cowgirl. The hope was that he would do the same for her puppies.

Chase looked around the room. "We'll send people out in teams to cover the island. Isla, do you have a feel for the most efficient way to divide up the island?"

She swung back around to her computers and walked her rolling chair toward the table. "I got a basic feel for the area. The north end has more visitors with more amenities, so we should send one team up there and maybe have the other two teams deal with the middle and south side of the island, which is less populated but more area to cover."

Chase looked at Hannah. "Someone will have to stay here and keep guard over Trevor."

Trevor rose to his feet. "Actually, I'd like to go out and help catch this guy."

Hannah's stomach tied into a knot. She stepped toward Chase and whispered, "I meant to tell you. He agreed to come with me only if he could help out."

Chase placed a hand on her shoulder, leaning close to her ear. "We'll have to talk later."

Hannah gritted her teeth. She did not fail to pick up on the irritation in Chase's voice. This was her own fault for not communicating with Chase sooner and for not running Trevor's idea by him first. She had just so wanted to accomplish the mission she'd been sent on to show Chase she was worthy of her appointment on the team. She'd gotten tunnel vision about getting Trevor to agree to a level of protection.

Chase turned back to the whole group. "All right then—Trevor and Hannah will take the north side of the island. Rocco and Selena, you can handle the area south of the ranch. Ian and I will go to the place along the lake where he was last seen."

Isla sat back down at her computers. "I'm going to send each of you a map specific to the area that needs to be covered."

Chase nodded. "Be in touch via radio. Check in on a regular basis even if you don't have any news."

Trevor stepped forward. "I brought a gun with me. I train regularly."

"No." Chase glanced in Hannah's direction. "I can't allow that. Too much liability."

Hannah had not realized Trevor had brought the gun with him after she asked him not to. One more way he wasn't being forthright with her.

The team loaded their respective K-9s and headed out. Trevor got into the passenger seat of Hannah's vehicle.

As she sat behind the wheel, she could not hide her frustration with the situation. It came out in her tone of voice. "You ready to go?"

"Sorry, I didn't mean to get you in trouble."

She shook her head and turned the key in the ignition. "Let's just get to work." After checking the directions on her phone and looking at the map Isla had sent her, she pulled out of her parking space and headed toward the ranch exit. The first stop would be the visitors' center.

Trevor had ruffled her feathers. As she drove, she prayed for a sense of peace to return. The road stretched before her, with a view of the lake and the mountains beyond. She felt herself calming down. "Look, this whole thing has been a little sideways from the beginning. I didn't count on that man coming after me. The attack didn't allow me to present myself in the most professional way possible. Guess I made a bad first impression."

"Maybe you're looking at this wrong, Hannah?"

He hadn't said anything about his first impression of her. "What do you mean?"

"We can protect each other. Are you open to that?"

Though she did think they could help each

other, something in his suggestion pricked her insecurity about how he saw her as a police officer. "I can't put you in harm's way. It goes against my mission as a law-enforcement officer."

"It's a choice I'm making." He leaned toward her. "I told you why. I could say the same about you."

"What are you talking about?"

"Given what happened, wouldn't you be more secure if you went off duty and into a safe house? Or maybe you feel like I do—that making yourself bait might bring some justice to the situation."

She had to hand it to him—Trevor was perceptive. "That thought had occurred to me."

"Well then." He settled back down into his seat. "That's something we have in common."

The hard edges around their relationship seemed to soften a bit. She flexed her hands on the steering wheel. "I don't want my life to be defined by what happened when I was ten. But I feel like it is."

"I get that. I feel the same way about what happened in Elk Valley when I was eighteen. It seems to govern so many of the choices I've made in my life."

She glanced at him, appreciating the warmth of his expression, before she put her eyes back on the road.

She shook off the intense feelings. Just because they had found a point of connection didn't mean they'd be picking out a china pattern together. She wasn't even sure what had made her think of such a thing.

"You still need to let me do my job," she said.

"I'm sorry I made you look bad in front of your boss," he said.

She drove on in silence, feeling the tight knot in her stomach return. She'd have to explain her choices to Chase and smooth things over. "I should've run the plan by him first. It is what it is."

Hannah turned into the visitors' center passing a large metal sculpture of a buffalo on the driveway leading to the parking lot. Once they found a spot, she unloaded Captain, and they headed toward a concrete building.

People milled around inside, looking at the displays about the wildlife and terrain. She spotted a ranger, an older man with a paunch, coming out of the gift shop.

The sight of the uniform caused a shiver to run down her back. The trauma of the attack was still with her. As if sensing the emotional shift, Captain leaned against her, his furry head brushing the back of her hand.

Trevor drew closer to her, as well. "You doing okay?"

Great, she was surrounded by empaths. It would be hard to hide any of her feelings.

She cleared her throat. "I'm thinking about asking that ranger if he knows who the guy is who came after me yesterday." She'd been so focused on today's assignment to look for the RMK that she hadn't stayed to talk to Isla about info she might have found out about her attacker.

The ranger offered her an inviting smile. She took a deep breath and moved toward him, hoping to get some answers on both of the cases.

Trevor stood beside Hannah as she got the ranger's attention. He was acutely aware of the people milling around him. Captain, in his K-9 vest, drew people's attention, but Trevor was tuned into anyone whose stare might be more menacing. To be out in the open like this was a risk, but he knew himself well enough that choosing to go into hiding would have been even harder. He had always been someone who made things happen, not a man who watched life pass by and let others do the work.

When the ranger turned toward her, Hannah spoke up. "Excuse me, I'm wondering if you have seen a tall blond man with a Labradoodle. The dog has a distinctive dark brown splotch on her right ear and the man usually wears sunglasses and a hat."

Trevor wondered if the RMK had a safe cool place to keep Cowgirl and the puppies. Having the dog with him would make the killer that much easier to spot. Certainly, he wouldn't come after Trevor with the dog in tow. He caught a flash of the brown uniform the rangers wore out of the corner of his eye. He whirled around and took a few steps toward the ranger, thinking it might be the park employee who had come after Hannah. Though he saw the ranger from the back, it was clearly a woman headed outside. He moved back toward Hannah. It wasn't just the RMK they needed to be worried about.

The ranger rested his hand on his paunch. "You must be with the Mountain Country K-9 unit. I saw the BOLO go out for that guy, but I'm not the one who called it in when he was spotted. Maybe he will make another appearance."

"That's what we're hoping for, so we can take him in," said Hannah.

"If he does show up, I'm sure we'll help you out as much as we can."

"We appreciate that." Hannah remained close to the ranger as her hand reached out to brush over Captain's head.

Her lingering indicated that she wanted to say something more but was hesitant. Her shoulders slumped. Trevor was pretty sure he knew what she wanted to ask. The trauma of the attempt on her life was probably still so fresh it was hard to talk about it.

He cleared his throat, hoping that he wasn't stepping out of line. "This officer is the one who was attacked by a park employee yesterday down by the lake."

Hannah gave him a sideways glance and an appreciative smile.

"I saw that report as well." The ranger turned toward Hannah. "I didn't realize it was you."

With a quick glance at Trevor, Hannah squared her shoulders, seeming to recover. "Do you have any idea who it might be?"

The ranger shook his head and ran his hands

through his thinning hair. "The problem is the description is pretty generic. Average height. Curly brown hair."

"I get that." Disappointment permeated Hannah's voice. "It just seems like he would be easy to track down if he works for the park service."

"I don't even know how many rangers are employed around the lake—quite a few. And we got seasonal workers, as well. I can tell you that no one was assigned to pick up trash in the area where the incident happened."

"That's interesting," she said. "Why would he have been over there then?"

The ranger shrugged. "It could be that he had some downtime and decided to use it to clean up. Most park employees take a lot of pride in keeping the park nice and not allowing littering."

Hannah thanked the ranger just before a mom and her young daughter came up to the ranger to ask him a question. The man turned his attention to the woman and her child.

Hannah looked at Trevor. "Thank you for asking the question about the attack on me."

"I hope I wasn't stepping on any toes. It made sense to try and get that information from someone who might know."

"No, I appreciate it. Tracking that guy down might be harder than I thought it would be," she said. "There was nothing distinct about him that I remember. No scars or tattoos."

"Still, if he works for the park service, that narrows it down quite a bit. He's got to know you can identify him. Do you suppose he might take sick days and lay low so he doesn't get caught?"

Hannah's hand fluttered to her neck. "Honestly, I think he'd want to get rid of me before I could attach a name to him and track him down. Maybe he's already taken the uniform off, so he blends in more. Even if he does call in sick, I don't think he'll leave the island until… I'm dead."

Her voice trembled with fear. He found himself wanting to take her in his arms and comfort her. Instead, he bumped his shoulder against hers. "We'll catch him. Just let me know what I can do to help."

"Maybe Isla has pulled up employment files and will find a match. Now that my memory has been jarred, if I saw a picture of him, I would recognize him."

"What do we do next?" Trevor asked.

"We need to focus on finding the RMK. We

should probably check all around this area inside and out. This is one of the busier parts of the island. Maybe we'll run into other rangers who might have seen him."

"We can split up and cover more ground faster." He angled away from her.

She grabbed his sleeve. "No, you stay close to me. That's the deal, right?" The look of insistence on her face reminded him of how quickly the tension could return to their relationship.

His intent had not been to antagonize her, but to try to be helpful. Why couldn't she see that? "Sorry, I didn't mean to step out of line. I know you're watching out for me."

"It's okay." Her voice softened.

With Captain by Hannah's side, they walked through the visitors' center and around the perimeter of the building, stopping at a birdhouse that was actually shaped like a Victorian house, with a tower-like structure on one end. Birds flitted around it.

He was struck by the view of the lake. There did not appear to be a single ripple and the mountains reflected perfectly in the water. The breeze rustled Hannah's red hair where it had slipped out of the bun. The soft wisps danced in the wind. The air smelled salty. He relished the moment of calm and quiet. It was the reason he liked coming out here.

Hannah looked off in the distance. "I came here all the time as a kid with my mom and dad."

"Good memories?"

"They are all marred by what happened." She rested her hand over her face, covering her eyes. Captain sat at her feet and gazed up at her.

It was the most vulnerable he'd seen her since the attack.

She carried such a heavy burden. He placed a hand on her arm above her elbow. Though she did not pull away, she stiffened at his touch. After dropping her hand away from her face and raising her head, she swiped at her eyes and lifted her chin a little higher.

He pulled his hand away. Hannah seemed to be doing battle between processing what had happened to her and trying to come across as strong. Her defenses had gone back up.

What could he say to break through the armor she seemed to think she needed to have around him? "I know this is hard."

"Everything has just gotten so stirred up inside of me by coming back here, but I think it's for a reason. God wants me to deal with this once and for all. Seeing that Jodie's killer goes to jail will help, but it's also about healing my mind and heart, getting beyond what happened."

What she said applied to him, as well. Feeling the softness of the breeze over his skin, he understood that silence was the better response to the struggle she was going through. He was coming to admire her. There was something endearing about the fortitude and tenacity of her character.

Seeming to break the power of the moment, Hannah slapped her thigh. "I'm hungry. That cereal didn't stay with me. Why don't we go get something to eat after we check out the area around Bridger Bay? I think I saw a sign for a food place around that area. Stopping for lunch will give us a chance to question workers who may have seen the RMK."

They returned to the parking lot. As they walked through the lot, he noticed the white compact car that had followed them on the road before they got to the ranch.

Once they were settled in the car, Hannah pulled a notebook from her belt. "I saw that white car, too." She spoke as she wrote. "I made note of the license plate. Isla can run it. It could be that the driver is just a tourist going to all the touristy spots on the island."

"Yes, could be. That's amazing, though."

"What?" She shoved the key in the ignition.

"You memorized that license-plate number with a single glance."

She shook her head and shrugged. "It's a skill you gain as a highway patrol officer." Before shifting gears, she rested her gaze on him. "But thank you for noticing."

The warmth of her response did not go unnoticed. They were both making an effort to create a workable professional relationship for the time that they had to be together.

She pulled out of the lot. Trevor gave a backward glance toward the white car, which was parked away from the other cars. No one was moving toward it.

In any case, it was a reminder that they needed to be on guard.

Chapter Five

As she drove toward their next destination, Bridger Bay, where there was a much-used beach and a campground, Hannah took note of the vehicle some distance behind them. It first appeared as a shimmering piece of metal in the distance.

Like much of the island, the area where Hannah drove was flat, surrounded by desert-like vegetation, lots of sagebrush and prairie grass. She had a view of the mountains off in the distance. The flat terrain and straight road provided visibility for a long way. As the car drew nearer, she saw that it was a Jeep, dark green in color.

Though the island was not bustling with activity, they had encountered several other cars on this stretch of road. The car zoomed toward them as if to pass. Hannah slowed and veered toward the edge of the road to allow the other vehicle room to get around them.

Instead, the car rammed her bumper. Her body was propelled forward and then snapped back by the seat belt. Her jaw clenched as she gripped the wheel.

Trevor put his hand out, bracing it against the dashboard. "What's going on?"

He barely had time to finish his sentence before a second, more intense ramming caused the SUV to veer off the road. They bumped along over grass and rocks. When she checked the mirror, the car was still coming after them.

Captain made a noise of distress from his kennel.

Hannah pressed the accelerator, seeking to avoid another collision as she aimed the steering wheel back toward the road. This time, the other car scraped the passenger side of her SUV.

She twisted the wheel to avoid full impact. Trevor groaned. Still accelerating, she swerved in a wide arc. Her back end fishtailed as she went off the road on the other side. She cranked the wheel toward the road.

An oncoming car honked its horn as it narrowly missed her when she sought to get on her side of the two-lane road. The green car was still behind them.

Heart pounding, she pressed the accelerator to the floor. Another car came up behind the green Jeep and several more moved toward them in the other lane. Traffic was increasing as they got closer to Bridger Bay.

Even though the green car hung back, allowing another car to get between them, her heart still raced. When she checked the mirror, the Jeep was no longer visible. He must have turned off. Maybe the driver realized he'd be caught if he continued to follow them.

After catching her breath, she glanced at Trevor. "You okay?"

He massaged the back of his neck. "I'll survive."

"Did you get a look at the driver?"

He shook his head. "Everything happened so fast. Do you think it was the RMK?"

Her heart had still not slowed down. "Not really his MO. But it's possible he's getting desperate."

"Well, if it wasn't him, I'll give you one guess as to who else it could be."

She waited for her hand to stop shaking before reaching for the radio.

"This is Officer Hannah Scott. We just had

an incident close to Bridger Bay. A green Jeep attempted to run us off the road."

Chase's steady voice came across the line. "Are you okay?"

"The SUV is a little dented up. We both might have a few bruises but otherwise okay."

"License-plate number?"

"No, I can tell you he's not following us anymore. He must have taken one of the roads or scenic turn offs before Bridger Bay," Hannah responded.

"Ian and I will go over there and have a look around. Rocco and Selena are farther south."

"Thank you," she said.

"I don't suppose you got a look at the driver?" said Chase.

"Neither one of us did."

"Now, after this, I'm not totally on board about you two being out in the open like that."

She was afraid he would say that. "We don't have enough personnel for me to be sidelined."

Chase did not answer. Static came over the radio.

"We're out here already. We can cover Bridger Bay and the nearby campsite. I don't know that we would be any safer at that ranch. Lot of people there, too."

Chase didn't respond immediately. "Point

taken. We just don't have any other choice if we're going to stay on the island."

"My turn is coming up." The sign for Bridger Beach flashed by her on the side of the road. "Over and out." Best to disconnect before Chase changed his mind. She hit her blinker and turned off.

She found a parking space that looked out on the long stretch of beach and the Great Salt Lake beyond. She pressed her head against the headrest, closed her eyes and thanked God for His protection.

Trevor's warm hand rested on hers. "That was some stellar driving back there."

His touch sent warmth through her. She pulled her hand away even as her insides melted. "All part of my training." It made her feel good that she'd impressed him, but she needed to keep things professional.

Bridger Beach was one of the most popular spots for people to try floating in the Great Salt Lake. This late in the year, more people were probably just enjoying walking on the white sand. Taking Captain with them, they got out and walked the beach, stopping to talk to several people, but none of them had seen anyone matching the RMKs description.

The wind whipped around them and the air smelled of salt as she scanned the area. It was probably not worth their time to wait for the people who were swimming to come in.

Trevor turned toward her. "What now?"

"The campground is not too far from here. Maybe we should drive through it and stop to talk to a few people. The RMK might be staying there. For sure, people would remember Cowgirl."

"Okay," he said.

Tents, RVs, campers and three cottages populated the campground. Each of the far-apart spots had a gazebo. Hannah drove slowly, knowing that spotting Cowgirl would be the most likely giveaway for their suspect. He might be taking the puppies out, as well, if he hadn't sold them. So far, the RMK seemed to be taking care of Cowgirl. She hoped the same was true for the puppies.

It seemed the RMK liked being spotted with the dog as a way of taunting the team. That's probably what his morning appearance was about—it was meant to instill frustration in the task force. Showing up on the island in such a public place was probably also intended to cause fear in Trevor. But to always have the dog in tow, and now, some puppies, would hinder the killer and make it that much harder to move stealthily toward his next intended victim. If he was staying on the island, it would have to be a camper or RV, not a tent—someplace the dogs would be safe if he left them.

She had to believe that searching the campgrounds was not futile. The door-to-door searches in police work could feel that way, and yet in her experience, being methodical usually turned up a lead.

They stopped at several campsites where people were outside cooking on the firepit or relaxing beneath a canopy. No one at the first two sites had noticed a man with a Labradoodle.

They stopped at a third site on the edge of the campground. An older couple sat beneath the gazebo in lawn chairs. Their truck camper was parked off to the side. The man rose from his seat as Hannah approached. Trevor followed behind her.

The man pointed at her SUV. "K-9 unit, huh?"

"Yes," she said.

"I used to train bloodhounds for the sheriff's department down in South Carolina. What kind of dog do you work with?"

Hannah perked up a bit. That meant the man was probably retired law enforcement. He'd be more likely to share info with her, and he probably was more observant than the average person. "A Newfoundland." She turned slightly toward the vehicle, where Captain was still secured in the back seat. "He's a good partner and a big ol' sweetheart."

The man took off his baseball hat and rubbed his thinning white hair. He studied Trevor for a long moment, probably wondering what his role was if Hannah already had a partner and why he wasn't in uniform.

"Trevor is assisting me in my investigation," she said. There was no need to share more details.

The man lifted his chin and nodded as if the explanation seemed to satisfy him. "Saw you driving through the campground. Looking for someone?"

Hannah nodded. "A tall blond man, usually wears sunglasses and a hat. He might have had a female Labradoodle with him who recently gave birth. The dog has a dark splotch on her ear."

The woman who had been sitting in the chair fanning herself piped up. "I saw a man matching that description yesterday evening."

"Here at this campground?" That meant that he must have stayed in the park last night before making his early morning appearance.

"Yes, I was taking Mr. Baby out for his evening constitutional." The older woman pointed at a basket by her chair that Hannah hadn't noticed before. A fluffy ball of brown-and-black fur was curled into a *C* shape.

Trevor stepped forward. "Where were you at when you saw the man?"

The woman pointed off in the distance. "There's a walking trail not too far from here."

Hannah's heart skipped a beat. This was the break they had been looking for. "Did you talk to the man at all?"

"Only briefly. His dog came up to me and was just so friendly. Our conversation was mostly about how cute the dog was."

Hannah piped up. "I don't suppose you saw his campsite or what he was driving?"

"We weren't close enough to the campsites for me to see which pad was his, and he didn't mention where he was staying or what he was staying in. The one thing I did notice about the dog was that it was clear she must be nursing puppies. Her teats were swollen, and her belly was stretched out as though she'd given birth recently."

"Thank you. You've both been very helpful."

"Mind if I meet your partner?" The husband's voice had a hopeful lilt to it, as if he was probably recalling his days of having worked with K-9s.

"Sure." Normally, she wouldn't have allowed someone to pet Captain while on duty, but the man seemed so overjoyed, and he and his wife had given her a break in the case. Plus, she could use an ally and a pair of eyes in the camp if the RMK was still here.

She opened the back car door and tripped the release on the kennel. Captain stuck his big furry head out so the man could pet him.

"What is his training specialty?" The man put his head close to Captain's.

"Search and rescue, mainly water."

After sweet talking to Captain for a moment and sharing a story about a dog he'd trained to search swamps, the older man thanked Hannah.

"Both the wife and I will keep an eye out for the man you're looking for."

Hannah handed him her card. "Call this number if you notice anything."

Despite her growling stomach, Hannah felt a

sense of elation as she and Trevor both climbed into the SUV.

She radioed Chase with the news, ending by saying that they should maybe set up a stake-out of the campground. "I know he might be moving from campground to campground, but it's worth a try. He may still be staying here. Someone is bound to notice or hear the puppies sooner or later."

"Yes, that makes sense," said Chase. "There are several campgrounds on the island, but it seems like a good strategy to focus on the place we know he stayed at."

She gripped the radio a little tighter. "Any sign of the green Jeep?"

"Negative. We searched the area where you thought he must have turned off and questioned a few people, but we didn't come up with anything. Hannah?"

"Okay, thanks." Her voice wilted from disappointment.

"I think you and Trevor should come back to the ranch for now, given what happened with that Jeep."

"Am I going to be part of the stakeout?"

"Meadow is one of the officers who stayed behind in Salt Lake in case there was another sighting there. Now that we know the RMK is staying on the island, it makes sense to have her help us out. The remaining members of the task force will stay in the city in case the RMK returns there."

"What are you saying?"

"I think the safest thing for both you and Trevor would be to come back to the ranch. With an extra officer, we should be able to proceed with the search. Meadow's K-9 has tracking skills, which will be a help."

Not what she wanted to hear. "Okay, we're going to pick up some food and then we'll head over there." She knew better than to argue with Chase. She already wasn't on his good side.

"See you in a bit," said Chase. "And, Hannah, you did good work today. I'm sure that car chase left you rattled, and you did your job, anyway."

"Thank you." Hannah clicked off the radio. The sense of elation she felt at having gotten a lead about the RMK eased the pain of knowing that she probably wouldn't be part of the stakeout.

The decision had been made. She needed to abide by what Chase wanted.

Trevor had heard the conversation. "Tough

break. You don't like to be on the sidelines any more than I do."

She smiled. One more thing they had in common. "I just don't know if we will be any safer at the ranch."

It could be that the RMK had already figured out the team had set up headquarters at the ranch. The bunkhouse was separated from some of the busier parts of the ranch, but the patrol vehicles would give them away. If the RMK had figured out where they were staying, it would just be a matter of time before he came after Trevor.

Trevor's heart went out to Hannah. She seemed to shrink in the driver's seat. Her features were less animated. The look on her face was pensive. He liked the exuberant Hannah he'd seen moments before, when her solid police work had moved the investigation forward.

"It wasn't safety that I signed up for when I made my decision to stay out in the open," said Trevor.

"Me, either." She turned the key in the ignition.

"If you weren't such a good police officer, so interested in justice, you would have hung up your gun and headed to a safe house yourself," said Trevor.

"True." She rolled through the campground and back onto the road. Within minutes, signs for the Island Buffalo Grill came up. It was short drive before they entered the parking lot, where several other cars were parked. As long as the fall weather remained nice, people still visited the island. This was his favorite time of year to be here—less heat and fewer bugs.

Trevor noted that there was no drive-through, which would have left them less exposed.

Hannah turned off the car. "As long as we're here, it won't hurt to ask the kitchen staff if they have seen the RMK or know the park employee who tried to kill me."

They stepped inside, where only two other people waited in line to give their orders. After Hannah ordered a cheeseburger and fries and paid, she asked the female clerk if she'd seen a tall blond man with a Labradoodle or puppies, and then described the park employee who had come after her. The clerk thought for a moment and then said, "No, I can't say that I have seen either of those men."

Trevor stepped forward and ordered a bison burger and onion rings.

While they waited for their food, they sat down at a table. Hannah stood up when she noticed a man wiping down a nearby table. She walked over and preceded to talk to him. The man shook his head. Once their meals came in to-go boxes, they headed out to the K-9 vehicle.

Hannah set her box on the console between the seats while Trevor dug into his onion rings. She took a couple bites of her burger and ate a handful of fries before starting the car and heading back toward the ranch.

They sped past one of the scenic turnouts. He thought he saw something in his peripheral vision. Trevor craned his neck to get a look through the rearview mirror. "The green Jeep is back there."

Chapter Six

After making sure there were no other cars close, Hannah spun the SUV around and pressed the accelerator. She could see the Jeep up ahead as it pulled onto the road.

The needle edged past seventy as she sought to close the distance between herself and the other car. She grabbed her radio and pressed the talk button. "Be advised. We are in pursuit of the green Jeep headed north from the Island Buffalo Grill. I could use some backup."

Chase's voice came across the line. "Headed in that direction. We're still in the area." Chase disconnected.

Her heart pounded as she kept her eyes on the road, passing the one car between her and the Jeep. The Jeep maintained speed as it turned off on a spur road that indicated it led to a trailhead.

She took the turn so tightly and at such a high speed that the tires spit up gravel that sprayed against the side of her vehicle. They headed up a twisty road, eventually coming to a dirt parking lot where only one other car was parked by a trailhead marker. The Jeep continued beyond the parking lot over the rough terrain. Hannah followed as both cars climbed a hill. The Jeep disappeared from view as it descended. When her SUV reached the top of the hill, she saw the Jeep, which was no longer moving. The driver's-side door had been flung open.

She didn't see the driver anywhere, and there was no indication of which direction he might have gone. Narrowing her eyes and leaning forward, she stared through the windshield. Her heart was still racing from the adrenaline rush of the pursuit.

"There," said Trevor.

Her gaze followed the direction Trevor pointed. A man in a khaki windbreaker and hat disappeared behind a rock formation.

There was no time to radio Chase and let him know what was going on.

She drove the patrol car to where the other car had been abandoned, due to the terrain being too rough to drive over. She and Trevor jumped out of the SUV, and Hannah deployed Captain. She headed toward the rocks with

Trevor keeping pace with her. Hannah drew her gun as they ran. They entered a huge rocky field containing plenty of big boulders that someone could hide behind.

They slowed, taking time to look for movement and listen for any sound that might indicate which direction the driver had gone. Her heartbeat thrummed in her ears and sweat trickled past her temples as they advanced deeper into the rocky field. She could see where the field ended and opened up into a forest of scrubby trees—beyond that was the lake.

A flash of movement above a large rock, like a bird fluttering low to the ground, drew her attention. She ran toward where she thought the man might be. When she saw him head toward the forest of short trees with tangled trunks, her suspicion was confirmed. Beneath the hat he wore, she couldn't see his face clearly. From this distance, he looked shorter than the RMK.

She ran ahead of Trevor while Captain kept pace with her. The man disappeared into the forest.

The forest grew denser with the trees not allowing her to see much beyond the tangled branches, even though many of the leaves had fallen to the ground. It was like peering through lattice. She stopped and Trevor came up beside her. Captain remained still while she listened for any noise that might tell her which direction the man had gone.

Her breathing seemed to grow louder in the silence. Both of them were gasping for air from sprinting.

A sudden rush of noise, breaking branches and the pounding of footsteps indicated which direction they should go. Pushing branches aside, they darted through the forest and reached a place where the trees were farther apart, opening up to tall grass and brush, and beyond that the beach that led to the lake.

As she scanned the landscape, she saw no sign of the man in the khaki coat. The brush provided a few places to hide and his neutral-colored clothes would camouflage him. She was fully aware that he might have a gun.

She lifted her firearm and took several steps through the grass. Captain brushed against her thigh as he heeled beside her. Though the dog was not trained to track, he had some natural skills and would signal with a muted bark if he thought danger was close.

Trevor squeezed her arm and pointed at a

bush. He must have noticed something. Treading lightly, they advanced through the grass.

As they drew near to the spot where Trevor had pointed, several birds flew up from the brush. The sudden movement and noise made her heart beat faster as she took a step back.

"Sorry," whispered Trevor. "I saw the branches moving and assumed it was a person."

"It's okay." She was already turning in a half circle, trying to figure out where the man had gone. He had to be hiding somewhere in the grass and brush. Once he headed toward the beach, he'd be easy enough to spot. So maybe he was choosing to stay in place.

A soft breeze rustled around the three of them as they stood still. The shrill cries of birds in the distance filled the air. Hannah scanned the area around her several times, looking for any sign of the man.

"I don't think we're going to find him today." Trevor kept his voice low. "Somehow, he got away."

Or he had found a good hiding spot.

She didn't want to give up, but Trevor was probably right. If he was still close, the man wasn't going to move as long as he thought he might get caught.

Maybe they could flush him out if he thought they were leaving. She turned to head back up the hill, glancing backward several times but still not seeing any signs of the man.

When they came to the Jeep, Hannah stopped to check the registration after noticing that the license plates were for Wyoming. Interesting. The paperwork in the glove box said the car belonged to Anise Withers. She wasn't sure what local resources Chase could tap into, but maybe the car could be brought in as evidence and checked for fingerprints. Certainly, Isla could trace the registration and Anise would be contacted to find out how she was related to the man they had just pursued.

They returned to her patrol vehicle and loaded up Captain. She radioed Chase to let him know what had happened. "I doubt he'll return to the Jeep, but we can watch it for a bit, out of sight."

Chase responded, "Give it a few minutes. I'm looking at a map of the area you're in. We're on the road he might have run out to and there is no sight of a man on foot."

"He found somewhere to hide out," said Hannah.

"If you think you got this handled, Ian and I

are close to the causeway. We're going to load up on some food for the team in Syracuse."

"Ten-four." Hannah lifted her finger off the talk button.

After they watched the Jeep for some time, seeing no sign of the man, she drove back toward the trailhead parking lot and then out to the main road. Though her food had gone cold, she munched on fries just to fill the hole in her stomach.

She was pretty sure the man who had evaded them was the same one who had come after her at the lake. He seemed to have some knowledge of the island. The only thing that didn't fit was the Wyoming license plates.

When they arrived at the ranch, they found Isla at her computers. She looked up from her screen. "Tough break. Chase told me what happened."

"We almost had him." Hannah slumped down on the couch and let out a heavy breath. Captain lay down at her feet. "I assume Chase and Ian are still out getting groceries?"

While staring at the screen in front of her, Isla ran her fingers through her dark hair. "Yes, I think he said something about meeting Meadow in Syracuse as well."

"Right, Chase said he was going to have her come over from Salt Lake now that it looks like the RMK is staying on the island."

Trevor sat down on the other end of the couch. He leaned his head back and closed his eyes, clearly exhausted. Maybe now he would see the wisdom of staying under guard at the ranch. She hoped Chase would let her go out with the rest of the team if she didn't have to take him along.

Hannah pulled out her scrunchie from where it had drifted down her head. She gathered the stray strands of her hair together to create a tidier bun. "Can you run a name for me? Anise Withers. That's who the green Jeep is registered to. The Jeep has Wyoming plates. I wonder if there is any connection to Elk Valley."

Isla pulled her chair closed to the table and tapped her keyboard. "That's easy enough." She looked at her screen. "Just give me a second. Here we go." She leaned closer to the screen. "The car is from Laramie and was reported stolen from Antelope Park about an hour ago."

"Where from?"

"The visitors' center," said Isla.

"So that means Anise was probably a tourist here on the island who had had her car stolen.

No connection to the guy who came after us." The information seemed to confirm her theory that the driver in the green Jeep was the man who wanted her dead.

A shiver ran down her spine. Jodie's killer was still out there, and he had been clever enough to acquire a car that wouldn't be traced back to him.

Trevor felt the fatigue settle into his bones. It was a good kind of tired, though like a day spent baling hay or fencing. It was rewarding to be helping make progress on the RMK case. Hannah was probably disappointed they hadn't been able to bring in the man in the green Jeep. Catching him would mean her life would no longer be under threat and she could focus on her work. She would get her life back.

There was a part of him that felt like his own life had been taken from him ten years ago. Guilt over the death of his friends had suspended him in time. He hadn't moved on. He should be married and with kids by now and yet, his friends had never been given that chance.

Isla tapped away on her keyboard. "While

you two were out and about, I was pulling up and compiling pictures of park employees."

Hannah rose to her feet. "Where did you find those? Don't you have to have permission to get employee records?"

"Yes," said Isla. "But the website is free to access, and most list their employees along with a photograph."

Hannah peered over Isla's shoulder. Trevor stood up, as well, and walked toward the screen.

"Give me a second," said Isla. "I'll eliminate the obvious ones that don't fit." She kept typing. "We are looking for a male under forty, medium build, brown curly hair." She lifted her hands from the keyboard and pushed back her chair. "It's all yours. I'm going to grab a bite to eat. We brought a little food with us this morning."

She retreated to the kitchen.

Trevor offered the chair to Hannah while he stood behind her. He leaned close enough that he smelled her floral perfume. The first photo came on the screen. A man with straight, dark brown hair and intense brown eyes.

"You saw him up close and for longer than I did," said Trevor. "But I just don't think that is the guy."

She studied the photo. "He could have changed his hairstyle, but I think you're right. The face is too symmetrical. The guy I saw wasn't good-looking." An image flashed through her mind. "His chin was pointed, and his eyes were close together."

They clicked through several more photos, shaking their heads each time.

Isla returned holding a sandwich on a paper plate. "Anything?"

"Not so far," said Trevor.

"Bear in mind that some of those photos might be older. I'm not sure how often the park updates their website." She took a bite of her sandwich. "It could be that he's a new hire. He might have transferred from another area around the lake that utilizes park rangers. I can do a search on those, too." Isla took a seat on the couch.

They filed through the last few photos. Hannah slumped back in her chair. Trevor squeezed her shoulder. "We'll find him."

Her hand brushed over his where it rested on her shoulder, sending a surge of warmth through him.

"I hope so," she said. "Remember what that ranger at the visitors' center said. That he didn't think anyone was assigned to pick up trash in that area?"

"Yes," said Trevor.

"What if he went back there because it's where Jodie died? He just needed the excuse of picking up the trash to revisit the place. He might go there often."

Trevor shook his head. "I don't quite get what you're saying."

Isla rose to her feet and tossed her paper plate in the trash. "I think I know what you're getting at, Hannah. Sometimes killers keep trophies or mementos of their crime and sometimes they go back to the place where it happened."

Hannah shuddered. "Kind of creepy."

"But he won't be going back there now that he knows he'll be recognized," said Trevor.

"You're probably right about that," said Isla.

Hannah's words came out haltingly. "But he'll stay around here until he can get to me."

Isla patted her friend's shoulder. "Why don't you give me that chair, and I'll see what other places around the lake have websites with employee pictures."

"I need to take Captain out for his walk, anyway." Hannah rose to her feet. Captain stood up from where he'd been lying on a rug, then wagged his tail and looked at her expectantly. The dog understood what she'd said.

"I'll go with you," said Trevor.

"I almost forgot." Hannah walked toward Isla and pulled a piece of paper out of her pocket. "That's the license plate of a white compact car that we noticed a couple of times. It might be nothing, but you got to follow every lead, right?"

"I can run it for you. No problem."

Trevor waited for Hannah after pushing the door open.

As they stepped out the door, Hannah commented, "Let's stay to the areas where there aren't very many tourists."

"Sounds like a plan," he said.

The ranch had plenty of open area with grass and trees, in addition to the numerous buildings and barns. They walked past a narrow three-sided barn that contained old trucks and tractors, and out toward a field surrounded by trees. He could just make out a barbed-wire fence in the distance. Some of the trees still had gold, red and yellow leaves on them.

"Isla seems nice," he said. "She certainly knows her stuff."

"I've enjoyed working with her. She's from Elk Valley. You never met her?"

He shook his head. "She may have moved there after I left. I know Elk Valley is only six thousand people, but I still didn't know everyone."

"She's been through a lot in the last few months," said Hannah.

"Really?"

"She's been trying to foster a child so she can adopt. An anonymous person called the agency and told lies about her being unfit to be a foster mom. Last month, someone set her house on fire. They never caught who did it, though we're pretty sure it's the same person who tried to discredit her with the foster agency."

"That is so unfair. Any inkling of who might be behind all that?"

Hannah shook her head. "I know she looked into ex-boyfriends and a cousin who was mad at her. But so far, she hasn't found anything solid. The team is doing as much as they can to help her. I hope things get resolved. She would be a great foster mom."

They came to a freshwater creek. The trickling of the water over rocks was soothing to

Trevor. Captain stood on the bank his focus on Hannah.

Hannah waved her arm in a half circle. "Dive in."

Captain lumbered into the creek and splashed around. He put his head down to get a drink and then splashed some more.

"Man, he loves the water." Trevor laughed.

"Newfoundlands are natural swimmers. They even have webbed feet," she said.

The giant fur ball of a dog romped through the water. Hannah tossed a stick into the river and Captain dove for it.

Watching the dog play lifted a weight off his own shoulders. Judging from the smile on her face, the moment was doing the same for Hannah.

Hannah commanded Captain to get out of the water. Once on the bank, he shook his big wooly body, spraying droplets of water everywhere. They both stepped back to avoid getting wet.

In her haste, Hannah crashed into Trevor and stepped on his boot. The back of her head collided with his face.

She whirled around and gazed up at him. "I'm sorry."

He bent toward her and touched her arm.

"No problem." She was near enough for him to feel her body heat as he looked into her green eyes. He found himself bending closer.

Both of them took a step back at the same time. As heat rose up his neck, he turned sideways and studied the rippling creek. What had that been about? He'd almost kissed her.

Hannah patted her bun and the back of her head with a nervous energy. She shot a sideways glance at him.

Captain let out a woof—maybe he'd picked up on the electric charge that had just passed between him and Hannah.

Hannah kneeled down and rubbed his head. "You big old teddy bear."

Captain returned the affection with some kisses on Hannah's cheeks.

Grateful that Captain had broken the intensity of the moment, Trevor stepped closer to rub Captain's ear. "What a good boy." As he leaned down, his shoulder brushed against hers. Even a brief touch reignited the warmth he'd experienced a moment before.

Several people had come out into the field where they were.

Hannah watched the group of five people for a moment. "We should probably go back inside."

He glanced over his shoulder as they headed back toward the three-sided barn. There were two men in the group, one of whom was wearing a hat that concealed his face. The other man was the right build to be Hannah's assailant, but his hair was black. He doubted the guy would show himself in such an obvious way. The arrival of the people milling around was a reminder that they could not take any chances. It would be easy enough for the RMK or the other man to hide in a crowd of tourists.

Chapter Seven

When they returned to the community room, both Chase and Ian were unloading groceries from the backs of their vehicles. Dash and Lola sat dutifully by the front door. Both dogs, the golden retriever and the German shepherd, held their heads high and sniffed the air, tuning into their surroundings.

Officer Meadow Ames pulled up in her vehicle, as well. Meadow got out and released Grace, a vizsla, from her kennel. She followed the dog while it wandered, sniffed and did her business. Because of her tracking skills, the dog should be useful to the investigation.

With a bright smile on her face, Meadow waved at Ian as he went inside with the load of groceries. The two of them had fallen in love and gotten engaged a few months ago.

Trevor and Hannah helped bring in the groceries. As the four of them carried the bags into the kitchen, she was grateful to have other people around. The tender moment between her and Trevor by the creek still had her rattled. Was it possible to be attracted to someone who you weren't sure you even liked.? And Trevor certainly was that. It wasn't just his obstinance about being protected, but the story of what he had done to Naomi ten years ago that still echoed through her brain. Perhaps her own mistreatment from men, cheating and being stood up, colored her judgement. All the same, if there was even a small chance Trevor was that kind of guy, it wasn't worth getting hurt again.

Chase placed a can of tomatoes, and some packages of hamburger and sausage on the counter. "I got all the stuff for spaghetti. Any volunteers to help out?"

"Rocco is a really good cook. Especially Italian," said Hannah.

"He and Selena should be back anytime now, but I need to get this sauce started," said Chase. "Maybe he can add his special touch and secret ingredients once I get it simmering."

Hannah put her grocery bag on the counter and peered inside. "Looks like you got ingredients for salad and garlic toast. I can help make those."

Trevor moved closer to Hannah. "I'll give you a hand with that."

Chase nodded. "You can prep that stuff if you want to, but the sauce will need to simmer through the afternoon."

Feeling a tightening in her chest, she pressed her lips together. She'd hoped that Trevor would go back into the living room, where Ian, Meadow and Isla were, so she didn't have to contend with the feelings of attraction every time he was close.

"Tomatoes and lettuce are in the bag at the end of the counter," said Chase.

She looked at Trevor momentarily. The eye contact made her heart flutter. She turned toward the cupboards. "I'll see if I can find you a knife and cutting board."

Chase opened a drawer by the stove and handed her a knife. It took her only a moment to retrieve a cutting board and a large bowl, which she sat by Trevor.

"I'll get the bread ready to broil," she said.

"I'm just glad this kitchen was stocked with some basics," said Chase. "There should be some vinegar and oil to make a dressing."

The kitchen filled with the smell of browning meat.

As she buttered the bread and put garlic and Parmesan cheese on it, she was keenly aware of Trevor's proximity. He sliced through the tomatoes with expertise. They finished the rest of the meal prep.

Hannah avoided Trevor for the rest of the afternoon.

By the time dinner was ready, Rocco and Selena had returned from their search for the RMK.

Chase greeted them as he carried a steaming pot of spaghetti sauce toward the table. "Dinner will give us a chance to debrief as a team."

Hannah set the bread on the table.

"Smells wonderful," said Meadow.

The rest of the food was placed on the table, then everyone took a seat and Chase said grace. Trevor sat across from her, next to Rocco.

After all the food had been passed around the table and everyone's plates were full, Chase addressed his comments to Selena and Rocco. Both of them were slumped over, as though that day had been a long one.

"Did you find out anything more about the RMK?"

They shook their heads in unison.

"Nothing solid," said Selena. "It sounds like Hannah got the strongest lead."

Rocco tore a piece of garlic toast in half. "So, are we going to stake out that campground tonight?"

"Yes," said Chase, "but we can't show up in our patrol cars. I asked around. The ranch has a van they use for tours that they can loan us. Ian, Meadow and Selena will be going with me. Two people will remain in the vehicle and two will be on foot."

"Hannah's not going? It's her lead," said Rocco.

"I think it would be better if she stayed behind with Trevor," said Chase.

Her stomach clenched. She didn't like being kept from the action of the investigation.

"Rocco, you'll stay here as well to stand guard through the night, so get a few hours sleep after dinner." Chase glanced over at Hannah. "Hannah will brief you on what happened with her and Trevor today."

Rocco nodded. "I heard a little bit from Isla. That same guy came after you in a car. Sounds like a cold case that just heated up." His voice was filled with compassion. "I'm sorry they never caught the guy who killed your friend."

Hannah shook her head as she set down her

fork. "I didn't remember his face until I saw him again."

Trevor added, "He works for the park service."

After dinner and cleanup, Chase and the other three left to set up the stakeout. The sky had already turned gray. This late in the fall, it got dark shortly after dinner.

"I'm going to get that rest Chase suggested." Rocco squeezed Hannah's shoulder as he walked past her. "Wake me in a couple hours so I can take over guard duty."

Hannah listened to Rocco's retreating footsteps as he moved toward the outside door in the kitchen, the fastest way to get to the bunkhouse. Cocoa followed beside him. Isla had already excused herself and gone to the bunkhouse.

Trevor sat opposite her on one of the couches.

He glanced around. "Now what?" His voice was filled with expectation.

The way he gazed at her caused her breath to catch. At the same time, she wanted to run very far away. Somehow, they had ended up alone together. "I need to take Captain for a walk."

He lifted himself from the sofa. "I'll go with you."

"I think it would be safer if you stayed here inside."

"You shouldn't go out by yourself, either," he said. "Maybe you should wait until Rocco wakes up."

"I'm a trained officer." She didn't want to be alone with Trevor and these blossoming feelings. "I can't *not* take him out. Stay inside. I won't be long." Her words held a force to them.

With Captain heeling beside her, she stepped outside, switched on her flashlight and broke into a run. The exercise was more for her to get rid of some of her twisted-up emotions than for Captain. As her feet pounded the dirt road, the dog kept pace with her, not questioning what she was doing.

The sprint left her breathless, but the burst of activity made her feel less tied up in knots. She bent over, resting her hands on her knees. Captain wandered into the tall grass to do his business.

Once he was done, she walked back toward the community room and bunkhouse. No exterior lights illuminated the outside of the community room. A warm glow emanated from the two visible windows. An undulating shadow caught her attention as it disappeared around the side of the building.

Was someone skulking around the building? She ran back to the community room and opened the door. Trevor's laptop was open on the couch, but there was no sign of him.

She drew her gun and hurried outside praying that nothing had happened to Trevor.

Trevor retreated toward the bunkhouse, where he'd left his gun. He'd seen shadows at one of the windows. When he'd run to the door, he thought he heard footsteps. Someone was out there.

As he'd stood on the threshold, he couldn't see Hannah's flashlight in the distance. Had something happened to her?

He entered the bunkhouse, where Rocco was snoring, grabbed his gun from the drawer where he'd put it and stepped outside.

A voice shouted at him from the darkness. "Police. Stop right there."

"Hannah?"

She stepped out of the shadows. "What are you doing out here?" She holstered her weapon.

"I heard a noise and thought I saw someone."

"I told you to stay inside." Her voice was filled with irritation.

"I was worried about you." Why was she so

defensive? Couldn't she see he was trying to protect her?

Her voice softened slightly. "I appreciate the gesture, but I can take care of myself."

She stared down at the gun in his hand. "What are you doing with that? Chase told you not to use it. It's bad enough you won't just go to a safe house. You don't need to get into a gun battle and end up dead."

He let out a heavy sigh. "I have a right to protect myself. I thought I could help you."

"Go back to your room and stay there with the door locked. You'll be safe in there with Rocco. I'm going to check the perimeter of the building." Each word was enunciated and delivered with intensity.

"I'm sorry." His words had some punch to them. The way she spoke made it sound like she was ordering him around.

"Why can't you just do what Chase says and what I say? Can't you see we're trying to keep you alive?"

"Yes, I know that." A note of irritation entered his voice.

"Captain and I will be back in a few minutes. I'll knock on the door and say your name."

Feeling like an errant schoolboy, he retreated

to the bunkhouse. After placing the gun on the table by the twin bed, he locked the door and sat down on the bed. It didn't seem to matter to her that his motive was to make sure she was okay.

She probably hadn't even felt the magnetic connection that had passed between them at the creek. He stared at the ceiling. The intense emotion had probably been driven by all the time they were spending together and the lightness of the moment. Resting his elbows on his knees, he placed his head in his hands. Had it all been in his imagination?

At least five minutes passed, and she didn't return. The room had only one window that looked out on the open field, and the trees and fence beyond.

Both of them thought they had seen someone outside the community room. Maybe that someone had been scared off, or maybe he was still lurking around, waiting for an opportunity.

He walked to the door and twisted the dead bolt so he could peer out. He wondered if he should wake Rocco but thought better of it. If he was going to be on guard duty all night, he needed his rest. This could be a false alarm. He hadn't heard the sound of a struggle or gunshots. It just seemed like she should be back by now.

He was torn between doing what she said and making sure she was safe. He wasn't sure why she was so resistant to his offer of help. Staring into the darkness, he took several steps away from the door.

He heard Captain barking in the distance and then saw a flashlight bobbing up and down, coming back toward the bunkhouse.

Trevor hurried back inside, locked the door and sat down on the bed.

A moment later, he heard a knock on the door. "Trevor, it's me."

He rose and opened the door. The noise had not awakened Rocco.

"Thank you for staying inside."

Not wanting to lie, he didn't say anything or even nod.

"Let's go back to the community room," she whispered.

He trailed behind her. They entered the quiet space. He sat down where he'd left his laptop. "Did you see anything?"

"I thought I saw movement by one of the barns. All the tourists should be gone by now. This place closes down a little after the dinner hour." Hannah paced the room, peering out each window.

"We both thought we saw a person moving around the outside of the building. I think someone was here."

"I agree," she said. "What we don't know is if he is still around or if it someone dangerous or just a tourist trying to have an after-hours look at the place." Hannah still hadn't sat down. Captain followed her with his eyes. With her hands on her hips, she stopped at one of the windows and peered out.

Guilt got the better of him. "Hannah, I have something to confess."

She turned to look at him. "Yes?"

"I left the bunkhouse for a moment. I only took a few steps outside. I was worried about you when you didn't come back."

"You shouldn't have done that." She sat down on the sofa opposite him. "I appreciate your honesty."

"Why does it bother you so much that I want to help keep *you* safe?"

She stared at the floor for a moment before looking at him. "Because it makes me feel like you think I can't do my job."

Her answer shocked him. "I never said that."

"You didn't have to." She sounded defensive.

"I don't like you assuming things about me. You don't know what's going on in my head." With each exchange, both their voices got louder.

With that stern look on her face, she opened her mouth as if to say something, then shook her head, stood up and walked away.

Captain made a groaning noise and lay down on the floor.

The moment of silence seemed to have calmed them both. "I don't want to get in an argument with you, Hannah."

She turned back around to face him. "It's just that I thought this assignment would go very differently. I pictured myself coming out here and convincing you to do in person what Chase couldn't get you to do over the phone, go to a safe house. I had no way of knowing that the first time we met I would be so...compromised because of what happened to me."

"Hannah, you have to let yourself be human. Anyone who had almost been drowned would have been...upset."

The tightness in her jaw and the hard angles of her features seemed to soften. "Thank you for saying that."

"I imagine your job is not an easy one. You have to deal with all kinds of difficult people and maintain control."

"Yes, that's true, and sometimes those people have had too much to drink or are bigger and stronger than me."

"I'm not trying to be one of those people. I just want to help catch the RMK. I feel an obligation," he said.

"I get that, but I don't want you to end up hurt or worse on my watch."

"I'm glad we had this conversation." He felt like he was seeing Hannah more clearly. She was a woman with a strong sense of responsibility and a desire to do her job well. The attacks on her had made her feel insecure about her abilities.

"Me, too." She headed toward the kitchen. "I think I saw some root beer in the fridge. You want one?"

"Sure," he said. They seemed to have at least called a truce.

Hannah returned and handed him a can. She sat down and took a few sips of her drink. He opened his laptop. He hadn't gotten much work done today. He read through a report he'd written about how a ranch he was a consultant on could expand their operation without adding much debt one more time before sending it. When he looked up, Hannah had closed her eyes and was resting her head against the back of the couch with her arms crossed over her chest.

"I'm not asleep," she said. "I'm just resting."

She must be tired. She couldn't have gotten much sleep while guarding him last night.

"You could tell I was staring at you without opening your eyes?"

She opened one eye. "Of course. I'm not going to fall asleep while I'm on guard duty." Her voice held a lighter tone that he had not heard before.

"I could use some sleep myself," he said. "It's been a long day."

She checked her watch. "Let's give Rocco a little more time. I'll wake him up, so I can get some rest. He'll be stationed outside your door and I'll just be next door."

They waited another hour in the community room. Trevor gave up trying to work and closed his laptop.

Hannah rose to her feet. "Let's go. It's been a long day."

She and Captain escorted Trevor outside and walked to the bunkhouse. After waking Rocco,

Trevor collapsed on the bed without changing out of his clothes. Sleep came quickly until he was jolted awake by the cacophony of frantically barking dogs. They had an intruder.

Chapter Eight

At the sound of Captain's barking, Hannah awoke with a start. The Newfoundland stood by the door. Outside, she could hear Cocoa barking, as well. After peeling back her covers, she jumped up and grabbed her gun belt. She'd slept in her clothes for this very reason—if an intruder tried to breach the security of the bunkhouse.

The other twin bed was still empty. The rest of the team must still be out on surveillance. Isla hadn't come to bed either though there were no lights on in the community room.

Captain continued to bark as she slipped on her shoes.

Two intense knocks on her door reverberated through the tiny room.

Rocco spoke with a staccato rhythm. "Intruder. I think he went toward the field where those trees are. I'm headed to check it out."

Hannah tied her shoelaces and bolted across the floor to click Captain into his leash. "Got it. I'll stay close to Trevor."

She swung open the door and stepped outside in time to see Rocco disappearing into the darkness. Trevor stood outside his room. His hair was disheveled, and he was bleary-eyed. "Trouble?"

"Yes, get back inside." She stepped toward his room.

A gunshot resounded through the air. Hannah leaped toward Trevor, taking him to the ground. The bullet had shattered the light above the bunkhouse. They were in darkness.

Hannah had taken off her shoulder radio to sleep and hadn't had time to reattach it. She had no way to let Rocco know the assailant was still close to the bunkhouse. Maybe he had been close enough to hear the shot.

She rolled off Trevor, who crawled toward the open door of his room. Another shot whizzed by him.

She could just make out Trevor putting a protective hand toward his head. "That was close," he shout-whispered.

"He's got a line on you. You won't make it to the room before being shot. This way."

She crawled toward the side of the community room, which would provide cover. The shooter would have to reposition to get a shot at them from this side of the building. Trevor came up beside her, and both of them pressed their backs against the wall. Captain panted and leaned close to her.

Isla was suddenly beside Trevor. "I have the key to the community room. I locked it up when I went for a walk."

"Good idea. Let's get inside. I can radio Rocco from there." The community room, which had two exits, would be safer than the bunkhouse room, which had only the one door for escape if the shooter chose to close in.

They moved along the outside wall and turned the corner where the door was. Isla edged in front of Hannah and pulled a key out of her pocket. In the dim light, she had to bend close to the knob to see.

Hannah pulled her gun and peered out into the inky night.

Isla and Trevor slipped in through the back door, entering the dark kitchen.

"Stay low, so we're not seen through the window." Hannah studied the area outside one final time. Not seeing or hearing anything, she followed the other two inside, locking the door behind her. Captain remained at her heels.

Crouching, they rushed past the counter into the living room. Isla turned on a single light. Hannah grabbed the radio and pressed the talk button. "Intruder is believed to be close to the premises. We're in the community room."

"Thought I heard shots. On my way back," Rocco responded.

"Exercise caution. Two shots fired from the north side of the building. That doesn't mean our perp is staying in one place."

"Got it. I'm going to see if Cocoa can track him." Hannah wasn't sure if that would work. Cocoa's training was for arson.

"We'll stay put," said Hannah.

Isla and Trevor had already taken up a position on the floor, their backs resting against the sofa. She kept the gun in her hand as she peered over the back of the couch out the window. She could barely discern the trees from the dark sky.

Still crouching, she proceeded to get closer to the window, lifting her head just a little above the sill and watching. She peered out several other windows, not seeing any sign of the person who had taken shots at them. He must be using a night scope to have gotten so close to hitting his target after the bunkhouse light was shattered.

Captain sat several feet from her, his head held high as if waiting for a command. She checked the other windows again. She should have seen Rocco and Cocoa by now or at least a bobbing flashlight. They couldn't have gotten far in such a short amount of time.

"Anything?" Trevor asked. He'd lifted his head just above the sofa.

Something must have happened to Rocco. "I'm going out there. Lock the door behind me."

Before Trevor could object, she and Captain hurried to the front door. She stepped outside.

She pressed against the building and peered out toward the barns and outbuildings. On the other side of the door, the bolt slid into place.

The sound of a dog's intense barking reached her ears. She and Captain sprinted in the direction of the noise through the darkness.

As her feet pounded through the grass and over the hard ground, she was aware that she could be running into an ambush. Slowing, she looked side to side.

The glow of a flashlight in the grass caught her eye. She sprinted toward it. The sound of the water rippling over rocks reached her ears. She was by the creek she and Trevor had been at earlier. The barking grew more intense, and she could see Cocoa pacing. The chocolate Lab was barely visible but for her K-9 vest.

When her eyes adjusted to the darkness, she saw that Rocco was lying on the ground by the dropped flashlight. She rushed toward him.

Before she could reach him, a force grabbed her from behind and dragged her toward the creek. Weight pulled her down and her feet grew wet. She saw flashes of a face, and brown curly hair, then he pushed her under and held her there with one hand on her neck and the other on her torso. The weight of the utility belt dragged her under.

She whipped her head back and forth while trying to pry his hand off her neck. With her other hand, she managed to pull her baton and hit his arm with it repeatedly. The pressure on her body let up enough that she was able to lift her head. She gasped for air before being pushed under again. This time, his hand was on her shoulder. His other hand braced the arm that held the baton so she could not get enough arc to hit him again.

She wasn't going to die tonight at this man's

hands, not when he should be in jail. Unable to see clearly, she grasped at the first thing she could get hold of, his shirt. She pulled him closer and then reached up, this time scratching his face. The man pulled back. She was able to get into a sitting position and hit him hard across the stomach.

He fell backward into the water. With the water rippling around her, she rose to her feet and raised the baton as he crawled toward the bank.

Captain had jumped in, blocking the man's easy escape route.

Wading through the calf-deep rushing water, Hannah prepared to land a blow.

The man turned on her suddenly, pulling a gun from a holster. "Back off or I'll shoot the dog."

Hannah put both hands in the air. She wasn't about to lose her partner. She called Captain toward her.

Still pointing the gun at her, the man glanced toward the buildings before crawling up the bank. He rose to his feet. Her breath caught. Was he going to shoot her? Once he was standing, he turned and took off running toward the trees.

Weighed down by wet clothes, Hannah dragged herself through the water and up the bank where the man had gone. She glanced over her shoulder, where she saw a bobbing light moving toward her. Trevor, maybe, or Isla. That must be why the man ran. He didn't want witnesses or to contend with more people. Yet, he had the gun all along. Why go to the trouble of trying to drown her?

An agitated Cocoa paced and whined beside his partner who lay motionless on the ground.

Please, God, don't let Rocco be shot.

She couldn't see much in the darkness. She shook Rocco's shoulder and said his name but got no response. She touched his neck.

Cocoa moved in closer and licked Hannah's cheek, as if to show support.

She let out a breath when she felt a pulse.

"Is he all right?" Isla asked as she came up behind her. Her flashlight didn't reveal any blood around Rocco.

"I don't think he's shot, just unconscious." Had he been used as bait to get Hannah close to the creek?

"You stay here with Rocco." She patted Isla's forearm. She had a suspect to catch. She took off running with Captain by her side.

Exhausted from her fight and weighed down by wet clothes, she willed herself to run in the direction the man had gone but did not get far before she slowed to catch her breath.

Trevor caught up with her. His hand rested on her soaking shirt. "I saw you running and came to help."

No matter what she said, it was clear that Trevor was going to be an active part of this investigation and right now she needed him to be.

"Your timing is perfect." She pointed in the direction the man had run. "He went that way."

"Got it." Trevor bolted ahead of her.

"Trevor!" she called after him. Despite that it was against protocol, she was grateful that he had come to assist her but was afraid for his safety.

She struggled to keep up as he disappeared into the darkness. She ran in the direction he'd gone.

A single gunshot filled the air. But it had not come from the trees where the man had gone. Instead, it seemed to have been fired toward where the barns and other buildings were.

She turned abruptly and sprinted toward where the shot had been fired, praying that she wasn't too late.

★ ★ ★

Upon hearing a gunshot, Trevor had sought cover behind one of the old trucks in the three-sided barn. The man who had assaulted Hannah had doubled back and run into the heart of the ranch, slipping between the buildings. Leaving his flashlight turned off and moving with a light step, Trevor had been stealthy enough to not be detected until they were close to the buildings. When the assailant had noticed him, he immediately took a shot, which went wild in the darkness. The next bullet might find its mark, though, if the guy got close enough.

Trevor crouched down behind the truck bed.

He could hear slow-moving footsteps. The man was searching for him and getting closer. Without a gun, Trevor had only the element of surprise on his side. If the guy got close enough, he might be able to jump him.

A threatening voice cut through the darkness. "You're in the way."

The words chilled Trevor to the bone. Judging from how loud the voice was, the man was very close. Trevor had gone after him thinking he only wanted to kill Hannah. His words indicated that he saw Trevor as an expendable obstacle.

Trevor's heartbeat thrummed in his ears.

Staying in a crouched position strained his leg muscles. The seconds between footsteps seemed to drag on. Then the padding of footfalls on packed dirt grew fainter.

He took in a breath. The assailant had moved past him without noticing his hiding place.

"Stop—police."

A shot reverberated through the air. Trevor lifted his head above the truck bed in time to see Hannah race by with Captain at her side headed in the same direction the culprit had gone.

He fell in behind her. Hannah looked over her shoulder at him just as he caught up. He scanned the darkness up ahead but didn't see anything. Hannah slowed, then stopped to look around.

She patted his arm. "Glad you're okay," she whispered.

They were nearly to the orientation building, which was locked up and dark.

He glanced around before edging closer to Hannah and Captain.

"Careful." His muscles tensed as he searched the darkness.

There were plenty of possible hiding places

where the guy could take a shot at them. Still, Captain would bark if the man was close.

Though he could no longer see the fleeing man, Trevor headed in the most likely direction he would have gone, toward the entrance to the ranch.

When they got to the parking lot, it was empty.

He couldn't hear anything, no car starting up or speeding away. "He must have parked his car somewhere around here, and that's why he had to come back through the farm."

Hannah still held her gun, though she dropped her hand to her side. She glanced down at Captain, who remained still. "If Captain doesn't sense that he's close, it means we lost him." She put her gun in the holster.

They trudged back through the farm.

"It's good you came when you did to help me chase the suspect, but you put yourself in danger," she said.

He was glad that she was accepting his help. "I don't mind. I'm in danger no matter what. We can work together on this. I want to catch that guy as much as you do. I want this to be over for you Hannah."

"You know how I feel about the RMK," she said. "I want it to be over for you too."

"Maybe we can help each other end both our nightmares."

"We're sort of up against the same thing."

Though the suggestion had been made before, it was the first time since their meeting that he sensed she had softened toward the idea of him aiding in the investigation.

"It's strange. He had a gun. Once I was out in the open searching for Rocco, he could have just shot me. Instead, he drags me to the creek."

"Something about this guy and water, huh?"

Hannah's shoes made soft squishing noises as they walked on the trail around the multiple buildings. The sliding door on one of the barns had been left open, revealing the darkness from within and reminding him of how and where so many of his friends had died. So far, the RMK had not made a move on him.

"Most murderers tend to use the same MO over and over," she said.

As they approached, light glowed from within the community room while the part of the bunkhouse he could see was still dark. "So the guy is fixated on drowning people?"

"It could indicate some deeper psychological

stuff that might be important. I've only had a little training in behavioral profiling, so I am not sure what is going on here," she said.

He reached for the door of the community room. When he jiggled the handle, it was locked.

Hannah knocked. "Isla, it's Hannah and Trevor."

Isla came to the door and opened it. Her expression, the raised eyebrows and bent neck, held a question.

Hannah shook her head as disappointment colored her words. "He got away."

Trevor let Hannah and Captain step across the threshold while he entered after they did.

In the community room, Rocco was sitting on one of the sofas with an ice pack pressed against the back of his head. Cocoa was lying at his feet.

Isla sat down in front of her monitors. "Just heard from Chase. They are calling off the stakeout. No sign of the RMK."

Hannah plunked down on the opposite end of the couch from Rocco. "I take it you got knocked out."

Rocco nodded. "The guy came out of no-where. I suspect I'm gonna have a bad headache in the morning. I'll go to Syracuse to be checked out soon as the sun comes up."

"I think he wanted to use you as bait to get me out there by the creek," said Hannah.

"Lot of premeditation in that," said Rocco.

Trevor peered out the window that offered a view of some of the farm buildings. The killers had something in common in that they both planned the murders to happen in a certain place, water and a barn. For the RMK, the barn must be symbolic. He wondered if that was true for the man who was after Hannah. He turned toward Isla. "Is there a reason why the guy would try to drown Hannah when shooting her would have been easier?"

Isla swung around in her office chair. "Sometimes killers want to recreate some trauma they themselves suffered."

Hannah leaned forward to stroke Captain's ear. "Like maybe he almost drowned once?"

"Or someone tried to drown him," said Isla.

Trevor settled on the couch opposite of where Hannah and Rocco were. It wasn't until he sat down that he realized how tired he was. His sleep had been interrupted. "You know, I think I want to go to bed."

Hannah turned toward Rocco. "You're probably not up for guard duty. I can take a post until the others get back from the stakeout. I have to change out of these wet clothes first."

Trevor shifted in his seat and ran his hands through his hair. "Do you think you should be out in the open like that, given what just happened?"

Hannah glanced in his direction but not with the usual look of challenge and defiance in her eyes. Instead he thought he read appreciation in her expression. "I suppose you're right. Maybe we should all just wait here and stay together until the rest of the team gets back."

With an injured officer and Hannah under threat herself, they were vulnerable.

Rocco rose to his feet. "I, for one, could eat some leftover spaghetti. Anyone else?"

"I'm good," said Isla. "Unless there is something a little lighter, like crackers or chips."

"I'll look," said Rocco.

As the room filled with the aroma of Italian spices, Trevor could feel his eyelids getting heavy. By the time the microwave dinged, he knew he wasn't going to last much longer.

The last thing he heard before he drifted off was the rustling of a potato-chip bag and Isla talking. "Hannah, if you want to come over, I have some more photos for you to look at."

He drifted off wondering if Isla had identified the man determined to kill Hannah.

Chapter Nine

After changing into dry clothes, Hannah grabbed a chair from the kitchen table and headed toward Isla's makeshift workstation. Trevor had fallen asleep with his head pressed on the armrest of the sofa. He looked serene and kind of cute when he slept.

She sat down by Isla. "I've pulled up more photos of park employees. I'll click through them—stop me if one catches your eye."

They filed through the photos. Each time Hannah shook her head. Only one even slightly looked like a possibility—a man with short buzz-cut hair. She leaned closer to the screen. "Do you suppose he's grown his hair out since this photo was taken and it gets curly when it's longer?"

"Could be," Isla said.

The face wasn't quite right. "I don't know."

Then again, she'd only seen her attacker when he was enraged.

"We'll put him in the maybe file." Isla clicked through the remaining photos.

Hannah studied each picture carefully before shaking her head. When she glanced over at the sofa, Rocco had fallen asleep, as well. The soft hum of light snoring filled the room.

"If he works for the park service," said Isla. "He's got to be in the system somewhere. The next step is to have Chase put in the paperwork for me to have access to employee records."

"You think the guy might be a recent transfer? Jodie was killed eighteen years ago. He must be from around here even if he hasn't always worked on Antelope Island."

Isla shrugged. "Or his picture didn't make it onto the website for some other reason."

"Maybe he stole the uniform, and he wears it so no one questions why he's always down where Jodie died," said Hannah.

"It's a theory." Isla pushed a piece of paper toward her. "I almost forgot."

Hannah took the paper and saw that the name Florence Black was written on it. "The owner of the white compact car?"

"Does it ring any bells?"

Hannah put the paper in her pocket. "No, Florence sounds like an older woman's name."

"She's seventy, according to DMV records," said Isla.

She pointed at one of Isla's screens, unable to hide the disappointment in her voice. "Two dead ends. No photo and no clear connection to the car."

"Don't give up. We'll keep digging." Isla offered her a supportive smile as she pressed her shoulder against Hannah. Her attention was drawn to the two sleeping people. "Everyone looks like a younger version of themselves when they're sleeping." Her voice was wistful. "Like a child."

Isla had had a great deal of personal heartache from the time the task force had first congregated in Elk Valley in March. Other team members, and Isla herself, had filled in Hannah on her ongoing battle to foster a child and the damage that had been done to her reputation. "How are you doing with everything that has happened? I'm sure the house fire was unsettling after you had already been through so much."

Isla's fingers hovered over the keyboard as she let out a sigh. "Someone sure wants to ruin my life and steal my dreams of adopting a child. That much is clear. I just can't imagine who would do such a thing."

"Any word on the status of the little boy you put an application in to foster? What was his name?" From the other members of the team, Hannah had heard that Isla had previously been ready to foster a little girl when an anonymous caller told the agency that Isla would not be a fit mother because she drank and had a drug habit, a total lie. No doubt, this was the same person who had set fire to Isla's house in Elk Valley.

Isla pulled her purse toward her and took out her wallet. "His name is Enzo and I am hopeful that I will be chosen to foster him." She flipped open the wallet to a picture of a dark-haired little boy with an infectious smile.

"So sweet," said Hannah.

Isla closed the wallet. "Even though I've given up on meeting Mr. Right, I didn't think the dream of adopting would be so difficult." She yawned and pushed her chair back a few inches. "How about you? I don't remember you ever talking about a boyfriend."

"My life is pretty much work and being a good aunt to my nephew and niece. I don't have very good radar for picking decent men. They present themselves as good guys and turn out to be the exact opposite."

"I hear you," said Isla. Her gaze fell on the sleeping Trevor.

Isla was as familiar with the specifics of this investigation as she was. "Do you think he was telling the truth when he said he really liked Naomi?"

Before Isla could answer, there was knock on the front door. "That must be the rest of the team." Isla rose to her feet to unlock the door.

Chase, Ian, Selena and Meadow shuffled in. Their slumped shoulders and weighted features communicated extreme exhaustion.

Trevor and Rocco stirred awake.

While everyone else sat down, Chase remained standing. "I'll keep this brief since we're all tired. We know the RMK is here on the island. We don't know why he hasn't come after Trevor yet. We'll continue our search tomorrow. Get some sleep, everyone. Ian and Rocco, you're bunking with Trevor. We'll need to post a guard outside, as well."

Ian offered him a weary salute. "We'll figure it out."

Chase's attention was drawn to Rocco, who held the ice pack to his head.

"Did something happen here tonight?"

Hannah stepped forward. "We didn't have time to radio you, but the attacker came after me again tonight."

Shock spread across Chase's face. "That means he knows we have set up headquarters here."

Hannah nodded.

Chase rubbed his chin. "If we're to stay on the island, there are no other options for a place to stay overnight other than in RVs, an expense we can't afford."

"We'll just have to double down on security," said Rocco.

Chase nodded. "That's the best option. Can I get a volunteer to stand guard outside the bunkhouse to watch both Hannah's and Trevor's doors?"

Ian raised his hand. "I can do it, but I'm only going to last a couple of hours."

"I can take over after I've had a couple hours shut-eye," said Meadow.

Chase glanced at the clock on the wall. "We'll convene for breakfast and assignments at eight a.m."

That gave them only four hours to rest. They walked out in silence to their respective rooms. Isla and Meadow plopped down on the beds opposite Hannah. After removing her gun belt, she lay down fully clothed. In case there was another interruption in the night, she would be ready. Selena came a few minutes later, after she'd walked Scout. The dogs settled down by their owners' beds.

Sleep came quickly to Hannah, but her dreams were of being pulled under water and drifting down deeper and deeper.

She was awakened when Isla made a rustling around.

She lifted her head off the pillow. "What's going on?"

"Someone phoned into Chase. Another RMK sighting over at Ladyfinger campground."

Would Chase let her be part of the search? Still groggy, Hannah jumped to her feet and grabbed her gun belt. There was a better chance of him saying yes if she looked ready. "When did the call come in?"

"Two minutes ago," said Isla.

Hannah ran outside, where Meadow was sitting in a chair. Grace rested at her feet. She was still fastening her belt when Trevor stepped out of the other room. Ian came out a few seconds later.

Chase, who looked fully awake and was holding what must be coffee in a tumbler, stepped out of the back door of the community room. "We're down to four officers. I sent Rocco into town to get his injury checked out."

"You're down to five." Trevor stepped forward. "You have me. I want to help."

Hannah's stomach twisted tight. Taking him along could be a liability. Then again, she didn't want to be left behind to guard Trevor and be cut out of the action.

"He did help me chase the guy after me last night," she said. "I was glad to have the back-up."

Her breath caught in her throat as her muscles tensed.

The decision was Chase's to make.

Trevor's heart pounded in anticipation. They might catch the RMK today, and he wanted to be there to see him taken into custody.

Chase studied him for a long moment. "You ride with Hannah. Given what happened last night, the two of you are probably safest staying with the team."

Trevor relaxed. "Thank you."

"I'll be in the front vehicle with Meadow. Ian and Selena, you take rear position in one vehicle. Hannah, you take the middle position to provide a measure of safety for you two."

They hurried to their respective vehicles and pulled out of the ranch, leaving Isla to man the radio. The main building was still dark as they rolled past it toward the ranch exit.

Hannah seemed focused on the road in front of her. He didn't know how to read her reaction to his inserting himself in the investigation. Even though the suspect had gotten away last night, he felt like they had worked together. Her attitude toward him seemed to have softened.

They followed the lead car on the straight road. It was nearly thirteen miles from the ranch to the campground, which was on the north part of the island. Shortly after passing the sign that indicated Ladyfinger campground, Chase pulled over into a parking lot. The other two vehicles pulled in beside him.

It was still early for the tourists to arrive, but some of the campers may have gotten up to greet the sunrise and hike the trail. There were two other cars in the parking lot.

Chase's voice came on the radio. "The suspect was spotted by one of the campers less than twenty minutes ago out walking Cowgirl. Meadow and I will interview the camper who called this in, as well as others in the area."

Hannah pointed through the windshield. "Ladyfinger campground only has five camp-sites and it looks like each one was occupied."

"Ian, you and Selena watch the parking lot. If people return to those cars, question them about what they may have seen," said Chase.

From the SUV, Hannah pulled the radio and pressed the talk button. "What do you want me to do?"

"You and Trevor take the hike up to Lady-finger Point. See if you spot anything."

Her voice went flat. "Roger that."

"Everyone, stay alert. It wasn't that long ago he was spotted. He could still be in the area."

She put the radio back in place. Her lips were pressed together in a tight line.

Trevor leaned toward her. "You're not happy with your assignment?"

"He gave us the least likely place for anything to happen. The farthest away from where the RMK was last spotted."

"He's probably doing that to keep me safe," said Trevor.

They opened their respective car doors and

Hannah deployed Captain. The trailhead map indicated the hike was less than a quarter mile.

He'd hiked this trail before, a relaxing walk. They moved past a field filled with sagebrush. In the distance was the Great Salt Lake and a marina that was no longer in use due to the lake shrinking and the water level being so low. He remembered seeing a news story about when it had closed down.

He stopped and turned toward the beach, which was between the trail and the marina. "That must have been where he was spotted down there."

"Yes, but he would have been closer to the campsites to be seen. Weird."

"What's that?"

"He was totally out in the open with the dog, like he wanted to be spotted," said Hannah.

His leg muscles tensed. Had they been lured out here?

The sagebrush gave way to rocks and boulders as they continued their hike. They reached the end of the hike that provided a view of the lake and Egg Island in the distance.

Chase's voice came over the radio. "None of the campers saw our perp head toward the parking lot and leave. That means he must have parked somewhere else. Let me know if you see a car anywhere."

"Roger that," said Hannah. "We are at the end of the trail looking out toward Egg Island. Got a three-sixty view here. I don't see a car anywhere."

Selena reported back that she also did not see any vehicles besides the ones in the parking lot.

Hannah clicked off her radio and continued to study the area. "My parents used to bring me here to spot the birds on Egg Island." She stepped toward a cement pad and peered through the viewfinder.

He'd done the same thing himself on his trips out here. As Hannah swung the viewfinder around, he had a feeling she wasn't looking for birds. "See anything?"

She pulled her eye away from the viewfinder. "I'm just wondering if he didn't park in the lot that connects with the campground and the trail, where did he park?"

Trevor gazed off in the distance. "I suppose he could have parked at the marina."

"Chase will find out exactly where he was spotted. It's a little bit of a walk to get back to the marina." She lifted her head and looked around. "He could have just taken Cowgirl on the shore by the marina. More private and less likely to be seen. I really think he wanted to be spotted."

"So the team would show up?"

Her voice had a chilly quality to it. "Yes."

"You think this is some kind of setup." The RMK would have no way of knowing that Trevor was going out with the team.

"Honestly, I think he takes the dog out when he wants to taunt us." She shook her head. "He's knows it will be reported."

Hannah peered through the viewfinder again. "There is something down there between the marina and the base of this hill." She stepped to one side so he could see. "It looks like a black box."

Trevor looked through the viewfinder. "Where at?"

"Over by that rock outcropping."

He swung the viewfinder. His eye caught something dark and out of focus. He inched it back until what looked like a dark colored box came into focus. "I see it." The object was too far away to discern anything more about it.

Hannah got on her radio to notify Chase of what they had seen. "The box could be connected to the RMK being here."

"Unlikely. Anyone could have left it there," said Chase.

"Permission to check it out," said Hannah. "We can probably hike down to it from here faster than if we had to drive around and walk out from the marina."

"Granted," Chase responded. "If that is what you want to do. We're going to continue with our inquiries down here."

Ian broke in. "One of the owners of the cars has just shown up. I'm going to see if he noticed anything."

The man who arrived at the parking lot must have been walking off trail. Trevor and Hannah had not encountered anyone on their way up.

Hannah signed off. They headed down toward the rocks where the object was. The wind grew stronger the closer they got to the shore, rippling his shirt and hair. Captain's long fur seemed to be flying in all directions.

They drew closer to the rocks, but he still couldn't discern what the cube shaped object was.

"I wish I had binoculars," said Trevor.

They both walked a little faster. The three of them traversed across flat open beach. He had the strange sensation they were being watched.

He looked off in the distance. From the empty marina to the rock formations, there were plenty of places someone could be hiding and watching.

Slowly, Trevor began to realize what they were looking at. "That's the kind of crate you put a dog in." There were blankets inside the crate but no sign of any dog.

Hannah pulled her gun. "This could be some kind of trap."

The RMK would have no way of knowing Trevor would be the one to find the crate. Was his intent to take out members of the K-9 team?

They took a few steps toward the crate.

Hannah relaxed her stance, bending her elbows and pointing the gun at the sky. "What is going on here?"

They drew closer. He kneeled to open the crate door as the blanket wiggled. "Well, how about that. Look what we have here."

Chapter Ten

Hannah laughed as a furry brown head emerged from beneath the blanket. She holstered her gun.

Trevor had already kneeled down to open the door of the crate. He reached in to grab a cinnamon-colored puppy. "Hello there, little potato." The puppy fit in his hand as he held it to his chest.

"They totally look like Cowgirl," said Hannah. "They must be hers."

There was a water dish and an empty dish that must have contained food. The RMK had not left them here to starve.

The blanket continued to ripple.

Hannah pressed in beside him as he lifted the blanket to reveal three more puppies—one yellow, one dark brown and one a combination of the others' colors. She reached for the yellow bundle.

Captain poked his head between Trevor and Hannah. His fur brushed against her cheek.

Feeling a sense of elation, Hannah pointed the puppy's face toward Captain. "Look what we have here."

Captain sniffed the furry bundle. The dog had always been gentle around anything smaller than him.

"They look well fed." Trevor put the cinnamon puppy back down by his siblings. His hand brushed over the dark brown dog.

"I'd guess they're about eight weeks," she said. "Time enough to be weaned."

Hannah's radio crackled. Chase's voice came across the line. "Hannah, what's going on?"

She put down the puppy and pressed the talk button on her shoulder. "You'll never believe what we found. It looks like the RMK lured us out here so we would find Cowgirl's puppies."

"No kidding. Are they okay?"

"They look like they've been taken care of," she said. "There's four of them."

"We'll be out there as fast as we can." Chase's voice intensified. "Hannah, please be careful. This could still be a trap."

He was right. What had she been thinking? She'd been so caught up in the sweetness of the moment. She stared at the wriggling, grunting fur balls. Her mood shifted as she rose to her feet. There was a stretch of flat land on three sides of them and a lake on the fourth. The rocks would not provide much cover. What better way to get someone's defenses down than for them to find puppies?

It wouldn't be beneath the RMK to use the puppies as some sort of bait. Her gaze darted toward the marina, where someone might hide, then to the trees in the distance.

"What is this?" After lifting the blanket that covered the floor of the crate, Trevor reached into the cage and pulled out a folded piece of paper. He opened it up and read it. Color drained from his face as his arm went limp.

Her own chest went tight in response to his sudden change of mood. "Trevor? Let me see." She reached down for the piece of paper. A typed note.

For the MCK9 task force. I can't easily elude you and care for them. I'm keeping their mama. I've grown quite fond of Killer. Tell Trevor Gage he'll be dead soon enough.

Hannah felt like a weight had been placed on her lungs. The paper rippled in the breeze.

"This will have to be taken in as evidence." She hadn't brought a plastic baggie with her. She put the note in her pocket.

Trevor rose to his feet and stood beside her. "From the way he worded the note, he doesn't realize I'm helping the team out."

If he was watching them now, he would figure it out.

Trevor squared his shoulders and placed a hand on her arm just above the elbow. "He can't get away with this. We're going to catch him."

While she appreciated his resolve and strength, the content of the note echoed through her brain and chilled her to the bone.

"Let's slip behind these rocks until the rest of the team gets here." She ushered him toward the side of the rocks that faced the lake. The least likely place for the RMK to hide. If he approached from that direction, they'd be able to see him from a long way off. They crouched behind the rocks close enough to the crate to keep an eye on the puppies.

Captain pressed against her on one side and Trevor on the other. She peered over the rim of the stone after pulling her gun. The smell of saltwater permeated the air around her.

The puppies continued to squeak and grunt in the crate.

"Why did he call the dog Killer?" Trevor asked. "I thought her name was Cowgirl."

"That's the name the RMK gave her. He sent pictures of Cowgirl with a collar that says that. We were able to track down the shop in an Idaho town where he purchased that collar."

"In Sagebrush, where Luke Randall was shot?"

Luke had been the RMK's sixth victim. "Yes, I wish the team could have gotten to him before it happened. They were so close to stopping that murder." Still holding her gun, she continued to study the area around her as she spoke.

She shifted her weight. Her knees had grown sore from resting on the sand.

"I feel like he's watching us," said Trevor.

"I get that." Her gaze bounced around to every possible hiding place, looking for any sign of movement or color that seemed out of place.

She was relieved when two patrol vehicles pulled up to the shore. Chase, Selena and Meadow got out, each deploying their K-9s. Chase pointed in two directions. Selena and Meadow both drew their guns and headed to search where Chase had indicated with their dogs heeling beside them.

Hannah and Trevor stood up and made their way toward Chase and Dash.

"Where's Ian?" Hannah asked.

Chase replied, "He stayed with your vehicle and to keep watch."

They led Chase back to where the puppies were.

A faint smile graced his face when he looked down at the puppies climbing all over each other. Chase was a man who didn't wear his feelings on his sleeve, so such a reaction from him was pretty huge.

He kneeled and opened the crate door, then drew out the multicolored puppy. "We'll have to get these little guys back to Elk Valley and have Liana take over their care."

Liana Lightfoot was the team's lead K-9 trainer in Elk Valley. She was set to adopt Cowgirl before the dog had been kidnapped.

"She'll be glad to see them," said Hannah. "Hopefully, we'll get Cowgirl back soon, too."

"Hopefully." Chase stared off into the distance before continuing. "I'll see if I can arrange a chopper to transport these guys."

Hannah could tell that Cowgirl's kidnapping weighed heavily on him.

She stared back down into the crate, trying to inject a hopeful tone into her words. "Looks like they're eating solid food. The blankets will probably have the RMK's scent on them so we can use them for the dogs to track him."

"Yes, all that is good," said Chase. "We'll see if we can get any prints off the crate as well."

Hannah pulled the note from her pocket. Her voice dropped half an octave. "He left this for us to find."

Chase took the note and read it. His expression registered only a minute reaction—a slight parting of his lips, and a subtle deepening of the furrow between his brows. "Our prints will be on this, but we can still send it in for analysis."

Hannah appreciated Chase's steadfastness in the face of such a threatening message.

Selena and Meadow emerged from where they'd been sent to search. They came out to meet the others. Trevor and Chase lifted the crate and carried it across the sand to where the vehicles were parked, then loaded it in the back of Chase's patrol car.

"Selena and Meadow. I want you two to continue to question the campers at the other campgrounds. Hannah, why don't you and Trevor come back to headquarters with me. One of you can ride with me and the other in Selena's patrol car. It's going to be a little cramped. We'll drive you back to your vehicle and you can follow me back to the ranch from there."

They drove back to where Ian and the other patrol car was. Hannah got Captain into his kennel and Trevor sat in the passenger seat.

She turned the key in the ignition and pulled onto the road. She drove toward the ranch behind Chase.

She knew Chase was concerned about Trevor's safety. That was why he wanted them back at headquarters.

The RMK had been on the island for two days, making appearances that he knew would be reported back to them, yet he had not attempted to come after Trevor. The reason for that was now clear. He had been hindered by having to take care of the puppies.

With those four tiny obstacles out of the way, it was just a matter of time before he had Trevor in his crosshairs.

Trevor couldn't stop thinking about the note the RMK had left. It made the threat on his life that much more real. Sure, the note had chilled him to the bone, but as he stared out the window, he felt something much stronger than fear rising to the surface.

For his dead friends and for the whole town of Elk Valley, he wanted this guy behind bars. The RMK had caused enough pain. Trevor knew he was the only one who could draw the RMK out into the open.

"Do you think he'll try to lure me to a barn, like he did with the other victims? Doesn't it make it that much harder to get at me?"

Hannah didn't respond right away, as though she was weighing what he had said. "The RMK is clever, and he's got to know that we've figured out his patterns. Because he doesn't want to get caught, he might change some of his MO to get to you."

"I agree. Otherwise the only thing I have to do to stay safe is stay out of barns, right." He tried to sound lighthearted.

"He could shoot you and then place your body in a barn." Her tone had grown serious. "My guess is that the barn is a sort of symbol of what the YRC represented."

"I'm the last one left of that friends' group from ten years ago," said Trevor.

"One of the RMK's notes on the recent victims said he was saving the *best for last*. We believe that's you, Trevor. His plan is probably to go after you, and then disappear, making him that much harder to catch."

"All the more reason to stay the course." He found himself praying silently, for courage, as the road clipped by. "The death that bothers me the most is Peter Windham. He wasn't part of the group that pranked Naomi or treated women badly."

Hannah kept her eyes on the road. "The fifth victim, living in Colorado at the time of his death. Someone who wasn't a member of the club wouldn't know that about Peter."

"You're probably right. Maybe Peter was just made guilty by association." He couldn't shake the sharp pain that threaded through his chest. "That is the saddest thing of all."

She nodded.

Hannah turned on the road that led to the ranch and followed Chase's car to the parking area by the community room and bunkhouse. Trevor helped Chase unload the puppies and carry them into the community room while still in the crate.

Isla rose from her desk. She stared into the

crate, making oohing sounds. "What a bunch of cuties."

Chase excused himself and stepped outside.

Hannah left the community room and returned a moment later with a towel. "I had an extra one. I need to pull those blankets for us to use for the dogs to pick up the RMK's scent." Kneeling, she drew out the blankets and put the towel inside for the puppies.

From the window, Trevor could see Chase pace around the building outside with his phone held close to his face.

Holding the water dish, Hannah rose to her feet. Her gaze followed where Trevor was looking out the window at Chase. "He's probably making calls to arrange for the puppies to be transported to Elk Valley."

"Who will take care of them once the puppies get there?"

"Liana Lightfoot, the team's K-9 trainer, will be there to meet them when they arrive," said Hannah. "She'll be overjoyed to see those puppies, I'm sure."

Hannah retreated to the kitchen and returned with a full water dish.

Trevor picked up the cinnamon-colored pup. He was the smallest in the litter, but from watching him interact with his siblings, he appeared to also be the most rambunctious.

Rocco entered from the kitchen. He must have been in the bunkhouse. "What do we have here?"

"The RMK left Cowgirl's puppies for us to find," said Trevor.

Rocco kneeled down and peered into the crate. "Of course, he'd want to unload these little guys. I imagine they made it that much harder to carry out the final part of his plan." He glanced nervously at Trevor.

Trevor drew the puppy close to him, resting it on his chest. He reminded himself of his resolve to stay on the island to draw out the RMK. The puppy licked the underside of his chin.

Hannah stepped closer to Trevor but looked in Rocco's direction. "How's your head?"

Rocco responded, "Just a bump. I'm cleared for light duty."

Hannah stepped toward the crate and kneeled to pick up an escaping puppy. The other two seemed happy to remain in the crate sleeping.

Still holding the cinnamon-colored puppy, Trevor sat down on the sofa.

Chase stepped into the community room.

"Chopper should be here before the day is over to transport the puppies. I'm going to need an officer to accompany them."

"I can go," said Rocco. "I'm supposed to take it easy today, anyway."

"Great," said Chase.

Rocco smiled. "It will give me a chance to say hi to Sadie and Myles." Rocco, who was from Elk Valley, had recently become engaged to a woman who lived there and ran a food truck. Sadie had a three-year-old son, Myles.

Chase put his phone away. "I'm headed back out to continue searching and questioning. Where are the blankets with the scent?"

Hannah handed one of the blankets to Chase. "We're staying here?"

"For the time being," said Chase. "We'll remain in radio contact. Someone needs to stay behind to watch over Trevor. Rocco can help out, as well, until the chopper comes. I'll make sure at least one officer is back before he leaves with the pups."

Hannah didn't say anything. She simply nodded and placed the puppy she was holding back in the crate. Her disappointment was palpable, though.

With his golden retriever, Dash, following

him, Chase excused himself. Trevor could hear his SUV start up outside.

The cinnamon-colored puppy had fallen asleep on Trevor's chest.

"Looks like you are pinned down," said Rocco. "Want me to take him off your hands?"

"Sure," said Trevor.

Rocco reached for the puppy, who grunted and wiggled when he picked him up.

Isla had returned to her computers. Hannah wandered into the kitchen with Captain trailing behind her.

Trevor found Hannah standing at the counter making a sandwich. Captain sat at her feet. "You hungry? We didn't get a chance for breakfast."

"I could eat." He stepped toward the counter and drew out two pieces of bread.

She pushed the packages of cold cuts and sliced cheese toward him. "I'm sorry about you being cut out of the action on account of me," he said.

She took a bite of her sandwich and shrugged. "Sure, I'm frustrated, but I understand. Chase is just trying to keep both of us safe. I respect his judgment."

He squeezed some mustard onto his sandwich. "But it's hard to deal with, all the same?"

"I just thought when this case landed in my backyard that I would be playing a bigger part."

"You are playing an important part. You're protecting me."

"Well, you've pulled my feet out of the fire enough times," she said.

"I think you've handled yourself like a top-notch officer, Hannah."

She lifted her chin as a rich warmth came into her eyes. "Thank you."

It seemed a mutual respect had grown between them. That was progress from where they had started out from.

After they ate, they both wandered into the living room.

Isla looked up from her keyboard. "I'm trying to track down all the part-time and seasonal park employees. I've made a call to the HR person who would have done the hiring. No answer, but I left a message."

"Thanks for doing that, Isla. Maybe that will get us a name to go with the face."

The afternoon dragged on into early evening. Chase and the others all radioed in that the K-9s had not picked up any trail and had not run into anyone who had seen the RMK or Cowgirl since the morning sighting. They were headed home.

It was nearly dinnertime when the chopper landed in a field not too far from the ranch. Trevor helped Hannah and Rocco carry and load the crate.

Rocco got into the chopper with Cocoa after hugging Hannah and shaking Trevor's hand.

Trevor pressed his hand on the crate. "Safe journey, little fellas."

He and Hannah stepped back as the helicopter blade whirled, stirring up dust all around them. They stood close enough that his hand brushed over hers.

As the helicopter gained altitude, she grabbed his hand and squeezed it.

What had her gesture communicated? That they were in this together, willing to fight for each other's lives and safety?

The sound of the chopper grew faint as it became a tiny dot in the expanse of sky.

Trevor stared all around and then back at the edge of the ranch, where the bunkhouse was. It occurred to him that maybe the RMK had not been spotted anywhere on the island since this morning because he had already moved in closer to the ranch and was biding his time, waiting for a vulnerable moment when he could come after his target.

Chapter Eleven

The team ate a late dinner together while the sky grew dark outside. The heaviness of frustration at the RMK having eluded them seemed palpable. The conversation was mostly about inconsequential things with long silences between comments.

Hannah cleared her throat. Time to address the elephant in the room. "Is there something different we could be doing to draw the RMK out?"

Chase put down his fork as if he was ready to say something.

Trevor interjected. "We could set a trap with bait, namely me."

"I'm not going to put you at more risk," said Chase.

"Seriously, I'll just go stand in a barn somewhere while you guys wait in the shadows." Trevor's words came across as sarcastic.

Ian snorted a laugh.

Chase smiled, as well. He placed his fork on the table. "Appreciate the sentiment, and I feel your frustration, Trevor."

Hannah wiped her mouth with her napkin. "Trevor and I were talking earlier, and we think he might change his MO since he has established a pattern for luring the victims into a barn to shoot them."

"I think that's possible," said Isla. "He's methodical and he's a planner. In order to catch us by surprise, he might try something different."

Chase scooted his chair back, rose and picked up his plate. "We know from the note left on the victims that were killed this past February that he always planned to go after Trevor. That's what he meant by *saving the best for last.*"

It had been clear from the beginning that this case was about revenge. Hannah recalled the contents of the note that had been left on the first two victims. *They got what they deserved. More to come across the Rockies and I'm saving the best for last.*

"What are you saying?" said Meadow.

"I think he sees this K-9 task force as an affront to his careful plan," Chase said. "He thought he was just going to carry out the killings. His anger has spilled over to the task force. That's why he kidnapped Cowgirl, and I believe he's taking delight in evading and taunting us when we are so close to catching him. He's clever and he's adaptable and driven by some deep-seated anger. So, yes, I do think he might change it up, and I wouldn't put it past him to try to target any one of us because he sees us as being in the way."

Hannah let Chase's words sink in but not the fear they had the potential to induce. The team would protect each other. "What's our next step?"

"Meadow, after a couple hours of sleep, you and I will go out on night patrol. We'll get the dog to scent off the blankets that were left in the puppy crate. Selena, you grab a nap, as well, so you can stand guard outside the bunkhouse. Ian, if you're not too tired, why don't you stay close to Trevor along with Hannah?"

After the dishes were done, the three officers left to rest up for an evening of duty.

Isla returned to her computers while Trevor worked on his laptop.

Hannah stood at the window staring at the night sky. The stars were stunning, and they would be even more beautiful if she could go outside and look at them but being exposed like that would be too dangerous.

Antelope Island was known as a great place to star-gaze because of the lack of interference from artificial light due to its remoteness. Memories of last time she and her parents and Jodie had laid on a blanket by the camper to watch the night sky whirled through her mind. The next day, Jodie had been killed.

It marked the end of her childhood and of innocence.

She glanced back at Trevor, who was fully concentrating on his laptop screen. His unruly hair partially covered one eyebrow. What would it be like to star-gaze with Trevor?

Why had that thought popped into her head?

Maybe because there seemed to have been some unspoken agreement between them as they'd watched the helicopter take the puppies away. She'd squeezed his hand to let him know that she was there for him. In terms of keeping each other safe, they had each others' backs. She hoped he understood that she hadn't meant anything more by grabbing his hand.

He had won her trust in that way…at least. That didn't mean her heart was open to anything romantic between them. She'd been hurt one too many times in that department.

Isla piped up. "Hannah, I just got an email from the HR person who hires the seasonal help for the park."

"She's working late."

"It came in several hours ago," said Isla. "I just now had a chance to check it."

Hannah moved across the floor. "What does she say?"

"She gave me three names of possible men that matched the description you gave. They all live in Syracuse. One works in the winter. The other two are spring-summer employees, so they would just be finishing up since it's September. David Weller and Frank Stafford."

"I wonder if they keep their uniforms so they could show up even when they weren't working and not draw attention."

Isla grabbed a piece of paper off her desk and picked up a pen. "She couldn't disclose their addresses, but I can easily match their names to where they live." Her pen whirled across the page. She handed Hannah the piece of paper.

"Thanks, Isla, you're the best." Hannah stared at the three names.

"The first two are the spring-summer employees, probably should look into them first."

Trevor closed his laptop. "I suppose one of the other officers will have to track them down."

That would mean drawing personnel from the RMK case, which might not be possible. "I think maybe we should find out more about them first." She wondered, too, if the culprit would stay away from his home for fear of being caught once they could attach a name to his face.

"I can help you with that, too." Isla turned her attention back to her keyboard. "I'll find if any of them have a police record and do a general search on them to see what pops up. That will help us start building a profile."

"I don't suppose there were photographs of the two men who just finished up their season," said Hannah.

"They don't usually do that for the seasonal help," said Isla.

"It might be helpful to talk to this HR person in the morning. Do you have her name and number?"

Isla grabbed another piece of paper and wrote down the contact information.

Hannah waved the pieces of paper. "I knew

once you did your hard work, Isla, we'd make progress." Her mood was elevated by the prospect of being able to identify the man who had come after her.

Shortly after Chase and Meadow left, Trevor and Hannah made the decision to retire. Isla stated that she still had some work to do.

When Hannah glanced at Isla's screen just before she prepared to leave the sitting area, she noticed that she had pulled up the Caring Hearts Adoption Agency website, the agency Isla had been working with to foster Enzo. The look on Isla's face was one of wistful longing.

Isla must have felt Hannah staring. She turned her chair toward where Hannah stood in the doorway.

"Still no word?" Hannah felt her own heart squeeze tight.

"Like looking at the website is going to give me answers." Isla shook her head. "I just wish I could get this thing cleared up and have that little boy in my life."

"I do, too. I've been praying for you. Let me know if there's any way I can help."

Hannah excused herself and headed toward the bunkhouse. Selena had already taken up her position with her K-9, Scout, sitting outside on a chair while Ian took a turn resting.

"Make sure you lock the door behind you," Selena said. "Isla has a key. I checked the room a few minutes ago to make sure it was clear."

Hannah watched as Trevor and Ian headed toward their room, closing the door behind them.

Selena gave a backward glance toward the men's sleeping quarters. "He's all right, Hannah."

"Why are you telling me that?"

Selena shrugged. "Just saying. You seem a little guarded around him and then I see you looking at him like… I don't know, there's some kind of spark between the two of you."

"No, that's not what's going on." She sounded like she was trying to convince herself. "I'm here to do a job and that job is being Trevor's protection."

"If you say so." Selena reached down to stroke her K-9's ear. The Malinois tilted his head in response.

Hannah glanced up at the huge sky and twinkling stars before stepping into the dark room with Captain. She couldn't get away from Selena's probing stare soon enough.

After taking off her gun belt, she removed

her shoes and threw back the covers. She pulled her hair free of the bun it had been in. She fluffed her pillow and lay down, staring at the ceiling. She could hear Captain breathing as he settled down beside her.

"Maybe I do have some feelings for Trevor." She turned on her side, barely able to make out Captain's brown head in the darkness. "What do you think?"

The dog emitted a sympathetic whine.

"Oh, what do you know about love, anyway?" She reached down to touch his head. What did *she* know about it? After her last boyfriend had cheated on her, she had simply closed the door on that possibility. She'd seen the worst side of men in her dating life.

She sighed and closed her eyes, slowly drifting off to sleep. She had the sensation of being pulled through the top of her bed, only it wasn't her bed. Water covered her face. She couldn't breathe. Air, she needed air. Above her was the soft-focus face of the man who had killed Jodie. His hand reached out toward her, slicing through the murky water.

She awoke with a start, her heart racing. The room was dark. Isla's bed was still empty. Captain was lying beside her, snoring.

A knock on the door startled her. Still shaken by the dream, she glanced toward where she'd left her gun.

"Hannah, it's me." As he lifted his hand from the door, Trevor wasn't sure what had happened. Selena and Scout were no longer posted outside. The chair was empty. The sound of Hannah's screaming had awakened him. Worried that something bad had happened to her, he rushed over to her door.

He heard footsteps and the door swung open. She stood there barefoot but still in her uniform. Her long red hair flowed freely, framing her face.

He breathed a sigh of relief. She was all right. "I heard you scream. What happened?"

"I didn't realize." She stared at the floor. "I had a bad dream." When she looked up at him, her eyes were glazed. "I saw him...in my dream." Her voice faltered. "He was trying to—"

He gathered her into his arms. She was crying and shaking as he stroked her hair and held her close. He hugged her for a long moment, relishing the warmth of her and grateful that he could offer comfort.

She stepped free of the embrace and swiped

at her eyes. "Thank you." She shook her head. "The dream just seemed so real." She noticed the empty chair. "Where's Selena?"

"The chair was empty when I left my room to see what was going on with you."

She stepped out onto the concrete pad and looked in both directions. "She must have seen something."

"We shouldn't be standing outside. I'll wait with you in your room until she comes back. Ian is still asleep."

She nodded and stepped aside. Captain stood wagging his tail. Hannah walked over to the window and peered out. "I wonder what it was that Selena saw."

"I don't know. I didn't hear a gunshot." He stood beside her, seeing nothing but the dark shadows of the trees. "You should probably stay away from the window."

She sat down on the bed, and he settled into the only chair in the room. The embrace had seemed so genuine, he was having a hard time reconciling that with the words he had overheard her say to Selena. That she thought of him as just part of the job. She sent such mixed signals.

The doorknob shook and he realized he hadn't locked it.

The door opened. Isla stood on the threshold. "What's going on?"

Hannah answered. "Selena took off. We think she must have been after someone."

"Oh, my. I hope it was nothing. I hate to think of either of those men being that close."

Yet it was a possibility. The man after Hannah had already tried to lure her out.

"I thought I'd wait here with Hannah until Selena got back," said Trevor.

Isla nodded. "I just came to grab my pajamas and toiletries. I'm ready to call it a night."

The old bunkhouse had no bathroom, so everyone had to use the one bathroom in the community room.

"You stayed up pretty late," said Hannah.

"One thing leads to another. I keep thinking of angles I could be working to move the investigation forward. Since both of our suspects, Ryan and Evan, seem to have fallen off the map, I thought I'd put together a list of people who might know where they are or had seen them. I intend to call them tomorrow if I have any downtime." Isla pulled pajamas, a robe and a bag from her open suitcase on the bed.

"Maybe one of the other team members staying in Salt Lake can assist with that," said Hannah.

"I intend to enlist their help. We still have to track down an address for Ryan. I'd like to put some time into that." Isla pulled pajamas, a robe and a bag from her open suitcase on the bed. She moved toward the door.

Trevor rose to his feet. "I'm going to lock the door behind you. Knock when you come back."

"Got it." Isla reached for the doorknob.

After she left, Trevor rose and pushed the knob in to lock it. Hardly high security.

He sat back down. Their eyes met. He longed to ask what she had meant by saying that she saw being with him as just part of her job, but he was afraid of the answer. Despite how guarded she could be, he was starting to have feelings for her. He couldn't assume that the feelings flowed both ways.

She was a hard person to understand with all the layers of armor she seemed to wear.

Feeling awkward, he got up and peered out the window. Shadows moved by the trees. He took a step back.

"You saw something." She half rose from the bed.

"Stay down." His eyes went to her gun, which she had pulled from the holster and placed on her bedside table.

When he looked back out the window, he saw no more movement.

A pounding at the door caused both of them to jump.

Selena's intense voice boomed through the closed door. "You all right in there, Hannah?"

"Yes," she said.

"Where's Trevor?"

"He's in here with me."

"Oh?" Selena sounded confused.

"When we saw you were gone, we figured something was up. I came in here to make sure she was safe." Tired of talking to the door, Trevor unlocked it.

Dressed in her robe, Isla stood behind Selena.

Hannah spoke over Trevor's shoulder. "Was somebody out there, Selena?"

Trevor turned slightly so Hannah would have a better view.

Scout panted and Selena appeared to be out of breath, as well.

"Scout got all restless and growly, started pulling on the leash. I commanded him to take off. We searched the whole area by the trees."

"There's a lot of wildlife around here," said Trevor.

Selena shook her head. "I don't think that's what it was. Because he's trained to track in all kinds of environments, Scout wouldn't be distracted by other animals, and he was insistent that something was out there."

Hannah came and stood closer to Trevor. He could feel her breath on his neck as she spoke over his shoulder. "At this point, it could have been the RMK or the man who is after me."

Selena put her hands on her hips and let out an audible breath. "I don't think he's coming back tonight. If it was either man, Scout's barking probably scared him away. It wouldn't hurt to have another officer on duty, though. I might wake Ian in a bit."

Trevor stepped out of the way. "Sorry, Isla, didn't mean to keep you waiting."

Selena moved toward her chair. "Why don't you all try to get some sleep?" She commanded Scout to lie down.

"I should probably get some shut-eye, too," said Trevor.

As he left the room, he noticed that Hannah had retreated back toward the nightstand, where she'd pulled out her phone. He wondered whom she would be calling at this time of night but knew that it would have to wait until morning.

He returned to his room. The RMK might have been watching them when they found the puppies. He could have followed them and discovered where they'd set up headquarters. Sleep came slowly. He tossed and turned at the thought that the RMK might be lurking around the ranch watching and waiting for his chance to move in to kill him.

Chapter Twelve

When Hannah woke up, Isla was still asleep. Selena and Scout must have come in sometime in the night, as well. Meadow and Grace were sleeping, too. She grabbed her toiletries and a change of clothes with Captain trailing behind her. She greeted Ian, who sat on the chair outside. Lola was lying at his feet, head up, still alert.

"You couldn't have gotten much sleep."

"I'll get more soon as Chase and Meadow wake up. They came in about two hours ago."

Everyone but her had put in a long night. She felt guilty. She showered and changed. When she came out of the bathroom, Trevor stood by a griddle flipping pancakes. The room smelled like coffee. Scrambled eggs rested in a frying pan on the counter.

"There was a mix in there." He pointed at

the cupboard. "Thought I'd try to help out some way."

She grabbed a cup of coffee. "Yeah, I know I feel like I'm not pulling my weight, but I have a plan."

He lifted a pancake with his spatula and transferred it to the plate he'd set out. "Oh?"

She wandered over to the refrigerator and opened it. "I texted Chase last night and asked if I could go talk to the HR woman Isla contacted. Her office is in Syracuse." She spotted some orange juice and pulled it out.

"I assume I'd be going with you?"

"Yes, of course, I still have to look out for your safety so the rest of the officers can concentrate on the investigation. The way I explained it to Chase was that the sooner we can get this man in custody, the sooner I can focus my full energy on helping catch the RMK."

"And what did Chase say?"

"He said it would be all right. I'll call the HR woman and let her know I'm coming in just a bit. I imagine she's not in the office yet."

They ate quickly and cleaned up. Trevor left a note letting the others know there were pancakes in the fridge that could be reheated.

They drove through the park and back over

the causeway. Hannah checked the rearview mirror. Only two cars were behind her. Traffic was light this early in the day.

Syracuse was the last town before the island, a place where people picked up supplies or stayed if they wanted something nicer than a camper or tent.

Hannah turned off the main street and drove a few blocks to the park employment office. She unbuckled her seat belt. "Why don't you come with me?"

She didn't notice anyone following them, but she couldn't take any chances.

Leaving Captain in his kennel, Hannah and Trevor stepped into an office where a blond woman wearing pink glasses who looked like she was barely out of her teens sat behind a desk. "Can I help you?"

"I'm Hannah Scott. We're here to see Lydia Strobel."

"You're catching her early. I doubt that she's busy yet." The woman pushed a button on her phone. "Lydia, Hannah Scott and her partner are here."

The assumption the receptionist had made caused Hannah to smile. To the world, she and

Trevor came across as two officers working on a case.

Lydia's voice came through the line. "Send them in."

When they entered the office, Lydia Strobel stood by the water cooler filling a water bottle. "Hannah Scott?" Her forehead furrowed when she looked at Trevor.

"Yes, and this is Trevor Gage. He's helping me out."

"I'm not sure what more I can tell you that I didn't already share with Isla," said Lydia.

In Hannah's experience, people were freer with giving information when questioned in person. But what she really hoped for by making the drive was to see if Lydia had pictures of any of the likely suspects.

"I am wondering if you can tell us about David Weller and Frank Stafford."

"I've only been in this position for four years. David has worked seasonally for many years. I'd have to look up his employment record to tell you exactly how many. This is Frank's third year with the park."

"Are both men long-term residents of the area?"

"Yes, I believe so." Lydia took a sip from her water bottle.

Both men must have been responsible enough workers to be hired year after year. "What can you tell me about the personalities of each man?"

"My interaction with both of them was pretty brief. You'd have to talk to some of their co-workers to get a more complete picture."

"I don't suppose you have a photograph of either of the men?"

Lydia took a sip of her water and set it on her desk. "Like I told Isla, we don't usually take headshots for the seasonal workers."

"Maybe something less formal," said Hannah. "A picnic or a work project a bunch of people were on."

Lydia sat down at her desk and put her hands on the keyboard. "Maybe something on our Facebook page."

It seemed like Isla would have accessed something like that since it was available to the public.

Lydia scrolled through, shaking her head. "Neither David nor Frank do any educational programs. That's mostly what we take pictures of." She looked up and lifted her hands from the keyboard. "Wait." She scooted her chair back and walked over to a file cabinet. "We do take a group picture at the end–of–the–season picnic. I don't have the one from this year yet, but here is the one from last year." She laid a photograph on her desk.

It was a posed photo, three lines of men and women in park uniforms. The front line was kneeling. Hannah scanned the sea of faces.

Lydia stood beside her. "There's Frank Stafford."

She pointed at a man in the middle row.

Hannah shook her head. The features were too sharp. The nose too big. Frank Stafford resembled an eagle.

Lydia continued to scan the picture. "I don't remember if David Weller was in attendance or not."

Hannah's eyes fell on a man in the back row. He stood in such a way that his face was half-concealed by the person next to him. She recognized the brown curly hair. "That must be David Weller."

"Oh, yes, there he is," said Lydia.

A chill ran down her spine as her heart pounded. The man in the photo was the same man who had come after her. David Weller was Jodie's killer.

★ ★ ★

Sensing a shift in mood, Trevor stepped closer to Hannah. Her face had drained of color.

"That's him. That's the man." Her voice came out in a hoarse whisper.

Trevor looked at where Hannah was pointing. His face was only partially visible. "Are you sure?"

Hannah nodded. "Can you tell me who David primarily worked with?"

Lydia took the photograph and walked back over to the file cabinet. "I'd have to look up the shift assignments." Her phone rang. She stepped toward her desk. "I can't do that right now but maybe later, and I'll send the information to Isla."

"Thank you, I'd appreciate that." Hannah spoke in a monotone.

Having looked at the face of a murderer, Trevor wondered if she wasn't in a bit of shock.

"Thanks so much. You have been very helpful." Resting his hand on Hannah's upper arm, he guided her toward the door.

Lydia picked up the phone and waved at Trevor and Hannah as they stepped into the reception area.

Once outside, Trevor opened Hannah's car door for her. He climbed into the passenger seat.

"You doing all right?"

She nodded. "I'll be okay in a minute. It's just seeing that man's face kind of put me in a tailspin."

He reached over and rested his palm on her wrist. "Understandable."

She startled when her phone rang. "It's Isla. I'll put it on speakerphone so you can hear it, too." She pressed a button and spoke into the phone. "Yes."

"Hannah, I've got addresses to connect to those names."

"We only need one. David Weller is the guy. Lydia had a photograph."

"That's good news," said Isla. "How are you doing? You sound a little shook up."

"I am. You know, it's been eighteen years since Jodie died. I can't believe that I might finally be free of this cloud that has hung over me for so long."

"Well, that's a good thing." Warmth permeated Isla's voice.

Trevor was grateful that Hannah seemed to be able to open up more to Isla than to him. It was clear the team members were close and supported each other.

"Yes, it is," said Hannah.

"Anyway, I have David Weller's address. Just wanted to let you know. Chase will probably want to send one of the other officers over there."

"That would be the safest thing. Wait. Is the address clearly a rented apartment? It wouldn't hurt for us to talk to the landlord or manager find out what kind of person David was."

"The address does have a 'half' attached to it so it's probably a basement or an above the garage unit." Isla read off the address while Hannah put it in her phone. "Hannah, maybe you should wait until another officer is available."

Though he understood her urgency in wanting to get the case resolved, Trevor wasn't sure going there was such a good idea.

"It's a weekday. The guy probably had to get to work, or maybe he's hanging out on the island all the time. Besides, Trevor is with me." She gazed in his direction. "We're already over here in Syracuse."

Her vote of confidence in his ability to assist felt good, but he still wasn't sure they should take a chance in going to David's place.

Hannah said goodbye to Isla. She glanced in his direction. "I can tell by the look on your face. You don't like this idea."

Was he that easy to read, or did she just know him so well from all the time they'd been spending together?

"I think talking to the landlord is smart, but what if David is around, he could come after you. Or if he knew you had tracked him to his residence, it might make him flee the state and he'd never be caught."

"We're here in town. The faster we can move this case forward, the sooner I get my life back." She let out a breath and gazed at him. "Please, support me in this."

"Okay, I get it. It's no different than me not wanting to go to a safe house because I feel so much personal responsibility about the murders."

"Why would you feel guilty?" She turned to face him. "In the transcript of your interview you said you really liked Naomi when you asked her to the dance." Her eyes narrowed as she leaned toward him, body language that demanded a clear answer.

At least his conscience was clear about that. "I did like her. I thought she was smart and funny."

Something in her expression relaxed when he gave his answer. "So why do you feel like all the deaths are your fault?"

"If I had spoken up all those years ago, the joke wouldn't have gotten so out of hand," he said. "Even if it's Ryan York who is behind all this, an atmosphere was set in the YRC that led to Seth dumping Shelly. I had influence. I could have changed things and called my friends out."

"I can't argue with you there." A note of irritation threaded through her words.

"Wait. Did you really think I would do something mean like ask a girl out as a joke?"

"I wasn't sure until now. Now that we've talked, I believe you were sincere in asking her to the dance."

"You thought I could do something like that?" Now he understood why there always seemed to be a barrier between them.

She laced her fingers together and stared at them. "I know how Naomi felt. Something similar happened to me in high school. A boy asked him out to a formal dance. I got all dressed up. Mom took me to get my nails done…and then he didn't show. The buzz around the school was that it was on a dare from his friends. I know how mean boys can be."

The anguish in her voice was so intense he wanted to hug her, to comfort her. "I'm sorry that happened to you. That wasn't right."

"It's not just that. My last boyfriend cheated on me. I guess I'm just jaded when it comes to men." She twisted the button on her uniform. "The group you ran with in the YRC didn't come across as stellar examples of manhood."

"Agreed. It wasn't who I really was, and Seth, Brad and Aaron never got a chance to mature and change. It certainly wasn't how my father taught me to treat women, the example he set with my mom. I'm not making excuses, it's just that I was young. I let my peers have too much sway over me."

Warmth came into her eyes as she reached out to touch his hand. "I'm glad we talked about this."

He was, too. He'd seen that vulnerable side of her again. He understood a little better why she was so guarded.

He studied her profile, the subtle spray of freckles across her nose and cheeks. If she was going to be more open from now on, what did that mean for him. Did he deserve to have love in his life when his friends had never gotten that chance?

She turned and put her hands on the steering wheel. "Back to work."

"Yup."

Once the car started rolling, her phone instructed her to turn. She glanced down at it. "I'm only a few blocks from the address. I'm going to circle the block before I stop. Keep your eyes peeled. Any sign of him, and I'll just drive on."

He watched the house numbers. An older woman in a muumuu stood staring at her flower bed at the house where David lived. No sign of David. That didn't mean he wasn't around.

Hannah circled the block and parked around the corner, out of view. "Let's try to catch the landlady while she's in her yard."

They got out. Hannah deployed Captain. Trevor remained close as they turned on the street where David Weller lived.

As they approached the house, he glanced around. Still no sign of David. All the same, he found himself wishing he had his gun.

Chapter Thirteen

Hannah's heart beat a little faster as they approached the blue house where David lived. All these years, he'd been here probably in this town. Only a short distance away from where she lived in Salt Lake.

The older woman was bent over her flower bed, pulling out weeds. She looked up when they stood at the short fence. The woman eyed Trevor and then Hannah. She hoped her uniform and Captain's K-9 vest would communicate that they were here in an official capacity.

The older woman straightened. "Can I help you?"

"Is this where David Weller lives?"

She massaged her lower back. "David rents a basement from me. He's not here right now."

That made her breathe a little easier. "Is he at work? When will he be back?"

The woman picked up the watering can that

rested on the edge of the flower bed. "He hasn't been here for days. He said he was going to take a little vacation before he started back at the job he does once the weather gets cold. What's this about? Has David done something wrong?"

There was no need to fill her in on the details of what was going on. "We just need to talk to him about an ongoing investigation. Did he say where he was going?"

The woman's gray curls bounced as she shook her head. "We don't talk that much."

Hannah assumed that David's *vacation* was spent hiding on the island trying to get access to her. He probably wouldn't return home until he succeeded in his mission.

Trevor stepped forward. "How long has he rented from you?"

"A couple of years."

"What kind of renter is he?"

"He's quiet and keeps to himself. Pays his rent on time."

"Anything unusual about him?"

The woman lifted her head and thought for a moment. "Didn't ever have any family visit him. I guess they moved away years ago. When he talked about his family, it sounded like he didn't like them very much."

"He was estranged from them?"

"Far as I know," said the landlady. "He mentioned having a mom, a dad and a sister. Come to think of it, I never saw him with friends or a girlfriend."

Interesting. Hannah pulled her business card out and handed it over the fence to the woman. "If he does show up, please call us right away."

The woman eyed the card. "You sure he's not in trouble?"

Hannah didn't think the landlady was in any danger from David. "Please just call us."

Hannah turned to walk away when Trevor touched her elbow and bent his head toward the garage, where the door was open. Hannah took a few steps and stretched her neck to see what Trevor was indicating. Inside was a white compact car just like the one that had been following them.

"Ma'am, is that your car in there or David's?"

"Yes, that's my car. I loaned it to David a couple of days ago because he said his car was in the shop, but he got it fixed, I guess."

David must have had the white car at the same time he stole the green Jeep.

"What kind of car did David drive?" Hannah asked.

"Not sure of the model. It was dark blue and had one of those racks on the top for hauling stuff—his mountain bike and his kayak."

More good information. She thanked the woman again before leaving.

Hannah could feel her mood lifting as they hurried around the block to the car. They had a description of the car David drove. Isla would be able to find out the exact make and model. She was getting a clearer picture of who David Weller was, personality wise.

After loading Captain, she slipped behind the wheel and waited for Trevor to buckle himself in.

"I don't think there's any need to waste precious time on staking out David's place," she said.

"Yeah, it's sounds like he's hiding out on the island," said Trevor.

"It's clear from the attacks that he knows I'm at the ranch. Maybe he's sleeping somewhere during the day and going to the ranch at night since that is when the attack occurred."

"He might change it up, though, now that that hasn't worked. It would be easy enough to blend in the tourist crowd until he saw his opportunity."

"True." As she drove, Hannah thought about the landlady's comment about David not seeming to have any social connections.

She turned onto the causeway, feeling a sense of excitement at the progress they'd made. Once they arrived at the ranch, they found Isla in the community room, along with Rocco.

"You're back," said Hannah.

"Yes, got to see my lovely lady and her little boy. Cooked a nice Italian meal together." Rocco smiled at the memory.

It must be hard to be away from someone you love. Hannah asked, "Did the puppies get settled in?"

Rocco nodded. "Liana made them right at home. Such cute little guys and girls." He rose from the sofa. "Meadow and I are on guard duty, by the way."

"Fine by me," said Hannah. "Chase might want to change up the plan once he hears what we found out."

"What is that?"

Isla piped up. "We have the name of the man after Hannah—David Weller."

"Progress," said Rocco.

"More than that. We tracked down his landlady. He hasn't been home for days."

"That means he's probably on the island twenty-four-seven," said Trevor.

Hannah moved toward Isla's workstation. "We need to find out what make and model of car David is driving."

"That won't take long now that we have a name," said Isla.

Hannah let out a breath and rested her hands on the table. A theory had begun to form in her mind. David's estrangement from family and apparent anti-social behavior was a red flag.

She thought about how the RMK repeated the pattern of shooting his victims in a barn because it was symbolic. David Weller liked to kill by drowning even when he had other easier options. Was the water symbolic? "Can you check on something else for me?"

"What's that?" Isla smoothed her dark brown hair.

"I'm curious if there have been other drownings in the area in the years since Jodie died." As a profile of David Weller emerged, Hannah wondered if David had killed before.

"Give me a little time," said Isla, "and I'll have all that information for you also."

Hannah stepped toward the kitchen with

Captain following behind her. Trevor joined her a second later.

She opened the refrigerator. "You want something to drink? Looks like there is some iced tea in here."

"Sure," he said. "Why are you having Isla look up if there were other drownings in the area?"

She handed him a can of iced tea. "As I learn more about David Weller, I'm starting to wonder if we're dealing with a serial killer."

Trevor felt a tightening through his chest at the idea that David Weller may have murdered before. As if he wasn't a sinister enough figure already. "If that's the case, your being able to identify him and connect him to Jodie's murder must have really set him off." He pulled the tab off the iced tea and took a sip. "He's gone all this time without getting caught."

"It's just a theory. We'll see what Isla comes up with."

"Scary though, to think about," said Trevor.

She nodded. "It's part of the job. The clearer the profile we have of David Weller, the easier it will be to catch him."

He saw the fear in her eyes. His knuckles brushed over her cheek. "I'm here for you."

She met his gaze. "I appreciate that." Her voice was soft and lilting.

Rocco poked his head into the kitchen. "Isla found something."

They stepped away from each other, though Rocco had probably noticed how close they'd been standing to each other. They both entered the seating area. Hannah took a seat beside Isla while Trevor and Rocco peered over their shoulders at the screen Isla was looking at.

"First, I looked up to see if David Weller had ever had any criminal charges brought against him."

Hannah shifted in her seat. "Anything?"

"No, not so much as a parking ticket, no restraining orders, nothing."

Trevor relaxed a little and took in a deep breath. Maybe that was a good sign.

Isla fingers flew across the keyboard. "Then I looked up to see if there were any other drownings, either accidents or homicides, in this area. There was one a few years after Jodie died." Isla brought up a page of a Syracuse newspaper.

Trevor read the headline. "She died in a pool in a Syracuse hotel." The article featured a photograph of a woman who was maybe in her late forties.

Hannah leaned forward, scanning the article. "Was it an accident?"

"When I pulled up the coroner's report, the cause of death was listed as inconclusive. She did have some alcohol in her system, but there was also some bruising on her wrists and neck."

Trevor looked closer at the article. "She was traveling by herself."

Isla typed some more. "Then we have this just last year. A man drowned in one of the freshwater springs here on the island. They do think it was a homicide. Those streams are not that deep. The man was hit on the back of the head. They never caught the guy who did it."

Trevor stared at the photo of the man. Probably about the same age as the woman.

"Any connection between any of the victims including Jodie?" said Hannah.

"None that I could find. The crimes seem fairly random."

"Man, woman and child," said Trevor. "Like a family."

Isla turned in her chair and looked at him. "Exactly." Her eyes lit up. She swung back around and typed some more. "I wonder."

"What are you looking up?"

"Trying to find out about David Weller's

family. Give me a minute. This might require some digging."

"The landlady said that she thought they had moved away from here," said Hannah.

Trevor and Rocco both stepped away. He wandered over to where Cocoa sat at attention, then brushed his hand over the dog's head and peered out the window that faced the gravel lot where the cars were parked. Outside, Chase had just pulled up in his vehicle, an expression of concentration on his face as he opened the door so Dash could dismount.

Chase entered the room. His face had a slackness that suggested fatigue.

Rocco, Hannah and Trevor all looked in his direction.

"Any developments?" asked Rocco.

Despite his obvious weariness, Chase squared his shoulders. "Actually, we got a little bit of a lead. The RMK was spotted at White Rock campground during the day yesterday. When we went to the campsite the witness had indicated, no one was there. That means he's moving around from campground to campground."

"Maybe sleeping during the day," suggested Hannah.

Chase shifted his weight and ran his hands

through his brown hair. "Yes, and then taking off at night while Cowgirl is sleeping."

"Probably to come watch the ranch to wait for his chance to get at Trevor," said Hannah.

"We don't know that for sure. Trevor hasn't been attacked while at the ranch," said Chase. "Even if he eluded us again, we gained some information from the witness. The RMK is in one of those vans that has a bed inside. He can conceal Cowgirl in there. No windows in the back. The witness thought it referenced a rental company on the side. He couldn't remember the name."

"We've found out quite a bit about the man who came after me," said Hannah. She filled him in on all they had learned about their suspect but didn't share her serial killer theory.

"That is some good police work," said Chase. "I just came back for some food and to grab a little sleep. We'll continue to search the island for both men."

So far, it had only been David Weller who had attacked them at the ranch. The RMK had yet to make a move. If the RMK had been watching when they found the puppies, he would know that Trevor was assisting them. They still needed solid evidence the RMK had figured out that they were using the ranch as their headquarters. Unfortunately, that evidence might come in the form of an attempt on Trevor's life.

Isla rose from her chair and stretched. "I have something to show you all that is quite interesting."

Chapter Fourteen

Hannah and the others hurried over to where Isla had settled back down in her seat.

"It took a little digging, but I found a picture of David Weller and his family. The dad was given some kind of award for a civic club he belonged to. The family had their picture taken together for the paper." She brought up a photograph. A younger David Weller with his mom, dad and sister. David looked to be in his teens. To a degree, Mom and Dad resembled the other two victims. Similar haircuts and a sort of suburban middle-class style. The round innocent face of David's sister stared out from the old photo.

Hannah's breath caught in her throat as she bit her lower lip. Just as with the parents, the resemblance was not exact, but David's sister looked to be about the same age as Jodie when she died.

Hannah put her hand over her mouth. "It's like he killed his family."

"Exactly," said Isla. "Like you said Hannah, the actual family is alive and well and no longer living in this area. I have one more tidbit for you."

"Go ahead," said Trevor.

"Out of curiosity, I wondered what David did for a living when he wasn't working at the park. He's a lifeguard at the indoor city pool and he teaches classes at a private school."

"We're talking about a guy who feels very comfortable in the water." Hannah recalled that the first time she'd encountered David he had shown up in a boat.

"Yes, maybe he doesn't have a lot of confidence in other aspects of his life, but he feels like he's in control when he's in water. It's not that he had trauma connected to being drowned," said Isla. "It's that he feels like the strong one in the water."

Hannah rubbed her goose-pimpled arms. The new information made her thoughts run in different directions all at once.

Chase excused himself to go get some food.

Hannah sat down on the couch. Trevor and Rocco wandered away from the computers, as well. If the deaths were connected, she understood now why David wanted her dead. He'd done his killings and then his work allowed him to return to the spot where the first one, Jodie, had happened. He could have continued for years without anyone connecting the deaths. "Isla, did any witnesses come forward for the other two deaths?"

"Not that I could find. I read the coroners' reports and the initial police investigations, which both went cold," said Isla.

The deaths would have remained unsolved if she hadn't recognized David at the beach days ago. She was the only one who could put him in jail.

Chase returned with a plate of food. "Isla, all this information is interesting in understanding who we're after from a behavioral and psychological standpoint. We know why he did what he did, but none of it helps us catch him."

Isla lifted a finger in the air. "Touché. My research has not been all focused on the forensic psychology of it all. I also was able to find out exactly what kind of car he drives through DMV records. I can pull up a picture of a similar model."

"The one David drove had a rack on it for bicycles and other outdoor equipment," said Trevor.

Chase took a bite of the hot dog he'd prepared. "License-plate number?"

"Yup," said Isla.

"That is solid. We can put out the information to the park police. We should be able to track him down that much faster," said Chase.

"I'll get the notice out, along with the photo of a similar model," said Isla.

"Maybe we'll have him in custody before the day is over," said Hannah. The possibility lifted her spirits.

Chase sat down at the table to finish his hot dog. Hannah took a seat opposite him. "Chase, we think both the RMK and David Weller may be watching the ranch waiting for their chance. I don't know that either Trevor or I are any safer staying confined here and it requires another officer to be pulled off the search to provide extra protection."

Chase held up a hand. "I know what you are going to ask. The attack on you occurred at night. Even the guy Selena saw tried to move in under the cover of darkness. That's the most dangerous time."

"You still want us to stay here during the day?"

Chase wiped crumbs off his fingers. "What we've got to do is beef up security at night for the two of you and to maybe flush the culprits out. We still need solid evidence that the RMK has zeroed in on the ranch."

Captain sauntered over to stand beside Hannah's chair. "Okay, we'll stay here." She reached down to pet him.

Isla pulled off her headset. "I just got a call. The RMK was spotted over by the Island Buffalo Grill without Cowgirl."

"I'm on it," said Chase, rising from his chair. "Dispatch Ian, Selena and Meadow. Whoever is close." Chase hurried out the door. "Maybe we can get him this time."

"I'll stay put," said Rocco.

Hannah sat down beside Trevor, who reached over and patted her hand. "I know it's hard to be out of commission like this."

She appreciated his show of support. The warmth of his touch lingered even after he pulled his hand away. She was a part of this team, and she still could make a contribution. "We should see what kind of food is in that kitchen. Maybe we can prepare something other than junk food for when the rest of the team shows up."

"Sounds good. I'll give you a hand."

Rocco paced the floor, looking out each window before stepping outside, probably to patrol the exterior each of the buildings with Cocoa.

Hannah and Trevor retreated to the kitchen. She inspected what was in the fridge and the freezer. "Looks like there is stuff for a roast in here." She put a bag of carrots on the counter.

Isla stood in the doorway. "I just got a call. David's vehicle was spotted." Her voice held an edginess to it.

Hannah turned to face her. "That's good news. Where at?"

Isla's jawline grew tight as she rubbed her upper arm nervously. "It's here on the ranch, over by where the horses are kept that people can rent for trail rides."

Hannah knew what she had to do. There was no time to seek Chase's permission. "We can get to him faster than anyone. The others are on the way to where the RMK was sighted." She raced toward the door. When she got outside, she didn't see Rocco anywhere. She had hoped for some backup.

She clicked on her radio. "Rocco, where are you?"

"I saw suspicious movement in the trees and had to check it out."

Trevor had followed her outside. "I'm going with you."

She didn't want to go into this alone and it would take precious minutes for Rocco to come back. She spoke into her radio. "Isla will fill you in when you get back." She turned toward Trevor. "Hop in."

Captain was already waiting by the back door of the SUV.

It would be a short drive to get over to the horse stables. She prayed they would be able to take David Weller into custody.

They arrived at the horse-rental area within minutes. Somehow, Trevor had a feeling David Weller hadn't come here to ride a horse for the afternoon. Maybe he figured he'd park his car in an out-of-the-way place, walk over to the bunk-house and look for a chance to get at Hannah.

He didn't see David's car anywhere.

Four people leaned on the fence watching the horses in the corral. Two of them were young children.

A man in a park police uniform walked toward the patrol vehicle as they got out.

Hannah held out her hand. "Are you the officer who phoned this in?"

The man nodded. "Just noticed it a few minutes ago." He pointed. "It's on the other side of that barn."

"Did you see the man who was in the car?"

"No. It was unoccupied when I walked over to it." The man turned slightly. "I have met David Weller, though."

"What can you tell me about him?"

"Bit of an odd duck. Quiet in an eerie way. Guess he's a hard worker. Shows up on time, mostly does cleanup."

Hannah thanked the man and asked him to stay close in case they needed backup. As he walked away, she glanced around. "I think we should park my patrol vehicle out of sight. And then watch the car to see if he comes back."

They hurried back to the SUV. Hannah found a hiding spot for the patrol vehicle behind a copse of trees. After deploying Captain, they walked the short distance past the corral. Several people rode horses toward the trailhead.

David's car was parked off to the side of the building where people paid for their rentals. A red station wagon was beside it. Hannah circled the vehicle and peered in the windows.

They both studied the area around them. "It would be a little bit of a walk to get over to the bunkhouse," said Trevor.

Hannah turned from side to side as if she was thinking about something. "David is employed by the park service. Even if he's not working right now, he might be in touch with other employees. Maybe he receives emails. That notice about his car went out to all park-service employees."

"You think he got info that might have tipped him off?"

"Could be he didn't want to have the car spotted too close to the bunkhouse," said Hannah. "And maybe word got back to him and he abandoned the car."

They stepped inside the building.

A short woman with black spiky hair, probably in her early twenties, stood behind the counter. "Did you folks want to go on a trail ride?"

"We're here on police business. Is that your red station wagon outside?"

"Yes." She eyed them suspiciously as she took a step back. "What is this about?"

"Did you see the man who parked the car next to yours?"

"That's employee parking. I didn't realize there was another car there." The woman came from around the counter and stared out the window. "He or she must have parked there after I got here."

"And when was that?"

"I started my shift fifteen minutes ago."

That meant they weren't too far behind David.

Trevor and Hannah stepped outside.

Hannah pressed the button on her radio. "Rocco, how are things there?"

"Quiet. What's going on with you? Any sign of David?"

"Just his car. I think we'll stake out the area and see if he comes back to it."

"You want me to come help?"

"Stay put. He might be headed your way."

"Ten-four. I'll run a patrol of the area."

"Stay in touch," she said.

Hannah turned to face Trevor. "Why don't we find a hiding spot? We'll give it a half hour."

They circled the building, not finding any place that provided a view of the car but would keep them concealed.

"Let's just watch from inside the building. We can see the car from that window."

They returned to the building, taking up a

place on either side of the window. While they waited and watched, a couple came in to pay for the horseback ride. They eyed Hannah and Trevor before turning toward the woman behind the counter.

"When is the next guided horseback ride?" The man stretched his arm around the woman's back and squeezed her shoulder. She peered up at him. Two people who were clearly in love.

Hannah moved her attention away from the window, toward the couple. Trevor couldn't quite read the look on her face. When he caught her staring, though, her expression changed. Had she given up on the possibility of love for herself, yet longed for it?

The spiky-haired woman said, "The next group leaves in half an hour."

Hannah's radio crackled and she pressed the talk button. "What's up, Rocco?" She walked toward the door.

Trevor followed her outside. He stepped closer to her so he could hear both sides of the conversation.

Rocco's voice came across the line. "Two things. There was a man on a mountain bike pedaling by here real slow, over by the road."

Her voice faltered a bit. "Did it look like David?"

"Couldn't tell for sure. He had a helmet on, and he was far enough away so I didn't have a clear view of his face. I just happened to be on the back side of the bunkhouse that faces that road. He seemed to be watching the bunkhouse awful close, and he zoomed off when I spotted him."

Hannah didn't answer right away. With her head still bent toward the radio, she leaned a little closer to Trevor. "You said two things."

"Yes—Isla heard from the rest of the team. The call was a false alarm. When they got there, they spotted a man who looked like the RMK. He said a man paid him to wear the sunglasses and baseball hat and show up in that area."

"A decoy," said Hannah.

"The rest of the team is headed back here. Chase thinks the RMK might be somewhere on the grounds."

Tension threaded through Hannah's voice. "The RMK wanted most of the team to be called away so Trevor would be vulnerable."

Trevor tensed, pressing his teeth together. "He's close," he whispered under his breath.

Hannah glanced up at him and then spoke into the radio. "We're headed back to the bunkhouse. We'll get there as fast as we can." She lifted her finger off the talk button.

Both of them stared out at the ranch. Plenty of people wandered through the farm.

"Let's get back to your vehicle." Trevor guided Hannah to where they had hidden the car.

Hannah was reaching to open the back door when Captain barked and stared out toward one of the other buildings. "What is it, boy?"

Trevor searched the area that had alarmed Captain, not seeing anyone who looked like the RMK.

Hannah shot a nervous glance at Trevor. "He might just be picking up on our fear."

She got Captain loaded into the kennel.

Trevor grabbed his seat belt and secured it as she pulled out from behind the trees and veered toward the dirt road that led back to the bunk-house. "Do you think David will go back to his car or has he ditched it permanently?"

"I'm not sure. He can't get around much without it. He may have a boat stashed somewhere. That first day when I saw him, he was in a small motorboat. Even that would limit where he could go. We need to have somebody watching that car all the same if there is even a small chance that he will return there."

"It just can't be you and me doing it, given what we think the RMK is up to?" said Trevor.

"If the RMK is lurking around here, you can't be out in the open," she said.

She took the winding dirt road that led to the community room with the bunkhouse behind it.

When they arrived, Rocco's patrol vehicle was the only one parked outside. They got out. Trevor could see tourists circling around some of the buildings that were closer to the community room, as well as people walking through the fields where the freshwater stream and trails were.

Chase and the rest of the team hadn't made it back yet. As they walked toward the door, Trevor noticed that Hannah had unclipped that strap that held her gun in place.

She sensed their vulnerability, too.

Chapter Fifteen

Even once she and Trevor were safe inside the community room, Hannah found no relief from the tension that snaked around her torso and made it hard to breathe. With two killers probably close by, it felt like they were under siege.

Rocco stood up from the couch. "Glad you made it back. Hannah, if you want to stay inside with Trevor, Cocoa and I will patrol the exterior of the building."

Hannah nodded. "We need to get someone watching David's car as soon as possible."

"I don't think it would be a good idea for me to leave the premises just yet." Rocco cupped his hand on Hannah's shoulder. "For now, I need to stay close to you and Trevor."

Isla emerged from the kitchen. "I just made a fresh pot of coffee if you guys want some. Chase and the rest of the team should be here soon."

Trevor moved toward the kitchen. "I'll get you a cup."

Rocco exited through the front door. Standing to the side, Hannah watched from the window as Cocoa heeled dutifully beside Rocco.

Trevor held a steaming mug out to her. She took the cup. "You might want to stay away from the window." Both men had guns and could take a shot from a hiding place.

"I'd say the same to you," said Trevor.

She took a tiny step back. "I'm being careful. I have to watch." After checking out of the other two windows in the community room and then going into the kitchen to look through the window that provided a view of the bunkhouse, Hannah was satisfied that neither man was approaching the house. She caught a glimpse of Rocco as he headed through the field toward the trees. He was vulnerable out there alone. When were Chase and the rest of the team going to get back?

She took a drink of her coffee, enjoying the warm richness of the liquid and the intense aroma. Then she walked back into the seating area. Isla was busy at her computers, and Trevor sat on a couch. After taking a sip of coffee, he put down his cup and rocked back and forth before rising to his feet. He was as rest-less as she was.

Captain rested on the floor with his head up looking around. He thumped his tail when he saw Hannah. She bent down to pet him and ran her fingers through his thick fur.

A distant pop caused Hannah to fall to the floor. "That was a gunshot. Get down."

Isla had already dropped to the floor.

After commanding Captain to follow, Han-nah crab-crawled to the front door and burst outside. She pressed close to the building and peered out, not seeing Rocco anywhere.

Trevor appeared in the doorway and then moved against the wall close to Captain.

"You need to stay inside," he said.

"So do you. I can't leave my colleague out there alone." She pressed the talk button on her radio. "Rocco, come in. Where are you?"

No response.

She dared not try a second time. The sound of the radio might give Rocco away if he was still in the shooter's crosshairs. He and Cocoa could just be laying low and trying to be quiet to avoid being shot at again. Or, he might al-ready be shot and bleeding out.

The notion paralyzed her for a moment. What should she do?

She rationalized that if he had been shot, it seemed as though his K-9 would have raised the alarm with barking. Rocco must be okay but unable to respond.

"I have to go out there," said Hannah. "I can't leave him stranded. He might be pinned down."

"Then I'm going with you," said Trevor.

Isla peeked around the doorway while she used the wall to block most of her body. "Which direction do you think the shot came from?"

Hannah shook her head. "I'm guessing this side of the house and more toward the trees." That's where the potential hiding places were, anyway.

"I'll stay close to the main radio," said Isla.

With Trevor following her, Hannah and Captain hurried in the general direction she thought the shot had come from.

Rocco's voice came across the line in a low whisper. "I think I lost him."

Hannah scanned the trees, catching a flash of movement. "I think I see him. I'm on it."

"Which way?"

"Not sure. He disappeared." Hannah gasped

for breath as she ran and tried to talk at the same time.

She hurried toward the trees, where she'd seen a flash of neon yellow that contrasted with the gold-, red-and rust-colored leaves that hung on the trees.

Wind made the dry leaves rattle as she and Trevor entered the trees.

"Over there." Trevor sprinted ahead of her.

She moved to catch up.

They came to a yellow mountain bike propped against a tree. Both of them slowed their pace, then stopped abruptly. Captain was on full alert.

The first gunshot came so close to Hannah's head that her ears rang from the intensity of it.

They both fell to the ground as the second shot zinged over them. Hannah pulled her gun, took aim and fired a shot.

Rocco's voice came across the radio. "I heard that. On my way."

Hannah wasn't sure which way Rocco would be coming from. "Approach with caution."

More shots were fired. They were driven deeper into the trees. They no longer had a clear view of the bicycle.

With her gun lifted, she watched the foliage.

She heard the breaking of branches off to the side but could not risk hitting Rocco. Her heart pounded as she watched and waited to see some sign of who was coming toward them.

Rocco and Cocoa emerged through the thick underbrush.

Hannah pointed. "He's over that way."

The three of them rushed in the direction they had just retreated from. When they arrived in the open area where the bike had been, she saw that it was gone.

"He's must be headed toward that dirt road," said Trevor.

"I'm going back to get my vehicle to see if I can head him off via the road." Rocco turned back around.

"Great, we'll pursue on foot," said Hannah.

With Captain by her side, she and Trevor moved toward where the trees opened up to a flat grassy area. Beyond that was the dirt road. There was no sign of David Weller or his bike. With her gun still drawn, she ran toward some brush that provided a degree of cover.

In one direction, the curved road was partially concealed by a rock formation. In the other direction, the road was straight. She could see the outskirts of the ranch in the distance.

When no shots were fired in their vicinity, she stepped out and moved toward the road. Mountain-bike tracks had left an impression in the road where it was soft, but they soon faded on the harder packed dirt.

Trevor pointed toward where the road curved. "He must have gone that way."

Rocco's car came into view on the part of the road that was straight. He slowed his vehicle as he approached. Then stopped with the engine still running while he rolled down the window and leaned out. "Any sign of him?"

"We think he went that way." She pointed.

"I should be able to catch him." He closed the window as the SUV rolled forward and sped away.

Rocco had rounded the curve by the rocks before Hannah could suggest he needed backup. The three of them and two K-9s would have been cramped in the car, anyway. The kennel took up most of the back seat. For sure, she could not leave Trevor unguarded.

"I guess we head back." They trudged up the road, toward the ranch.

After nearly five minutes, Rocco's voice came across the radio. "He's not here. I should have caught up with him if he stayed on this road."

"Where could he have gone?"

"I passed a sign for a trailhead a ways back."

Hannah looked off in the distance, where a trail led up a rocky hill. She could just make out a bicycle as the sun glinted off the metal. The neon yellow of the rider's clothes was also evident. The rider remained still at the peak looking in their direction, then disappeared over the other side. How menacing.

Hannah still had her hand on the radio. "I think we lost him."

Disappointment permeated Rocco's voice as it came through the radio. "I'll get turned around and come so you guys can use my patrol vehicle. Neither you nor Trevor should be out in the open for too long, but we can't all fit in the vehicle."

Hannah let go of the radio. They were standing out in the open, easy targets for a man with a gun, if he was close. They still didn't know where the RMK was.

Trevor reached for her hand and squeezed it. "He can't get far on just a bicycle."

The muscles around her mouth tightened. "Yeah, but he knows this island and all the possible hiding places. He's managed to evade us so far."

"He can't hide forever," said Trevor.

Clearly shaken, she pressed her face into her palm. "We're so close to catching him."

His heart squeezed tight over how distressed she was. "We'll get him. You have a great team of officers backing you up."

She lifted her head, revealing the tears forming in her eyes. "Sometimes it feels like this will never end."

He wrapped his arms around her and drew her close. "We'll do this together."

She turned her face up to look into his eyes. He longed to comfort her and ease the pain he saw on her face.

"I know I have to keep believing that and not lose hope." Green eyes stared at him, searching. Her gaze held a magnetic pull he could not resist.

He bent his head and kissed her. She seemed to melt against him as her hand rested on his chest.

His heart pounded as he breathed in the floral scent of perfume.

The sound of an approaching car cut the kiss

short. They both stepped away from each other at the same time.

Heat rose up his neck. He looked toward where Rocco's patrol car had come into view. He stopped the car, got out and deployed Cocoa.

"We'll walk back," he said, handing Hannah the keys.

Once they were settled in the patrol car, an awkward silence surrounded them. What had that kiss even been about? Had he just caught her at a vulnerable moment or was she opening her heart to him?

He wasn't even sure of his own feelings. He had so wanted to comfort her.

He cleared his throat.

She started talking before he could say anything. Her words had a nervous rapid-fire quality to them. "I just hope Chase understands why I left the community room. I don't know why those guys are taking so long in getting back, anyway…" She glanced in his direction and then continued to talk about the case.

Okay, so the kiss had made her nervous or confused her.

Hannah drove on the dirt road and turned into the ranch. In order to get back to the bunkhouse, they had to go past the busier parts of the ranch. Trevor found himself scanning the crowds and clusters of people, looking for a blond man in sunglasses and a hat. He doubted Cowgirl would be with the RMK if he was getting ready to make a move.

When they arrived at the community room, there were two other patrol vehicles parked in the dirt lot. Chase and the others were back.

Inside, Chase and Ian were sitting at the table sipping coffee.

Chase looked up as they entered and addressed his comments to Hannah. "Isla filled me in on the excitement. I've sent Selena to watch David Weller's vehicle. It was ill-advised for you to leave the protection of the community room, but I understand why you did it."

"I couldn't leave Rocco stranded out there while he was being shot at."

"I get that. Where is he, anyway?"

"He's walking." Trevor felt the need to defend Hannah. "We both needed the protection of a vehicle."

"I am trying to make smart choices." Hannah pulled a strand of red hair behind her ear. "But I feel an obligation to help out as much as I possibly can."

"I know that." Chase put his coffee mug

down. "All the same, as much as possible stay close to the community room and to Trevor. He's in just as much danger as you are."

Ian rose to his feet and picked up his cup. "I'm going to get some sleep."

Chase said, "We have the RMK's scent on the blankets from the puppies. Grace, Meadow's dog, is trained to track. If the RMK is at the ranch, maybe she can find him."

Trevor tugged on Hannah's sleeve. "We were in the process of trying to get that roast in the oven when we were interrupted."

Maybe if they were alone and working on something together, they both would relax, and they could talk about the kiss.

Hannah followed him into the kitchen. She searched the cupboards until she found a large roasting pan. "How about I cut potatoes while you brown the meat?"

"Sounds good." He moved toward the refrigerator and took out the roast.

They both worked in their respective areas. Trevor found a frying pan and oil. He removed the meat from the packaging, enjoying the sizzle when he placed it in the hot oil.

Hannah cut potatoes with an intense energy.

Trevor placed the browned meat in the roasting pan. "Now what?"

She turned back toward the counter, grabbing a cutting board. "I think I saw an onion in the produce bin."

He took the cutting board, retrieved the onion and a knife, then stood beside her at the counter while she continued to work on the potatoes.

Her shoulder brushed against his sending an electric charge through him. "Listen, about that kiss. I didn't mean to be forward. I don't know where I stand with you."

She sliced through the potatoes, making rapid pounding noises on the cutting board. She turned toward him. "It's all right. Maybe we both just got caught up in the moment."

It felt like a rock had dropped in his stomach as he tried to sort through his confused feelings. "Sure. That must have been it."

She turned back toward her task. She'd made it clear she didn't want him reading anything into the kiss.

They finished putting the roast together without any further conversation other than exchanges about the logistics of the cooking.

The day wore on. Trevor spent his time trying to focus on the work he could do on his laptop or phone. When Ian woke up, Chase sent him out to continue to search the ranch. Selena radioed that there still was no sign of David Weller returning to his car.

While the room filled with the aroma of the roast cooking, Hannah retrieved a book from her patrol car and sat down on the opposite end of the couch from Trevor to read.

She offered him a quick nervous smile before turning her attention to her book. Even that brought back the memory of how right it had felt to hold her and kiss her.

The team regrouped with all but Rocco who took over the stakeout on the car, so Selena could have a break. Ian as well was still searching the ranch. They ate dinner together after Chase said grace.

"I'll stand guard outside the bunkhouse. Meadow and Selena, I'd like you two to continue to search the grounds at night. Your K-9s have the best training for finding the RMK. Take a power nap if you need one. If David Weller doesn't show up for his car under the cover of darkness, he's probably not going to come back to it. We won't continue the stakeout on the car. I can't waste precious personnel if it's proving to be a dead end."

"There must be something I can do?" said Hannah.

Chase pushed his chair back from the table. "I can't risk your safety, Hannah. If David Weller only has a bike for transportation, he's not going to go far from the ranch."

"I understand," she said.

Hannah's disappointment was palpable to Trevor. "Hannah thought David might have access to a boat. He was in one the first time he came after her. He could be getting around that way."

"Could be. That limits him, too."

Isla piped up. "Hannah, I'll pull up some pictures of boats and you can tell me which one best matches the one you saw."

"The marina's not in use," said Chase. "Where would he dock it?"

"It was a small craft. There are hundreds of little inlets around the lake where he could pull it up on shore. I know most of them from having come here as a kid," said Hannah.

"Would you be able to point them out on a map?"

Hannah shook her head. "I'd have to show them to you in person."

"Maybe Hannah and I and another officer could check the sights out in daylight," suggested Trevor.

"Maybe. We'll see what tonight yields." Chase rose holding his plate. "I'll be patrolling outside with Dash. Hannah, you stay here with Trevor."

Trevor spent the rest of the night finishing the work on his laptop.

After about an hour, Hannah put down the book she'd been reading and rose from the sofa. "I finished this. I'm going to grab my Bible from my bag." I'll just be a minute."

Isla rose from the sofa, where she'd been watching something on her phone with headphones. "I think I'm going out for a walk to get some air. Lock the door behind me."

"Can do," said Trevor.

After Isla left, Trevor tapped the keys on his laptop as he assessed the profit margins on a cattle ranch that was considering expanding into other livestock and updating some equipment.

Trevor massaged his temples. His eyes hurt from staring at a computer screen. Hannah should have been back by now.

The radio on Isla's desk fizzled with static and then a voice came through the line. "Isla, Chase…are you there?" The voice was Selena's.

Why wasn't Chase picking up?

Trevor walked over to Isla's workstation. He pushed the talk button. "Selena, it's Trevor. Isla just stepped out. Not sure what is up with Chase."

"We spotted a guy slinking around the grounds. Tall, like the RMK, but we couldn't get a good look at him. He could be headed your way."

"Thanks. I'll go let Chase know."

Trevor hurried into the kitchen. Before opening the back door, he peered out the window that provided a partial view of the bunkhouse.

Chase was lying on the ground outside the bunkhouse. The door that led to the men's sleeping area had been flung wide open. Dash was nowhere in sight.

Heart pounding against his rib cage, Trevor's first thought was concern for Hannah's safety.

He ran toward the back door when the knob shook. Isla or Hannah would have spoken up and Isla probably would have come to the front door.

Someone was trying to breach the locked door. He froze, watching the shaking doorknob.

He pulled himself from his paralysis. He needed to get his phone in the other room.

Just as he turned to go, a gunshot exploded outside. The intruder was trying to shoot the door open.

Chapter Sixteen

The blast of a gunshot caused Hannah to jump. She'd taken way too much time looking for her Bible when she should have stayed with Trevor. She grabbed her firearm from the side table. Captain barked when they stepped outside.

She took in the scene. Chase was lying on the ground. Where was Dash? She checked for a pulse. Alive but unconscious. No sign of a gunshot wound.

Inside her room, she could hear her phone ringing. No time to go back to get it. She'd left her utility belt behind, as well.

It sounded like the shot had come from outside the community room. She ran around the corner. A man stood by the back door, covered in shadows.

"Police—put your hands up."

The man turned around, fired a shot in her direction and took off running. The shot had gone wild. Her feet pounded the hard earth as she followed the man into the darkness.

The man's baseball hat had fallen to the ground as he headed toward a cluster of buildings and sheds. In the moonlight, she saw blond hair…the RMK. As she drew closer to the buildings, she lost sight of him. She slowed down, scanning the areas around the buildings, listening for any sound that might be out of place. Her eyes had not yet adjusted to the darkness when she reached an open-sided shed. She aimed her gun at the interior of the structure as her eyes scanned for movement. Stillness answered back.

Her heartbeat thrummed in her ears. She swallowed to produce some moisture in her mouth. She gripped the gun with both hands, ready to take a shot.

Backup would be nice, but her radio was back in her room.

Captain brushed against her leg, reminding her that she was not alone in this fight.

Satisfied the perp was not hiding in the shed, she worked her way toward the next building.

Footsteps behind her caused her to whirl around. "Trevor, I almost shot you," she shout whispered.

He stepped closer to her and spoke in a low

voice. "No way was I going to leave you out here alone."

His words brought her consolation. She'd felt so much confusion after their kiss. He seemed to not want to make a big deal of it, so she'd said something to let him off the hook. "It's too dangerous for you. It's the RMK for sure and he has a gun."

"This is the first clear attack on me. We have to get him."

She admired his courage, and his desire to protect her touched her deeply, but this was too risky for him. She leaned close to him. "Go back."

Had the other officers been close enough to hear the shots? Maybe she would get some backup.

Her desire to take in the RMK gave her the courage to keep going.

She took off running, only to find Trevor beside her. There was no time to argue. She had a chance to take in the RMK.

Staying close together, they weaved through the buildings. Without a flashlight, it was hard to see anything in the shadows. The moonlight provided only a small amount of illumination.

They pressed against the stone wall of a round

structure and circled it. She stared at the sky in frustration, letting out a heavy breath. He wasn't here. Somehow the RMK had managed to get away without making discernable noise.

"We should head back," said Trevor. "We're not going to flush him out. Maybe he slipped away."

She gripped her gun tighter. If she had had her radio, she could have called more of the team in and cornered him. "I should have handled this differently. I just want to catch him so bad." Her voice came out in a hoarse whisper. "It's best to assume he's still close, waiting to take a shot at us even if we can't hear him. Move with caution."

Using the buildings as cover whenever possible, they worked their way back to the community room, breaking into a full-out run once they were in an open area. When they arrived, the front door was unlocked. They entered to find Isla sitting beside Chase, who was holding an ice pack on his head. Dash was at his feet.

"You're okay." Chase grimaced and adjusted the ice pack. "I've got the others out looking for you."

"We were in pursuit of the RMK," Hannah

said. "It was him for sure. I saw his blond hair when his hat fell off."

Chase's voice became solemn. "That means he's here on the grounds." He rose to his feet. "Trevor, you never should have left the building."

Hannah lowered her voice. "This is partially my fault. I thought I was only going to be in my room for a minute. I shouldn't have left my post."

Trevor spoke up. "He was firing shots at the back door. I moved to escape out the front door, and I saw Hannah running. I knew I couldn't leave her out there alone."

"Everything happened so fast, I heard shots, I didn't have time to grab my radio," said Hannah. "I know that I could have handled things better." She stepped toward Chase. "But we almost had him."

Chase touched her arm. "We both played this one poorly. I can't believe I got knocked in the head. I turned away for a second."

"What happened to Dash?"

"We found him tied to a tree. The RMK is very good with dogs. He must have grabbed Dash right after he hit me," Chase said.

"He has to have been watching this place

closely. He knew where Trevor was sleeping. He kicked that door open first."

Trevor collapsed in a chair. "When he didn't find me there, he must have looked in the community room window and saw that I was alone."

"We never should have let this happen. Isla, get on the radio, we need to call everyone in for the night. I want two people on shift outside guarding the bunkhouse, one sitting and one patrolling."

"Since this place is so vulnerable, what if Hannah and I returned to my RV with one other person to stand guard."

Chase shook his head. "Like Hannah said, we're being surveilled closely. There is too much danger that the RMK or Weller would see us leave and follow. You wouldn't be any safer at the RV and you'd have less protection."

"But David doesn't have a car," said Trevor. "Hannah would be safer."

Isla spoke up. "Actually, I've been watching the park-police reports and a car was reported stolen about an hour ago not too far from here."

The news was like a jab to Hannah's stomach. That meant David was more mobile.

Chase spoke up. "The smart thing is for all

of us to get as much sleep as possible with the guard shifts I set up. I don't want another attack to happen tonight. We'll play offense as well. Whoever is not on guard duty or sleeping will go out to track the RMK. If he's still lurking on the grounds, we'll find him."

Isla moved toward her worktable.

"If we could catch David Weller," said Hannah, "I could be more of a help instead of a liability."

"No one thinks of you that way," Isla responded.

Chase looked at Hannah for a long moment as though he were thinking about something. "I'll escort the two of you back to the rooms."

Chase's tone indicated a level of frustration that Hannah shared. To be this close, to know that he was out there watching them and not to be able to bring the RMK in, was upsetting.

Trevor, Hannah and Captain followed Chase and Dash outside. Hannah said good-night and retreated to her room. After setting her gun on the nightstand, she called Captain over to her.

She rubbed his furry head. "You did good out there tonight, big guy."

Captain licked her hand.

"Now lie down and get some sleep." She put her face close to his. "That's a good boy."

Captain settled on the floor beside her bed. She reached over to turn off the nightstand lamp.

Hannah got into bed fully clothed and pulled the covers up around her. She wondered why Chase had looked at her for a long moment and then not said anything. Did he think she was a liability, or was she projecting her insecurity on him, just like she'd done with Trevor?

She longed for the comfort of his arms around her.

She could feel tears warming the corners of her eyes. From the moment she'd turned onto the causeway to the island, nothing had gone as she'd hoped. She certainly didn't think she would find herself falling for Trevor Gage.

She stared at the ceiling. Captain had risen to his feet. He licked her arm where it was exposed.

She turned to face her partner and rub his ears. "Thanks for always being on my side."

She drifted off to sleep, barely waking when both Isla and Selena came in some time later. Meadow must be on guard duty.

She turned on her side and pulled the blanket around her shoulder, praying that tomorrow would be a more fruitful day and that they all would have a safe night's sleep.

The next morning, when Rocco had invited Trevor to help cook breakfast, he'd jumped at the chance to keep busy. The smell of sausages filled the air. Trevor got out the orange juice then broke eggs to be scrambled.

Rocco watched the sausages while also pouring pancakes on the griddle. He seemed quite skilled at cooking. Trevor recognized Rocco's last name. There had been a detective named Manelli on the original case, most likely Rocco's father. Catching the RMK was probably as personal to Rocco as it was to Trevor.

The rest of the team slowly shuffled in, grabbing cups of coffee and retreating to the seating area.

Just as breakfast was ready to serve, Hannah appeared at the door and looked into the kitchen. "Rocco, you're going to want to see this since you were the one who transported the pups. Trevor, you might like this. Come see what Isla has set up."

The rest of the team had already gathered around the monitors.

On the screen was a woman Trevor didn't recognize. The woman's dark hair, pulled back in a single braid, offset her caramel-colored skin. She was holding Cowgirl's cinnamon-colored puppy. The other three pups played at her feet in some sort of outdoor pen.

Isla pressed a button on her keyboard. "Liana has a message for all of you."

Liana waved and drew the puppy closer to her face. The puppy licked her cheek as its little legs ran a marathon. "Hey, everyone. I thought you could use some good news. All the puppies are in good health and very active, as you can see." She bent over and picked up the multicol-ored puppy. Both puppies wiggled in her hands.

Isla leaned forward. "What are the plans for those little guys?"

"We'll start working with them to see if they can be trained as compassion K-9s like their mom." She bent her head toward one of the pups and then looked at the screen as her voice filled with longing. "Any sign of Cowgirl?"

Chase piped up. "She's been spotted several times. It looks like she's being well taken care of."

"I just hope she's recovered soon. I miss her." Liana bent to put the pups down.

Trevor had noticed that the woman's eyes had glazed right before her face went off screen. The atmosphere in the room had grown heavy.

Hannah leaned close to Trevor. "Liana was supposed to adopt Cowgirl. She'd bring her to the Elk Valley PD, where the task force has its HQ, every morning for her work as a therapy dog and then home every night."

Rocco edged toward the screen. "Hopefully soon, Liana, those of us who live in Elk Valley will be back there to see those little guys grow and learn."

"Yes, for sure," said Liana. "I hope you all have a productive day."

"We'll do our best," said Chase.

Liana waved goodbye and managed a smile that didn't quite reach her eyes before the screen went black.

"She's pretty broken up about Cowgirl," said Hannah.

The others nodded in agreement.

"Let's eat breakfast," said Chase. "Whatever it is, it smells good."

After the food was brought out, each of the team members took a seat, as did Trevor.

"I can say grace if you like." Trevor addressed his comment to Chase.

"That would be great," said Chase as he bowed his head and pressed his hands together.

"Lord, we thank You for this day. For the way this team works together and for seeing how healthy and active the puppies are."

Several people laughed.

Trevor continued, "We ask that you protect each and everyone around this table as we work today to bring in these two men who have caused so much havoc. Thank You for this food—please bless and nourish it to our bodies."

Several people said, "Amen."

Trevor raised his head and opened his eyes, allowing his gaze to rest on each of the officers for just a moment. He'd come to a place of respect for the dedication and tenacity he saw in each of these men and women. Their desire to see justice done had restored his faith in law enforcement.

The food was passed around and compliments flowed as people dug into their meals. No one seemed to want to talk about the case.

Isla cleared her throat after setting down her fork on her empty plate. "I have a bit of news that might affect what we do today. It seems that today is the first day of the Kite and Balloon Stampede that's held on the island."

"So that means more people on the island?" Meadow grabbed the last sausage off the serving plate.

"An extra twenty thousand," said Isla. "Most of the activities are at White Rock Bay up north, but I'm sure some people will filter down here."

Chase said, "More traffic too I bet."

"Yes, they launch the balloons off the road sometimes," said Isla. "I imagine things can get pretty backed up."

"Gonna complicate things for us doing our job," said Rocco. "It's a lot easier to hide in a crowd."

"I think we will concentrate our efforts on locating the RMK closer to the ranch for now." Chase pushed back his chair and stood up. "Ian, you stay here with Trevor, Hannah and Isla. The rest of us will search the ranch out of uniform. I don't want to draw attention to ourselves. We'll still have the dogs get a scent off the blankets that were left in the crate with puppies."

"Even though Scout is trained for wilderness terrain, he can handle crowds just fine," said Selena.

The four officers left. Trevor watched through

the window of the community room. Already, it looked like there were more people than usual milling through the ranch.

Ian called Lola to his side. "I will be outside patrolling the area close to here." He tapped his radio. "Stay in touch. It looks busy out there."

"I'll be inside with Trevor," said Hannah.

Isla returned to her worktable.

Trevor grabbed his laptop from the bunk-house and settled down to get some work done. Captain rested on a rug at his feet.

Hannah took a seat opposite Trevor and began reading something on her phone, then rose to look out each window. She sat back down with a heavy sigh.

It was clear she was restless.

Trevor said, "Why don't I get us all something cold to drink?"

"That sounds nice," said Hannah. "I'd take an iced tea if there are any left."

"Isla, you want anything?"

"I'm good," said Isla.

Trevor went to the kitchen and opened the refrigerator. He grabbed the last iced tea and a soft drink.

He thought he heard Hannah say something like "What's that?"

Captain let out a single bark.

When he returned to the sitting area, Isla had risen and pushed back her chair.

Hannah rushed across the room with her hand hovering over her gun.

Chapter Seventeen

At the sound of someone rattling the front door, Hannah had risen to her feet. The door burst open.

Two young men tumbled into the community room. They were both dressed in baggy pants and oversize hoodies.

At the sight of Hannah, they put their arms up in the air.

"Whoa," the taller of the two men said.

The second man took a step back. "We were just having a look around the ranch."

"This building is not open to the public," said Hannah. "There should be a sign outside."

"We didn't see any," said the taller man.

"We're sorry," the other man added.

"No problem." She put the hand that had been hovering over the gun at her side. "Sorry to have scared you."

Trevor had risen to stand beside Hannah. "Enjoy your time at the ranch."

The two men left by the door they'd come in by.

"That door should have been locked." Hannah stepped toward it, then examined the door.

"Let me see," said Trevor. He leaned in to have a closer look at the doorknob. "It appears to be broken."

"No surprise there. It's old." She stared at the outside area by the door, not seeing the sign that indicated the bunkhouse wasn't open to the public. She stepped farther out—the sign had been on flimsy wooden post. Someone could have pulled it up.

"Can you fix the lock?"

"Maybe if I had some tools," said Trevor.

She circled the building, looking for the sign. The bunkhouse was close to a thick forest with trails and bird-viewing areas. She spotted at least a dozen people wandering through the trees.

Ian and Lola came around from the other side of the bunkhouse. "Everything okay?"

"The lock on the front door is broken and the sign saying the area isn't open to the public is gone."

"I'll look around for it," said Ian. "You should get back inside."

All the extra people milling through made her nervous. When she returned, Trevor was taking the doorknob apart using a knife as a screwdriver.

"Not sure if this is a good idea," said Trevor. "I'll get it all torn apart and not be able to put it back together. Besides, it looks like the locking mechanism when you twist this—" he pointed to the elevated button in the middle of the doorknob "—won't go down. The knob probably needs to be replaced."

"Neither one of you should be standing here," said Isla. "Let's go inside."

Hannah pushed the door into place behind her. The knob was wobbly. This wasn't good. Not only did it mean the tourist could wander in here, but it was also one less point of protection against the two men. The other door had probably been damaged from the RMK shooting at it, as well. The place was hardly high-security and now it was even less so.

"Isla, can you print up a sign we can put on the door that says the building isn't open to the public?"

"Sure, in just a minute." She lifted her head

above her screen. "Want to know what I have been working on?" There was a hopeful lilt in her voice.

Hannah walked over to Isla's worktable. There was a grid on one of her screens with names in the squares. She looked a little closer. "It's a work schedule."

"Remember when you interviewed the HR woman who hired David? She was going to send me the shift schedule to see who worked the most with David and might know something about him that could help us catch him."

Hannah pulled up a chair. "Yes, I remember. What did you find out?"

"David mostly worked alone doing cleanup and maintenance, but there were a few times he did work projects with other park employees. I've got two names for you. Thought you might want to interview them. Won't take but a second to track down their phone numbers."

"Thank you. That could be helpful. I'd like to find out if they know where he stashed that boat."

"Okay, give me a minute." Isla had already put her finger back on the keyboard. She clicked through several screens and then wrote down two phone numbers beside the names she had already written down. Her phone rang. She looked at the phone screen. Her jaw fell. "I have to take this call." Her voice had changed.

She rose and walked into the kitchen, closing the door behind her but leaving it ajar.

Hannah could hear Isla's muffled voice but not any words.

"Wonder what that was about?" Trevor looked up from his laptop.

Hannah shrugged. It had certainly changed Isla's mood.

The call ended but Isla did not return to the seating area. No sound of Isla opening cupboards or turning on a microwave emanated from the kitchen.

Something was wrong. Hannah pushed back her chair. "I'll go talk to her."

She opened the kitchen door. Isla was leaning against the counter with her bent head resting in her hands.

"Hey…" Hannah's voice was soft. "Everything okay?"

Isla lifted her head. Her eyes were filled with tears. "That was the adoption agency." She sniffled. "My application to foster Enzo was turned down."

Hannah felt like a knife had gone through

her own heart. Her throat grew tight. "I'm so sorry." She held open her arms and gathered Isla into them.

She held her friend tight while she sobbed.

Isla pulled away and swiped at her eyes. "If you don't mind, I'm going to go lie down for a while." She stepped toward the door but then turned back. "I'll tell the rest of the team when I'm ready. If anyone asks, I don't mind you letting them know."

"Sure, I understand," said Hannah.

"Thank you for being a friend." Isla lifted her head and managed a smile. "I'll get through this. God is faithful, and I will trust his timing in everything."

She admired her friend's steadfast faith. "You'll get this thing cleared up and have a child to foster. I know you will."

"Thanks. I won't give up hope." Isla left through the back door.

Hannah watched from the window as she headed to the bunkhouse, feeling her own eyes warm with tears.

She returned to the sitting area with a heavy heart.

Trevor was leaning forward on the sofa petting Captain. "Everything all right?" He sat up straighter.

"Isla is really hurting right now. Her application to foster that little boy got turned down."

"What a tough break." Trevor shook his head. "That must have knocked her off her feet."

"She's going to rest for a while." Hannah sat down on the opposite end of the couch from Trevor.

"I got the impression she really wanted that in her life, to have a child."

"She would be a great mom. She has the support of her grandmother to help raise the kid since she's not married and I think she's like me, that she's kind of given up on meeting Mr. Right."

Trevor turned so he was facing Hannah. "What made you give up?"

The question had such weight to it considering her attraction to Trevor. "I just got tired of being hurt by men and living that cycle of hope and disappointment every time it didn't work out when I saw the guy I was dating for who he really was."

She lifted her head and met his gaze. The

light in his eyes and the softness of his expression drew her in.

"I'm really sorry that your life has gone that way. You deserved better."

His words were so filled with compassion it was as if she'd let out a breath she'd been holding for years. "What about you?"

"What do you mean?"

"You must be about my age and yet you're not married or with anyone."

He shook his head for a long moment. "Maybe I was punishing myself. Like I didn't deserve that kind of happiness because of what happened ten years ago."

"Self-forgiveness is a thing Trevor." She knew the words were for herself as much as him.

"It would be good to move on, wouldn't it? For both of us." He studied her long enough that his stare made her uncomfortable.

She looked away and stood up, feeling like there should be something more said between them. The conversation made her nervous and afraid. Was she ready to give her heart to this man?

To hide her agitation, Hannah moved over to Isla's work area and grabbed a piece of paper from the printer. "I'll just handwrite a note that says this building is closed off to the public. I don't want to mess with Isla's computers."

After making the sign, Hannah picked up the piece of paper that had the names of the two people who might be able to shed more light on David Weller. She pressed in the first number but got no answer, not even a voice mail.

"Dead end." She shook her head and looked at the piece of paper. "Maybe this woman, Maggie Dunne, will be helpful."

Hannah pressed in the number and waited. A woman's crisp voice came across the line. Hannah asked some preliminary questions and explained that she was with law enforcement. It seemed that Maggie had tried to befriend David because he seemed kind of lonely.

"We talked quite a bit. Over the season, I invited him to a few things that the other employees were doing together. He always had an excuse."

"Do you know if David owned a boat?"

"Oh, sure, just a small motorboat he invited me to go out with him on it. I went, but I was a little concerned that he thought I was interested in him romantically, which was not my intent. I kind of gave him the cold shoulder after that."

"Do you know where he kept his boat when he was on the island?"

"I know when I went out with him, he launched from a little inlet that was a short hike from the Garr Ranch."

She tensed. David liked to have his boat close to where she was right now. Hannah tried to remember if her family had ever docked near the ranch. "You launched the boat from an area by the ranch?"

Trevor raised his head from his laptop, as if what she had said sparked his interest.

"Yes, we left the car in their parking lot just outside the ranch entrance and walked from there."

Now she had an idea of where the docking area might be. Hannah thanked the woman and disconnected from the call.

"That sounded a little more hopeful," said Trevor.

"David might have his boat close to here. I want to go out and search the bay."

"Not alone."

"Maybe Ian and Lola can go with me," she said.

"I'll go with you too. I should not stay here alone anyway."

She pressed her radio. "Ian, are you there?"

His voice came over the line. He sounded out of breath. "Lola picked up a scent. We had to follow it."

"Oh, good. Hope it leads somewhere." Disappointment settled around her. Going down to the water would have to wait.

Hannah disconnected from the radio, crossed her arms and stared out the window for a long moment. "We're going to have to wait on that. The others might come in for lunch soon."

"Speaking of which. Why don't I go grab us something to eat?"

"Sure, I'm hungry," she said.

Trevor set his laptop on an end table and moved to the kitchen.

Captain rose from the rug where he'd been lying and whined. "I'll take him out real quick to do his business."

Hannah opened the door. Captain ran outside. She stepped across the threshold but stayed close to the building.

Plenty of people milled around the other buildings and in the woods closer to the bunkhouse. Her heart beat a little faster, but she couldn't say why.

Captain had wandered around the corner of the building out of sight.

She stepped away from the community room and called out to her K-9.

Her attention was drawn back to the woods. A man in a hat and sunglasses stepped out from the trees. He looked right at her before turning and disappearing into the trees.

Her throat went tight as she pressed the button on her radio. "Ian, the RMK is here not too far from the bunkhouse. I'm in pursuit."

"I'll get there as fast as we can." Ian's words were jumpy. He must be running.

Meadow and Chase responded that they had been searching not too far from the bunkhouse. "We're on it," said Chase.

Though she did not see him anywhere, Ian would be close by if he and Lola had been hot on the RMK's trail. She ran toward where the RMK had gone. Captain had come back around the building and was a few paces behind her.

She entered the trees where several people were standing by the bird-watching signs, looking up. Her heart raced as she scanned the area. Her eyes were drawn to a man she saw only from the back who was wearing a baseball cap.

Though he was not running, he was moving at a steady pace.

She hurried to catch up with him. He disappeared in the thickness of the trees. When she looked over her shoulder, Captain was still behind her.

She pressed her radio. "Ian, where are you?"

"Just got back to the bunkhouse."

It didn't make sense that he was that far away. Hadn't Lola just been on the RMK's scent?

She increased her pace, moving in the direction she'd seen the RMK go. She stepped into an open area. She could see the lake in the distance.

Sensing that someone was behind her, she whirled around, The man in front of her wore sunglasses and a baseball hat, but it was not the RMK.

David Weller grinned at her. "Did you think I wouldn't see the notices sent out to employees describing the man you've all been looking for?"

She'd been tricked.

She reached for her gun just as he grabbed her arm and yanked it behind her back.

She needed to buy time, to try to break free.

"You killed my friend because she looked like your sister?"

"So what if I did." He pushed her arm up higher causing pain to shoot through her body.

She angled side to side trying to get away. Maybe someone would see them struggling before he got her to the water to drown her. Ian might find her if she could only delay long enough. If she could throw him off his game mentally, she might have a chance. "And that man and that woman who looked like your mom and dad. You killed them too."

David grew very still, snaking his free arm across her chest and pulling her close. He hissed in her ear, "I could never live up to Mommy and Daddy's expectations. They ridiculed me. My sister too. They got what they deserved."

It was clear there was no psychological separation between the symbolic parents David had probably killed and his real parents.

He had all but confessed to the killings. She only hoped she would live to testify against him.

When she tried to twist her body, he held her so tightly she could barely move.

She wrapped her leg behind his so she could trip him. They both fell on the ground.

His hands clawed at her as she crawled to get away. He jumped on top of her back with her stomach pressed against the ground.

A hard object hit the side of her head.

She could smell salt in the air and hear Captain barking as she lost consciousness.

Chapter Eighteen

Trevor rushed outside when Hannah and Captain hadn't returned after he'd pulled sandwich stuff from the fridge. Ian and Lola raced toward the community room.

Ian pointed. "Hannah is in pursuit of the RMK. Get back inside."

"No way," said Trevor. "Hannah might be in danger."

Ian was already several paces in front of him and probably realized that arguing was pointless. The two men hurried toward the trees. Ian slowed down and looked from side to side. "Something is not right. Lola is not picking up any kind of trail like she did before."

Chase's voice came through the radio. "We're getting close to the community room, but I don't see you."

"We're in the trees," said Ian.

Trevor stopped a man who had binoculars around his neck.

"Did you see a woman in a uniform around here?"

"Yes, just a few minutes ago. She went that way."

Both men ran in the direction that the bird-watcher had pointed.

They came to an open area, where they could see the beach in the distance. Some people were flying kites along the beach. Several people were out on the water in boats of different sizes. A balloon floated over the water.

Trevor shook his head. "Where did she go?"

Then he heard it, a faint but distinct barking. Lola's ears perked up and she licked her chops.

"That's Captain," said Ian.

They ran toward the sound of the barking, moving around a rock formation that had blocked their view. They found Captain pacing the shore and barking. Trevor scanned the water, allowing his gaze to rest on each boat. A short distance from the shore, a man in a motorboat looked over his shoulder at them. He pulled down his baseball cap lower on his face before increasing his speed. He had something in the boat covered in a tarp.

Alarm bells went off in Trevor's head as he continued to watch the man. Wind caught the corner of the tarp. Trevor thought he saw what looked like a foot, but why would the RMK kidnap Hannah? "I think that's our guy," said Trevor.

Both men glanced along the shore. They needed a boat.

Ian ran toward a man who had just brought a small craft up on the beach. Trevor called Captain and followed Ian and Lola.

"Official police business. I need your boat."

The man stepped away from his boat. "I'll help push it back into the water."

Ian, Trevor and the two dogs jumped in. Once they were in deep enough water, Trevor yanked the pull cord to start the engine, then steered so they were headed in the same direction as the boat that Hannah was probably in.

They passed several other boats but did not see the one they were looking for anywhere.

Trevor steered around a bend. What did the RMK have in mind, anyway? Was this some sort of trap to get at him? If the RMK had been watching at all, he must have noticed how often he and Hannah were together.

Both dogs seemed to be on high alert, with their heads lifted as they sniffed the air.

Trevor shouted above the hum of the boat engine as he scanned the glassy lake. "He's probably going someplace secluded." But where?

Trevor steered closer to the shore and away from the larger boats. Up ahead, he saw trees close to the shore. He headed in that direction. Once around the trees, they entered a C-shaped cove that was framed by a long shoreline on each side covered in rocks and scrubby trees. Up ahead was a man dumping Hannah's body into the water close to the boat. The immobile body barely made a noise as it hit the buoyant water, falling close to the rim of the boat. The man put his hand on Hannah's head and pushed her under.

Ian's hand hovered over his weapon, but he did not draw it. They were still too far away to get an accurate shot. Their boat was already moving at top speed.

The wind blew the man's hat off and Trevor saw the brown curly hair. David Weller.

David's head shot up. He straightened from where he had been bent over holding Hannah's head under water. He started the boat up and sped back toward the open part of the lake, leaving Hannah behind. She floated face-first in the water.

"We have to get to her," Trevor shouted.

Ian looked at the fleeing man and then back at Hannah.

"Take over," said Trevor.

Ian scrambled toward the back of the boat to steer. The boat slowed and drifted in the exchange between the two men as they drew closer to Hannah's floating body.

Trevor shouted the command at Captain he'd heard Hannah use. "Save."

Without hesitation, Captain leaped out of the boat and paddled toward Hannah. Trevor jumped into the water, as well.

Ian sped off toward the other boat. Swimming in the salt water was arduous. He had to get to Hannah. Captain seemed to take the buoyancy in stride as he got closer to his partner. Still not moving, Hannah had flipped sideways in the water. Captain reached her and tugged on the collar of her uniform to turn her so she was face up, then dragged her toward the shore.

Knowing that Hannah was in good paws, Trevor swam in the direction that Captain went to get to the nearest dry land. Captain brought

Hannah ashore with her legs still resting in the water. Trevor reached her seconds later, kneeling over her as water dripped from his hair.

His heart squeezed tight at seeing her pale, lifeless face. She still had a pulse, but she'd probably swallowed water. He began to perform CPR, pressing below her rib cage and then placing his lips on hers. She gurgled. He turned her head to the side. Water spilled out of her mouth.

Still dazed, she looked up at him, reaching her hand to touch his cheek. "Hey," she said.

Her voice made him think of a summer breeze.

He rested his hand on hers. "Hey there. Glad you're okay."

Captain moved in and licked Hannah's forehead. Hannah laughed as she sat up and reached out to touch Captain's dripping wet jowls. "My buddy."

"He saved you."

"I imagine you both worked together," she said.

"I was afraid I'd lost you. I don't know what I would've done if—"

His words were interrupted by the sound of gunfire.

★ ★ ★

Stunned out of the moment of warmth and connection that had passed between them, Hannah's attention was drawn over Trevor's shoulder as he turned to see the source of the gunfire.

David Weller's boat had run aground at the tip of the peninsula that led into the cove. From his boat, Ian must have fired a shot at him as David neared the rocky shore, where his boat now was. David ran toward the shelter of the rocks and trees.

"He'll have to come back close to here. I can catch him," Hannah said. She tried to push herself to her feet, but her knees buckled.

He reached out to steady her by grabbing her elbow. "You're still weak. Give me your gun."

He was right. In her state, there was no way she could catch up with him. She handed him the gun. Trevor took off running. Captain stayed close to her as she tried to keep up but fell several paces behind him.

As they neared the place where they would collide with David Weller before he took off down the beach, she prayed for more strength.

Trevor got farther ahead of her.

David emerged from the trees, his face red

from exertion...or was it rage. Her world seemed to move in slow motion as David turned, saw Trevor, lifted the gun and fired.

Trevor's whole body flung backward as the arm not holding the gun flailed in the air, but he did not fall to the ground. He took aim and fired a shot, then kept running, though his steps seemed much more weighted.

Ian and Lola emerged through the trees as David headed up the beach and dove behind some brush. Lola ran ahead of her partner.

David edged out from behind the bush and fired at Lola. The dog lurched. Her whole body twisted.

Fearing that Lola had been hit, Hannah's heart stopped.

The German shepherd remained standing with her head down. Ian commanded her to stop probably fearing she would be shot if she got closer to the suspect. Trevor had gone out ahead of Ian and Lola.

She saw now that his sleeve was red with blood. Trevor had been hit in the arm that he didn't use to shoot with. A scream got caught in her throat.

She willed herself to go faster, though her muscles felt like mush.

Beyond the brush where David had been hidden was a rocky field. She caught movement, a flash of color. David was running the other way through the rocks.

"That way." She was closer than the other two men, but she could not hope to take on David without a gun. Trevor rerouted himself and headed toward the rocks still holding the gun. Ian and Lola were right behind him. They disappeared behind a large boulder.

Hannah reached the edge of the rocky field with Captain. She heard noise, like one rock crashing into another, and then a gunshot.

Her whole body lurched at the sound. What if Trevor had been shot again? This time fatally?

Captain let out a low growl. Then silence enveloped her. Her heart was still pounding from the exertion of trying to keep up. She stepped toward the rocks. David Weller came out from behind a boulder only yards away from where she was. His back was toward her. She crouched down behind a rock when he glanced her way. When she lifted her head above the rim of the rock, she saw that he was headed toward the boats.

Summoning all the strength she had left, she bolted toward him and leaped in the air, hoping to land on his back. If she missed, he would have time to shoot her. She sailed through the air, hit her target and knocked him down on his stomach. He'd dropped the gun a few feet from his hand.

"Police, you're under arrest." She was so out of breath her voice lacked conviction. She wasn't sure if she'd be strong enough to subdue him for long. Her knees were on the middle of his back and one hand secured his wrist.

David twisted and pushed her off. Just as he dove for her, Trevor emerged from the boulder field.

He landed a blow across David's jaw that caused him to fall backward. He was clearly weakened from his gunshot wound but he held the gun on a stunned David. "It's over."

David sneered. "You look like you're about to fall over."

Ian and Lola came to stand beside Trevor. Ian held his firearm as well, while Lola stood at the ready to take down the suspect.

"Don't even think about it," said Ian. "Put your hands in the air, where I can see them."

David complied though rage was still evident in his eyes. His features were taut, and his teeth showed through his parted lips.

Lola edged closer as Ian moved in to handcuff David Weller, who watched the dogs with wary eyes.

Hannah ran toward Trevor. "You've been shot."

He touched his arm. "I think I was just grazed."

Trevor was putting on a brave face, but she had a feeling he was in pain judging from how blood soaked his sleeve was. "All the same, we need to get you to a hospital."

"I'll take this guy back," said Ian. "If the two of you want to bring his boat in. There is not enough room for all of us in the other boat. He's not going to try anything with Lola close by."

Hannah led Trevor down to the other boat.

They journeyed back up the shore. The rest of the team was there to meet them. Chase ushered Trevor and Hannah back to the bunkhouse and into his car, then they took off to the hospital in Syracuse.

She sat with Chase in the waiting room after Trevor was put in a wheelchair and pushed down a hallway.

Chase leaned his shoulder against hers. "I'm sure he's going to be okay."

"That's what he thought." She still couldn't

let go of her fear. What if the wound was worse than it appeared?

Chase rested a hand on her arm. "I can tell you look worried."

"I care about him."

"Care about him? I've seen the way you look at each other. I would say you passed caring about him a while ago."

Her cheeks flushed, and she smiled so widely it almost hurt. "Okay, more than care about him. I think I love him. He's truly a decent man, everything I ever wanted in a life partner."

"I agree. I wasn't sure from the interviews, but having spent time with him, I see now that he is the real deal."

She let out a breath. It was good to say out loud what she had been thinking for some time. To admit it to herself. She had been so closed off to the idea that any man could be gentle and courageous and loving, that she hadn't been able to believe that Trevor was exactly that.

Chase picked up a magazine that had been lying on the chair beside him and flipped through it. "I wouldn't be surprised if there wasn't another engagement in the task force soon."

"No." She slapped his magazine lightly.

"You never know," he teased.

She knew it was what she wanted. But the big question was how did Trevor feel about her? Their relationship had had so many mixed messages, she still wasn't sure where he stood.

"Engagements are always nice." The smile faded from Chase's face and he got a faraway look in his eyes. Was he thinking about his own life? It seemed that the loss of his wife and baby was the thing that defined him, just as Jodie's death had held a grip on Hannah. Perhaps in the future, Chase would find some measure of happiness, and maybe even love, if all his energy wasn't focused on catching the RMK.

Chapter Nineteen

A spike of pain shot through Trevor's arm as he sat on the couch looking at his phone.

Ian and Isla were in the kitchen. Meadow and Selena had taken their dogs to search the premises, using the scent off the puppy blankets, a reminder that the RMK was still out there, still a threat to his life. It was unclear if the RMK had left the island or was still looking for a chance to come after Trevor.

Rocco muttered something about getting some rest and left the room. Chase and Hannah sat on different couches both looking at their phones.

Earlier, the team had eaten dinner together and raised their water glasses in a toast to David Weller being taken into custody. He would be charged with Jodie's murder as well as attempted murder of Hannah. A case would have to be made against the other two drownings of people who resembled his mother and father. Hannah could testify as to what he had confessed to her before knocking her unconscious.

The sky had grown dark.

After his arm had been treated, they had driven home with little conversation passing between him and Hannah. Not that there wasn't something on his mind. Being shot had changed his perspective on his choices. If the bullet had been a few more inches to the left, he might not be alive. More than anything, he wanted a chance to be alone with Hannah so they could talk.

Hannah rose to her feet. "I think Captain needs to go outside for a bit."

Seeing his opportunity, Trevor also got up. "I'll go with you."

"I don't think that is a good idea," said Chase.

"Selena and Meadow are out there." Trevor gave Chase a steely glare that he hoped communicated that he wanted some time alone with Hannah. "I have lots of protection."

Chase nodded seeming to understand. "Stay close to the buildings."

Hannah had already stepped out the door with Captain when he caught up with her. While Captain wandered around, he came to stand by Hannah. Selena walked by with Scout and nodded in their direction before disappearing around a corner of the building.

"Quite a day, huh?" His mind raced with what to say and how to say it.

"For sure," she said.

"I bet it feels pretty good to close the book on Jodie's death."

"Yes, now I can get on with my life and put my full energy into catching the RMK." She turned to face him. "I know this must be hard for you knowing that the RMK is still out there. You probably hoped he'd be in custody after you took such a risk in staying out in the open."

He stepped a little closer to her. "Being shot has made me rethink some things."

She gazed at him, shaking her head.

"I think maybe I was willing to take such risks because my life didn't matter to me that much, but it does now."

"Are you saying you're willing to go into a safe house?"

"Yes." He stepped closer to her.

"What changed?"

"My life matters to me more now because I want to spend it with you. Hannah, I'm in love with you. I don't want to throw my life away over something that happened ten years ago, and I don't want to be stuck because of it. It's time to look forward, not to live in the past. I can see a future now and I want it to be with you."

"Oh, Trevor. I feel the same way. I just wasn't sure where you stood."

He touched her face. "Hannah, will you marry me?"

"Yes, of course, I will." She gazed up at him.

He bent his head and kissed her. This time there was no doubt what the kiss meant. He wrapped an arm around her waist and drew her close.

After a long moment, she pulled away from the kiss but remained in his embrace. "I don't want to be away from you for even a minute. I'll volunteer as a guard at the safe house."

"Funny way to start out a relationship, but it'll be a great story to tell our kids." He kissed her again.

Captain stood a few feet away from them, watching. His dark coloring blended with the night but is eyes shone.

When Trevor pulled free of the kiss, he saw that Chase, Isla and Ian had all come outside.

"About time you two realized what you are to each other," said Chase.

Selena and Meadow had drawn closer, as well. The whole team applauded and spoke words of congratulations.

Trevor embraced Hannah and kissed her to another round of applause. He relished holding the woman he wanted to spend his life with.

Don't miss the stories in this mini series!

MOUNTAIN COUNTRY K-9 UNIT

MILLS & BOON

Montana Hidden Deception

Amity Steffen

MILLS & BOON

Amity Steffen lives in northern Minnesota with her two boys and two spoiled cats. She's a voracious reader and a novice baker. She enjoys watching her sons play baseball in the summer and would rather stay indoors in the winter. She's worked in the education field for more years than she cares to count, but writing has always been her passion. Amity loves connecting with readers, so please visit her at Facebook.com/amitysteffenauthor.

Visit the Author Profile page
at millsandboon.com.au for more titles.

Behold, I will do a new thing; now it shall spring forth; shall ye not know it? I will even make a way in the wilderness, and rivers in the desert.
—*Isaiah* 43:19

DEDICATION

For Ann Marie, whose strength, perseverance and vibrant personality shine through in everything you do. Your friendship, support and guidance over the decades have been a light in my world, especially through the darkest times.

Chapter One

Nina Montgomery began to carefully make her way down the steep incline. It was a perfect day to visit Mulberry Creek State Park. The rolling Montana sky seemed to stretch out forever from here. She'd departed from the trail to reach this higher elevation, hoping to get a few pictures of the newly hatched eaglets. What she had thought would be a good vantage point hadn't turned out to be that great. She'd gotten a few shots with the fancy Nikon camera her family had given her when she'd finished nursing school last year but doubted they were going to be anything spectacular.

It was no matter. The day was beautiful. The air was warm. The sun was shining. She'd just seen a momma raccoon with her kits trotting by. Nina loved springtime. Everything was fresh and new.

This is the day that the Lord has made, she thought. It was bright and glorious and perfect.

With measured footsteps, she edged her way downward. It would be mildly disastrous to take a tumble out here. If she twisted her ankle, it could take hours before someone else came this way. Nina already knew from past visits that cell phone reception could be spotty on this side of the park.

Almost to the trail now, she began to relax as the incline evened out. She held up her camera again. Last week, by chance, she'd taken a few good shots of a doe with her twin spotted fawns nestled in the woods. She stood still, using her zoom lens like a binocular.

She let out a gasp of surprise.

What was that? On the other side of the trail, movement.

Was it a bear? It was low to the ground, tucked in among the shrubbery. Rooting around.

No. It was too small to be a bear.

Her heart thumped harshly in her chest.

Was it a cub? That would not be good. Where baby was, momma was sure to be nearby. Her mind instantly whirled, trying to remember what to do if confronted by a bear. Make yourself as big as possible and try to appear frightening? Or curl into a ball and play dead? She couldn't recall.

Then the creature stood and she realized it wasn't a bear at all.

It was a man.

Odd.

He knelt down again, as if he'd only needed to stretch a moment.

Intrigued, Nina stood there watching him. Now that she was focused on him, she could see the man wasn't really rooting around at all. He wore thick black gloves along with his black sweats and his black hoodie. He had a garden trowel and he was digging a hole. What was he doing?

This was *really* odd.

Click.

Click.

Click. Click.

Almost reflexively, she snapped a few pictures.

Then she shook her head. What was she doing? It wasn't like her to spy on someone. He was probably just burying a time capsule. Or maybe he was geocaching. That had become popular lately.

Nina really had no idea what it entailed, other than leaving objects where other people could somehow find them. Did that include burying them?

Common sense told her she should keep moving. Just mind her own business. But her curiosity was burning hot and insatiable. She continued to move closer to the trail. For a moment, she contemplated simply asking what he was doing. But the man seemed to be working frantically now. Something about his movements, the way he viciously stabbed at the earth with the trowel, set her nerves on edge. Didn't people use their phones while geocaching? She wasn't sure, but that made her wonder if he was doing something else. But what?

Almost unconsciously, Nina slipped behind a tree. There was no way off this trail without strolling past the stranger. Suddenly, she did not want to do that. Instead, she lingered in her hiding place, feeling a bit foolish, but the old adage *better safe than sorry* swirled through her mind.

He stood again. This time he cast a glance over his shoulder. His features were mostly hidden under the hoodie he wore. Dark sunglasses covered much of his pale face. As she peered through thick branches, Nina thought it looked like he was scanning the area. She hoped the dense pine boughs would provide coverage for her.

He lifted a metal box that his body had been blocking. It wasn't much larger than a shoebox. For a moment, he just held it, almost reverently, then he lowered it into the hole.

At least he's not burying a body.

Nina pressed a hand to her chest, startled by the thought. Her heart pounded against her palm and she realized that this situation was making her more than a little uncomfortable.

The stranger grabbed the trowel again and with choppy, hurried movements, began filling the hole back in with the pile of dirt he'd accumulated. He tossed another glance over his shoulder. This time his gaze seemed to slowly scan the area. Could he sense her out there, watching?

Nina's heart was pounding so hard now she thought she could hear the blood sloshing through her veins.

Was she being ridiculous?

Maybe.

Better safe than sorry.

Moving slowly, she pulled her phone out

of her pocket. No reception. Just as she'd expected. She stuffed it back inside. It was probably for the best. Who would she text and what would she tell them?

Don't worry about me. Watching a man dig a hole while I hide behind a tree.

Thinking of trees, she wished she'd found a bigger one to hide behind. She was grateful she'd thrown on dark jeans and a navy T-shirt this morning. It wasn't exactly camouflage, but at least it wasn't something that would stand out.

After what felt like forever, the man rose. She realized now he had a backpack. He shoved the thick black gloves and trowel inside. Then he scanned the area again. Thoroughly. Was he looking for someone? Something? Or was he just trying to commit the place to memory so he could come back later?

Dangling the backpack in his hand, he began to make his way out of the woods. He didn't have far to go. Maybe twenty feet or so. Nina saw that he held a can of spray paint. First, he glanced up and down the trail, which caused her to look as well. There was no one in sight in either direction. Then, with his back to her, he shot a quick blast of black paint against the white bark of a birch. It was subtle, not something that would grab the attention of anyone hiking by. But it was obvious enough that someone looking for it would find it again.

The hole he'd dug was straight back from where he'd marked the spot. His hand tapped restlessly against his thigh. A minute later, he took a step into the tree line then stopped, as if debating what to do.

With a growl, he whirled and stomped out to the trail.

Nina realized she was holding her breath, pushing herself up against the tree as she tried to remain invisible and praying he would be on his way. She felt so alone, so secluded. It made her long to be at her family's ranch where there were kids and chaos. Really, she wished she was just about anywhere but here.

In another moment, he took off down the trail. Though his movements had seemed frantic, hurried, while he'd been digging, he seemed to be moving at a leisurely pace now. Or perhaps she was mistaken. Was his pace leisurely…or hesitant?

She watched him go and then her eyes swung across the path. From her position, she could just barely make out the black dirt covering the freshly dug hole.

Detective Mateo Bianchi was desperately trying to enjoy his day off. It was tough. Days off provided too much time to think. He'd hoped spending time at the Mulberry Creek State Park would refresh his mind, cleanse his spirit.

Leave him feeling invigorated.

Instead, it left him feeling drained. It wasn't due to jogging the trails, either. No. It was seeing all the families. Happy families with bickering kids, excited kids, exhausted kids.

Being here made him think of Josh and Nate. It made him miss them with that wretched ache that never went away. This was the sort of day where he and Jolene should've brought the twins to the park, had a picnic, enjoyed a hike.

But they were gone. Dead. His entire family. Killed in a horrific car crash two years ago. And he would probably never stop feeling as if he were to blame.

Maybe he didn't deserve to have a relaxing day.

Nate and Josh never would. Gone before their seventh birthday.

As his shoes smacked against the hard-packed

earth, he glanced skyward, wondering for the millionth time why God had let it happen.

Knowing he wouldn't get an answer, he blew out a breath and tried to relax by taking in the view as he jogged along this out-of-the-way path. He scanned the brilliantly vibrant new spring foliage. It was admittedly beautiful against the flawless azure sky. He pulled in a lungful of fresh, clean air.

The trail curved and he glanced down in time to avoid a man rushing around the corner. Mateo stepped back and they barely missed smashing shoulders. They guy had his hood up, head down, and didn't even acknowledge Mateo.

Fine by him. He wasn't in the mood to chat with anyone, anyway. That's why he'd chosen this trail. It was on the edge of the park. There wasn't much to see, so it didn't get as much foot traffic as some of the others.

He glanced at his watch as he jogged along. It was nearing dinnertime and, as if it had just gotten the memo, his stomach growled. Maybe it was time to turn back. He wasn't a great cook but he was pretty good with the grill and he had a steak marinating in the fridge.

He slowed, ready to pivot, and nearly skidded in his tracks.

A woman stood inside the tree line, holding a metal box. Her long strawberry blonde hair was falling out of her ponytail. Dirt was smudged across her creamy-smooth cheek. Her pale green eyes were wide in surprise.

There was a pile of dirt at her feet.

Stranger still, she wore disposable gloves.

Her face scrunched, as if in embarrassment. "Detective Bianchi."

He arched a brow, surprised she remembered him from the one time they'd met. "Nina Montgomery, right?"

She gave him a hesitant smile and nodded. "I suppose you're wondering what I'm doing."

"Yes." He realized he was staring at her. She was such a strange, unexpected sight standing there in the trees, and he'd seen a lot of strange things over the years. "You could certainly say that."

She walked toward him, holding the box out in front of her like an offering. "It's an interesting story," she began.

"Can't wait to hear it."

"Hey!"

Mateo turned to see the man he'd nearly bumped into earlier racing toward them.

"Drop that box!"

His arm was outstretched and Mateo had seen enough weapons, even from a distance, to know the man was aiming a gun at them. He darted forward.

Nina let out a shriek, but instead of dropping the box as commanded, she dashed into the woods and took off running. Mateo tore after her, grateful she'd headed for the thickest foliage. He heard the unmistakable blast of a gun, muted by a silencer but audible all the same. Bark exploded on a tree off to their side.

Mateo grabbed Nina's hand as they ran. It made dodging foliage cumbersome, but it was better than being separated as the greenery became thicker and thicker. They dodged around trees, tore through bushes, and jumped over a few fallen logs.

The gunman was now shooting indiscriminately through the thick copse of trees. Bullets seemed to be flying on either side of them, taking out bark or sending up clumps of dirt as the slugs tore into the ground. His spine tingled—burned—with anxiety as he imagined a bullet tearing through his back.

Or Nina's.

God, protect us! The prayer took him by surprise. He hadn't prayed in years, but if he was going to start again, now seemed like as good of a time as any. The last time he'd prayed, he'd been begging for his child's life. It seemed God hadn't listened then.

Would he listen now?

What was in that box? How was Nina involved in this?

Though he barely knew the woman, his instincts told him she was not complicit in a crime. He knew both of her brothers and their wives. They were good people. Law-abiding people.

Was this a case of being in the wrong place at the wrong time?

What was it with her family? They were virtual trouble magnets. He had just helped her brothers through some pretty trying ordeals. Just last fall, her brother Seth had landed himself in the hospital after helping solve a child trafficking case. Nina had hovered over his bedside, scolding Mateo for questioning him while he was recovering from a concussion. She'd had spunk, but she hadn't deterred him.

Mateo risked a glance over his shoulder and saw nothing but trees.

"Who is that guy?" he asked.

"No idea." She tossed a quick look at him but kept moving. "It's a long story. I'll tell you all about it as soon as I can."

She would tell him later. That was for sure. Right now, he needed to concentrate on keeping them alive.

The park was enormous, covering thousands of acres. Would anyone hear the shooting? Would they question what it was, where it was coming from? Or would the sound be too muffled as it traveled over the dips and hills, through the trees and down the trails?

They ran and ran. The bullets had finally subsided. Either the man had run out of ammo or he had given up. Was he trying to track them, though? He looked over his shoulder, wondering if they'd left a trail through the trees. The greenery was fresh, new, and seemed to have sprung back into place. The ground was covered with last year's leaves. He didn't think they were leaving footprints anywhere.

"Here." He tugged Nina sideways then pulled her in beside him behind a massive boulder. It was one of many they had passed and wouldn't stand out any more than the others as an obvious hiding spot. "Get down."

She didn't hesitate, simply dropped down beside him. In the chaos, he hadn't realized she was still clutching the box. He saw it now, though, tucked under one arm.

Again, he wondered what it was holding that was so important.

She let out a soft groan.

"Are you hurt?" he asked, his voice low and concerned.

"Just apparently not in great shape," she whispered. "Stitch. In my side. Ouch. Or maybe I shouldn't be running after guzzling a bottle of water."

The Nikon camera dangling around her neck snagged his attention. "Any chance you got a picture of the guy?"

"Actually, yes."

Mateo felt hope spring up, but Nina immediately quashed it when she made an apologetic face.

Her voice was low as she spoke. "Unfortunately, he had his back to me the whole time. I honestly don't even know why I took the pictures. It was just a reflex. I'm sure I don't have anything useful."

"You never know. We'll have someone look at the pictures." *As soon as we get out of this*, he added silently.

He swiped sweat off his brow with the back of his hand. Then he scoured the forest, looking for any sign of the shooter. Had they lost the guy? He pulled his phone from his pocket. On a positive note, it was fully charged. Yet that didn't do a lot of good when they had no reception. Regardless, he sent off a few texts because he had to do *something*.

Nina shifted beside him. The box was now settled at her feet. She pulled off the disposable gloves that still baffled him and shoved them into the fanny pack she wore. When she glanced up at him, her expression was questioning.

Mateo gave her a warning look but didn't have to tell her not to speak.

She nodded to let him know she understood. Then she gave him a strained smile, as if to tell him she was okay. He patted her shoulder and then turned his attention to the woods. Mateo was grateful she was holding it together so well. He knew a lot of people would melt down under so much pressure. Being shot at? Chased through the woods? Targeted?

It was a lot to deal with. He'd been in law enforcement for more than a decade now and he still felt plenty rattled over what had just happened.

Yet there she sat, doing what sounded like deep breathing exercises. Or maybe she was simply trying to relieve the stitch in her side. He realized then that her eyes were closed and her hands were folded. In prayer? Probably.

They crouched there, hidden behind the boulder, both listening. They were so close their shoulders were touching. It was the only way to be sure they were both secreted. He glanced at his phone every few minutes, but none of the texts appeared to have been sent. Fifteen minutes passed. Then twenty. If he'd been alone, he may have begun creeping through the woods.

But he wasn't alone. He was with Nina and he was unarmed. A helpless sensation slithered through him. He hated feeling like he was cowering in the bushes, but for now he knew hiding was their best option.

He had so many questions for this woman.

Thirty minutes slipped by. He was torn because he didn't want to act hastily. He needed to be sure they weren't being stalked. Yet the longer they stayed hidden, the more time it gave the perp to get away.

Finally, he stood slowly and peered over the boulder.

His heart pounded as he waited for the sound of a gunshot.

Chapter Two

Mateo had been glancing at his phone periodically. The scowl he wore let her know his text still hadn't gone through. Nina had contemplated sending a few texts of her own. But to what end? To whom? Her family? The last thing she wanted was to terrify them, to have them try to race to her rescue and potentially end up in danger themselves. No, she'd leave it to Mateo to report the situation.

When he stood, she found herself bracing for the worst. No shot came. In fact, there seemed to be no sign of the gunman at all. Mateo held out a hand and she reached for it. His strong fingers wrapped around her own and he hoisted her up. Her legs tingled from sitting crouched for so long.

"Do you think he's gone?" Her palms were sweaty and anxiety still buzzed down her spine.

"Not sure." Mateo turned to look at her. She

hadn't remembered how dark his eyes were, almost as black as his hair. A worry line rested between his brows. He was taller than she remembered, too. She barely reached his shoulders. His gray thermal shirt stretched tautly across his chest. He looked formidable as he stood guard.

Nina was grateful that he was with her now. Detective Mateo Bianchi seemed to be the sort of man you would want on your side. What would she have done if the gunman had come back and she'd been alone? What if he'd sneaked up on her in the woods and Mateo hadn't been there?

She had a hunch he'd have shot her and she'd be dead right now. What had she stumbled upon? What could possibly be so important that someone would shoot at them? Had it only been a few hours ago that she'd been snapping photos of the eaglets? How had her day gone so completely sideways?

Nina wrapped her arms around herself, trying to keep it together.

"I think you need to tell me what's going on here." Mateo studied her face a moment before his gaze dropped to the box and then returned to her with a questioning look.

Nina told him everything, starting with how she'd been trying to get some photos of the eaglets. She described seeing the man in the woods and realizing he was burying something.

"Why didn't you just keep on walking?"

She winced. "I admit, I was curious at first. Then… I don't know. After I watched him for a minute, the situation started to feel off. People aren't supposed to litter. Burying something in the state park seemed odd to me. His behavior seemed strange and it made me think he wouldn't appreciate seeing me waltzing down the path. I started to get nervous, so I hid behind a tree until he left."

He arched a brow. "And then?"

"I was going to go back to my car, but my curiosity got the better of me." She could feel heat flood her cheeks at the admission. God had given her a great deal of common sense and most of the time she used it. She wasn't sure why today had been so different.

Then again, if she had gone to the parking lot, she would've run into the man on the trail when he'd backtracked. Would he have suspected her then? Would he have confronted her or just let her go? She would never know.

"You dug up the box."

She nodded though his tone implied that probably hadn't been a smart move. He was right, but she could hardly take it back.

"You just happened to have disposable gloves to wear to keep your hands clean?" His pitch was skeptical.

Nina knew it was a legitimate question and even understood his incredulity. She patted the fanny pack her brothers liked to tease her about. "I'm a nurse, if you recall."

"I do."

"I keep a few emergency items in here. Gauze, scissors, tape, some antiseptic wipes." She unzipped the pack to give him a view of what was inside. "A few pairs of disposable gloves. I worked in the ER long enough to realize accidents happen all the time. I like to be prepared. I've never had to use my supplies for anything worse than a kiddo with a skinned knee, but you never know."

"I see." He knelt down in front of the box then gave the latch a tug. "It's locked."

"Yes." She shrugged. "When I realized I couldn't open it, I was going to put it back where I found it. I thought about letting a park ranger know on my way out today, but then you came along."

"Then we were shot at." He pinched the bridge of his nose. "Why didn't you drop the box when he told you to?"

Why hadn't she?

"I barely remember him saying that. All I remember is that I heard him yell. I saw a gun and my instinct was to run."

"It was a pretty good instinct. The trees are so thick out here, he wasn't able to get off a clear shot. Running into the woods likely saved our lives. I wonder why he came back."

She thought about that a moment. "After he marked the tree, he seemed hesitant to leave. At one point, he even went back into the woods."

"Did you ever get a good look at him?"

"No. He had his hood up the whole time and sunglasses on. Even when he was in the woods."

"I ran into him on the trail." Mateo's gaze flittered around, still taking in their surroundings. "I didn't get a good look at him, either. He had his head down and his face was covered. Seemed like he was in a hurry to get out of the park."

"He must've changed his mind."

"Obviously, whatever is in that box is pretty important to him. I'm going to bring it to the station and find out what's inside." He eyed the fanny pack that she'd zipped shut. "Did I see a plastic bag in there? I know you've touched the box, and I doubt we can lift any prints off it after it was buried in the dirt, but it might not hurt to try."

Nina pulled the plastic grocery bag out and handed it to him. "I keep a few in there in case I come across litter."

His lips twitched. "Right. I gather you're not a fan of littering."

"No." She watched as he bagged the box. Then he checked his phone. She could tell by his expression that he had no news. She felt jittery and wanted nothing more than to leave the park. "Can we get out of here now?"

"Maybe."

Mateo was hyperaware of his surroundings as his eyes scanned the forest. Birds chirped above him and a chipmunk stared him down, scolding him for invading the pristine space. Other than that, he and Nina seemed to be alone out here. He saw no questionable movement, heard no troubling sounds of someone approaching.

Still, he hated being weaponless. With Nina beside him, he wasn't about to take any chances.

He glanced at her. Her cheeks were rosy and

her green eyes seemed to glint in the sunlight. She looked young—so innocent and delicate—though he knew she was old enough to have graduated from nursing school.

She had also mentioned she worked in the ER, so maybe she wasn't as delicate as she appeared. He had to assume that took nerves of steel some days. That probably explained how she'd taken being shot at so well.

He cleared his throat when he realized he'd been gazing into her lovely eyes a few seconds too long. What was wrong with him?

"Uh, yeah." He kept his tone low, just in case. "I think we're in the clear."

"Good," she said decisively, "because I do not enjoy being shot at. That is not a good way to spend the day."

It took him a moment to realize she was trying to bring some levity to the serious situation.

His lip quirked. "Being shot at is not one of my favorite things, either."

"I suppose you've had more practice at it than I have." She shrugged. "Considering that this is my first, and hopefully last, time."

Surprised by her humor, he nodded his agreement. "I have been shot at a time or two, so I agree. I could do without that particular sort of excitement."

"You didn't shoot back." Her eyes scanned over him as if searching for a hidden weapon. "I suppose that's because you're off duty." Her tone held curiosity rather than censure. "At least, I assume you are since you're at the state park and you were out for a jog."

It was a stark contrast to Jolene's reproachful voice that, even now, years later, slammed through his brain.

Honestly, Mateo, do you even know how to enjoy a day off? Who carries a gun to the county fair? For once, can you act like you aren't on duty?

He rubbed his fingers over his forehead, as if he could scrub her words away. The last few years with her had been rough. She had complained about his job nonstop, had made him feel as if it was nothing but an inconvenience to her. He had tried to explain that, with all the ugly things he'd seen, he appreciated the added protection of a weapon.

Even on his day off.

So today, out of respect for her, he had eyed the gun locker that held his sidearm and had decided to leave it behind. He didn't want to think of Jolene right now. He needed to push her out of his mind so he could concentrate on the current situation.

"I'm not armed," he admitted.

Her gaze darted around the forest as if fearing their pursuer was lurking just out of sight.

"We're going to head back, but I don't want to go the same way we got here." He didn't have to voice his concern that the man could be waiting for them, either on the trail, or lingering a ways off. "We'll cut through the woods but head toward the fire tower."

The structure stood near the entrance of the park. It was the biggest tourist attraction in the place. Once they were out of the thickest part of the trees, it should be visible and they could use it to guide them to the ranger station.

She frowned and patted her pack. "A compass is one thing I don't have with me."

He tugged the long sleeve of his thermal shirt up an inch, allowing her to see his wrist. "Fortunately, this good old-fashioned watch has a built-in compass."

The watch had been a gift from the twins, given to him on the last Christmas they'd had together. Sure, Jolene had paid for it. But Nate and Josh had proudly told him it had been their idea and they had picked it out. They'd thought it would be useful for the family camping trip planned for the following summer.

It was a trip they'd never gotten to take.

He tucked the memory away and studied the compass for a moment. Then he nodded toward the east. "Heading this way should lead us to the fire tower. We'll stay in the woods but walk parallel to the trail. Sound good?"

"Getting out of here sounds great."

He picked up the bag holding the box. The sooner they got out of here, the sooner he could find out what was inside.

They were quiet for a while as they pushed through brush and brambles. Mateo checked the compass periodically to be sure they were still on track.

"Thank God you came along when you did," Nina said, finally breaking the silence.

He frowned. "We were shot at and you're thanking God?"

"For the fact that you came along? *Yes*." She gave him a quizzical look. "Don't tell me you don't believe in God."

"I do believe." He inwardly grimaced over the fact that a conversation with a woman he barely knew had headed in this direction. He believed, all right. He wouldn't be so angry with God right now if he *didn't* believe. No way was he getting into all of that.

Then again, he reminded himself, he had prayed today. More than once.

God had heard his prayer, answered it, because they were both alive and safe.

His phone chimed and Nina looked at him in surprise.

Mateo was surprised as well.

He tugged it from his pocket.

It was a text from Officer Lainie Hughes, one of the three people at the department he'd sent a message to, hoping that at least one would go through. He had known she was on duty today, so she'd been sent the first message.

"You have service?" Nina asked.

"Barely," he admitted. "But one of my texts went through to one of the officers in the department. She said the park rangers were alerted and that back up is en route." He glanced at his watch. "But the shooter could be long gone. The last shot fired was edging on an hour ago. That would be more than enough time for him to have jogged back down the trail and gotten out of the park."

He tried placing a call to Officer Hughes.

It didn't go through, so he typed another

text instead, then watched in frustration as the screen indicated it had been sent but not delivered. He shoved the phone back in his pocket, grateful that help was on the way.

While behind the boulder, he'd indicated to Officer Hughes that shots had been fired. Now, he had to assume that the park's entrances were being blocked off by rangers and that the park was being systematically evacuated. It was too bad that the shooter, if he had any sense, had probably hightailed it out of there already. It was unfortunate the text had taken so long to go through.

"Do you hear that?" Nina asked.

He froze. "What?"

Had she heard someone stalking them? He'd been so lost in his own thoughts, he realized he hadn't been paying attention. A stupid and potentially dangerous move.

Then he heard it.

"Sirens," she said.

Yes, sirens. Help was on the way.

That realization seemed to give Nina renewed energy as she quickened her pace.

"Let's veer this way," he suggested after glancing at the compass again. "We should hit the trail sooner rather than later. We're far enough away from where we entered that it's unlikely the perp would be lingering. Besides, if he hasn't vacated the park already, I suspect the approaching sirens will have him on the run."

In a matter of minutes, they were back on the trail, near the incline they had tumbled over. The fire tower loomed in the distance. Though Mateo didn't believe the shooter was still hanging around, he remained vigilant just in case. Desperate criminals were known to be unpredictable and he had to believe the man was desperate to retrieve the metal box.

Nina's phone erupted in a cacophony of sounds, a myriad of alerts as text messages from various people finally came through. She pulled her phone out and scrolled as they hustled along.

"My family just heard about an active shooter in the park. They're checking in to see if I'm okay." She began tapping out replies. "I'm going to let them know I'm fine. I'm not going to tell them I was the target. At least, not right now. If I did that, the whole family would think they need to race to my rescue."

Mateo smirked at that.

"Good call. I met your family when I was helping your brothers out. I think you're right. They'd be here in a heartbeat. Since I'm sure the park is being cleared out, the last thing we need is more people showing up." He tilted his head to the side, listening as the hum of a motor caught his attention.

"That sounds like a side-by-side," Nina said. "We have one at the ranch."

The sound got louder, indicating the vehicle was headed their way. It rounded a bend and Nina was right, it was a side-by-side.

Officer Lainie Hughes was behind the wheel. She waved when she spotted them. A moment later, she reached them.

"Am I ever glad to see you," Mateo proclaimed.

"Likewise." Lainie eyed them up. "You're both okay?"

"Fortunately," Mateo said.

"I commandeered this from one of the park rangers. Hop on." She patted the empty seat beside her. "I'll fill you in on the way back to the parking lot."

Nina slid in first then Mateo. With three of them on the bench seat, it was a tight fit, but he wasn't about to complain.

"The rangers have been emptying out the park, checking everyone as they leave, taking down license plate numbers. You know the drill. So far, no one has admitted to seeing anything. A handful of parkgoers claimed they thought they heard a few rounds shot off, but they assumed it was firecrackers."

"He was using a silencer," Mateo said.

"I expected as much," Lainie admitted.

They reached the parking lot, which was mostly cleared out of cars, except for several cruisers. It was swarming with law enforcement and park rangers. Mateo presumed the other three lots, located in different areas of the park, would look about the same.

"I should have asked…" Lainie said to Nina. "What lot are you parked in?"

Mateo hadn't thought to ask, either, believing she was parked here as it was closest to where she'd been hiking. Yet he should have confirmed.

Nina was quiet for a moment. Mateo wondered if she was lost in her own thoughts and hadn't heard Officer Hughes.

"Nina?" He noticed the frown on her face. Her hand trembled as she tucked a stray lock of hair behind her ear. Perhaps the adrenaline rush was wearing off and she was crashing, coming back to the reality of the situation. "Are you okay?"

"I...yes, I'm fine. However, my vehicle is not." She pointed to a cherry-red Trailblazer. One of the last left in the lot, other than his white Tahoe.

His heart kicked in his chest when he realized what had caused her distress.

"That vehicle there—" he gestured to it "—is yours?"

"Yes, the one with the slashed tires is mine." Her troubled eyes locked with his. "Detective Bianchi, do you know what this means?"

Yes, he sure did know.

"It means," he said slowly, "that if your attacker knows what car you drive, he clearly knows your identity."

And *that* put a whole new spin on things.

Chapter Three

Nina couldn't take her eyes off her Trailblazer. Mateo circled the vehicle and she followed. All four tires had been slashed. She shuddered. Not just because of the damage, but because of the realization that her attacker had apparently been armed with a knife as well as a gun. Worst of all, clearly, he knew her. What did the slashed tires mean? Was it just supposed to slow her down? Was it a warning? A threat? It felt like a threat. If he knew what SUV she drove, what else did he know about her?

What if God hadn't sent Mateo to her when He had? What if the man had overpowered her and dragged her off the trail and into the woods?

She could *not* let her mind go there.

"Nina?" Mateo sidled up next to her. His hand floated in the air a moment, as if he wanted to reach out and give her assurance, but then it fell to his side. "Are you okay?"

She had never been good at lying. Now didn't seem the best time to start.

"Actually," she said, "I don't think I am."

"I can talk to Officer Hughes. She can take you home. Better yet, she can take you to your family's ranch. I suspect you'll be safer there."

Nina pulled her gaze away from the shredded tires.

"I want to go to the station with you." Her eyes locked with his. "I want to see what's in that box."

His brow furrowed and he was clearly ready to protest.

Nina did not give him the chance.

"Please, Detective. I've been chased, shot at, and my tires are slashed. Don't you think I deserve to know what's so important to this guy?"

"I guess it wouldn't hurt to have you come along to the department. I can take your official statement." He shrugged. "Who knows, maybe something in that lockbox will help you figure out who this guy is. I mean, he clearly knows who you are, which leads me to believe that even if you didn't recognize him, you likely know him as well."

She nodded slowly. "I thought of that. I've been wracking my brain, trying to place him. It's hard when I don't even know where to start. I grew up in Mulberry Creek. It could be someone I went to school with. Someone I worked with in the past, or present, or volunteer with."

"Could be someone from your church."

She frowned at him.

"I'm not ruling anyone out," he said.

"Are you always so cynical?"

"Yes." He motioned toward the only other civilian vehicle in the lot. "Let's go. The crew here is capable of handling things. Officer Hughes is currently viewing the security footage of the parking lot. She'll meet us back at the station."

He opened the door of the white SUV for Nina. She hopped inside.

"I'd like to check in with the officers on scene, if you don't mind," Mateo said. "Will you be okay if I do that? I won't go far and I won't be long. You'll be safe."

"Of course." She nodded for emphasis. "Take your time."

He gently closed her door.

She watched as he strode over to a group of uniformed men and women. He looked so confident, strong and capable. He shoved his hands into his pockets as he spoke with the group, as if he was completely relaxed after the whole ordeal.

Nina settled into the seat and realized his vehicle smelled like him. Like woodsy soap and faint cologne. It was comforting. In fact, everything about Mateo was comforting.

She realized she also found his dark good looks and his deep, smooth voice appealing. In fact, she found everything about the man quite likeable.

You were just shot at, she thought, *and now you're thinking of Mateo's espresso-colored eyes.*

"I do love espresso, though," she murmured to herself.

As she waited for him, her gaze scanned the lot, the woods on the edge, even drifted to the tower behind them. She had been coming to this park for as long as she could remember. How many picnics, hikes and leisurely days had she spent here with her family?

Would she ever feel safe coming here again?

The memory of being shot at, the intense fear she had felt, slammed into her. It had been a terror unlike anything she had ever known.

She closed her eyes and leaned her head back.

"Breathe," she muttered under her breath. "Just breathe."

She was exhaling slowly when Mateo opened the driver's-side door and climbed in. She glanced at him. He quirked a brow at her but didn't say anything, just started up his Tahoe and slowly drove from the lot.

"Is there *anything* about the man that seemed familiar?" Mateo asked once they were out of the park. "His stance? His tone?"

Nina desperately tried to recall something, anything, that would be helpful. She came up blank.

"No," she said, feeling as if she were letting Mateo down.

He must've heard the defeat in her voice.

"It's all right," he said soothingly. "It's been an afternoon. You have a lot to process. I'm sure your mind is spinning."

It *was* spinning and she was grateful that he recognized that.

"If anything comes to you later—"

"I'll be sure to let you know."

"I've got to be honest… I'm concerned about your safety. When is your next shift at the hospital?"

"The hospital?" Nina echoed. Then she recalled she had mentioned she had been an ER nurse. "Oh, I don't work in the ER anymore. I'm a hospice nurse now. Have been for the past three months."

"Really?" Mateo's tone implied he wasn't sure what to make of that. "That sounds...heavy."

"It can be, yes," Nina said. "I'm supposed to work the day after tomorrow."

"Any chance you can have someone cover for you?"

Nina frowned. She hated the idea of shirking her responsibilities. Though, it was a new client, one she hadn't met, which made allowing someone to replace her a bit less difficult.

"Nina, your life could be on the line here." Mateo's tone was soft but his words hit hard.

"I know," she murmured. "Yes, I'm sure if I explain the situation, my supervisor can replace me for a day or two."

"You may need to be out more than a day or two."

"I can't even think about that right now."

Her phone rang and she tugged it from her pocket. It was her mother. She silenced the call and instead sent a text simply stating she couldn't talk at the moment, that she was fine, and would check in soon.

Then she powered off the device.

"Not ready to talk to anyone yet?" he asked.

"It's my mom. If I answer, she'll sense how wrong everything is, force the truth out of me, and then panic until she sees for herself that I'm okay. It's best if I can just cut to the part where she can see that I'm okay. I'll tell my family what happened, I sure won't be able to keep it a secret, but it's best if I do it in person."

"Good plan. Your family is pretty great. They'll be sure to keep you safe."

"Do you have family?" Nina voiced the question without thinking. Mostly, she was trying to make conversation, trying to distract herself from what had happened in the park. Mateo's frown and hesitation made her wish she could take the question back. Before she had a chance to try, he spoke.

"Of course. I mean…yeah, I have parents, you know." He cleared his throat. "They're retired and spend a good deal of their time traveling the country in their RV. I also have a sister. Mara. She lives in Bozeman. She's a kindergarten teacher."

"That's nice."

That's nice? She mentally chastised herself, embarrassed that she couldn't think of anything else to say. Maybe it was best to say nothing because his hesitant tone implied it was something he did not want to talk about.

They finished the short drive to Mulberry Creek in silence.

Once at the police department, he escorted her inside to his office where she—again—went over the details of what she had seen. This time he took notes and his questions seemed even more thorough than before. Nina wished desperately that she had better answers for him. Yet, try as she might, she could not make out anything familiar about her attacker.

A knock on the door grabbed their attention.

"Come in," Mateo called.

The door was already open a crack. Officer Joe Rollins, whom Nina vaguely knew because he was close in age to her brothers, came in.

"I'm just letting you know we managed to get the box open. You said you wanted to go through the contents yourself. It's ready whenever you are."

"Great!" Nina stood up so fast her chair squealed as it slid backward.

Mateo glared at her.

She shot him a look right back. "Please don't make me beg. You said yourself, since this guy knows me and I probably know him, the contents might give me a clue as to who he is."

Nina had no idea if the evidence would rattle anything loose in her brain, but she had to try. She wanted this man caught. The thought of him lurking out there, strolling the streets of Mulberry Creek, possibly bringing harm to others, did not sit well with her.

"Fine." Mateo stood. "You can stay to the back of the evidence room."

"Perfect." She grinned at him. "I promise I'll stay out of the way. You'll hardly know I'm there."

You'll hardly know I'm there.

Nina's words seemed to taunt Mateo. He knew she was there all right. He was far too aware of her presence. It had been impossible to ignore her excitement as he'd led her to the evidence room. He was also very aware of how that exuberance faded with each item he pulled out of the box.

So far, Officer Rollins had helped him log nearly a dozen items, primarily jewelry. They'd taken pictures, jotted notes into the log book, and inspected the items from every angle, looking for initials, engravings, or any type of clue.

Nina sighed.

Mateo glanced up at her.

"Sorry," she muttered, "it's just that the box is almost empty and nothing is familiar."

He shrugged as he gingerly held a Rolex in his gloved hand. Officer Rollins had done a quick internet search and deemed the Rolex was high-end and worth a small fortune. "It was a long shot. We both knew that."

Officer Rollins finished logging the watch then bagged it up.

Next, Mateo pulled a zippered sandwich bag out of the lockbox.

Officer Rollins let out a low whistle. "Those are all American Gold Eagle coins. My grandad is big into coins. Has quite the collection. I'm not nearly the expert he is, but I'd say you're looking at well over ten grand in that bag."

"This guy's bounty is definitely adding up," Mateo agreed. His rough calculation had the contents at close to a hundred grand.

Once the coins were processed, Mateo pulled out another piece of jewelry.

Nina pushed away from the wall where she'd been leaning, though she was careful not to get too close.

"That's stunning," she said.

Mateo held up the diamond-studded crucifix so she could get a better look. It was a large pendant hanging from a gold chain.

"Truly beautiful." Her brow furrowed. "I…"

He waited. When she said nothing, he gave her a verbal nudge. "You what? Have you seen this before?"

"I don't think so." She shook her head, looking uncertain. "Maybe? I'm not sure. It grabbed my attention, but that could be because it's so striking."

He motioned her forward and she came in for a better look. It laid flat against his gloved palm.

She bit her lip as her eyes scanned over it. Finally, she glanced at him. "I just don't know. I want so badly to be helpful. Now I'm not sure if it's truly familiar to me or if I just want it to be."

She looked so utterly disappointed.

"Don't worry about it," Mateo urged. "There are a few more items left. Let's get them logged and then wrap this up."

He pulled out a few more antiques that he suspected would be worth a fair amount.

Last, he retrieved a large ruby brooch. No one had to tell him it was quite valuable. The size alone made that clear.

"What happens now?" Nina asked.

"We'll run the items through the system," Officer Rollins chimed in. "It's likely they are stolen. It's such an eclectic mix. Hopefully, at least a few of them will turn into leads."

"We'll also get an expert for appraisals," Mateo added. "I'm curious about the overall value. Also, bringing in someone from the field may help us figure out where some of these items originated." He spent a few minutes finishing up with the evidence, then peeled off his gloves and led Nina from the room.

Officer Hughes caught them in the hallway.

"Sir!" she called.

He pivoted.

"You asked for an update on the incident in the parking lot," she said. "The security cameras picked up a man slashing Miss Montgomery's tires. He was, as you described, the attacker. Dark clothes, hoodie pulled up. There isn't a clear shot of his face. He was quick about it, then darted away out of camera range. He wasn't picked up anywhere else in the park. I suspect he had a change of clothes in that backpack. Or, all he'd really have to do is peel off the hoodie and his look would change. Regardless, though we don't have anything useful yet, we'll go over footage from the other parking lots for the entire day."

Mateo nodded. "I appreciate the update."

Officer Hughes hurried off, likely to deal with the next crisis.

Mateo turned to Nina. "Are you ready to go home?"

She wrapped her arms around herself and nodded. Her hair had been put neatly back into a ponytail and, after a trip to the restroom, the smudge on her cheek had been cleaned off. Still, she looked rattled and he wished he could do something to make her feel better. He knew she probably just needed time to process and work through everything.

"By home, I mean your family's ranch," he clarified. "Are you okay with that? I can take you there now."

"Would it be too much to ask to stop by my house first?" She gave him an apologetic yet hopeful look. "I'd like to pick up some clothes. I could have my parents or one of my brothers take me. However, once they find out what happened, I know things are going to get chaotic. They'll have a million questions and go into protective mode. They'll probably want to put me in a bubble and lock me away. I know you're busy. If you don't have time, I completely understand. I'd go myself, if I had a vehicle."

"It's not a problem," he said. "In fact, I'd rather take you. Once you get situated at the ranch, I plan on having a police presence there. I'd prefer once that's in a place that you didn't leave."

"A police presence." She blew out a breath. "I can't believe this morning I was excited about eaglets. Now I need police protection."

"I'm also going to take a cruiser instead of my personal vehicle. If this guy is watching us, I want it to be clear you are under police protection. I'm hoping that'll be a deterrent."

Once he'd checked out the vehicle he needed, they headed toward the door.

"Detective Bianchi, I want you to know I appreciate everything you did for me today. I know you're going to catch this guy," she said.

He had worked hard to earn the title of detective and usually he enjoyed hearing it. Not now, though. It sounded too formal coming from Nina's lips.

"Call me Mateo," he said gruffly. "After running for our lives together, 'Detective Bianchi' sounds a bit too formal."

She smiled at him. It was her first true smile

of the day, lighting up her eyes and setting a dimple in her left cheek free. His heart seemed to swirl in his chest. Perhaps he should have kept the formality in place.

Too late now.

"Where are we headed?" Mateo asked.

Nina rattled off the address.

"I feel like I know that place but I'm not sure why."

"I bought the house from my sister-in-law, Holly," Nina admitted. "I know you were there last year, working on her case."

"That's right." He used his key fob to unlock a cruiser with the department's logo on the side and then opened Nina's door for her. She thanked him as she got in.

He was intent on keeping the conversation light as he drove toward her home. Thinking the best way to do that was to ask for updates on her brothers, he did just that. All the while, he remained vigilant, needing to be sure they were not being followed.

"Eric and Cassie recently had twins."

His heart pinched though he knew that they had been expecting twins. He couldn't help but think of his own boys.

"Ethan and Matilda," Nina continued. "Named

after Cassie's grandparents. Wyatt is really excited about being a big brother. Seth and Holly are expecting a baby boy in about a month. Chloe is not nearly as excited about being a big sister. I'm pretty sure she'll change her mind once the baby is here."

He continued to pepper her with questions that had nothing to do with the attacker. She seemed to relax and was all too happy to talk about her new nieces and nephews.

In no time, he was turning off the blacktop and onto a gravel road.

"Second mailbox on the left?" He was pretty sure that was correct. He'd been here a few times last year when Holly and her daughter Chloe had been attacked.

"Good memory," she said.

"How long have you had the place?"

"Almost half a year. I had been renting, but when Holly married my brother and mentioned she was selling her house, it seemed like it was meant to be."

"Cute place."

Mateo eyed the pale blue house with white trim and shutters. A white front porch held flowerpots filled with magenta hydrangeas.

"Thanks." Nina beamed at him. "I kind of

love it. I grew up with a house full of siblings then had four roommates in nursing school. It's really nice to have a place of my own."

He maneuvered the vehicle so it was facing the road. He was sure they hadn't been followed, but he was anxious to be on their way again.

Nina hopped out and he hustled after her.

"I'll be quick." She had already pulled out her key and quickly slid it in the lock. "I'll just throw stuff into my biggest suitcase. If I forget anything, someone at the ranch is sure to have something I can borrow."

They stepped into the entryway. A suspicious scent assaulted Mateo's senses. He realized, almost subconsciously, that they were about to die.

"No!" He shouted the word as Nina reached for the light switch. In one swift movement, he latched onto her arm, tugged her back out the door and shoved her across the lawn, propelling her forward. "Run!"

Even as they raced across the grass, the unmistakable scent of natural gas still lingered in his nose. They were halfway to the tree line when—

Boom!

The blast blew him forward, slammed him into Nina. He instinctively wrapped his arms around her, protecting her body with his. They hit the ground as the world around them exploded.

Chapter Four

Nina slammed against the hard-packed earth, her mind swirling in confusion as pain from the jarring tumble ricocheted through her body.

"You okay?" Mateo asked, his voice gruff. He shifted and it was only then that she realized he'd landed on top of her. He'd shielded her, if the blood trickling down his temple was any indication.

"I'm fine." Her response was breathless and her voice wobbled. "But you're hurt."

"Nope, I'm good." He scrambled off her then held out a hand, but she was already clambering to her feet.

"My *house!*" Her words held equal parts disbelief and horror as she caught sight of the inferno blazing behind them. She swayed and Mateo reached out to steady her.

With his hand firmly against her back, he said, "We need to get out of here. This was a natural gas explosion. You didn't flip the light switch or do anything to spark it. I think it was set remotely. I have no idea how far away the guy is."

He didn't need to spell it out for her. Nina understood he thought the attacker may be nearby. The very thought made her blood run cold.

They were instantly on the move, jogging on shaky legs to the cruiser.

"Close enough to know we went inside?" Nina guessed.

Mateo didn't answer.

He didn't need to.

Nina could sense his tension and it only added to her own. She tossed a worried glance over her shoulder and wouldn't have been surprised to see the man lingering in the tree line. Or racing after them, gun raised.

All she saw was her house, her home, blazing. Already, ash and smoke permeated the air, mixing with the debris from the blast.

Mateo ushered her into the cruiser. She tumbled inside, frantically looking around at the disaster. How could everything have changed so quickly? It was almost incomprehensible. Only moments ago, she'd been looking at the home she'd been so proud of purchasing on her own.

She was vaguely aware of Mateo calling in the incident. Her mind seemed to fluctuate between disbelief and horror. She was in shock, she knew, and needed to shake herself out of it.

"The fire department is on the way." Mateo's tone was terse as the cruiser tore out of the driveway. "Officer Rollins is only a few minutes out. He'll get here quickly to keep an eye on the fire until the trucks arrive. I hate leaving the scene, but if this guy is still hanging around here, I don't want to give him the chance to take another shot at us."

She knew he meant literally and the somber realization pulled her from her stupor.

"I don't get it." Nina pulled in a breath, blew it out again, trying to calm herself as trees whizzed by in a blur. She realized he had turned north, headed toward the ranch, rather than south, which would lead back to town and the direction the emergency vehicles would be coming from. "What in that box could be so important? Sure, some of the items may be worth a lot of money, especially when added all together. But enough money to *kill* for?"

She just couldn't grasp the lunacy of that.

She turned to face him, studying him.

Mateo's expression was grim. His eyes swung

from the road in front of them to the rearview mirror as he kept watch from all directions.

"Yeah." He glanced at her, their eyes locking only briefly before he returned his attention to the road. "This all seems a bit excessive. Too excessive. My gut instinct, and a decade of experience, are telling me that there's way more to this than some potentially stolen items."

Reality slammed back into Nina then full-force. She realized Mateo was still bleeding from the wound that he'd received during the blast. His dark hair seemed to be matted with blood, but he'd apparently swiped away the trickle that had slid down his cheek.

"You're hurt." Her heart lurched. She shifted in her seat and fumbled to unzip the fanny pack her brothers always made fun of. She pulled out a large gauze pad and tore open the package. "Let me help with that."

He shot her a sideways look. "It's fine."

"It's not." She gently pressed the gauze pad to his temple. "You blocked me from the flying debris. Are you hurt anywhere else?"

"No."

"You're lying," Nina accused. She pulled a butterfly bandage from her supply.

He shot her a look.

She shot him one right back. "What I meant to say is, thank you for protecting me. Did you get hit anywhere else?" She deftly attached the bandage over his wound.

He hesitated and it was clear he didn't want to admit to anything.

"Mateo, either you give an honest answer or I'm going to assume the worst."

"Fine. Something hit me in the back. Clipped my shoulder." He scowled. "It clobbered me, but don't think it cut me. Doesn't feel like it's bleeding. Just sore."

Sore.

Nina assumed it was much more than sore. She was certain he'd been pummeled by debris, yet he refused to utter a word of complaint. Her admiration for this man seemed to grow by the minute.

"We're just about to the ranch." He pointed out the obvious in a clear attempt to distract her. "How are you doing? Ready to face your parents?"

Nina let out a mirthless laugh. "Not even a little. I wish I didn't have to tell them. But—"

"The rumor mill in Mulberry Creek is running strong. They'd find out anyway."

"Right." She leaned back in her seat and

sighed. "The story better come from me. And you. You'll stay to help fill in the details, right? You're not going to just drop me off in the driveway?"

He slid her a look. "I'm not going anywhere for a while. Not until I get an update on your house."

Her house.

She couldn't let herself think of that right now. It was only a house. It was replaceable.

Almost as an afterthought, she flipped down the sun visor and was relieved to find there was a built-in mirror on the backside. She gasped when she flipped it open. She had something— soot, perhaps—smudged across her face. There was debris in her hair. Grass, twigs...splinters?

She groaned. "You could have warned me that I'm a disaster."

He quirked a brow. "My mother would not approve of me telling a woman she's a disaster."

"Now is not the time for chivalry." She managed to find a wet wipe and began to clean up her face. "I'm not being vain." She finished with her face and started to pluck at her tresses, all the while wishing she had a comb in her fanny pack, but alas she did not. "It's just that my parents *cannot* see me like this."

"It's nice of you to care so much."

She shot him a look, wondering for just a moment if he was mocking her.

"Your family seems really close."

"We are." She continued to try to tidy her hair. "You probably know my older sister, Ella, died several years ago. The first few years were tough, but I think in the end, it brought us closer together. I'm the youngest of the family. Whether I like it or not, my parents will always think of me as their baby girl."

"Is that a bad thing?" His brow furrowed, as if he were genuinely curious.

"It can be overwhelming sometimes. Yet I know it's only because they love me. So, no, it's not a bad thing." She gave herself another once-over. Satisfied that she'd cleaned up as best she could, Nina flipped the mirror closed and readjusted the visor again.

Mateo flipped on the blinker, indicating he was about to turn into the driveway and pass under the wrought-iron arch that announced Big Sky Ranch in chunky iron letters. The winding driveway split in two. Mateo took the branch to the right, which would lead to her parents' home, and Eric's, if he were to keep driving. Seth's house was in the other direction.

Nina felt a wave of comfort when she spotted the log structure. It had just been rebuilt—due to a fire, ironically.

It wasn't the place she had grown up in. Eric and his family had taken that over and lived just up the hill. Even so, she'd spent plenty of hours in this new house. It didn't matter that the building was new, home was where the heart was. And there was plenty of heart in this log abode to go around.

Mateo hadn't even parked the cruiser when her parents, James and Julia, rushed out onto the porch.

"Looks like they've been watching for you."

Nina's heart pinched. Her family had been through so much this year. She knew how worried her parents must be. She realized belatedly that she should have at least mentioned that Mateo was bringing her home. It was probably a shock to see a cruiser come down the driveway. Her parents' thoughts were probably bouncing in all sorts of directions. Probably none of them good.

The moment he stopped the car, she leapt out. Her mother rushed to her, a look of relief etched onto her pretty features.

"I'm okay." She knew they were the words

that they would need to hear. "My car has a flat tire, so Mateo brought me home."

Her mother squeezed her into a hug, while her father went to shake Mateo's hand.

"Good to see you, Detective," he said. "Though I wish for once we could meet under less stressful conditions. Thank you for bringing my girl home."

"Happy to do it," Mateo replied.

"Tell us what happened." Her mother's critical gaze scanned over her.

Nina knew, despite her efforts to clean up, she was still a mess. "How about we go inside?" Nina motioned toward the house. "It's a long story. You'll want to sit down."

"That's a good idea," Mateo said. "I'll stay a bit, if that's okay, in case you have any questions."

"Of course." Her mother looped her arm through hers, as if she needed to keep her close.

Truth be told, Nina cherished her mother's presence.

As they walked into the house, she pulled in a breath to try to clear her head and steady her emotions. Some of the earlier shock was wearing off and, for just a moment, she wanted to curl into a ball and sob.

Nope. She couldn't, wouldn't do that. At least, not now. She needed to stay strong for her family. They would be worried enough once they heard about all that had happened. While they would offer her their full support, as they always had, she didn't want to make the situation any harder on them than it was already going to be.

Coco, her chocolate-colored cocker spaniel, greeted them on the other side of the door.

Nina immediately knelt and scooped the dog into her arms. "Hey, there."

Coco pressed her head against Nina's cheek. Calmness instantly swept over her. She loved this girl and seeing her always brought Nina joy.

"Who is this?"

Nina pivoted to look at Mateo. His eyes seemed to light up at the sight of her furry friend. He held out a hand, which the dog eagerly sniffed.

"This is Coco."

Mateo scratched the dog's ears and Coco immediately looked smitten. "Why wasn't she at the park with you?"

"My nephew, Wyatt, has really been missing his mom lately." Nina knew Mateo had worked the case involving Wyatt's mother's murder.

Mateo nodded. "Understandable."

"Coco's a certified therapy dog."

"Really?" Mateo's eyebrows hitched in interest.

"I've wanted a dog for as long as I can remember. When I moved back to Mulberry Creek last year, I started searching rescue organizations. Coco was pulled from a hoarding situation. She was just a puppy, the tiny runt of the litter. The conditions were deplorable. I knew I had to have her. It was love at first sight." She pressed a kiss onto the top of Coco's head. "I knew right away she was something special. I think, maybe because she knew what it was like to come from a miserable situation, she's good at sensing emotions in others. I decided to get her certified and I haven't regretted it."

"Huh. I've heard of therapy dogs," Mateo said. "I've never met one. K-9 officers, sure. We have one on the department. But not therapy dogs. What do you use her for? I mean other than Wyatt?"

"I often bring her to hospice care with me to help soothe the families I work with, only at their request, of course. Sometimes I take her to the Senior Center, or the nursing home, when I volunteer." Nina smiled at the dog affectionately. "It goes without saying she's great with people, really in tune with their emotions. Wyatt adores her. Cassie called this morning to ask if they could borrow her for the day. I couldn't say no. Besides, while I normally do take her to the park with me, it's easier to take photos without her tagging along. Dogs have to be on leashes, understandably. And I'm not quite coordinated enough to maneuver her leash and my camera."

Her mother nodded. "When Cassie heard about the shooting at the park, and that you were there, she thought you might need Coco more than Wyatt. She said to give you her love, but she couldn't stay. The twins are colicky and Eric had his hands full."

"It was sweet of her to bring Coco back." Nina was trying to delay the inevitable conversation, but her mother had reached the end of her patience.

"Tell me," Julia demanded, "how are you, really? I cannot believe that shots were fired at Mulberry Creek Park. It's always been such a quiet, relaxing getaway for us. When I couldn't get you on your phone, I have to say, I started to panic. There are already so many rumors going around, but nothing has been substantiated yet."

"There'll be a press conference," Mateo said. Something like a shooting, especially in a state park, was a big deal. A "critical incident," he had told Nina earlier. "The police chief will be speaking. Probably later this afternoon."

Julia pressed her hand to her heart. "Oh, my."

"Let's sit down." Nina glanced at Mateo and motioned for him to follow, lest he get the notion he should make a hasty retreat before she dropped a verbal bomb on her parents.

They all took seats in the living room. Her parents settled on the sofa, and she and Mateo each took one of the cozy chairs across from them.

"So, the park? The shooter?" Julia's gaze darted between Mateo and Nina. "Did you see him? Were you a good distance away? Were you safe?"

"Well…" Nina hedged.

Mateo gave her a subtle nod of encouragement.

Best to just drop that bomb and get it over with.

"Actually, the shooter happened to be after… me."

Mateo thought it was a good thing Julia was sitting when Nina hit her with the news. If not, she may have collapsed. As Nina's parents listened to her describe her ordeal, her mother looked appropriately horrified. Her father, James, a brawny, recently retired rancher, looked like he was ready to bolt out the door and hunt down the attacker himself.

Mateo sat back in his chair as he let Nina take the lead. Coco sat at her feet. Her head rested on Nina's lap and she stared adoringly at her owner. Nina absently petted the dog, even as she continued to answer her parents' questions.

"I'm sorry, hold up a minute." Julia held a hand in the air as if to halt her daughter's speech, but maybe it was actually to pause a moment to let her mind catch up to Nina's words. She visibly shuddered. James reached out a hand to steady her. "Your *house* blew up?"

"Yes." Nina winced then looked at Mateo as if silently pleading for his help. "It did."

"I understand how disturbing this is to hear." He leaned forward, addressing her parents. He used his calmest, most professional voice. "But we need to focus on what's important here. Nina is *safe*."

"Yes," Julia murmured. "God was watching over her. And *you*."

Had God been watching over him? Mateo

supposed He had. It was almost a foreign thought to him these days, to feel watched over, protected by the Creator. A niggling little voice reminded him that God had not been the one to put distance between them.

He cleared his throat, not ready to ponder that right now. Besides, Nina's parents needed answers and reassurance. "I can tell you, the entire Mulberry Creek PD is on this case. We're making it a top priority."

"A shooting in the park of all places." James looked disgusted. Then realization sank in. "Wait a minute. You said he slashed your tires? And he blew up your house. He knows who you are."

Nina winced. "Yes."

"You're being targeted." Julia's eyes widened in alarm. "The shooting in the park? That seems impulsive. But your house? That was premeditated. Intentional."

Yes, it was. Mateo was well aware of that and did not like the implications one bit. He had a hunch that this guy was going to be relentless now that Nina was on his radar. He'd been up against criminals like this before. The only way to stop them was to catch them.

He wasn't going to be the one to tell Nina's parents that she was not going to be safe until this man was behind bars. He knew they were still trying to process all the information that had been thrown at them, but they would figure it out soon enough.

Mateo wasn't even sure if Nina had come to that conclusion yet. She was an intelligent lady and would figure it out sooner rather than later.

Just because she'd survived the explosion did not mean that she was safe.

He glanced at her. The look in her eyes as they latched onto his made it clear that, yes, she had already come to that conclusion. She was well aware that her life was still in danger. He admired her calm and knew it was for her parents' benefit. He had to assume that inside she was quaking. She wasn't going to let her fear show. Not here, not now, at least.

"Mateo, I cannot tell you how grateful I am to you for taking care of Nina." Julia pulled in a shaky breath. "If anything would have happened to her. I can't even—" She cut herself off and pressed a hand to her lips, as if finishing the sentence was too difficult to bear.

"Yeah, I get it. Losing your child is every

parent's worst fear." Mateo inwardly grimaced. He hadn't meant to say that. Hadn't meant to go there. They probably thought he was referring to their oldest daughter, Ella. They would have no way of knowing he'd been referring to his own loss. He was not about to tell them. Instead, he hurried on. "But we're not going to let that happen."

"I don't understand how anyone who knows Nina could want to hurt her." Julia turned to James, who patted her hand.

"It makes no sense." James scowled.

"You're right," Mateo agreed. "He's not rational and that makes him unpredictable. It's likely that little he does will make sense."

He realized too late that that was the wrong thing to say.

"He's not going to stop." Julia's voice was strained and Mateo noticed she squeezed her husband's hand so hard her knuckles turned white. "He's going to keep coming after her."

"Don't you worry," James reassured her. "She'll stay here. We won't let him get close enough to harm her."

Nina bit her lip. Mateo could see how much she hated this. Not for herself, but she hated putting her parents through such grief.

"Promise me." Julia's gaze held Mateo's. "Promise me that you won't let anything happen to my baby girl."

"Mom." Nina shot him an apologetic look. "I'm not Mateo's responsibility."

"Actually, you are," he disagreed. "As a paid officer of the law, it's my job to protect anyone in danger."

As a paid officer of the law? Had he actually said that?

Yes, he had.

Why? Because it was easier than admitting she wasn't just anyone. How was it possible that in just one short day, this woman had pressed her way into his heart? Granted, today wasn't the first time he'd met Nina. If he were honest with himself, he'd have to admit he'd admired her fiery spirit when she'd tried to shoo him out of her brother's hospital room after a vigorous round of questioning last fall. She'd been firm yet polite. Professional. Determined. Protective.

Beautiful.

He inwardly winced because that was *not* relevant right now. Nor was it a reason to remember that it had taken him days, weeks maybe, to put that encounter out of his mind. She had made an impression on him that day.

There was no denying he was feeling all sorts of fluttery emotions that he hadn't felt in years. And not so fluttery emotions. Because he also felt a hard determination to keep the attacker from ever getting close enough to hurt her again.

"Promise me," Julia pressed, pulling him back to the moment.

Mateo knew he shouldn't; knew better than to make a promise like that. Yet he wanted nothing more than to keep Nina safe. Even after what they'd been through today, he couldn't say he knew her well. But he knew her *well enough*. Knew that he admired her spunk and respected her coolness under pressure. Knew that looking at her now, all disheveled and vulnerable, yet still undeniably lovely, caused something inside him to stir. The sort of something he hadn't felt for a very long time…attraction toward a woman. And not just a physical attraction because, yes, she was alluring, but it was more than that. She was sweet and caring, and loved her family passionately. And her adorable dog.

"I'll keep her safe." The words flowed from his mouth, solid and strong. "I promise."

He felt that promise all the way down into his soul. In that moment, he knew he would keep Nina safe, or die trying.

Chapter Five

It had been a long while since Mateo had sat on an overnight protection detail. His duties as a detective often pulled him in other directions. Yet here he sat, in the dark, on the Montgomery's covered front porch, tucked away in the shadows. His shoulder ached something awful. He'd taken a look at it earlier, when he'd gone back to the station for his vehicle and had managed to have a few minutes to himself. It was badly bruised, as he'd suspected, but whatever had pummeled him in the explosion hadn't broken the skin. Regardless, it made leaning back in the chair less than comfortable. Still, this was where he needed to be.

Chief Barsness had only been mildly surprised by the request, but hadn't balked at it.

Mateo could blame the unexpected change in duties on Julia Montgomery, her insistence that he promise to watch over Nina. That would only be a half-truth. It wasn't just because of his promise to her mother that he was sitting there. It was because he didn't want to leave Nina's protection to anyone else.

A ridiculous sentiment, he knew, because in any other situation, he'd trust the other members of the MCPD implicitly. In all honesty, he realized as he sat there in the dark, taking in the sounds of the night—the rustle of the leaves, the chirping of distant frogs—he did trust those on his force, but he'd *wanted* to be there.

Usually at times like this, when it was too still, too calm, his mind would wander to his boys. Tonight, though, his thoughts kept straying to how close he and Nina had come to dying. If she'd flipped the light switch, there would have been an entirely different ending to this situation. For both of them.

A creak cut through the night. The sound, though nearly inaudible, seemed to reverberate through his brain. It sent his senses on high alert. He silently sprang from the Adirondack chair he'd been stationed in. Quickly, quietly, pulling his sidearm, he moved noiselessly across the porch.

If he wasn't mistaken, the sound had come from the back of the house. He knew a screen door off the sunroom led to a cement patio that overlooked the backyard. Was the creaking sound that of rusty hinges? Had someone sneaked past him? Bypassed the front of the house? Perhaps cut through the woods? It was possible as the ranch was surrounded by acres and acres of thick trees.

The Montgomerys knew he was there on patrol and he'd assumed they were all sleeping soundly in their beds. They were counting on him to keep them all safe.

And he would.

He rushed around the side of the house, prepared to take a would-be intruder down. He only hoped that the trespasser hadn't managed to get inside yet. Doubtful, since he knew the Montgomerys had locked up tight. Even if the screen door had opened, he was sure no one could easily breach the entry door that led inside.

As he rounded the side of their home, he stopped in his tracks. Instead of seeing someone trying to break in, as he'd anticipated, he saw someone move away from the house. A small light led the person's steps. It was directed toward the ground, and muted, but to him it looked like an unnecessary beacon.

Why would anyone be leaving the house in the middle of the night? What could they possibly be thinking?

He was certainly going to find out.

He hustled after the person, sure it wasn't an intruder after all, but not holstering his gun just in case. A gentle breeze fluttered the leaves on the trees, making a whispering sound that muffled his footsteps. He glanced over his shoulder, scoping out the yard behind him as best he could in the dark, then he whipped back around, following his quarry.

Mateo was only vaguely familiar with the layout of Big Sky Ranch. Yet the person he was now silently stalking seemed to have a keen sense of awareness as to where they were headed. The light, he now realized, was a flashlight app illuminating the way down a trail. If Mateo was not mistaken, the trail would come out at the main ranch house, the original structure on the property, which was now inhabited by Nina's brother, Eric, and his wife, Cassie.

He shook his head in bewilderment, positive beyond a doubt, that the figure he was quickly gaining on was Nina.

But why? She had seemed afraid earlier. The

fact that she was outside, alone, in the middle of the night, was baffling.

What in the world is she doing?

Anger and frustration sizzled up Mateo's spine. He had vowed to keep this woman safe and here she was running through the woods at night. As if she had no regard for her own safety.

"Stop right there." His words sounded hard, cold, as they shot through the night in an undertone only loud enough for her to hear. He was only feet from her now.

She whirled, clapping her hand over her mouth, allowing a whimper to escape as she likely sealed a full-fledged scream inside.

"Mateo." She growled his name under her breath, as if he was the one at fault here. "You scared the ever-loving daylights out of me."

He closed the distance between them, slipped his fingers around her bicep, fully intending to tow her back to her parents' home. Back to safety. "You're fortunate that's all that happened to you. There are far worse things than being scared. Like dying."

He gave her arm a gentle tug and was surprised he was met with resistance.

"I know." She kept her voice low, as he had, as if they both feared danger was lurking in the darkness. It very well might be. "That's exactly why I need to get out of here."

"Where do you plan on going?" He glanced around, feeling as if they were targets standing there in the darkness. Nina must've felt the same because she turned off the beam of light she'd been using.

"Where? Anywhere but here," she said grimly.

"You think it's wise to leave the safety of the ranch?"

"Yes." The single word held so much weight. "Mateo, this person shot at us. Then blew up my house. What if he comes after me here? I can't risk him hurting my parents. My brothers and their families live on this property. Eric and Cassie just had twins and they have Wyatt. Seth and Holly have Chloe and a baby on the way. I can't be here with them. I can't put them at risk. If anything, anything at all, happened to them, I would never forgive myself. Please tell me you understand."

Understand that level of guilt? He understood more clearly than he cared to admit. He wouldn't tell her that, though.

"Exactly what were you going to do?" he demanded.

She shifted the hefty camping pack she wore.

For a moment, he thought she wasn't going to answer.

"Eric just bought an old beater of a ranch truck for doing chores. He keeps a spare key in the kitchen at Mom and Dad's. I swiped it out of the drawer. My plan is a bit hazy at the moment because I haven't had a chance to come up with something solid. Quite frankly, my only thought right now is that I need to get away."

"You were just going to take off? No warning? Just disappear?" He huffed in annoyance. "Don't you think that would scare your parents to death?"

She let out a matching huff of annoyance. "I left a note."

A note.

He scraped a hand over his face. Right. He could just imagine how well a note would go over with Julia and James.

"I get that you're scared, but this harebrained plan...running through the woods alone at night, stealing a truck and taking off without knowing exactly what you're going to do, is just the sort of thing that might get you killed."

"Harebrained?" Nina's voice held an edge. "And I wasn't *stealing* the truck. I was *borrowing* it. I would have come up with a plan as soon as I got far enough away from my family to think clearly."

It was obvious she was mad.

Maybe even a little hurt.

He couldn't think about that too much right now. He wasn't anything too happy either. If she had disappeared on his watch…well, he didn't want to think about it. He was grateful for the squeaky screen door because, other than that, Nina had the stealth of a cat. He wouldn't have realized she'd run off until she'd torn out of the driveway in her brother's truck.

"We can't stand out in the open arguing like this." His eyes zoomed around as he realized just how far away from the house they were, closer to Eric's place than her parents'. Standing out here felt all kinds of wrong. He didn't like being in the open. Certainly didn't like Nina out here, even if he was armed. "We need to get back. If you really think you need to leave—"

"I do."

He didn't see any point in arguing with her. She was stubborn. More than that, she might be right. Helping her to disappear for a while suddenly seemed like the best option. Not necessarily for her safety, but definitely for that of her family. He would've recommended leaving town before, but had assumed she'd be opposed to the idea of leaving.

"Okay then, this time we'll be smart about it. We'll make a plan to get you someplace safe. Somewhere far away from your family." He was already flipping through possibilities in his mind.

"Fine." Her tone was terse, but then she seemed to soften. "I'm sorry, Mateo. You may not think I made the best choice just now, but I'm just worried about my family. If you have a better plan, I'm open to it."

"You should have discussed this with me sooner."

"I didn't really get the chance. My parents were hovering. Also, I was afraid you'd tell me I should stay."

"Let's get back inside for now. We'll go from there."

This time when he tugged her arm, she didn't resist.

They traipsed back up the path through the woods. Neither said a word. Without a light to guide them, they moved slowly, but he wasn't willing to take an unnecessary risk.

Guilt niggled at him. He'd come down hard on her. Too hard. It was clear she was acting out of selflessness. Love for her family had motivated her. Yet that did nothing to mitigate the danger she was in. Walking outside at night, creeping through the woods, was reckless in his eyes.

Nina walked silently beside him. Not sulkily, but contrite, if he wasn't mistaken.

An apology was on the tip of his tongue. Before he could utter the words, a flash up ahead snagged his attention. Not the same sort of light that had emanated from Nina's phone. No, this light flickered.

Nina grasped his forearm, her grip ironclad, indicating she had noticed as well. He appreciated the fact that she didn't utter a word, seemingly understanding that danger lay ahead and, right now, they had the element of surprise on their side.

"Stay here," he whispered, his mouth right next to her ear.

He darted forward, tugging his arm from her grip.

The light up ahead glimmered and seemed to glow, vaguely illuminating the silhouette of the man holding the flame. His arm rose, hoisting the burning object higher.

"Freeze!" Mateo shouted. "MCPD! Stop where you are."

The man faltered for a split second then whipped the burning object toward the house. An explosion of flames erupted when the Molotov cocktail fell short of its target. Instead of being hurled through the window, it erupted on the Adirondack chair Mateo had vacated to chase after Nina. The piece of furniture went up in a whoosh of flame.

Nina let out a shriek of anger and fear.

The figure took off running.

"Get your parents out of the house!" Mateo shot off the warning before giving chase. He called for backup on his shoulder radio even as he ran. Then he prayed.

Please, God…watch over Nina's family. Get them out of the house safely.

He had to trust that Nina would do just that because he desperately wanted to catch this guy.

The night was inky-dark and the man had dressed in black. Though Mateo gave a valiant effort to catch the perp, dodging through the thick brush, trying to make out the figure in the darkness, listening for any hint of snapping branches, it wasn't long before he realized that his effort was in vain.

Mateo stopped running and leaned against a tree, more for camouflage than anything else. Ears straining, he only heard the natural sounds of the night that he'd been listening to on the porch earlier. The woods weren't familiar to him, so it didn't make sense to push forward. He had to assume the attacker was running blindly as well.

After a moments' pause, he pushed away from the tree because he suddenly feared the guy would backtrack and launch a sneak attack on Nina and her family. He thought it unlikely, but decided it was better to head back to the house than to take any chances.

When he arrived, he found Nina and her mother standing in the driveway, huddled together. The porch light shone down, lighting up the mass of charred wood that had been a chair.

James, her father, held a garden hose that spouted water on the remainder of the smoldering furniture. The porch had major damage, but the house seemed to have been spared.

A cruiser tore down the driveway, lights flashing in warning but sirens silent, just as Mateo strode out of the woods.

Officer Baker, a rookie, tossed the door open

and leapt from the vehicle. His gaze immediately locked with Mateo's. "Sir? What do you have?"

Mateo headed for the young officer. "The suspect tossed a Molotov cocktail. He missed the window. The damage appears to be contained to the front porch." He eyed the smoking mess. "I gave chase, but lost him in the woods, so I came back. I was concerned he might backtrack."

The officer's gaze flitted around. "I'll do a perimeter check."

"Good idea." Mateo strode toward Nina and her family when the officer took off. "Everyone okay?"

"We're fine. I pounded on the door to alert my parents, then I grabbed the hose until Dad took over." Nina untangled herself from her mother's embrace. "The attacker got away."

It wasn't a question and it certainly wasn't an accusation. Yet Mateo felt a sting of disappointment all the same.

"Yeah. He got away."

Again.

Nina could feel the frustration emanating off Mateo. She didn't like that he seemed to be so hard on himself. His gaze still scanned the yard, completely on guard and still in protection mode.

"You scared him off," she said. "Stopped him from hurting anyone. Thank you."

She felt a niggling stab of guilt. If she hadn't run off, hadn't given Mateo a reason to trek after her through the woods, he would have been sitting in a prime position to catch the man who had thrown the homemade fireball. He would have been where he'd intended to be.

"Yes." James finally gave up his effort with the hose. The fire was out and even the smoldering had dwindled. "I second my daughter's sentiment. Thank you. You saved us tonight from what would have surely been something disastrous."

"Just doing my job."

"Going above and beyond," Julia chimed in.

As if their thoughts were in unison, and very likely they were, both of her parents turned to face her.

Julia frowned. "What were *you* doing outside? It's the middle of the night. Someone is after you. What in the world were you thinking?"

Nina knew there was no sense in denying

what she'd been up to. Her parents hadn't found the note on the kitchen table yet and she could hardly race inside to tear it up without raising suspicion. Besides, her plans hadn't changed. Quite the contrary. After this latest attack, she was even more convinced that she was doing the right thing.

"I'm leaving." Her statement hung in the air, unanswered, as if her parents couldn't process what she was saying. "Right now. I'm leaving the ranch. It's not safe for me to be here. Not safe for me, and worse, not safe for my family."

"You don't need to worry about us." Her father sounded confused by the sentiment. "We want you here. We want to help protect you."

"But I *am* worried." Nina's gaze darted between her parents. "I worry about you. But I also worry about my nieces and nephews. You can't tell me that you wouldn't be devastated if something happened to them."

"Of course we would," Julia said with a frown, "but—"

"There's no point in arguing," Nina cut in. "I couldn't bear it if something happened to them. After tonight, there's no denying he knows I'm here. Do you think he's going to stop? He's been relentless so far. I can't take that chance."

Her parents exchanged a pained look.

Her mother sighed. "As much as I hate to admit it, perhaps you're right. I'm worried about everyone's safety, but most of all, I'm worried about *you* since you're his target."

"Exactly." Nina was relieved her mother saw things her way. "*I'm* the target. If I move on, hopefully he won't come back."

"Okay—" her mother nodded "—we'll pack our bags right now. Your father and I will take you somewhere far from here."

What? No.

That was not what Nina had had in mind at all. If her parents were with her, they would still be in danger. She shot a frantic look Mateo's way, hoping he would also think it was a terrible idea. Thankfully, he seemed to agree.

"I don't think that's wise," he said. "You might just be putting yourselves in danger, along with Nina."

James huffed. "I'm hardly going to send my daughter off on her own and hope for the best."

"Of course." Mateo's tone was conciliatory, calming. "That's why I think it's best if I take Nina somewhere. I'm equipped to protect her."

Her parents shared a long look.

"I don't like this at all," James finally said. "I don't like any of this. But I don't think we have any other option."

"Where would you go?" Julia demanded.

"I have a few places in mind. I think it's best if I don't say where." Mateo's gaze swung between her parents. "The less you know, the better."

Nina nodded, silently letting him know she agreed.

Everything was happening so fast, her world seemingly spinning out of control. She was relieved that he was willing to take charge.

"What do you think?" Mateo directed the question at Nina. "I've got a few options. Places that are off the beaten path. Somewhere no one would think to look for you. Obviously, I haven't worked out the details, or even decided yet which place might be best, but I've got a pretty good idea."

To be honest, she wasn't entirely sure what she thought. She hadn't had enough time to really wrap her head around the suggestion. On the other hand, he had a plan, which was more than she had. Furthermore, it got her away from her family and, therefore, would hopefully get them out of harm's way.

"Let's do it," she said.

Less than fifteen minutes later, they were loaded into Mateo's SUV. Her mother had packed enough food to last them days, ensuring they wouldn't need to stop anywhere. Nina had her backpack loaded with clothes Holly had lent her. She and her sister-in-law were typically close to the same size, though now Holly was hugely pregnant. She had given Nina free reign over her wardrobe since Nina had lost all of her clothing in the explosion.

Officer Baker had checked in, letting Mateo know that he hadn't seen any sign of the intruder. The man had gotten away somehow. Perhaps he'd hiked in and had hidden a vehicle somewhere.

Coco let out a sigh of contentment from the back seat where Nina had buckled her in to her doggy car seat. Her original intention was to leave the dog behind, but once they'd gone in the house to pack up the food Julia had insisted on, Coco had made it clear she wasn't pleased with that idea.

So here they were. Mateo, Nina and Coco, cruising down the back roads in the dead of night.

Nina prayed that they were heading toward safety.

Chapter Six

Nina was pleasantly surprised by what Mateo had warned her was a hunting "shack." It was small and rustic, but it also had indoor plumbing and other amenities that she would never take for granted.

Like electricity and semicomfy furniture. There was a fridge, stove, and essentially a fully functioning kitchen. It was far from fancy, but she'd been picturing a ramshackle place with an outhouse at best.

It was far enough out of town that it was private, surrounded by trees, with the nearest house miles away. Yet close enough they could drive back and forth easily while doing some investigating. Still, it had taken them nearly an hour to arrive tonight because Mateo had insisted on a roundabout route to be sure they were not followed.

The loft held a single bedroom, which Mateo

insisted Nina and Coco take. There was a futon in the small living area downstairs. Mateo assured her it was perfect for him. It would station him near the front door and windows on the off chance that someone had tracked them there.

She was dragging by the time she lugged her backpack inside. Mateo had a duffel bag, his go-bag, which he kept in his SUV so that he wouldn't have to stop by his place for anything. He carried in the generous food supply from Julia while Nina settled in upstairs.

Coco trotted down the steep wooden staircase after Nina, who yawned hugely, after checking out the loft.

Mateo glanced up from where he was stashing the last container in the refrigerator. The cooler stuffed with every ice pack her mother owned rested at his feet. He looked as fatigued as she felt.

"All settled?" he asked.

"Yes." She moved to the well-worn chair and dropped down, her body feeling heavy with fatigue. "What's the game plan?"

He dropped onto the futon and arched a brow. "Game plan?"

"You know what I mean." Coco plopped her bottom at Nina's feet and placed her chin on

Nina's knee. She stroked the dog's long, silky ears lovingly. "We're not going to just hang out here, waiting for this guy to be caught, are we?"

"Not exactly." Mateo leaned forward. "I want to go over some details of your life. I have questions about your job, your volunteer work. The people you hang out with."

She nodded. "I understand. I've been wracking my brain, trying to figure out how I could possibly know this man. But I've lived in Mulberry Creek most of my life. What if it's someone I knew as far back as high school?"

"Always a possibility. Recognizing you is one thing. But who would recognize your vehicle?"

Nina's eyes widened as she realized what Mateo was getting at. "It would have to be someone I've been in contact with recently. I've only had that vehicle two, maybe three, months. I drove an old beater through nursing school. When I started working in the ER, I worked mostly night shifts and slept most days. My schedule was all over the place and I didn't have time to look for something new. I didn't actually get my vehicle until I started working for hospice."

"Good." Mateo nodded and looked pleased. "That narrows the suspects down a bit. We don't have to go all the way back to high school because it's not just *you* they recognized but your vehicle."

"Right." She yawned again.

"The thing is, it's kind of a flashy color. The kind that gets noticed."

Nina wrinkled her nose, almost apologetically. "I wanted four-wheel drive. I need something reliable to get around because hospice sometimes brings me to places out in the country. You know what Montana winters can be like. Cherry red wasn't my top choice but the price was right. The color *does* stand out."

Mateo chuckled. "I'm not criticizing your choice. I'm just saying it's noticeable and makes sense someone connected it to you. I also noticed you had a decal on the back window that says 'Blessed' and, while it's subtle, it would still be an identifier."

"Makes me kind of wish I still had my old beater," she muttered. "No one ever paid attention to that."

"It's barely past daybreak," Mateo said. "I don't think either of us got a wink of sleep last night. What do you say we both get some rest? I think it would do us some good to sleep. We'll be able to come at this with clearer heads. Besides, we don't know what the next few days, maybe even weeks, will bring. I, for one, want to be at the top of my game."

"Me, too." Nina fought the urge to yawn. Again. "Sleep is sounding way too appealing right now."

Mateo cocked his head toward Coco. "What kind of guard dog is she?"

"A useless one." Nina chuckled then sobered. "Everyone is her friend. She's well trained and doesn't typically bark, not even at strangers. But do you think we need a guard dog?"

"No." Mateo sounded positive. "I can guarantee we weren't followed. Not only did I take precautions, but there was simply no traffic on the back roads we took. The man I borrowed this place from is a retired sheriff, a friend of my dad's. He won't tell a soul that we're here."

She felt herself relax at Mateo's obvious confidence. She didn't think he'd say they were safe if they weren't. Sure, she knew there were no guarantees, but she understood that in his professional opinion they were as safe as they could get.

For now.

"Was your dad in law enforcement?" she asked, curious about his family.

"He was. Worked as a deputy until he retired several years ago." Mateo motioned around the cabin, which Nina no longer thought of as a shack. "I spent some time here when I was younger, joining them on hunting trips. Not once did we see another soul out this way. It's a good place for us to hide out for a while."

Satisfied with his answer, she rose from her chair. "Coco, let's go. Get some rest, Mateo."

"Will do."

With great effort, Nina climbed the staircase again. She went straight to the bed in the small loft, flopped down without bothering to peel back the covers—only vaguely aware of Coca taking the liberty to snuggle in beside her—and fell into blissful slumber.

She awoke several hours later, feeling refreshed but absolutely starving. She stretched and gave herself a moment to gather her wits about her. The memory of the events of the day before came crashing back.

She sucked in a pained breath at the realization that her house, all of her belongings, were gone. Her heart thudded painfully as she recalled the explosion, the blaze. Then she reminded herself that it could have been so much worse. Her family, as far as she knew, was safe.

When it came down to it, that's all that really mattered.

She swung her legs over the bed. Coca stirred beside her.

"Did you have a good nap, sweet girl?"

The dog yawned.

Clattering from downstairs grabbed Nina's attention. She realized then that a savory aroma filled the air.

She also realized that Mateo was awake.

If he'd even slept.

A quick glance at her watch let her know it was well after lunchtime. She was surprised she'd slept so long considering all that was going on. Then again, she'd been utterly exhausted. Both physically and emotionally. So she was going to choose to give herself some grace.

She hustled down the staircase and found Mateo in the kitchen.

"Is that my mom's stew I smell?"

Mateo glanced over his shoulder and flashed her a grin. "It is. It sure came in handy that your mom had all those frozen meals. I popped the biscuits in the oven to warm. Everything should be ready in just a few minutes."

Nina's stomach growled.

He chuckled. "I can relate."

Coco whimpered.

Mateo stepped away from the stove. "I'll take her out."

"I'll set the table." She easily found what she was looking for in the limited cupboard space. By the time she had the table set and food set out, Mateo and Coco were back inside.

They took the only two seats at the tiny table.

Nina lowered her head to say a silent prayer. She was aware that Mateo waited for her to finish before dishing himself up.

"Did you sleep?" Nina took a roll and spread a thin layer of butter on it.

"A little." He set the soup ladle back in the pot.

He hadn't looked at her when he'd said it, leaving her to wonder how "little" was little. She knew he hadn't slept nearly as long as she had, but he did look more refreshed.

They ate in silence for a while, both of them clearly famished. Nina hadn't had an appetite the night before when she'd sat through dinner with her worried parents. She'd skipped breakfast this morning in lieu of the nap she'd just awakened from. Now her appetite seemed to be making up for a few missed meals.

"Your mom is a great cook." Mateo set his

spoon down. "I'm pretty mediocre myself. Do you take after her?"

"I try. I do like to cook, but there's nothing that beats Mom's home cooking." She swirled her spoon through the stew. "Do you have any information to share?"

"Officer Hughes confirmed that none of your pictures show this guy's face."

"I'm not surprised. I didn't think any of them would be useful."

Mateo's phone buzzed. He grabbed it off the table and read the incoming message with a frown.

"Something wrong?"

"Seems we've hit a bit of a roadblock already. Officer Rollins called earlier and now he's touching base again."

"What kind of roadblock?"

"We have to start this investigation somewhere, so we decided to start with one of the places you volunteer. He went to the Senior Center with pictures of the items found in the lockbox. We had all of the photos put into a few three-ring binders. I have one—picked it up from the station last night when I got my vehicle—because we're hoping it'll be useful when interviewing people. Rollins wasn't getting any answers, so he mentioned your name, hoping it would loosen some tongues if they knew it would help you out." Mateo grimaced. "Apparently that backfired. One of the visitors got it into her head that you were in trouble. And not in trouble like being shot at, but in trouble like you had done something wrong and might be headed to jail."

Nina's eyes widened. "What?"

"It seems that a Mrs. Marjorie Wallace told him she had warned you but you wouldn't listen." His brow creased. "Just what is she referring to? What did she warn you about? You don't really seem like a troublemaker to me."

Nina pressed a hand against her forehead and groaned. "Mrs. Wallace is always telling me that Coco is going to get me in trouble. According to her, people cannot bring pets into public buildings. I've explained that Coco is a service dog. She wears a vest when we're working. I even showed Marjorie the certificate we earned. But she's very old school and is always telling me dogs belong outside. She insists I'm violating all sorts of health codes."

"Even if she thinks you're at fault, it seems she has your back. Sounds like she was pretty riled up on your behalf. She's determined not to speak with Officer Rollins. And apparently has convinced the others not to as well."

"That's not surprising." Nina pushed away her empty bowl and leaned back in her chair. "She has a very commanding personality."

"Officer Hughes offered to give it a try. Maybe she can make a visit when Mrs. Wallace isn't there."

"She's there daily," Nina said. "And believe me, even if she isn't there, she'd be sure to get the word out. The only way you're going to get anyone to look at those photos and give you any information, is if I go there myself. I need to convince them I'm not in trouble. At least, not the way they suspect."

"I don't think so."

"Why not?" Nina frowned at Mateo but she was sure she could guess the answer. "I'll be safe if I'm with you. Obviously, you should lead the questioning, but I know how this group can be. Very stubborn once they have their minds made up. I'm going to have to convince them it's okay to share if they know something."

She knew how members of the Senior Center liked to talk, at least, under the right circumstances. She was willing to try anything if there was a possibility it would help them find the attacker. There was no doubt that the confrontation at the park was already big news in their town. People would be hungry for information and, for once, the gossip mill could be an asset.

"All right." Mateo pushed away from the table. "I'll get these dishes done. Then I don't see what a quick unannounced visit could hurt. If we get answers, it would be worth it."

Nina leapt to her feet. "I'll wash. You can dry."

In no time at all they were in Mateo's Tahoe, headed back to Mulberry Creek with Coco once again buckled into the backseat. The drive passed quickly as Mateo and Nina made small talk. She suspected he was trying to put her at ease. He needn't worry; there was something about him that was calming. He held an unpretentious air of confidence. She felt safe with him. And she was more than a little intrigued by him. He asked questions about her life, to find out more for his investigation, she was sure. But it didn't feel like he was prying.

By the time they hit the edge of town, Nina realized she hadn't been able to ask *him* a single question. She wanted to know more about him, and it wasn't just because he was the man protecting her. She wanted to know more about him as a person, not a detective.

"I've been thinking." Mateo tapped his fingers on the steering wheel. "It might be worthwhile to stop at Junkin' Treasures."

"I've heard of that. Is it an antique store?"

He turned his blinker on, routing them toward the downtown area. "Pawn shop. I know the owner, Jimmy. He's usually pretty helpful. I'd like to see if he's familiar with any of the items in the binder we put together. I know they weren't stolen from him, but he'd be able to give me an idea of what some of the items are worth. Or maybe this guy has tried to move some of the pieces through Jimmy's store. Not likely, but it's possible."

He pulled up in front of a large brick building. "This is it. Let's see if we can get some information."

Nina had never been in a pawn shop before, yet it was about as she'd expected it to be. A musty smell hung in the air. Rows of overcrowded shelves were lined with goods, possibly even some hidden treasures. A local rock station was being piped in through speakers in the ceiling. And the place looked like it could use a good cleaning.

What she had not expected was the way the proprietor's face lit up when she and Mateo walked through the door. Somehow, she had a hunch the enormous smile the guy wore was not for her.

"Mateo! My man!" Jimmy ducked around the side of the counter and strode straight for them. "Long time no see." He held up a hand, clearly waiting for a high-five.

For a moment, Nina wondered if Mateo would leave him hanging. Then he gave Jimmy's hand a powerful albeit somewhat awkward smack. Nina realized casual high-fives were not Mateo's thing.

"Good to see you, Jimmy." Mateo shifted the binder he held. "Listen, I'm wondering if you could help me and my friend, Nina, out."

"Hi, Jimmy." Nina smiled at the man and wiggled her fingers in a wave of greeting.

"Nice to meet you. Any friend of this guy is a friend of mine."

"Oh, really?" Nina asked, arching a brow. "You must think pretty highly of him."

"Yup, sure do." Jimmy nodded for emphasis. "Did he tell you what he did for me?"

Nina cut a quick glance to Mateo. His expression was that of stoic patience. Then she shook her head. "He didn't mention anything."

"This guy here—" Jimmy jabbed a finger in Mateo's direction "—pretty much saved my business. You see, a few years ago, I was having trouble with someone shoplifting. My most expensive items kept going missing, but even with security cameras, I couldn't catch the guy. Turns out the thief was an employee of mine. He'd made himself a key and snuck in at night, would mess with my cameras, and take off with the goods. I never would've suspected him. Trusted him like a friend. But our guy here came in and rooted out the scheme in no time."

Mateo cleared his throat and lifted the binder.

"Sure. Right." Jimmy rubbed his hands together in anticipation. "What do you got?"

Mateo motioned at the counter and Jimmy nodded, leading the way.

"I'm not sure what I have exactly." Mateo set the binder down but didn't open it. "I suspect stolen items. I'm wondering if you could help me get an idea of what these items are worth."

"Sure thing."

Mateo slid it Jimmy's way. "Have at it."

Jimmy opened the binder. He went through it slowly, meticulously, studying each page without saying a word. Yet the way his brow creased in concentration led Nina to believe he was taking this task quite seriously.

After several long minutes, he flipped back to a page in the middle. He tapped his finger on the photo depicting the collection of stamps. "I remember these."

"Are you sure it was that exact set?" Mateo asked.

"Positive." Jimmy nodded emphatically. "This is a unique collection of antique postage stamps, pre-Civil War era, and valuable. A guy came in, quite a while ago, asking me if I was interested. It's not the type of thing I typically sell, but I was willing to haggle a bit. We couldn't come to an agreement on price. Truth be told, I got the impression he didn't really want to sell. I think he just wanted to get an appraisal out of me."

Nina's heart skittered and she wanted to jiggle all of Jimmy's information free. She shifted a glance at Mateo. He looked a million times calmer than she felt.

"Do you recall the guy's name?" Mateo asked.

Jimmy scratched his head with one finger. His brows puckered. "Nope. I don't." He paused, then turned around and motioned to the mess behind him. "I took his name down. I'm pretty sure it's here somewhere."

Nina scanned the space. There were notebooks, receipt books, loose sheets of paper, and a plethora of odds and ends scattered across the space.

"Then again, could be I brought it back to my office," Jimmy admitted. "I don't keep that quite as tidy as I keep this area."

He thought this was tidy? Oh, goodness. Nina couldn't even imagine how disastrous his office could be.

"Can you give me a description?" Mateo asked.

"Older fella. Maybe close to eighty. Walked a little hunched over. I remember, I had a real nice hand-carved cane at the time. I thought maybe he'd be interested in it, but he didn't take too kindly to my suggestion. He was a cantankerous sort. Tried to talk me into giving him more than what the value was. A guy's gotta have some room for profit, so, like I said, we couldn't cut a deal."

Nina bit her lip. She didn't want to blurt out the obvious. Close to eighty? That couldn't be their guy. So how did he tie in?

"How long ago was this?" Mateo asked.

"Oh, a good three, four, months ago. He gave me his name and number in case I changed my mind. I knew I wouldn't—" Jimmy shrugged "—but I don't throw much away. Never know when you're going to need something. His information is around here somewhere."

Would he ever find the guy's number in that mess? Nina wondered and then winced at the uncharitable speculation. This could be organized chaos, as far as she knew.

"Jimmy, it would be real helpful if you could remember the gentleman's name. More helpful still if you could track down his number."

"I can sure try," Jimmy agreed amicably enough. "I keep thinking I need to come up with some sort of filing system, but just haven't had the time. Guess now would be a good time to work on that."

"I'd appreciate it," Mateo said.

"As for the value of the items, I'd say we're looking at close to a hundred grand. That's a high-end Rolex and, as I mentioned, the stamps are worth a good deal, not to mention the coins. The thing is, there's lots of jewelry there. Might be that no one would be interested in, say, that gold locket. But looks to me that it's pure gold. There are companies that buy that sort of thing, melt it down, and give you a fair price for it. Places you can find on the internet, even."

Mateo nodded slowly. "That would make these items almost impossible to trace once our guy decided to part with them."

"Yup."

Mateo grabbed the binder. "We'll let you get back to work."

He nudged Nina toward the door. She waved a goodbye to Jimmy. He grinned back, but then turned and immediately began sorting through papers. It looked like he was a man of his word.

They exited the building and Mateo hustled her to his SUV, parked right outside the pawn shop.

"That's not our guy that he was describing." Mateo's words echoed Nina's thoughts as he opened her door for her while scanning the sidewalk. "But whoever he is, it's possible he has information. If he was trying to sell the stamps to Jimmy then maybe he sold them to someone else."

"If our attacker bought everything fair and square, why would he be willing to kill over the items?"

"I agree, it doesn't make sense." Mateo paused

thoughtfully. "I hope Jimmy comes up with something for us. The sooner, the better."

Mateo hadn't been certain that allowing Nina to visit the Senior Center was a wise idea, but they hadn't had a lot of other options if they wanted to start getting some answers. His opinion on that changed when he escorted Nina through the door.

The place was bustling with activity. The open space was full of tables and the tables were full of people. At the back of the room, he spotted what looked like an ice cream bar. A long table held large tubs of ice cream. Smaller bowls with nuts, fruits and candies were beside it. At the end was a variety of syrups and whipped cream.

"Today is the ice cream social. I forgot about that." Nina shrugged. "On the bright side, with all of these people here, hopefully one of them will know something."

It seemed as if everyone in the place swiveled to see who had arrived once the door whooshed open.

A spry elderly woman with unnaturally red hair jumped up from her seat. She scurried over to Nina with the agility of a teenager.

"Goodness, girl! What are you doing here?" She pulled Nina into a quick hug. When she released her, she scowled at Coco, who had taken a seat next to Nina's feet. The dog wore a vest with the words Therapy Dog inscribed on it. "Did you come for the ice cream? Oh, you shouldn't have that mutt in here. I told you she'd bring trouble. She shouldn't be around the food." The woman's eyes zipped around and she whispered, "A cop was here looking for you."

"I heard," Nina whispered back. Then louder, added, "That was just a misunderstanding."

"It's about that dog, isn't it? I warned you."

The woman, Marjorie Wallace, Mateo was sure, scowled at him then.

"And who are you?" she demanded.

"This is Detective Bianchi," Nina said.

"Detective?" Marjorie scowled. "That seems a bit excessive for violating a health code."

Mateo remained silent as Nina spent the next several minutes explaining that she, herself, was not *in* trouble. But rather, she'd *faced* a bit of trouble. She spoke freely of being attacked in the park.

By the time she was done with her story, a crowd had gathered around. A few dozen older citizens of Mulberry Creek, who all looked as ravenous for news as they did for their ice cream, leaned in to listen.

"I heard about that," one gentleman said. "It was in the news. Been a lot of talk about it yesterday and today." He scooped up his melted treat and shoved a big bite in his mouth.

Mateo wondered if it was wise that Nina admit she was the one in the park but then realized it was too late to take it back. Besides, the attacker already knew who she was, and in a town this small, it was likely to get out anyway.

"You see," Nina said, "I could really use your help. We're trying to track down my attacker. We're hoping you could look over some photos, see if anything looks familiar. We don't know that these items are the reason behind my attack, but we have to start somewhere."

And with that simple explanation, the gathering of ice cream eaters readily agreed.

Even though Nina had told Mateo she would let him head the questioning, it turned out that she had a knack for getting this lively group of people talking.

Many of them commented on the items in the binder. Some were sure they'd seen some of the objects before and then decided they'd maybe seen a similar item before. Or maybe they'd owned something just like it in the past.

When all was said and done, they'd had a whole lot of conversation, but not one comment had resulted in anything he'd take as a substantial clue. There was a lot of interest in the binder and Nina's story. And when it became clear they weren't going to get anywhere, he decided it was time to move along.

He gave Nina's arm a gentle nudge.

She glanced up from a conversation about a brooch in the binder. Everyone thought it was pretty, but no one had seen it before. Mateo didn't need to say a word. She understood by the look he gave her that it was time to go.

"It was lovely to see you all." She stood and pushed in her chair. "I sincerely thank you for trying to help. But I think it's time for us to be on our way."

"You be careful, young lady." Marjorie looked at Coco. "Maybe you should get yourself a bigger dog. An attack dog. Something that can protect you."

"Thank you, Marjorie." Nina gave Coco's leash a gentle tug and the dog got to her feet. "I appreciate your concern."

"Thank you all for your time," Mateo said.

"If any of you think of anything that could re-late to the case, please give the police depart-ment a call."

He gently took Nina by the elbow and led her to the door. Not because she needed the prodding, but because he suspected that this lively group would waylay her departure if given a chance.

Nina blew out a sigh as they exited the build-ing. "I was hoping someone would recognize something."

Mateo barely heard her. Someone—a man dressed in torn jeans, a ball cap pulled low over his face—was lurking around his SUV. Mateo watched as he lifted the windshield wiper and stuffed something under it. A threatening note?

Was this their guy?

"Go back inside. Now." He gave Nina a gen-tle shove toward the building. Then he took off down the sidewalk. The guy spotted him, whirled and began to run like his life depended upon it.

Had this guy done something other than mess with his windshield wiper? Thoughts of Nina's burning house came to mind and he wondered if a car bomb was a possibility. Or a tracking device.

"Stop!" Mateo shouted.

Several people on the sidewalk darted out of the way as the chase continued. The guy dodged people as he ran. He nearly knocked down an elderly couple—maybe on their way to the ice cream social—who righted themselves as Mateo sped by.

He looked over his shoulder once to be sure Nina had complied with his request. She was no longer on the sidewalk. That glance almost cost him the chase as the guy ducked down an alley. But Mateo caught a glimpse of him and tore down the potholed path after him.

"Stop!" he shouted. "Police!"

To his surprise, the runner skidded to a halt. Something a perp almost never did. The kid—Mateo now realized this guy was probably college age—spun around. His hands flew up in the air and his eyes bulged in fear.

"I'm sorry! I'm sorry!" he sputtered. "I didn't mean to do anything wrong."

Mateo quickly closed the distance between them. He had his hand on his weapon, but the kid didn't appear to be armed, so he didn't draw it. "Why did you run?"

The guy blinked at him. "Because you started chasing me. It was just reflex, I guess."

"What's your name?"

"Tucker. Tucker Holden, sir."

"What were you doing to my Tahoe?"

The kid looked around frantically. Mateo realized a crowd was beginning to form behind them. He heard sirens nearing and assumed Nina had called for backup.

"I was just…" Tucker looked miserable. "I saw you and Nina pull up together. I volunteer at the Senior Center and I was just finishing my shift. I was leaving a note for Nina."

"What kind of note?"

"Just a note of support. Nina's always doing nice things for other people." He scrubbed both hands over his face.

Mateo wasn't sure what to make of this guy.

Was he telling the truth?

Or was Tucker Holden, if that was really his name, a would-be cold-blooded killer?

As Mateo's backup arrived and began to swarm the alley, he hoped they'd have an answer soon.

Chapter Seven

Nina pushed around the noodles on her dinner plate. She typically loved her mother's casseroles, but her stomach had been in knots ever since Tucker had been arrested. She knew him, but felt they had only recently transitioned from acquaintances to friends. Their volunteer paths crossed on occasion. She hadn't seen him at the center today, as he'd been back in the kitchen trying to keep up with all the dirty dishes.

"No appetite?" Mateo guessed. "I know it's not that the food is bad, because this is delicious."

"I can't stop thinking about Tucker. Do you think he's the guy?"

A storm was brewing and thunder rumbled in the distance. The day had turned dark and dreary, matching Nina's current mood.

Mateo set his fork down. "I think the fact that he lied about his whereabouts during the time of the attack in the park raises a major red flag."

Yes, it did, Nina knew. Tucker had been brought in for questioning. When asked, he had said he was working during the time of the attack. Checking in at the Good Stuff Café, with owner Sal Goodman, had been easy enough. Sal had verified that Tucker had *not* been working.

"He said he panicked."

"That is what he said." Mateo's tone was wry. "He also used that excuse for the reason he took off running."

She tilted her head, studying Mateo's unreadable expression. "You don't believe him?"

"I don't want to speculate. I like to look at facts. He has a connection to you. He's roughly the size of the guy who chased us through the park. He lied regarding his whereabouts. When questioned again, he said he was fly fishing, but we can't corroborate that, either."

"Yet."

"Right." Mateo nodded. "Then there's the fact that apparently he's had an unrequited crush on you."

Nina groaned and put her face in her hands. "I had no idea."

This particular nugget of information had

come from Marjorie Wallace. Seemingly, Tucker had confided in Marjorie as the pair had become chummy over their love for Monopoly. When Marjorie had found out Tucker had been taken in for questioning, she'd tracked Mateo down at the station to tell him.

While the woman was hoping the admission would help Tucker, it also gave him motive. Could he be upset with Nina for turning him down multiple times? It seemed excessive, but Mateo told Nina he'd seen far stranger cases. Maybe being turned down, paired with having his box full of belongings confiscated, had pushed him over the edge.

"He asked me to go to the Fall Festival at church last year." Nina pushed her plate away because there was no point in pretending she was able to eat. "And there was a dance at the Senior Center that volunteers were encouraged to attend. I declined both because both conflicted with my work schedule."

"According to Marjorie, he's head over heels for you." Mateo lifted his eyebrows. "You really didn't suspect?"

"No. I thought he was asking as a friend." Nina hadn't suspected his crush. She had thought they were in comfy friend territory.

Tucker was quiet, not the least bit outgoing. He didn't even really talk to her that much. Now that she knew about his crush, she could imagine how hard it had been for him to ask her out. If that's what he'd been doing. He was a loner, for sure. Had she angered him by turning him down? While she wanted to see her attacker caught, she didn't want her attacker to be Tucker. Yet, now that she thought about it, she recalled catching him looking at her. She'd thought it was a coincidence, no big deal. But had there been malice behind that interest? Anger that she'd turned him down?

"What about the note he left?"

It had actually been a Bible verse combined with a note.

The fear of man bringeth a snare: But whoso putteth his trust in the LORD shall be safe.
Stay safe, Nina.

Mateo shrugged. "Maybe it was a backhanded threat. You know, the bit about a snare."

Could he be right? Or was Mateo just used to looking for the worst in people?

"If he wanted to encourage you, as he said, I don't get why he didn't just talk to you," Mateo said. "Why sneak around and put a note on my vehicle?"

"I don't know. I'm sure he saw I was with you. You are rather intimidating."

He frowned. "You find me intimidating?"

"The first time we met, yes." She shrugged. "You wanted to interrogate my brother and would not take no for an answer."

"I wanted to *interview* your brother. I knew he was one of the good guys. There's a difference." He chuckled. "You were pretty formidable yourself. I recall you tried to have me removed from his hospital room."

"He was injured. He needed to rest."

"I was trying to wrap up a big case. I needed his testimony."

Her lips twitched. "You got it."

"And you stood by his bedside the whole time, making sure I didn't rile him up too much."

That was true. She had worked at the hospital back then, and while she hadn't been on duty, she had taken advantage of her hospital privileges by not leaving Seth's side for much of the time.

She was surprised and a bit flattered that Mateo seemed to remember that long-ago encounter as well as she did. She pushed away from the table and began to clear it. "I'll take care of the dishes. You mentioned you wanted to check your emails."

"If you're sure."

Nina nodded. She needed to keep busy. Her mind kept wandering back to Tucker and she found herself second-guessing every conversation they'd had.

The rumble of thunder rolled closer as the sky continued to darken. She could feel the storm moving in. Leaves trembled on the trees. Rain had begun sprinkling down but she was sure they were in for much worse. Pushing the curtain aside, she glanced out at the tree line. The gentle rain began spattering in large hard droplets against the windowpane. The wind picked up and the trees seemed to swirl against the sky. Forks of lightning split through the steely gray clouds. She let the curtain fall back in place.

It was unlikely her attacker was out in the woods, watching. Not with this weather coming in.

She hoped. The thought made her shudder.

"Are you cold?" Mateo was sitting at the table, reading his email from his phone so he could stay caught up on his work. Nina knew he'd had to touch base with the police chief, and had been given approval for concentrating on Nina's case for the time being. That included sequestering her away.

"A little." Though that wasn't why she'd shuddered, it wasn't a lie. The temperature had dropped now that the storm was moving in.

"I could start a fire," he offered.

"I'll be fine." She gave him a smile and began scrubbing the few dishes they had used. A feeling of restlessness settled into her bones. The cabin was so small and she was full of nervous energy.

She was trying to stay out of his way to let him get some work done. He was now jotting something in the notebook that had been in his briefcase. She wondered if it had to do with her case, or another. She wasn't naïve enough to think that hers was the only one he was working on right now.

Despite her curiosity, she didn't want to disturb him. Earlier, Officer Hughes had let them know she'd interviewed Nina's pastor and the church secretary. Neither had recognized any of the items in the binder. They had logged over a dozen photos and every one of them seemed to be a dead end.

Just like the photos on her camera.

She quashed down her disappointment.

The roar of thunder caused the cabin to vibrate. The rain beat down and Nina could hear the wind howling through the trees.

Mateo flipped his notebook shut and moved away from the table. "The storm is really picking up. I didn't realize it was supposed to get so bad."

The lights flickered as thunder boomed again.

Mateo moved from the kitchen as Nina dropped onto the battered recliner.

The lights flickered and then went out completely, leaving the cabin gloomy but not completely dark. Though, with night falling, it would be dark soon enough.

"Mateo?"

"It's okay. It's just the storm." He pulled the curtain over the sink closed because Nina had accidentally left it open just a crack. For a moment, she thought it was strange there was a curtain over every window, even the smallest ones, but then remembered that the cabin was owned by a retired sheriff. He probably had the coverings for just this reason. To keep anyone from being able to see in. Was that paranoia? Or just good planning?

Maybe it was a bit of both.

Next, he went to the kitchen cupboard and pulled out a jar.

No, Nina realized, not a jar. A candle.

He found matches in the drawer.

His efficiency made it clear he'd scoped the place out and knew exactly where the items were that he was looking for. He placed the candle on the fireplace hearth. It was dim enough that Nina suspected it wouldn't draw attention through the window, but cast a lovely warm glow that took the edge off the gloom.

The relentless rumble of thunder made the cabin perpetually shudder.

Nina trembled and wrapped her arms around herself. Coco roused from her spot on the rug and trotted over to Nina.

"Is she afraid of storms?" Mateo asked.

"No." Nina scooped the dog off the floor and into her lap. "But she senses I'm not crazy about them."

He settled onto the futon. Though he was seated, Nina thought he still looked alert. She noticed his gun was holstered and easily within reach. She was sure he was right about the storm knocking out the electricity. Yet it was reassuring to know he was prepared should it turn out to be more.

He braced his elbows on his knees and leaned forward, studying her. "You're afraid of storms?"

She winced. "I used to be terrified, to be honest. We were in a terrible storm when I was younger, maybe five or six. My family was on the way home from an out-of-town wedding. Dad thought we could beat the storm, but it moved in faster than expected. Back then, we didn't have a cell phone, didn't carry around the internet in our pockets and purses to check the weather on a whim. We got caught in a deluge. He had to pull over because he couldn't see the road in front of him. The wind picked up. We could hear trees breaking and falling. I was sure we were going to be crushed. I was sitting in the very back of Mom's minivan with Ella. She held my hand and whispered over and over that everything was going to be okay. My brothers were in front of us, their noses pressed to the glass, trying to take in everything."

Mateo's lips quirked. "I don't know Eric and Seth well, but I can picture them doing that." Then he turned serious. "You and Ella were close?"

"She and Eric were twins, so I guess you could say they had a special bond." Her memory flittered back in time. There were years when thinking about Ella would hurt so badly she felt as if her heart would break all over again at any simple memory. She was mostly past that now and could remember her sister with fondness. "But I was the baby of the family. She watched over me. I adored her and wanted to be just like her when I grew up."

"I'm sure she'd be proud of you now."

His words touched Nina's heart. "I hope so. It's because of her I decided to become a hospice nurse."

He nodded slowly. "I wondered why you'd chosen that path. You're so young. So vibrant. I hope I don't sound insensitive, because I admire what you do, but it seems like such a morose job for someone as young as you."

The fact that he had mentioned her age twice did not slip past Nina's notice. Was he bothered by her age? Or only surprised by it in relation to her chosen profession?

"You don't sound insensitive, but on that note, I don't find it morose." She often found it difficult to explain how she felt about her career. "Yes, there's a lot of sadness, but there's also a lot of hope. The hospice program I work for is Christian based. It's an honor to be with those who are slipping from this life to the next, knowing that Jesus is waiting for them there."

He leaned back, his expression unreadable.

"You don't agree?"

Coco whimpered and slipped off her lap. She trotted over to Mateo.

Nina wondered what that was about. Coco seemed to be in tune with people's emotions. Nina believed God gave dogs the gift of feeling others' emotions in a way that humans couldn't. She had no proof of this, and sure, she could be wrong, but she'd seen enough service dogs in action to think that something special was happening here.

He cleared his throat. "You make it sound so simple. I think death is a lot more complicated than that."

Complicated wasn't a surprise. Mateo seemed like a complicated man.

"It's only complicated to the people left behind," Nina murmured. "I know you said you have some family around. You didn't mention a wife. Is there anyone special?"

His eyes shot to hers.

She felt her cheeks redden because she knew it was a nosy question. "I'm just wondering if I'm keeping you from someone."

He paused a few beats. "No, there's no one."

Coco let out a soft whimper and laid her head on his knee. He smiled faintly at her and gave her shoulders a vigorous rubbing.

Nina watched the scene with a mixture of interest and concern. She'd seen Coco do the same thing countless times before. What kind of troubling emotion had Coco sensed emanating from Mateo? Sadness? Anxiety?

She wanted to ask but she'd already been a bit too curious. Instead, she let Coco do her thing. Mateo continued to pet her and Nina was sure she could see some of the tension melt from his shoulders. Coco sighed as if relieved.

When he glanced at Nina again, he gave her a faint smile.

"Sorry, I didn't mean to pry," she said. "I just want you to know how grateful I am that you're here with me." Worried how that would sound, she hurried on. "When I sneaked out of the house, I had every intention of taking off on my own. I wasn't looking forward to it. Honestly, I was scared to death, even though I felt it was the right thing to do to keep my family safe. I'm glad I'm not alone."

"It's no problem." Mateo leaned back. Coco wriggled around beside him, making herself comfortable while staying close. "Just doing my job."

Right. His job.

Of course, she knew that, but she didn't like the reminder. An unreasonable part of her wanted him to be there because he *wanted* to be. But he was right. He was guarding her because it was his job. Nothing more, nothing less.

She couldn't help but wonder, though, was he trying to convince her of that? Or himself?

Mateo wished the lights would come back on. He wanted the storm to stop. This conversation with Nina had started to feel far too personal.

He did not do personal.

He didn't want to talk about himself. Nor did he want to bring up the case right now. Nina was already wound tight enough. Besides, at this juncture, there was nothing new to discuss, so best to let it rest and not bring it up at all.

Conversely, while he would like to get to know Nina better, he knew asking her about herself was a bad idea. He already knew enough to do his job. No need to be nosy and try to find out more. Because if he did, he would have to admit to himself that he was only asking because he was curious.

He needed to stay professional.

Mind whirling, he tried to think of something neutral to talk about.

"Other than Mrs. Wallace, the people at the Senior Center really seem to like Coco." He stroked the dog's head. She leaned into him. Maybe he should get a dog. No. He'd thought about that before. As much as he'd like to, he wasn't home enough.

Nina's eyes sparkled. "Yes, most people do."

"I've met K-9 dogs. Search-and-rescue and bomb-sniffing dogs. But I've never seen a therapy dog at work before. What exactly does she do?"

Nina arched an eyebrow and pointed at him.

He tried not to notice how pretty she looked in the flickering of the candlelight. Instead, he glanced down at the dog resting beside him, her head on his lap.

"She takes naps on people?"

She chuckled. "Not exactly. I believe she senses when people are upset. I mean we sense when others are upset, but I think dogs feel it on a deeper level. When she senses heavy emotions in people she…" Nina paused, as if searching for the right words. "Well, I guess she loves on them and usually that helps bring a sense of calm."

It took him a moment to wrap his head around what Nina was saying. She had clearly given him a pointed look.

"Wait." He jerked his hand back as he looked at the dog soaking up his attention. She lifted her head and blinked at him, awakened by his sudden movement. Here he'd thought he was doing the little rascal a favor by petting her. Was it the other way around? He narrowed his eyes at the cocker spaniel and she stared back at him. Those deep brown puppy-dog eyes seemed filled with emotion. "Are you saying she's sensing something…from me?"

"That's what she does. Yes."

Mateo glanced from Nina to Coco then back at Nina. "You think she's sensing heavy emotions from me? And what, using her special puppy powers to calm me?"

Nina laughed lightly. It was a refreshing sound, even if her laughter was over his question.

"Don't sound so horrified by that. There's

nothing wrong with being stressed and needing a little calming with her—" she made air quotes with her fingers "—'special puppy power.' I don't know anyone whose emotions are even keel all the time."

Here he thought he'd hidden his emotions so well.

He glanced at the dog again, feeling as if Nina's furry friend had betrayed him. He was unreasonably annoyed by that.

"I can tell you're carrying something heavy." Nina's words were gentle. "Coco isn't the only one who can sense that. Want to talk about it?"

Suddenly it seemed like the shack was closing in on him. No one had asked him that in ages. The last person had been Mara, his sister. Yes, he'd had a few friends who had tried to get him to open up, but he'd always shut them down. It was part of the reason he'd left Bozeman, where his parents and sister resided. The town where his family had perished.

He'd moved to Mulberry Creek for a fresh start. To get away from sympathetic glances and prying questions. Only, instead of the fresh start he'd hoped for, he felt unfilled and alone. So very alone.

He did not want to talk about Jolene and his boys. Not ever.

Only now, somehow with Nina, he felt like he did.

But he couldn't. He and Nina didn't have that kind of relationship. They had *no* relationship at all, really. Other than that she was in danger and it was his job to protect her.

Right. Keep reminding yourself of that, buddy. Because you seem awfully close to forgetting.

Yet he knew, with almost complete assurance, that if anyone would understand, it would be her. He could not cross that line, though. It would be too easy to slide down that slippery slope.

He needed to keep things professional.

"Did something happen with your job? Did a case go sideways?" Nina asked.

It was a good guess. He'd had his share of tough cases. Seen his share of rough, unpleasant things. But nothing compared to what he'd gone through in his personal life.

"No. Not my job." Why had he admitted that?

"Something personal then."

Nina's tone was soft and the look she gave him made his insides stir, made his cold hardened heart beat a little faster. She was looking at him like she cared. But what did that mean? Did she care the same way she would with any other person Coco had taken notice of? Or did she care about him in the same way he was coming to care about her?

It wasn't as if he could ask.

Yet maybe he *could* open up to her and tell her about Jolene and the boys. He found himself wanting to. Nina was so open and honest. He felt as if she would listen and try to understand what he'd gone through and how it still affected him.

But no, he couldn't.

The thought terrified him. Ridiculous that the big, tough detective was afraid of opening up to someone. Besides, the timing was all wrong.

He was working a case right now. Nina's case.

"I'm sorry." Nina winced. "I don't mean to pry. Just because I told you about Ella, that doesn't mean that you have to share anything with me. I thought maybe you wanted to talk, but, clearly, I was wrong."

Actually, she was right. He wanted desperately to tell her so. It had been so long since he'd confided in someone. Now it seemed impossible to get the words out. Like they were all locked up inside and he'd lost the key.

Coco whimpered and nudged his hand. He was tempted to yank it away, but it was too late. Nina had seen. A slight crease rested between her brows but she didn't say anything. He glanced down at the dog, giving her an accusatory look. Coco's head was tilted to the side as she gazed up at him. It was silly, impossible, he was sure, but he was certain the dog was looking at him with concern.

Could she sense his emotions? That seemed ludicrous. And yet…

He couldn't deny that in this moment his emotions did seem to be a swirling mixed-up jumble.

He gently slid Coco's head from his lap. She let out a sound of disappointment before she trotted over to Nina.

"Mateo?"

"I should do a perimeter check."

"It's still raining." She frowned. "I really don't think anyone is out there."

"I won't melt." He shrugged. "And we can't be too careful."

He strode toward the door and out into the wet evening though he didn't believe for one second there was anyone out there. Leaning against the side of the cabin, barely sheltered under the eve, he pulled in a deep breath. Then exhaled slowly. He needed to find this attacker, needed to put him behind bars.

Then he needed to send Nina and her pesky pooch back to her parents' ranch. *Then* he could get back to status quo.

Because having them both here…was just causing too much chaos for his battered heart.

Chapter Eight

The next morning the sky was heavy with clouds, leaving Mateo wondering if they were in for more bad weather. Much to his relief, the electricity had been restored sometime in the middle of the night. It was reassuring to know that while they were sequestered, they weren't so far from civilization that they were forgotten by the rest of the world.

He hadn't slept well the night before. The storm, his strained conversation with Nina, and the questioning of Tucker were all on his mind. They hadn't had enough reason to hold the guy, so he'd been released. Mateo didn't know what to make of the questioning. It bothered him that Tucker had lied. He should've known better. But did that make him guilty? No. However, Mateo wasn't convinced of his innocence, either. He was going to stay neutral on the matter until they had more facts.

He'd stayed outside far too long last night in the rain. Nina had gone upstairs before he'd come back in. She'd gotten the hint he hadn't wanted to talk anymore.

He heard the loft door open, followed by her soft footsteps on the staircase.

"Good morning." She wore a tentative smile as she entered the kitchen. "What do we have planned for today? Is visiting Golden Acres still on the agenda?"

Whether Tucker was guilty or not, there was no denying they still needed more evidence. That evidence would either prove his guilt or innocence.

"It is." Mateo lifted his cup and took a sip. He was grateful that Nina didn't mention last night. He felt a bit foolish now for running out into the rain, but at the time he'd just needed to get away. "There's plenty of coffee left if you'd like to help yourself."

Coco did a wiggly little dance at the door.

"Looks like we need to take care of business first. We'll be right back." She grabbed the leash she'd hung on a coat hook. After clipping it to Coco's collar and sliding her shoes on, they went outside. Mateo stood and watched through the window. He was sure they were safe outside, but there were no guarantees. He wasn't going to take any chances of Nina disappearing on him. She walked Coco to the edge of the forest and let her do her thing. Then Coco trotted toward the door and they came back inside.

Nina quickly filled the dog's food and water dishes then took a seat across from him. He had a cup of coffee waiting for her.

While he was grateful she hadn't brought it up, he wondered if he should apologize for last night. He didn't really want to talk about it. Definitely didn't want to draw attention to his cantankerous behavior, but he was afraid guilt would get the better of him. Before he could think it over too long, his phone rang.

He glanced at it and then shot Nina a hopeful look before answering. "Hey, Jimmy. Tell me you have something for me."

"I do. I decided this place could use a good organizing. I've been cleaning up since you left. At least, when there hasn't been anyone in the store."

"Uh-huh," Mateo said. "And?"

"I found the guy's name." Jimmy sounded pleased with himself. "Have his number, too. You still want the info?"

"You know I do."

"I'll text to it to you in a minute. Just thought I'd mention that I remembered something else. This guy, name's Lyle Weintzel, by the way, said his wife was in a nursing home and the cost was eating up his savings. Said he'd maybe stop by with some other items for me to look at, but he never did."

"A nursing home?" Mateo's interest was piqued. "Did he happen to say which one?"

"Boy, I'm not sure."

"Any chance it was Golden Acres?" Mateo knew he risked the power of suggestion, but threw it out there anyway.

"You know…" Jimmy paused, as if thinking it over. "I think he did say that. Said it was a nice place and he was happy with the care she was receiving."

"Thanks, Jimmy."

"Sure thing. I hope this pans out for you. I'll send the information now."

They said a quick goodbye and then Mateo's phone pinged with the text.

It was the man's name along with his phone number.

"Do you have a lead?" Nina asked.

"Sure do. Jimmy came through for me. The

man with the stamps? His name is Lyle Weintzel. Do you know him?"

Her brow furrowed. "I don't think so. Should I?"

He shrugged. "Probably not. But Lyle's wife is in a nursing home."

"Golden Acres?"

"Jimmy thinks so. I get that it's a big place, so you're not going to know everyone. But if his wife really is there, that could be a connection."

"Are you going to call him?"

"Since this is our only lead so far, and it's shaky at best, I don't want to give him the chance to blow me off." Mateo tapped on his phone, looking up the man's address. "Looks like he lives on Birch Street, right near the downtown area."

"We're going to go see him?"

"Yes. I want to speak with him in person."

Nina finished off her coffee. "Let's go."

He admired her gumption and they left without delay.

Lyle's place was easy enough to find. The street was lined with older homes. His appeared to be meticulously well-kept. Colorful flowers bloomed in the flower bed that lined the front porch.

A Ford truck, several decades old but devoid of rust, sat in the driveway.

Mateo parked at the curb. He glanced around. The street was quiet with only a few people out in their yards. It was the middle of the work-day, so he wasn't surprised. A few vehicles rolled past but none of them caused him any concern.

"Let's go see if he's home." Mateo grabbed the binder. "We're due for a real break in this case."

They quickly strode up the sidewalk. Mateo knocked firmly on the door. When no one an-swered, he knocked again.

"Hold yer horses!"

"At least he's home," Nina murmured.

The door was tugged open and a frail-look-ing elderly gentleman frowned at them. "I wasn't expecting company."

"I'm sorry, sir," Mateo began, "but if I could just have a few minutes of your time?"

The man's bushy white eyebrows narrowed in suspicion. "Why?"

"I was told you own a rather unique stamp collection."

The man's eyes lit with interest. "That so? You in the market to buy them?"

The way the man spoke, it sounded as if he was still in possession of them.

Mateo sidestepped the question. "Do you still have them?"

Was it possible he didn't know they were missing? Or had Jimmy been mistaken about the items?

"I do." The man looked at Nina. "You look familiar. Do I know you?"

"I'm not sure." She gave him an endearing smile. "I heard your wife is at Golden Acres. I volunteer there on occasion."

He snapped his fingers. "That's right. You're the dog lady!"

"Uh, yes."

He peered over her shoulder. "Well, where is she?"

"In the car," Nina said. "We left the windows open a crack for fresh air. And it's not too warm out today."

After last night's storm, it was downright chilly.

"Awww, go get her, would ya?"

"I'll do it." Mateo trotted down the steps. He heard Lyle pick up the conversation.

"I've seen that dog around but haven't had the chance to greet her personally," he said.

"You like dogs?" Nina asked.

"Who doesn't?"

Mateo returned with Coco on her leash.

Lyle winced when his back cracked and popped, but that didn't stop him from bending over to pet the pooch.

"What a good lil' girl you are," he said.

Mateo's eyes met Nina's. She flashed him a grin. Seemed everyone adored Coco. Mateo had to admit, the dog was hard not to like, even if she was a fluffy little traitor.

"All right," Lyle said as he creakily straightened again, "you wanted to see my stamps?"

"I do."

"Come on in." Lyle held the door open and stood back to allow them entrance.

Mateo was immediately struck by how clean the house was. Everything seemed to be in its place. There was no clutter, no stacks or piles of anything. The furniture and carpet were dated and worn, but appeared to have been treated with love. The scent of lemon furniture polish clung to the air.

"You have a very nice home," Nina said.

"Thank you." Lyle glanced around the room as if trying to see it through Nina's eyes. "The missus was a fussy housekeeper. I know it's silly, but I don't want to disappoint her by letting this place go to the dumps."

"It's not silly," Nina assured him. "It's very sweet."

"You two have a seat," Lyle ordered. "I'll go fetch the collection."

Mateo and Nina did as instructed, Coca resting near Nina's feet.

She leaned closer to Mateo and whispered, "I thought his stamps were in the lockbox? How can he still have them?"

"Either he has a similar set and Jimmy was mistaken," Mateo said, "or they aren't here after all."

A few moments later, they had their answer.

Lyle stomped into the living room. He rubbed a hand over his face. "They're gone. My stamps are gone. So's my cash. Nearly a thousand dollars of emergency money. It's gone."

Mateo rose to his feet. "Have you let anyone, other than us, into your house recently?"

Lyle frowned. "Just family. Don't get much company other than my kids and grandkids."

"Have you noticed any sign of forced entry?"

"No." His brow wrinkled in thought. "Can't say that I have."

"Do you lock your doors?"

"Yes. Of course." He hefted an aggrieved sigh. "Mostly."

Mostly. Mateo was afraid of that.

"Sometimes I forget," he admitted.

"When is the last time you remember seeing your collection?"

Lyle shot him a suspicious look. "Why all the questions?"

Mateo took out his badge and held it for Lyle to inspect. "I'm with the Mulberry Creek Police Department. I have reason to suspect your collection was stolen. When you said it was here, I was hoping I was wrong and we could just be on our way."

"Stolen." Lyle spat the word. "Right out of my house?"

"Do you recall when you saw them last?" Mateo pressed. "It's important. Then I'll fill you in on what we know."

"Pretty sure the last time I saw them was when I brought them to the pawn shop guy. Jerry, I think. Must've been a few months ago, at least."

"Jimmy," Mateo lightly corrected.

"Jimmy." Lyle slapped his thigh. "That's it. Did he take my stamps?"

"No," Mateo assured him.

"I think I need to sit." Lyle collapsed into the threadbare recliner.

Coco made a sound of commiseration then trotted over to him. She rested her head against Lyle's knee. Lyle leaned forward and scooped the small dog up, placing her in his lap. She didn't protest, simply pressed her head against his chest. She sat patiently as he methodically stroked her fur.

Nina's heart went out to the elderly gentleman. Mateo had handled the situation as gently as could be expected. Lyle looked utterly flabbergasted as he realized that his home had been violated. He looked around, as if inspecting everything with a newly critical eye.

Mateo gave him the binder and when Lyle flipped to the page with the photo of his stamps, his expression hardened. "That's them. That's them right there."

Nina hadn't really doubted, but it was good to have confirmation.

Lyle stroked Coco mindlessly, methodically, as he took a big breath. "It's hard to believe someone was in my home and I didn't even notice."

"Did you talk about your collection at the nursing home?" Mateo asked.

"My wife is very proud of my stamps. They've been in my family a long time. It's come up a time or two."

"Where did you keep them?" Mateo asked.

"In a shoebox under my bed," Lyle said. "Same place they've been for decades."

Nina and Mateo shared a look. She was wondering if perhaps his wife had unwittingly shared Lyle's secret.

It became clear quickly that while the stamps were Lyle's, he had no idea who could have taken them.

Mateo and Nina stood.

Cocoa jumped off Lyle's lap.

He stood as well.

"If you think of anything, anyone suspicious, or remember any incident that happened here that didn't seem important at the time, give me a call. Even if it's something small." Mateo handed him a card.

They left with a promise from Mateo that Lyle's collection would be returned to him as soon as possible.

"Well, that was a bummer," Nina said as they slid into Mateo's Tahoe. "I feel bad for the guy. His stamps were stolen and he didn't even realize it."

"At least they were recovered." Mateo winced. "Unlike the money."

They were only halfway down the block when Mateo's phone rang. He glanced at the screen. "It's Lyle."

Nina wondered if they'd forgotten something, but she was certain that other than the binder and Coco, they hadn't taken anything in.

He answered, telling Lyle he was on speakerphone because he was driving.

"I just thought of something," Lyle said.

"Yeah, what's that?"

Mateo shot a quick look at Nina.

"You let me look through that binder that you have. I was in a rush to get to the page with my stamps, but something has been needling at me since you left." Lyle paused then huffed out a breath. "Now, I can't be certain, mind you, because I was flipping through the pages so fast, but I'm pretty sure I recall seeing that nice ruby brooch before."

Nina's heart skittered.

Mateo's voice remained calm, but Nina noticed how his hands tightened on the steering wheel. "Do you recall where?"

"Sure do. A nice lady by the name of Beatrice Walker."

Nina knew that name.

Lyle continued. "Her husband's a resident of Golden Acres. I've seen her around with him. He's in a wheelchair but she takes him out into the courtyard every chance she gets. She's always dressed real fancy. I think they probably come from money. I guess it's possible it's not the same brooch. But it sure does look a lot like it."

"Thank you, Lyle," Mateo said. "That's very helpful."

"You think so?" He sounded hopeful. "You think it might help catch this guy?"

"If your suspicion pans out, it sure might," Mateo said. "Thank you for telling me. I'll be in touch."

Mateo disconnected and turned to Nina.

She arched a brow. "Next stop, Beatrice Walker's house?"

He nodded. "You know it."

It didn't take long to track down Beatrice's address and drive to the other side of town. Unlike Lyle's home, hers was in a fancy neighborhood. The brick two-story home was picture-perfect. No chipped or peeling paint in sight.

On a hunch that Beatrice would not approve

of Coco in her immaculate home, they left her in the car. The windows were open far enough to ensure the cool breeze would keep her comfortable.

Nina noticed everything about the home looked pristine. She thought Lyle was right. This family had money.

Mateo rang the bell. She could hear the sound reverberating through the house. It took only a few moments before a lovely elderly woman opened the door. Her hair was as white as a cotton ball, her sparkling blue eyes as bright as a sapphire. Her face was perfectly made up, as if she were on her way out the door.

"Mrs. Walker?" Mateo asked.

"Yes? Can I help you?"

Mateo held out his badge. "I do hope so. Could I ask for a few minutes of your time?"

She blinked at him in confusion then worry. "Are my children all right?"

Nina had to guess her children were middle-aged, but mothers never stopped being mothers.

"We're here about a ruby brooch."

That statement got them through the door.

Beatrice led them to the kitchen where she offered them coffee. They both declined and then, while seated at the kitchen table, Mateo got down to business. He explained what they had discovered, how a gentleman had recalled seeing her wear the brooch at Golden Acres, and why they were there now.

He slid the binder toward her, opened to the page with the item in question.

Beatrice stared at them in disbelief. "I thought I lost that brooch. I've looked high and low for it. I finally assumed that it must've fallen off. The clasp was wobbly at one time, but I'd had it fixed. It belonged to my mother."

Nina gritted her teeth at the confirmation. What kind of rotten person stole from the elderly?

"You're *sure* it's your brooch?" Mateo asked.

"Very sure." Beatrice stood and hurried out of the room. In a matter of minutes, she was back, holding a picture frame. She held it out for Mateo and Nina to view. "My husband and me."

Nina thought it looked like the sort of picture taken for a church directory. It was a close-up and the brooch affixed to Beatrice's emerald-green blazer was clearly the same brooch that was in the binder. The ruby was massive and the gold enclosing it was ornate.

They went through the same round of questions with Beatrice as they had with Lyle. She perused the binder, looking at every photo carefully, but none of the items, other than her brooch, was familiar to her.

From her vantage point Nina caught sight of the diamond-crusted crucifix again as Beatrice turned the pages. It niggled at her. She was sure she'd seen it. But where? It couldn't have been recently or she wouldn't be having such a terrible time trying to remember. Had it belonged to a resident at Golden Acres? No. Residents of the nursing home weren't allowed to keep anything valuable with them. The rooms weren't private like rooms in an assisted living facility. The residents' doors were not locked in case they needed immediate care, which would've left valuables vulnerable.

A visitor then?

She was so frustrated with herself. She wished she could remember. Or maybe she was completely wrong. Maybe she had only seen something similar at one time.

They wrapped up their visit after Beatrice obtained a promise from Mateo that the brooch would be returned to her.

Because Golden Acres seemed to be the common link, they headed there next.

Mateo let Nina sign them in then she introduced him to the director of the nursing home. She gave her permission for him to question the residents as long as they were willing.

Nina suspected many would be willing. Most of the residents were hungry for company. Nina didn't know everyone at Golden Acres, but she'd grown close to a few residents. Primarily those who came to visit Coco in the large comfortable room Nina had dubbed the parlor. That was their first stop.

A small group of women was seated around a table, playing a card game.

"Hi, ladies." Nina edged up to the table. "How is the game going?"

Mildred, a woman Nina had known from the Senior Center before she'd become a resident at Golden Acres, greeted her warmly.

"What are you up to today?" Mildred asked the question as she gave Mateo a thorough once-over. "And who do you have with you?"

"This is a friend of mine. His name is Mateo." Nina introduced him to the group, naming the women as she went around the table.

"A friend." Mildred's eyes lit up. She grinned conspiratorially at Nina. "A very handsome friend, too."

Nina flashed Mateo a look that was half apology, half amusement. "Mildred, he's not that kind of friend. Not the sort you're implying. He's just a...pal. A buddy."

"Mmm-hmm," the woman hummed. "I've heard that line before. It's almost always nonsense."

Nina laughed. "I assure you, this time it's the truth."

"We'll see." Mildred sounded very sure of herself. "Time will tell. I have a knack for sensing these things."

"I'm here for a reason..." Nina pushed ahead.

"To let me visit with that lovely pup of yours?" Wilma asked. The woman adored Coco and Nina knew she would keep her all to herself if she could. She held out her hand from the other side of the table, reaching for Coco's leash. "May I?"

"Of course." Nina led Coco around the table and handed the leash off to Wilma. The woman smiled down at Coco, who began nuzzling her knee.

"What really brings you by?" Mildred asked, circling the conversation back around.

Nina dove into the issue at hand, explaining everything in detail for what felt like the thousandth time.

"How exciting," Mildred declared. "I love a good mystery. Let's take a look at that binder of yours."

Nina wasn't expecting much. She certainly wasn't expecting Mildred to recognize the pendant that took up the first page. It was the piece that had seemed so familiar to Nina, but that she couldn't place. "Why, this belonged to Gloria Hanson."

Yes!

The moment Mildred said the name, everything clicked. She had met Gloria at the Senior Center. Now that her memory had been jostled, Nina could clearly envision the woman wearing the pendant.

"She had a nasty fall," Mildred continued. "Why someone her age was trying to go into the cellar is beyond me. I know my limitations and I would never do such a thing."

"That's right," Nina murmured, remembering now.

Mildred flipped the page again. "Oh! This one here! This belongs to Beatrice Walker. I'm sure of it. I know it went missing a few months ago. She thought she'd lost it."

"Yes, it's hers." Mateo kept his tone conversational but Nina knew he was absorbing every word. "We've spoken with her already. She'll be reunited with her brooch soon."

Mildred nodded her approval. Her eyes widened when she spotted the Rolex. "Well, I do believe this belongs to Chester Crenshaw. It was a gift from his eldest son and he was terribly proud of it. Always telling anyone who would listen that his son was quite the moneymaker. Showed it off every chance he got." Mildred glanced at Nina. "Do you remember him, dear?"

Chester Crenshaw.

"Yes. I knew him from the Senior Center, though not well." She locked eyes with Mateo as a shiver shimmied down her spine. She tried to silently convey that she had so much more to tell him about Chester Crenshaw, that it wasn't something she wanted to share in front of this group of women. He gave her an almost-imperceptible nod to let her know he understood.

Mildred continued to page through the binder as the ladies sitting with her craned their heads to view it, too. When she got to the end, she flipped it closed.

"That's all. I only recognize those three items." She glanced around the table at her group of friends. "I assume none of you recognized anything or you would have piped up."

"Not a thing," Hazel said.

"Only Beatrice's brooch," Wilma conceded.

That made sense as Nina knew the other two women had been residents of Golden Acres for quite some time. Nina didn't ever remember them visiting the Senior Center, which was where Mildred recognized both the pendant and the Rolex from.

Was the Senior Center the common link? They had begun to think it was the nursing home after identifying the owners of the stamps and brooch.

A thought occurred to her.

"Mildred, do you know if either Gloria Hanson or Chester Crenshaw had a spouse here? A reason to visit?"

"Not that I'm aware of." Mildred rubbed her temple as if trying to coax her memories loose. "But I could be wrong. I do believe that Gloria had a good friend here. I think I remember her mentioning that during one of our Thursday knitting meetings held at the Senior Center. Though, for the life of me, I can't think of who. She's been gone nearly a year now, you know. I can't seem to remember many details that far back." The woman looked perturbed over her memory loss.

Mateo placed a hand on her shoulder. "It's quite all right. You've been very helpful."

Mildred beamed at him. "Have I? It's been the longest time since I've felt useful."

"You have," he assured her.

Nina frowned as she glanced around. "Wilma, where's Coco?"

Wilma looked startled. She looked down at her hand, which was no longer holding the leash, as if surprised by the question. "Oh, dear. I must've let go of her."

Nina spun around, her eyes darting across the room. "It's not like her to wander off."

Mateo reached over and grabbed the binder off the table. "Thank you all so much for your help. It was nice meeting you, but we have a dog to find."

Nina waved a hurried goodbye as she hustled out of the parlor.

"Coco is welcomed here," Nina said, "but that was with the agreement that she would be kept under control at all times. While I'm sure she's not wreaking havoc, she certainly isn't supposed to be wandering about freely."

Nina's shoes slapped against the linoleum floor as Mateo kept pace with her. She glanced into each room they passed by.

"Does she have a favorite friend here? Someone she might wander off to see?" he asked.

Just then, Nina spotted a furry fanny with a stubby little tail that wiggled as if in overdrive. A purple leash trailed behind.

"Coco." Nina's voice was firm, commanding, as she hustled down the hallway to her dog. The spaniel's back end was sticking out of the corridor and when they rounded it, they realized she was chomping on something.

"What do you have?" Nina demanded.

But Coco had swallowed whatever she'd been munching on, leaving no trace of evidence. Nina whirled, looking up and down the hallway. No one was in sight. Then she grabbed the dog's leash.

"Do you think she got into something she shouldn't have?" Mateo asked.

"I think someone probably gave her a treat without getting permission," Nina admitted.

"It happens. Most people ask, but some just take the liberty of tossing her a snack." She winced. "I'm so embarrassed. Usually, she's better behaved than this. She hasn't been a therapy dog for long, but I thought we had the rules down."

She noticed the clock on the wall. "It's getting close to dinnertime. Do you want to question anyone else? We don't have much time before everyone begins filing into the dining room."

"Not today," Mateo said. "I have a feeling there's something you want to share with me."

Nina's eyes flitted up and down the hallway as her thoughts swirled back around to Chester Crenshaw. "Yes."

A chill cascaded down her spine.

Both Chester and Gloria were tied to the Senior Center and both had perished in falls, though the falls were nearly a year apart. Both had also had items stolen from them. Her thoughts fluttered to Tucker. He'd been volunteering at the center at least that long. Could he be the attacker after all?

"We need to talk, but not here." Nina kept her voice low. She didn't think anyone was within hearing distance though she wasn't going to take that chance.

Coco dropped to her haunches and scratched at her neck with her back foot, causing her nametag to jingle. It sounded ridiculously loud to Nina's ears. She scooped Coco up and headed for the door. Since her hands were full, Mateo signed them out.

She appreciated that he waited until they were a distance from the lot before questioning her.

"Okay. What do you know?" He gave her an expectant look as they headed out of town.

"I knew Chester Crenshaw. Not just from the Senior Center. What Mildred didn't mention was that he also died from an accidental fall."

"'Accidental.'" Mateo arched a brow. "Go on."

"He slipped in his kitchen. Hit his head on the tile floor. Never regained consciousness." Nina pulled in a breath. "His family wanted him to pass in familiar surroundings. They'd brought him home from the hospital. I was his hospice nurse."

"So we have two deaths. Both of them falls, yet because they were elderly, I assume the falls weren't looked into."

"Correct. But there's more."

He looked at her expectantly.

"When I'm working with a patient, I do my best to give the family privacy. Yet sometimes it's impossible not to overhear conversations." Nina paused briefly. "Mateo, his two sons were arguing. Quite loudly. One son accused the other of stealing a coffee can full of money. He mentioned that since their dad had lived through the Great Depression, he didn't trust banks and his life savings was stored inside the house. In the kitchen cabinet. In a coffee can. He didn't say how much, but I got the impression it was quite substantial. He also mentioned a missing watch. I assume now he meant the Rolex."

"How long ago was this?"

"I haven't been with hospice long." Nina ran a hand through her hair as she thought about it. "I'd say this happened a month ago, at the most. Our agency keeps record of everything, of course, so they could confirm the exact date."

Mateo didn't say anything for several long moments.

When he finally spoke, he looked grim.

"We don't have enough information to open a full-blown investigation into these deaths. I do agree, given the circumstances, they seem suspicious. I'll try to do some digging. One thing that has become obvious, whether it's the Senior Center, the nursing home, or your work in hospice—all of which are tied to the stolen goods, and therefore the attacker—*you* seem to be the common link."

They had known from the start that there had to be more to this case than a man burying trinkets in the park. Even if the items had been stolen, which they obviously had been, and worth a great deal of money. But what if these deaths were not accidental? Two falls resulting in the passing of at least two of the people who'd been robbed. Could they be dealing with a murderer?

A sense of dread cascaded over her.

"That's not our only problem." Mateo's voice was terse and Nina realized he had spotted something in the rearview mirror.

She whirled around in her seat to check out the road behind them. Her heart nearly exploded from her chest. A vehicle was behind them, gaining fast. That in itself wasn't what had her heart racing.

That she could blame on the gun sticking out the window, pointing right at them.

Chapter Nine

How had they been followed? Had someone put a tracking device on Mateo's Tahoe? The car behind them seemed to have come from nowhere. Nina dug her phone out of her purse, intending to call 911.

Boom.

The sound of gunshot split the air. Nina let out a shriek of surprise.

The SUV skidded as a tire blew. It fishtailed and Nina knew they were going to roll an instant before the vehicle actually did. She dropped her phone, the call unfinished.

"Hold on!" Mateo's voice was a growl.

The impact was juddering, every bone in her body felt as if it was being slammed around. She clenched her teeth in an effort to keep from crying out. Everything blended together as Nina's seat belt held her, almost painfully, in place. The airbags deployed. The vehicle slammed onto the roof, then back again, once...twice... she couldn't keep track.

Coco yipped from the back seat and Nina was grateful for the doggy car seat her niece and nephew had giggled over.

It felt as though they'd hit a brick wall when they came to a jarring stop.

Nina slowly opened her eyes. The airbag that had held her in place was already deflating. She twisted around to see Mateo slumped against the driver's door. His deployed airbag was also shrinking by the second. The window was cracked and a large tree was on the other side.

That, she realized, was what had stopped them in place.

At least they had landed right-side up.

"Mateo." Her voice was shaky. Pain ricocheted through her body but she didn't think anything was broken. Her heart skittered in her chest when Mateo didn't move. "Mateo!"

It was then that she saw the blood trickling down the window, pooling from a gash she could not see.

Coco whimpered from the back. She twisted around to find the dog securely strapped in place, staring at her. Frightened but seemingly unharmed.

In an instant, she remembered what had caused the crash. Someone had been pursuing them. They'd been chased then shot at. The tire had exploded.

Right.

Was that person still out there?

Most likely.

Swiveling her head, she scoped out their immediate surroundings for danger.

Mateo still hadn't moved. She saw the spider-webbing of glass throughout the window and suspected he'd hit his head. Hard. Probably when the SUV had slammed against the tree.

She needed to tend to Mateo, though nothing in her ever-present fanny pack would be a cure all for this dire situation. Then she needed to get him mobile so they could get out of here.

With great effort, she pushed the door wide. She shoved the airbag out of the way. They couldn't just sit there. It was too dangerous. She needed to formulate a plan. There didn't seem to be a part of her body that wasn't aching as she wiggled her way out the door. She nearly fell, still dizzy and disoriented from the crash, as she slid gracelessly from the vehicle.

And came face-to-face with a masked man.

She let out a yip of terror. Coco let out a commiserating yip of her own.

"Finally caught up to you."

"Who are you?" Nina demanded.

"Not for you to know."

She could see his eyes through the mask, but not much else. They were brown. Not as dark as Mateo's. But colder. So much colder.

What color eyes did Tucker have? Had she ever paid close enough attention? She couldn't remember. This man was the same size, but his voice was chilling.

"Looks like he smashed his head hard. Is he dead?" He motioned with his gun. From this vantage point, Mateo looked ghastly pale against the blood-streaked window. He was unmoving. "You're a nurse. Figure it out."

Her heart was hammering but she tried to ignore the gun pointed at her head. Leaning inside, she reached across her seat and pressed two fingers to Mateo's carotid artery. The pulse beating under her fingertips brought a wrenching sob to her lips.

The man mistook her sob of gratitude for one of despair.

"One down, one to go. Grab his gun."

She was *not* about to correct his misassumption.

"His gun," the man growled.

She moved without delay this time. If Mateo flinched, or moaned, made any sign of life at all, she suspected this man would shoot him point-blank. With shaking hands, she slid Mateo's gun from his holster.

Don't move, Mateo. Don't make a sound. Let him believe that you're dead.

His chest rose and fell, almost peacefully, and she prayed this man would not notice.

"Put the gun where I can see it."

The weapon felt foreign in Nina's hand. She came from a family of avid hunters, even her mother was good with a gun. But not Nina. She'd never had a desire to learn the skill. While she didn't have a problem with others hunting, she couldn't stomach the thought of doing so herself. She'd never learned to shoot.

This guy didn't have to tell her not to try anything with the gun because she didn't know how anyway. In that moment, she felt so utterly helpless. So alone.

But no, she wasn't alone.

God, please protect us. Watch over Mateo. I don't see a way out of this, but I know You can make a way where there is no way.

She turned, holding the gun gingerly, taking no chances he would see her as a threat.

"Toss it."

Nina did as she was told. The gun flew through the air and landed in the brush.

"Where are your phones?"

"I'll get them." Nina tugged Mateo's phone from where it was clipped to the dashboard. She fumbled with the airbag as she dug around for her phone on the floor.

Nina held them out to him. She longed to finish the call she hadn't been able to send, but couldn't. Not with this man watching her every move.

"Drop them."

She followed his command and he stomped on each, shattering the screens.

"Now toss them."

She picked them up and whipped them into the woods, realizing he didn't want his fingerprints on anything. Mateo's cell disappeared as his gun had, but her phone hit a tree and bounced back to the ground.

"Good enough," he snarled. "Now let's move."

The order seemed to reverberate through her.

"Okay." She took a step toward him. More importantly, she took a step *away* from Mateo.

It was the only thing she could think of to do that would protect him. She had to get this man away from him before Mateo awoke. *If* he awoke. A frisson of misery coursed through her. It was killing her that she couldn't tend to him. She ached to help him, get him to safety. But the best thing she could do right now was try to keep him safe the only way she knew how. By leading the danger away from him. "Which way?"

The masked man pointed, motioning with the gun. "Go in front of me. Don't forget, I'll be right behind you. Try to pull anything and you're a dead woman."

Nina had a horrible hunch he planned to shoot her whether she cooperated or not. Yet she couldn't argue with him. Not when Mateo was only feet away, utterly out cold and unable to fend for himself at the moment.

Coco whined miserably but Nina didn't dare look back. She took one step then another. Her battered body seemed to gain strength as she moved.

They trudged through the woods. Nina was only vaguely familiar with this area. The hunting cabin was miles away, but the area was still very rural. If she wasn't mistaken, Mulberry

Creek—which was more of a river, really—ran nearby. They had passed over it quite a ways back where it rushed under the road.

Every now and again, she felt something jab her back. She knew it was the tip of the handgun and that he was taunting her with it. She kept walking, her heart pounding, her mind reeling. Was Mateo okay? Would this man stop at the vehicle on his way back? Was Mateo still in danger?

Probably. The realization terrified her.

"Are the items in the box really worth killing for?" Nina asked.

"You're not allowed to ask questions."

"Really?" Nina hated how her voice trembled. She did not want to give this man the satisfaction. "I assume you're going to kill me. What would it hurt if you answer me first?"

They came to a ridge. Nina could see the water flowing below. She knew then what he planned to do. He would shoot her, allowing her to tumble over. Her body would be carried away by the water. Would anyone ever find her? It was possible that they wouldn't.

Stop, she told herself. *You're not dead yet. You have a brain. Use it.*

Keeping herself as far from the edge as she could, she gave him an imploring look.

"Why are you stealing from the elderly? Why are you burying their treasures? Are you hoarding them for later? Or is it all for the thrill?" She was not going to admit she suspected he'd killed at least two people.

"The thrill?"

His voice had an edge and she knew she'd offended him. He gripped the gun but his hand had fallen to his side.

Keep him talking. Find a way out of this.

"That's how it looks to me. Like you're just in this for the thrill of it."

"You know nothing, you nosy woman. Why couldn't you just leave well enough alone? You stole from me!"

Stole from *him*? What about the people whose lives he'd infiltrated? He'd taken their precious items. He'd possibly done worse.

"You're the one that stole." She tried to keep the quiver from her voice. She did not want him to know how afraid she was. "All of the items in that box belonged to other people. You had no right to them."

"Because of you—" he waved his gun her

way "—everything, *years* of planning, has been ruined. I think you need to pay for that."

Was there anything she could say to calm this angry killer?

Mateo came to with a jolt. His awareness that something was terribly, horrifically, wrong had snapped him back to reality. He stuffed down a groan as pain ricocheted through his head. He blinked hard, trying to clear his hazy, blurry vision. Nausea swelled up but he chose to ignore it.

"Nina?" His voice was hoarse, muted. When she didn't answer, he twisted his head away from the tree he'd found himself looking at through the spiderweb cracks of his window. Now he faced her empty seat. Horror filled him when he realized her door was open and he couldn't see her anywhere.

Coco whimpered and the sound terrified him because he knew Nina would not take off and leave her dog behind. Granted, she wouldn't leave him behind, either, but that thought took a few more seconds to surface.

Or would she?

Had she gone for help?

No.

In that instant, Mateo remembered they had been followed. Shot at. Someone had been after them. He had to assume that *someone* had taken Nina while he'd been unconscious. He wanted to yell in frustration, but that wouldn't help anyone. He reached for his sidearm.

Gone.

Of course it was. He hoped Nina had it with her for protection, but he doubted that.

The only way to help her was to get moving. It took him too long to get out of the vehicle, past the floppy airbags, and out Nina's door since his was jammed against the oak. He caught sight of his face in the side mirror. The amount of blood made him do a double-take. He quickly shrugged out of his jacket and swiped his face clean, then held it against the wound for a moment to see if it was still bleeding. It was a relief that it didn't seem to be.

Coco whimpered.

"Don't worry, little one." He reached for the back door and tugged it open. "I won't leave you behind." He released the dog from the safety straps that had undoubtedly kept her from harm. When he had her out of the vehicle, the spaniel wriggled in his arms. He placed her on the ground and watched as she trotted off toward the woods. She looked like a pup on a mission. No hesitation.

Coco was a therapy dog. She was *not* a tracker. Mateo knew that much. He also knew that she was a dog who loved her owner. When Coco took off for the brush, he followed, having no doubt that she was looking for her master. Realizing that, in his addled state, he'd forgotten her leash, he commanded her to heel.

The dog froze in place but gave him an imploring look, as if torn between wanting to be obedient and needing to race toward her beloved Nina. She didn't trot back to him but she did wait for him to catch up. Mateo realized Coco had stopped next to a shattered cell phone in a purple case. It was Nina's, he knew. The phone looked broken beyond use; he grabbed it and stuffed it into his pocket anyway.

They got moving again and Coco obediently stayed close but was always a step or two ahead of him. He was okay with that. What he would not be okay with was letting her run off. If he lost Nina's cherished furry friend, she would be heartbroken.

If she's alive. He clenched his teeth and banished the thought from his brain. Nina was alive. She had to be.

Please, God.

As his head thudded in pain, and his vision remained blurred, it was the most articulate prayer he could scrounge up. The best plea he could muster in the moment. Yet he felt the weight of it, so heavy and intense it could have knocked him to his knees.

Maybe it should have.

Mateo suddenly felt the urge to drop to his knees and pray as he hadn't prayed in years. He couldn't do that, couldn't take the time. Nina needed him to find her. Needed him *now.* So he would pray as he ran—or more like stumbled through the woods.

He still felt lousy, weak, bleary-eyed. The throbbing in his head had not subsided, but he couldn't worry about any of that now. It occurred to him that he was blindly following a dog into the woods, deeper by the minute. What if she wasn't leading him to Nina? Was it possible she was just running?

When Coco stopped and sniffed the air then the ground and began to move again, he relaxed. They moved through the woods for what felt like forever, but he was aware it maybe only felt that way because he was in rough shape.

An angry voice reached Mateo's ears.

Then a softer, gentler voice. Nina.

Thank You, God. She's alive.

"Coco, come." His voice was low but firm.

The dog hesitated then reluctantly obeyed. Mateo scooped her up in his arms because it would do no good to have her race to her master's side.

He couldn't hear what Nina was saying, but it was undoubtedly her. He edged forward slowly, trying to be quiet. He felt awkward as an ox after the accident. And helpless. He had no weapon and held a squirming pooch in his arms. His coordination was questionable at the moment.

God, help us because I'm too much of a mess to help myself, let alone Nina.

He could see them now. A man dressed in black had his back to Mateo. Nina stood in front of him. The man waved his gun in the air.

"Stop talking!" he yelled, his anger reverberating through the woods. He raised his hand as if to pistol-whip Nina. "You nosy, meddling—"

Before Mateo could react, Coco leapt from his arms. She let out an angry bark at the stranger. The man whirled and the dog lunged at him, clasping the hand with the gun in her jaw. She held on tight, like the proverbial dog with a bone. Mateo was surprised she had that sort of feistiness in her, but he realized Coco was only protecting the person she loved.

Nina shrieked in surprise and ran to Mateo, calling for Coco to come.

Everything happened fast then. The man kicked at Coco but missed and she leapt away. The gun went flying when the dog released his hand. Mateo could see blood streaming from his fingers. The guy let out a feral-sounding scream as he clasped his injured hand with his good hand.

Nina broke through the tree line, Coco at her heels. Mateo only briefly contemplated tackling the man, but he was not at full strength. Not even close after the rollover. Mateo couldn't see where the gun had landed. Was it at the man's feet, within easy reach? Best to go on the offensive.

"Run!"

Mateo let her lead the way, knowing neither one of them knew where they were or where they were going. They had one goal: to escape. He was determined to stay behind Nina, to put himself between her and a bullet should the man decide to shoot. He was about to tell her not to slow down because of him. Then he realized she'd been in the accident as well. That was probably why she wasn't moving as quickly as he knew she was capable of. He prayed they were moving fast enough.

He glanced down once and was satisfied that Coco was keeping stride with them. She had found Nina and was not going to let her out of her sight.

"We need to make a plan." Mateo, an avid runner, was embarrassed that his voice came out in a huff. His head was hurting fiercely and nausea swirled. He had a concussion, he was sure of it, though there was nothing he could do about it.

Nina glanced over her shoulder then slowed. Finally, they came to a standstill. He knew she sensed he needed a break. It was a blow to his ego, but he wasn't going to argue.

"I have a plan." She looked in the direction they'd been headed. "When he had me stand at the edge of the cliff, I noticed there's a foot-bridge up ahead. If we cross over, maybe we can lose him."

Coco whined.

They both glanced down. She was scratching manically at her neck and whimpering.

Nina frowned. "What's the matter, Coco?"

"She was doing that earlier."

Nina knelt and pulled her dog close. "Do you have a thorn? Did a sticker bush of some sort get you?"

He watched as she ran her finger around Coco's collar, looking for whatever was causing the dog discomfort.

"What is this?" Nina's brow creased as she popped off Coco's collar. "That's not a thorn."

Mateo knew instantly what he was looking at. A tiny black object affixed to the inside of the dog's collar. A small tuft of hair had come off when Nina removed the collar, having gotten stuck on the backside of the device. It had been tugging at Coco's skin, making her uncomfortable.

"That's a tracker." His gaze swiveled around the forest. Were they being stalked right now? Probably. "At Golden Acres, when she went missing—"

"That's how he followed us." Nina tore off the tracker, popped the collar back on the dog, and took off. "Come on!"

Mateo hurried after her, his adrenaline kicking in, helping him ignore the pain. When he spotted the footbridge ahead, he groaned. It was ancient.

They slowed.

"That doesn't look safe. I don't think we can cross."

She eyed him. "We can't. You must outweigh me by fifty pounds."

At least.

"But I can. And this—" she held up the tracking device "—has to. It's the only way to get him off our tail."

"I don't—"

He didn't have the chance to finish his protest. Nina hustled to the bridge. He understood her rush. Time could be running out. If this man was easily tracking them, he may only be a minute or two behind. Mateo assumed the guy had spent time looking for his gun or he'd be on their backs by now.

Or perhaps he was taking his time because he had a tracking device that would eventually lead the way.

A protest dangled on the tip of his tongue but he leaned down and grabbed Coco instead. Kneeling next to her, holding her collar, he began to pray as Nina crossed the wobbly bridge. It swayed under her weight. The weathered rope that held the planks in place looked frayed, worn. He could hear it creak. Groan. Moan in protest.

The water rushed below.

Please, God… The prayer, on a constant loop, filled his mind.

Mateo watched her cross, and his gaze drilled into her back as if he could hold her up by his sheer will.

She stopped halfway then whipped the tracking device across to the other side. It was so small, he didn't see where it landed, but he didn't need to know.

When Nina turned around, he realized how afraid she was. Her jaw was set. Her eyes were wide. She looked terrified yet determined. His admiration for her soared. Admiration and… yes, he could admit it to himself. It would be ridiculous to deny it.

He was falling for her.

He could hear the bridge complain continuously under her weight. *Please, God…*

She stopped when she reached the end and stepped onto solid ground. He rushed forward, ready to pull her along. But as she knelt, he realized she was taking something out of her fanny pack.

A small scissors.

"For gauze," she whispered. "Or a rickety

old bridge." She opened it wide and began to saw away.

The urge to grab her and run hit Mateo hard, but he decided to give her just a moment.

Coco had stilled, her attention now on the woods.

Nina quickly moved to the other side of the rope bridge and did the same.

Coco growled.

Nina leapt to her feet. Her eyes large and questioning.

"I think he's coming." Mateo whispered the words as he scooped up Coco. Together they rushed into the thickest part of the foliage. They crouched down, making themselves as small as possible. Then they waited.

So much time passed that Mateo began to wonder if Coco had misled them. He placed the dog on the ground between them, where she sat obediently, as if she understood the gravity of the situation.

The brush to their left rustled.

Coco stiffened but remained silent as Nina held a gentle hand against her neck, holding her in place next to her body.

They watched as the attacker trudged out of the woods. He held the gun in a hand that was smeared with blood. In his other hand, he held a cell phone. He still wore his mask as he moved to a spot right in front of them. The man studied the phone screen then glanced up at the bridge. He hesitated only a moment before he made his way to the unsteady crossing.

Mateo realized the gunman probably assumed Mateo, who was roughly the same size, had crossed without incident.

The man took a step onto the bridge.

Nina reached out her free hand and latched onto Mateo's fingers, holding them tight. He squeezed back because it was the only support he could offer in that moment.

Their attacker took a step. Then another. Finally reached the middle of the bridge.

The bridge creaked.

Groaned.

Whined as if in misery.

Pop.

One side of the rope bridge gave way. The man let out a guttural yell and dropped to his knees. His phone and gun fell from his hands, flying into the water below. He gripped the wooden slats that made the walkway as—

Pop.

The other side of the bridge gave way and

the whole thing swung toward the wall of the cliff on the far side.

He crashed into it but held on.

Nina let out a whimper.

The man was no threat to them, though he was climbing the slats of wood now that the bridge had turned into a makeshift ladder.

"Should we do something?" Nina whispered.

"It looks like he's going to climb to safety. The best thing we can do is get out of here before he sees us. Hopefully, he'll assume we've crossed to that side and look for us there."

They stayed hidden as they watched through the branches.

In a matter of minutes, the man had managed to scramble to the top. Once he reached solid ground, he bent over, hands on knees, his chest heaving as if he needed a moment to catch his breath.

"I think he had the scare of his life." Nina didn't sound sorry about that.

Mateo rose, pulling Nina with him. She was only an arm's length away. And then she was closer, in his arms, pressed against his chest. He held her tight as she trembled, and he wished he could wash all her fears away. Despite the wrongness of the situation, it felt right to have her in his embrace. As if she belonged there.

"I didn't want to kill him," she murmured, "so I'm glad he made it to the other side, but I don't know what it's going to take to get him to leave us alone."

Mateo knew that nothing short of death, or being caught, was going to get this man out of Nina's life.

Chapter Ten

Nina slipped from Mateo's arms as they watched from their hidden vantage point. The man looked right and then left, as if trying to decide which way to go. Without his phone as his guide, he seemed a bit lost. He had no way of knowing the now-useless tracking device was only feet away. He let out a howl of frustration and kicked at the ground hard enough to send dirt into the air.

Coco whimpered and huddled against Nina's leg. She bent and rubbed the dog's head in an effort to comfort her.

Take off your mask, you coward. The thought seemed to play on repeat in her mind. But her silent plea went unheard. How could they be so close to having answers, so close to catching this guy, yet so far away?

Now that he was safely on the other side of the river, they could easily take off back toward the road. Yet it seemed wise to let him believe they were on his side of the river as well. Let him go off on a wild-goose chase as he tried to track them down. She understood why they were staying put, staying out of sight, for now.

A moment later, still clearly furious, he stomped off and disappeared into the woods.

Mateo swayed. Nina reached out a hand to steady him.

"You hit your head. There was blood on the window. I was so scared—" Her voice cracked as tears burned. His face was still a bit of a mess, though he'd clearly made an effort to clean himself up.

He slid a finger under her chin and looked into her eyes. "Hey, I'm okay."

She nodded. "You have no idea what a relief it was to see you come through those woods. He thought you were dead, you know. That's the only reason he left you behind. You looked like you were in pretty rough shape. He didn't question it."

"I hate that I wasn't there to protect you." His hand fell to his side.

"You did protect me. You came after me." She studied his face. "How are you feeling?"

"I'm fine."

"Now isn't the time for sugarcoating, Mateo. I'm a nurse, remember?"

He nodded.

She reached over and felt the lump on the side of his head. Her fingers came away with crusted blood. She opened up her fanny pack and took out an alcohol wipe to scrub them off. It was time to put away her emotions and act like the professional she was. "You need to see a doctor. Are you dizzy?"

He pursed his lips and didn't answer.

"Considering how you swayed, I'm going to take that as a yes. Nausea?"

Again, he hesitated, but after she shot him a disapproving look, he nodded.

"Any vomiting?"

"No."

"Blurry vision?"

He glanced away and she took that as another affirmative.

"How bad?"

"It's getting better. It was pretty bad when I first came to."

She blew out a breath. He'd been knocked unconscious, had a lump on his head, and was suffering from nausea and double vision.

"You have a concussion."

"I know."

"You should rest, but that doesn't really seem to be an option right now." The sky was darkening and she was afraid another storm was moving in. They couldn't spend the night out here. She looked around, suddenly feeling disoriented. "We need to get back to civilization. Which way do we go?"

"Uh." Mateo looked baffled by the question. He eyed their surroundings. "I'm not sure."

"Your compass, Mateo." Her tone was gentle as she gave the reminder. Confusion was another sign of a concussion.

"Oh."

He lifted his wrist and stared at the watch, moving it close to his eyes then away again.

Nina bit her lip as she watched him squint, trying to make out which way the arrows pointed. She knew they had to head west to get to the road. It should be an easy hike as soon as they started moving. At least, it would've been easy under normal circumstance. She wasn't so sure now, with Mateo's vision blurred and his head concussed.

She gently reached out and clasped his wrist in her fingers. He gave her a startled look. The smile she gave him felt forced. Worry niggled at her, and she didn't want him to know. She didn't like the state he was in.

"Let me look." It took her only a moment to determine which direction they needed to head. She let go of his wrist but clasped his hand instead. He didn't argue and she was glad. She doubted he realized she was holding his hand so it would be easier for her to lead the way. It would do no good to have him stumble or stray.

It was slow going as they trudged out toward the road. Coco walked slowly behind them, as if she, too, sensed Mateo was struggling.

"I heard him yelling at you." Mateo's voice sounded strained and Nina assumed it was from pain. "Did he reveal anything?"

Disappointment zinged through her. "I tried to get him to talk. He didn't reveal anything. I couldn't even get him to admit to stealing the items."

"What *did* he say then?"

"He was furious that I stole from him and accused me of ruining everything."

"Right. It's a little bit harder to steal from the unsuspecting elderly once law enforcement is on to you," he mumbled. "I can't help but wonder how long this has been going on. The items that have been identified seem to have been stolen somewhat recently. But are there other boxes buried in the park? Or somewhere else?"

"I did ask why he buried the box in the park." She let out a little huff. "He told me it was none of my business."

"He's a real chatty fellow, I take it," Mateo said wryly. "I hope you didn't ask him about Gloria and Chester."

"No." Nina shook her head. "I didn't want to anger him. He was mad enough about the items in the box. I didn't dare ask him if he murdered someone."

Mateo stumbled over a branch and Nina's grip on his hand tightened. She needed to get him out of here. He needed rest, not to be making a strenuous trek through the woods when he couldn't even see clearly.

Coco whimpered.

"Do you need to take a break?" Nina asked.

"No." Mateo sounded annoyed that she'd asked. "I want to get out of these woods and get back to work."

Nina saw no point in telling him that was a bad idea. He wouldn't want to hear it, so she'd deal with that later.

"I need a break," Nina said.

Mateo gave her a skeptical look. She knew

he was about to argue that they were not going to take a break on his account.

"I'm starving." Nina was telling the truth, not just using it as an excuse to stop. "I really wish we had some water."

"I could chug a gallon," Mateo admitted.

"I don't have water, but I do have a snack."

Mateo's stomach growled. "Guess I'm starving, too."

She unzipped her fanny pack and pulled out two peanut butter granola bars. She handed him one. "I wish I had more."

"Hey, this is better than what I have. Which is nothing." He tore open his wrapper.

Coco watched them with interest. Her nose twitched as she scented the treat in the air. Then she plopped her head down on her paws and looked forlorn.

Dog food was one thing Nina did not have with her.

She broke her granola bar in two, intending to share with Coco. Before she had a chance, Mateo had handed the dog *his* granola bar. The whole thing.

"Mateo!"

"What?" His eyes widened as he looked at Nina then back at the dog. "Oh, no. Was there something in there that she can't have? Something bad for her? I know a lot of human food is bad for dogs. I should have asked." He looked like he wanted to take the treat back, but Coco had gobbled it up already.

"No, it's fine. It's just that you said you were starving."

"I am. But so is she and she doesn't understand what's going on. I couldn't have her thinking we were being neglectful. You said that she came from a neglectful hoarding situation. I guess I thought maybe that meant she hadn't been properly fed. I didn't want her to worry."

Nina was sure she could literally feel her heart swell in her chest. "That is the sweetest thing anyone has ever done for me. Even if it was actually done for my dog." She handed him half of the granola bar she held, instantly noticing that he didn't lift his hand to take it. "Please. I'll stress if you don't eat something."

"Okay." He took the proffered snack.

It only took them moments to finish.

Thunder rumbled overhead.

Mateo glanced skyward. "Sounds like we're in for another storm. Hopefully, we can get back to the SUV and take shelter. It's not ideal, but I think it'll take our attacker a while to get back across the river if he even tries. At least now he's without a weapon." He squinted at Nina. "Speaking of which, what happened to mine?"

"He made me toss it along with your phone."

"I figured as much. That reminds me, I have your phone." He pulled it out and toyed with it a minute. As Nina suspected, her cell was hopelessly beyond use.

"We should keep walking." Nina would like nothing more than to allow Mateo to rest a bit longer but now, with another storm coming, it was more important than ever to find shelter.

"Coco was really something special earlier. I didn't get a chance to tell you this, but the second I let her out of her safety seat, she was on your trail. You know, I read somewhere that dogs can smell their owners from several miles away. When she took off after you, I wasn't sure how far you'd gone. But she was determined to find you. It's obvious she adores you."

"The feeling is mutual." Nina felt a wave of gratitude. "I saved her life when I brought her home with me. Today she saved mine."

Thunder rumbled again. Louder this time. And with it, another sound that was entirely incongruous.

"Did you hear that?" Mateo asked.

"Yes." Nina stilled a moment, canting her head to the side, straining her ears. The wind had picked up, but she was sure she could hear sirens in the distance. "Is that what I think it is?"

"I hope that means help is on the way."

The very thought got them moving faster.

Hope swelled in Mateo's chest. The wailing of sirens grew louder, cresting over the echoes of the incoming storm. They followed the sound as Coco now trotted ahead of them. He hated that he was so unsteady on his feet. Hated the feeling of inadequacy because, try as he might, he still could not see clearly.

"How do you think they found us?" Nina asked.

"Not sure."

Flashing lights could be seen through the trees, letting them know they were close to the road. The vehicles kept going, first one then another. He and Nina were hustling along now. So close to reaching the help that they needed. They broke from the forest and spotted the two cruisers pulled over less than a mile down the road. The emergency vehicles were parked next to a tan car. Mateo was certain it was the vehicle their attacker had been driving.

A third cruiser approached and slowed as the driver spotted them. The car came to a stop and Officer Lainie Hughes buzzed down her window.

Rain began to fall then. Big, pattering drops.

"Mateo!" Lainie cried. "What a relief. Get in."

He and Nina did not need to be told twice. He rounded the vehicle and nearly collapsed into the front seat. Nina and Coco slid into the back.

"The guy that ran us off the road is out there somewhere," Mateo warned her. "But I don't think he's nearby." He gave her a quick rundown of what had transpired.

When he was finished, Lainie radioed the two officers parked right up the road to give them an update. Next, she called for backup so they could check the woods in the area the man had disappeared.

Mateo waited for her to finish.

"How did you find us?"

"We had a call about a rollover spotted in the woods." Lainie went on to describe how a teenager was on the way to town to meet up with friends. "Her family owns this land, their house is right around that curve. First, she spotted the abandoned car on the side of the road. She slowed to be sure no one was inside needing assistance. Then she noticed there was another vehicle, with extensive damage, smashed up against a tree down the incline. She got out to inspect and realized the car was empty but there was blood smeared across the window. She called 9-1-1 and gave the license plates number of both cars. We realized real quick that the Tahoe was yours. The other vehicle was stolen. No surprise there."

"Where is the girl now?" Nina asked, her voice full of concern.

"As soon as we realized one vehicle was Mateo's, and the other most likely belonged to the perp, we told her to head somewhere safe. We've already received confirmation that she's back home with her parents."

That was a relief.

"Would you mind pulling up ahead?" Mateo asked. "I should assist Officers Rollins and Baker."

"I'm sorry," Nina said, not sounding the least bit so, "but *no* you should not. That's a terrible idea. You have a concussion."

Lainie cut a narrowed-eyed gaze his way. "You could have mentioned that."

Nina continued. "You should be resting and, instead, you just hiked through the woods."

He was grateful that she didn't blurt out in front of Officer Hughes that he had blurry vision. And that he'd been stumbling around. As her superior officer, Mateo felt she didn't need to know that.

"Now what?" Nina asked. "Do we go back to the hunting cabin?"

Mateo shook his head and immediately regretted it when he was sure he felt his brain slam around from one side of his skull to the other. He hated to admit that Nina had a point. He'd probably be more of a hindrance than a help right now.

"I don't think going to the shack is a good idea. We know he used the tracker on Coco's collar to follow us. While he doesn't know exactly where we're headed, he may be able to figure it out as there's not a lot of residences out this way." He pinched the bridge of his nose, fighting against pain and nausea, and willed himself to think.

Where could they go on short notice?

Certainly not back to the ranch.

His house? No. By now the perp had probably figured out who he was. Especially since he'd clearly been at Golden Acres earlier where Mateo had introduced himself and had been asking questions.

"My place has a great security system." Lainie gave a one-shoulder shrug. "If you don't have another safe house in mind, you're welcome to stay with me. I've been putting in extra hours, so I'm hardly there. We can run to the shack to grab your things."

It was a generous offer, considering the danger they were in. Mateo was tempted to turn it down, but they were running treacherously low on options.

"Thanks, Lainie. I think we'll take you up on that." He shifted in his seat and tried to gather his thoughts. "There are a few things I'd like to take care of first. For one, someone needs to track down Tucker Holden. Find out where he was this afternoon. Better yet, have someone take a good look at his right fingers. Coco got a hold of this guy's hand when she realized he was going to strike Nina. I'm not sure how much damage she did, but there was a lot of blood. There would definitely be evidence of a dog bite."

He gave her an update on what had transpired at the nursing home. The discussion with the ladies, then Coco disappearing and their later realization she'd been tagged with a tracking device.

"That means our guy was at Golden Acres this afternoon." Lainie's voice rose in excitement. "Are there security cameras?"

Mateo was wondering the same thing and it would've been his next question for Nina, if Lainie hadn't asked it first. He glanced over his shoulder and shot Nina a questioning look.

"Yes, there are some. I'm not sure there's one in the area where we found Coco."

This guy was likely familiar with the nursing home, so Mateo had to guess he'd chosen a spot where he wouldn't be caught on camera messing with the dog. However, that didn't mean a camera hadn't caught him somewhere.

"We'll need a warrant, but it's imperative we get that security footage. We also need to look into every male that was working this afternoon."

"That could be a lot of men," Nina said. "It's a large facility. There's medical staff, cooks, cleaning staff. It's a weekday, so there were probably supply deliveries as well."

He frowned. "We'll also need to look at the sign-in book in case this guy was just a visitor."

He didn't have high hopes that the book would be of any help. No one monitored the sign-in. It was just as easy to jot down a fake name as it was to bypass the registry and not sign it at all. Still, he didn't want to overlook any detail that may help.

"I'll let Chief Barsness know we need a warrant," Lainie offered.

He was about to protest when he felt Nina's hand land on his shoulder. She gave it a tight squeeze. "That would be very helpful, Officer Hughes. If I had my way, Mateo would be headed to the ER right now to be looked over."

He shot a scowl at her over his shoulder. He was not going to the ER. There was too much work to be done. They were getting close now, he could feel it. "I've been looked over. You said I have a concussion. I've had one before and, if I recall, there wasn't anything a doctor could do about it anyway. You already diagnosed me and I trust you."

"I'm glad." Nina flashed him a sweetly smug smile. "Then you'll trust me when I tell you that you need stitches. That gash is too much for a butterfly bandage. Whether you like it or not, you need a trip to the ER. The nurse says so."

Well, he'd walked right into that.

Chapter Eleven

Lainie pulled her vehicle directly into the garage and immediately lowered the door. The less her neighbors saw, the better. Mateo didn't want small-town gossip spreading that Lainie had company. It might be too easy to figure out just who her guests were.

Though law enforcement was scouring the woods for the attacker, the guy had had a head start. If he followed the river, he would be out of the woods by now. The main road was less than a mile from where the footbridge had been. Officer Rollins had met the Dawsons, whose daughter had found the vehicles. He had discovered they had built the footbridge years ago, when their kids were small, to get from their home to their favorite picnic area on the other side of the river. They were warned to be on the lookout for the gunman.

Officer Baker had retrieved Mateo's weapon and phone.

Mateo itched to be in on the investigation but Nina wouldn't allow it. They had made a quick stop at the hunting cabin to gather their things, including one last casserole from Julia and Coco's dog food.

Then they spent what felt like forever in the ER. But Mateo knew that the doctor had given him priority and stitched him up expediently.

While Nina had waited in the ER with him, Lainie had run into a store to purchase two disposable phones, one for each of them. It was the best she could do under the rushed circumstances. They had already set them up on the drive to the house. While the cheap phones were not ideal, it sure beat being without communication.

Lainie had been in touch with Officer Baker so they could stay apprised of the situation. As soon as she had Mateo and Nina settled, she was going back out to assist with the search. He hated being left behind but knew he had no choice.

Lainie led them into her house. It was cozy, with ordered piles of clutter scattered throughout. Mateo could relate. Working odd shifts, being called in for overtime, and being wiped out physically and mentally when you were home wasn't always conducive to the best housekeeping. Not that her house was messy. It looked more like organized chaos.

"Sorry, I only have one guest room," she said. "You'll find it at the end of the hallway."

"Not a problem," Mateo assured her. "As long as you have a couch, I'm good."

She checked her watch. "I still have several hours left of my shift. I apologize, the fridge is pretty empty. It's been a hectic week." She winced. "Not that I have to tell you that."

Nina lifted her mother's chicken and dumpling casserole. "Not a problem. We'll save you some."

Lainie smiled. "Thanks. I'll grab groceries at some point. Mateo, there's a linen closet at the end of the hall. You'll find bedding there. I'll set the alarm before I go and you can expect me back shortly after midnight, unless something comes up."

"Thank you, Lainie." Nina gave her a grateful smile. "It's gracious of you to offer us a place to stay."

"Don't think anything of it." Lainie motioned toward Mateo. "The detective here would do anything for any one of us. The police force is like one big family." She strode to the door. "Stay safe, you two. I'm guessing our perp has his hands full right now, but if something comes up, the department is just a shout-out away." She stopped in her tracks and whirled around wearing a guilty expression, as if something had just occurred to her. "Before I go, there's something I should probably show you. Follow me."

Nina placed the casserole on the counter as she and Mateo both lugged their bags along with them. Coco's nails clicked across the kitchen's tiled floor.

Lainie stopped in the middle of her living room. It took Mateo a moment to figure out what he was looking at. He blamed his rattled brain for the delayed reaction. "An evidence board."

Blocking most of the big-screen TV was a large chalkboard, held in a wooden frame, on wheels. It had been ages since he'd seen a chalkboard. This one was clearly covered with details of Nina's case.

Lainie winced, as if embarrassed. "Sorry. I know we have something similar back at the station, but this case has been weighing on me.

It helps to clear my head when I can just get everything out." She motioned at the board. "Gran was a schoolteacher and got to keep it when she retired because they'd switched to whiteboards. Gramps saved this for me because I had so much fun with it when I was little."

Mateo chuckled. "What would he think if he knew you were tracking a murder suspect with it?"

She grinned at him. "He'd be proud, for sure. Gramps was a detective for the Seattle PD for two decades. He's the reason I went into law enforcement. Anyhow, this is what we know so far." She turned her attention to Mateo. "Have I missed anything?"

Mateo and Nina shared a look.

"The only thing missing is the new information from this afternoon." Mateo eyed a piece of chalk, his fingers itching to get everything updated.

"Feel free to add anything you feel is relevant." Lainie winced. "Or if you think this is stupid, feel free to ignore it altogether."

"It's not stupid. It's brilliant." Mateo was impressed with the information she'd included. She had a great attention to detail. "We'll update it and maybe later we can all go over everything together."

Lainie's eyes glittered with excitement. "Perfect. Now, I better get going." She took off toward the door again.

"Keep me updated," Mateo called after her.

"Sure thing," she replied over her shoulder. Then the door that led from the kitchen into the garage banged shut, announcing her departure.

Nina let the large backpack drop from her shoulder. She moved closer to the board. "That lady has been busy."

He nodded. "I'm impressed. I have a whiteboard similar to this in my office. It helps to see everything laid out like this. While we were at the shack, I kept details in my notebook, but it's just not the same."

Nina's stomach growled. "I'm still famished. The casserole from Mom won't take long to reheat. I'm going to pop it in the oven, get Coco settled. Then get myself settled. You should relax a bit. After we eat, we can go over everything again."

Mateo's new phone rang. He hadn't adjusted the volume and cringed at the blaring sound.

"It's Lainie." He had figured so before glancing at the screen as he hadn't had a chance to give his number to anyone else yet. "Hey, there. Do you have news already?"

Nina's eyebrow quirked and she took a step closer.

"I just got word that Tucker Holden is missing."

"Tucker's missing? I'm putting you on speakerphone for Nina's benefit." He looked at the phone but it blurred. Nina reached over and pressed a button so he could continue the conversation. "Define missing."

"Chief Barsness went to his parents' house himself. He's not taking too kindly to the fact that this man has tried to kill you more than once. First with the explosion, then the rollover. When he arrived, Tucker's mom claimed he was in his room. However, when she went to fetch him, he was gone. Chief believes she didn't know he'd left. The problem is she couldn't recall exactly when she'd seen him last. Apparently, he's been spending a lot of time in his room since his visit to the station."

"This guy keeps looking guiltier and guiltier," Mateo said.

"His mom is sure he took off because he's scared."

Mateo fought down a groan. "That seems to be his excuse for everything."

"Could be true," Lainie said, "but I agree. He keeps making some very bad choices. I've got to go, but I'll let you know if I find out anything else."

They disconnected and Mateo placed the phone on the coffee table. He wanted to turn the ringer down, but didn't want to prove to Nina yet again that he was still having some trouble with his vision. He'd let it go for now.

"Mateo, I can't believe it's him." Nina ran a hand through her hair. "All we know for sure is that he put a note on your vehicle."

"Are you willing to stake your life on that?"

Nina bit her lip. Then shook her head. "No. I suppose not."

"I know you think I'm jaded, and maybe I am, but there's a reason for that." Mateo's tone had gentled. "I've learned the hard way you can't let your guard down. You can't let your heart rule a situation. Just because you want him to be innocent, doesn't mean he is."

Nina sighed out a breath. "You're right."

Coco made a whining sound deep in her throat that grabbed Nina's attention.

"You're hungry, aren't you? And I'm sure you need to take care of business. Let's go, girl." She pointed a finger at Mateo. "I know you won't rest. But at least try to relax."

"Sure." He wanted to agree but his mind was spinning. He really needed to eat. Then update the evidence board. After that, maybe he could follow the nurse's orders and relax.

Maybe.

"Mateo, you told me you would relax," Nina gently chided. She eyed him as he intently studied the chalkboard.

"I am relaxing." Mateo motioned to himself. "I'm sitting in a cushy recliner instead of scouring the woods for the attacker. I got cleaned up. I've been fed. We've updated this board with everything we know. We've tossed around ideas. I'm actually feeling pretty good."

She bowed a brow at him.

"I'm not lying."

She laughed lightly. "I didn't say that you were."

"I'm not exaggerating, either."

He winked and his teasing caused her heart to flutter.

"You do certainly seem to be on the mend."

"It was your mother's dumplings and your nursing skills. Thank you for finding me some ibuprofen and getting me hydrated. It's made a world of difference. If you're implying I should take a nap, that's not going to happen. I've never been a napper and that's not going to start today."

"I didn't say you had to nap. You need to stop straining your brain. What I really want," Nina said, "is for you to stop staring at the board as if your life depends on it."

He turned somber and she realized she'd said the wrong thing.

"*Your* life might depend on it."

Nina shifted on the couch, jostling Coco a bit. She hoped Lainie didn't mind Coco being on the furniture, but she really needed the connection right now.

"You know what? I know it's important, but I'm really tired of talking about this case. We aren't going to figure out anything more tonight," she said.

"You're probably right." He shifted in his seat and Nina noticed he no longer winced when he moved. "What do you want to do? See if we can find a movie?"

"I don't think I could concentrate on a movie."

"Same."

"Maybe we could talk about something other than this case," Nina suggested.

"Such as...?"

"Mateo, when this is over, would you consider going out to dinner with me? Or a movie? Maybe both?" Her words surprised her. She had been thinking about this though hadn't exactly intended to ask him. Not yet. But, really, now seemed to be as good a time as any.

He stared at her a moment, silent, and she wondered if his concussion was messing with his comprehension. Then again, they'd been having a perfectly logical conversation only moments ago. Yet he seemed confused.

She felt the need to clarify. "Like, on a date. Not tomorrow or anything. But when this case is solved. I'm guessing it would be a conflict of interest to start something now."

"Oh." He cleared his throat and frowned.

She did not take that as a good sign.

"I was wondering if that's what you meant."

Not knowing what to say, she just looked at him expectantly.

"Look, Nina, I'm flattered."

Her heart sank. "But...?"

"But...it's not a good idea."

She mentally tossed his answer around for a moment, trying to make sense of it.

"Not a good idea because I'm not your type?" Nina studied him quizzically. She had thought she'd felt a connection between them. She supposed it could have been one-sided, but she had been sure she'd sensed interest from him.

"You don't seem like the sort of person who is into casual relationships," Mateo stated. "Neither am I. But the crux of the problem is, I'm not husband material. In fact, I'd make a terrible husband."

"Says who?" Nina demanded.

"My wife."

Nina's stomach jolted. Suddenly, her feelings toward Mateo felt all kinds of wrong. "Your wife?"

She rewound her memory. Hadn't he said he wasn't married? Had she misunderstood?

He winced, though she didn't think it was from pain. At least, not physical pain. "Late wife." He paused, as if debating what to share. "I made a terrible husband. She told me so. I made a lousy husband for her and, since my lifestyle hasn't changed much—I'm still a detective, I still work awful hours, my head still gets tangled up in my job—I'm pretty sure I'd be a terrible husband still."

Nina was at a loss for words. He was widowed? His wife—deceased wife—had told him he was a terrible husband?

"That seems like a very cruel thing to say."

He shrugged but his tone turned wistful. "The thing is, she was probably right. It's the last thing she ever said to me. Right before she dragged our six-year-old twins out to the car."

Nina's stomach twisted. Mateo had children? Twin sons? Had his wife taken them away from him? He didn't seem the sort of man who would allow that.

"You have sons?" she pressed.

He was silent for a long time; his gaze seeming lost and far away. Her heart dipped because she sensed where this story was going. Coco whimpered, crawled off Nina's lap and trotted over to Mateo. She placed a paw on his knee and stared up at him woefully. After a moment, he patted his lap, a clear invitation, and the dog accepted.

A sound escaped his throat, somewhere between a sigh and a groan of misery. "This isn't something I talk about."

Nina wanted to tell him it was okay, he didn't

need to talk about it now, but maybe he *did* need to talk about it.

"I'm a good listener, Mateo."

"I do feel like I owe you an explanation. Jolene and I had a fight that last night. It was one of many over the last years of our marriage. She said she was leaving me, for good. I'd just gotten home from work. Her car was packed with suitcases. She was furious I was late again, always tied up on a case. I thought she just needed time to cool off. I was exhausted, so I let her go." His voice trembled. "She pulled out in front of a semitruck just a few miles from our home."

Dread trickled down Nina's spine.

"The semi hit the driver's side. Nate was in the back seat, directly behind Jolene. They were killed instantly. But Josh…" He pulled in a shuddering breath. "He made it through the wreck. He spent over a week in ICU. He didn't regain consciousness, but every day he held on, the doctors became more hopeful. *I* became more hopeful. I knew the road to recovery would be long. I prayed…oh, how I prayed…that he would come back to me."

"What happened?" Nina coaxed, her voice soft, comforting, full of compassion.

"A blood clot." Mateo cleared his throat. "A blood clot formed and broke loose. It stopped his heart. It happened so fast. I had gone down to the cafeteria for a sandwich. When I came back, he was gone. Just like that."

Nina's heart clenched. Tears welled behind her eyes and then a few trickled down. She wiped them away, not knowing what to say. Mateo's heart had to have been shattered. "I'm not going to ply you with platitudes. Just know, I am very, very sorry for your loss. I understand it had to be devastating."

"Devastating. Yes." He looked at her then. "I'm sorry if I led you on. Sorry if I made you think there could be anything between us. There can't be. I don't have it in me."

"You don't think you could love that way again?" she asked.

"I don't think I could survive *losing* that way again." He shook his head. "There's no way you can understand that and you're naïve if you think you can."

His words took her by surprise.

"Are you certain about that?" Her tone was calm but firm. "I assure you, I am well acquainted with the intricacies of life and death. I'm a hospice nurse, Mateo. I'm honored to have the job I have. I help people slip away from often-painful bodies into the glorious Kingdom of Heaven. I do what I can to be sure their last days are filled with dignity and compassion. I lost my sister when I was fifteen. I was there, right by her side, when cancer stole her from us, sending her from this life to the next. I held her hand as she died."

Regret flitted across his features.

"I know. I'm sorry. That was insensitive of me to say. For the record, I don't think you're naïve. Far from it. I think you're vivacious and smart. Beautiful and determined. Young." He finally met her gaze. "I'm too old for you."

She hadn't expected that. "Really? How old are you?"

"I'm thirty-three."

She narrowed her eyes at him. "You're nine years older than me, Mateo. That hardly makes you ancient."

"Yeah? Well, some days I feel ancient."

"You've dealt with a lot."

"It's made me feel old and jaded."

"You can work at changing how you feel," Nina said softly.

"It's not that easy," he huffed.

"Few things worth fighting for are easy," Nina countered.

"I don't want to ruin you...the way I ruined my wife. When we met, she was lively and always looking to have fun. Because of me, she turned angry, bitter. She hated my job, hated when I was gone, hated that I had to take emergency calls. I can't blame her. Being married to a law enforcement officer is rough."

Nina leaned forward. "Were you an officer when you met?"

"I was."

"She knew what she was getting into."

"I think at first the uniform seemed glamorous to her. Eventually, the novelty wore off. Reality set in, and it wasn't a reality that she appreciated. I knew how much she had come to despise my job. If I'd only quit one of the hundreds of times she'd asked me to."

Nina knew where he was going with this. "You can't live your life wondering what-if. Do you really think that would've made her happy?"

He shrugged. "I honestly don't know. I feel like she changed a lot over the years. I'm not sure anything I could've done would've made her happy."

"Then don't you dare blame yourself. Don't you dare feel like you weren't a good husband." Nina leveled her gaze on him. "Her unhappiness was not on you. We all need to be responsible for our own happiness."

He didn't say anything for a long while, simply sat there, stroking Coco.

Nina let him stew in his thoughts.

Finally, he looked up, appearing lost and forlorn. "I have a lot of baggage. Too much. Dating again has never even crossed my mind. I'm not good enough for you, Nina. I'd only weigh you down."

Nina stood and crossed the room to him. She pressed a kiss onto his forehead then scooped Coco off his lap.

"I don't believe that for one minute. You are a wonderful person, worthy of love. Sleep well. I'll see you in the morning."

With that, she turned and headed for the spare bedroom before Mateo saw the tears that were spilling from her eyes.

Chapter Twelve

Nina sat forward on the edge of Lainie's plaid couch. Her elbows were propped on her knees and if she stared any harder at the chalkboard, she thought she might make it implode. All of Lainie's notes tied together so nicely.

Who was the attacker?

She wanted the answer to jump out at her.

Of course, it hadn't yet, and it wasn't likely to soon.

Though Lainie was supposed to have the day off, she had volunteered to do some investigating instead.

Earlier, she and another officer had delivered Nina's Trailblazer. Unbeknownst to her, Mateo had seen to it that the tires had been replaced. Now, with his SUV destroyed, Mateo had insisted on having it here in case of an emergency. It was tucked away in the garage, out of sight.

Now he was in the kitchen throwing together a peanut butter and jelly sandwich, one of the few things Lainie had ingredients for.

Oh, Mateo. Nina had been trying hard to concentrate on the clues in front of her but her mind continued to swirl back to Mateo and his story. While she had suspected he'd been through a lot, she certainly had not expected anything close to the story he'd told. He'd been married. He'd been a father. She had seen first-hand how horrific her sister's death had been for her parents. Mateo had lost two sons. They'd been so very young.

She could almost not fathom the depth of his pain. Nate and Josh. Her heart ached for Mateo.

The very idea that he wasn't good enough for her was ludicrous. But she'd awakened this morning with the realization that now was not the time or the place to discuss romantic involvement.

Solving this case had to be a top priority.

She heard Mateo's phone blaring from the kitchen. He really needed to turn that ringer down. He strode into the room holding his sandwich in one hand, his phone in the other. Coco trailed after him, licking her lips. She had a dab of peanut butter on her chin.

It was difficult to tell who Mateo was speaking with, so Nina sat patiently.

When he disconnected, he didn't keep her waiting.

"That was Lainie. She spoke with Al Crenshaw, the oldest son of Chester Crenshaw. The one you said made the accusations against his brother." Mateo waited for Nina to confirm with a nod then went on. "Your hunch was right. He stated he believes his brother stole the funds *and* the Rolex that's missing. He didn't want to turn his brother in, and he had no proof, so he let it go. Lainie showed him the watch we have on file and he was able to provide a receipt. Furthermore, she got footage from a neighbor's security camera. Someone is seen breaking into the house the night Chester supposedly tripped and fell."

"And Gloria?" Nina was curious about the other "accidental" death.

"Officer Hughes has been busy. She met with one of Gloria's three daughters. Not only was the pendant missing, a very expensive pendant valued at several thousand dollars, but also an extensive collection of sterling-silver cutlery."

Nina's brow furrowed. "Did they report that?"

"Gloria had been 'decluttering' her house—

that was her daughter's word—for the past year or so. They thought perhaps Gloria had sold the cutlery and just hadn't mentioned it. However, she had three different sets and had promised one to each of her girls."

"Making it unlikely that she sold them."

"She touched base with Jimmy down at Junkin' Treasures. The sets never came through his store. He also reached out to some of the other pawnbrokers in the area and none of them were familiar with the sets, either. I can't imagine an eighty-two-year-old woman would travel more than a thirty-mile radius. That's what Jimmy's phone calls covered." He made his way to the chalkboard. After taking a bite of his sandwich, he started filling in the information they had just learned. "Jimmy did have an interesting thought. Real sterling silver, which this was, could be melted down. Just like he mentioned with the gold. It would sell for a good price. The amount Gloria had would have been far too much to fit into that box."

"You think this guy managed to have it melted and sold?"

Mateo shrugged. "I'm just saying it's a possibility. There are buyers out there interested in silver for the purpose of melting it down, so yeah, that would make it a bit harder to trace. We have no proof that's what happened. Not yet. It's just an interesting theory that Jimmy brought up. Furthermore, this daughter of Gloria's—she's the only one of the three that still lives in town—told Lainie that she's the one who found her mother. She said something odd struck her that day. When she arrived, the back door was ajar. According to her, her mother didn't use the back door. She didn't mention it, though, because she had no reason to think it was relevant. In the chaos of finding her mother's body after what she assumed was an accidental fall, she forgot about it."

"That's not proof someone else was in the house that night, but it does make it seem possible."

Mateo jotted a few more notes on the board. "I think the department now has reason to look into both deaths thoroughly."

"Has the department gotten the security footage from Golden Acres yet?"

"We should have it by the end of the day."

"You and Officer Hughes have been busy."

Mateo smirked. "If I didn't know better, I'd say she's after my job."

Nina's eyes widened. "Oh, no."

He chuckled. "She'd make a good detective."

"Does the department have room for another detective?"

"Not at the moment." He cleared his throat. "I've been thinking for a while that maybe it's time to make a career change."

She stared at him, speechless.

"It's just an idea I've been tossing around." He shrugged. "Back to the case."

They went over everything again.

While the Senior Center could be a possible connection, because of Gloria and Chester, the two also had a connection to Golden Acres. Gloria visited a good friend often, and Chester visited his brother almost daily.

This made the nursing home the one common factor with a connection to *all* of the items they'd found owners for so far.

"If Golden Acres is the place that connects everyone, does that mean Tucker is off the hook?" she asked.

Mateo finished the last bite of his sandwich and shook his head. "He's not off the hook until I see his right hand. Or better yet, until we have someone else in custody. Besides, he volunteers at the Senior Center. But we don't know for sure he doesn't have a connection to

Golden Acres. I'm pretty frustrated with that kid for taking off."

Nina winced at his use of the word "kid" because Tucker was twenty-one. Only a few years younger than she was. Her heart dipped. Is that how Mateo thought of her, as a kid, too? Sure, she was only twenty-four. But didn't her life experiences count for anything?

Mateo was going a bit stir-crazy being inside Lainie's house all day. He was used to being out in the field, working a case. It was hard to do so from his colleague's living room where all he had was the chalkboard.

They were close to wrapping up this case. He was sure of it, could feel it in his bones. That's why not being actively involved at the moment was so hard to take. Mateo reminded himself that he was keeping Nina safe, which was more important than anything right now.

He couldn't leave her alone. While he could call another officer in for a protection detail, the thought didn't sit well with him, either. He needed to be with her to truly know that she was safe. Meanwhile he needed to trust his department was doing everything it could do to catch this perp.

Even worse, he felt awkward with Nina today. He was embarrassed that he'd shared his story with her. It was probably Coco's fault, the way she was all-comforting and whatnot. He shot an irritated glance at the dog, though he knew he really had no one but himself to blame. A part of him had wanted to share with Nina.

He hungered to have someone look at him the way Nina often did. Like she trusted him, admired him, maybe even adored him. That wouldn't do. And was exactly why he needed to put a stop to any misplaced feelings that may arise.

He had ruined his fun-loving wife.

He wouldn't risk turning Nina, sweet, joyful Nina, into a bitter woman.

Why had he shared all of that with her? Was he trying to scare her off? Maybe.

She was rattling around in the kitchen, doing the dishes or maybe trying to scrounge up something to make later for dinner.

Or maybe she was just avoiding him.

But no, that was not Nina's way. That was something Jolene would have done.

Don't you dare feel like you weren't a good husband. Nina's words from the night before whispered through his mind. *Her unhappiness was not on you. We all need to be responsible for our own happiness.*

Was that true? Would he ever be able to stop feeling like he hadn't tried hard enough? Like he hadn't been good enough?

With an effort, he pushed the thoughts away.

He was jotting a note down, the chalk screeching across the board in a way that reminded him of his grade-school days, when his phone rang. He'd finally turned the ringer down, so this time it didn't make him feel like jumping out of his skin.

Picking it up, he expected it to be someone from the station.

He didn't recognize the number.

"Detective Bianchi."

"Detective, my name is Hector Gomez. My wife, Maria, is a resident of Golden Acres."

Mateo's interest was instantly piqued. "How did you get this number?"

"I called the station. Someone there gave it to me," the man said gruffly. "Is that a problem?"

"No. It's not a problem at all. I was just curious." Mateo had asked them to give out his new number in just this sort of instance. "What can I help you with?"

"My wife, she was talking with her new

friend, Mildred. Apparently, there was a discussion about a variety of stolen items. Would one of those items happen to be a collection of gold coins?"

Mateo's brow curved. "Why do you ask?"

Nina's gaze was on him; he could feel her curiosity like it was a physical thing. He didn't want to risk a break in the conversation by filling her in right now.

"I haven't told my dear wife that they've gone missing, but when she told me about this book of yours, I couldn't help but be hopeful. Would it be possible for me to see this book? I'd like to know if the Mulberry Creek Police Department is in possession of my collection."

"I think a viewing of the binder can be arranged."

"So you have them?" The relief in the man's tone was palpable. "You have the coins?"

"Can you tell me a bit more about them?"

"Gold coins." He paused. "In a black collector's book. Do you have them or not?"

One problem with having so many people view the photo binder was that Mateo wouldn't be surprised if someone came forward trying to claim an item that didn't belong to them. He inwardly grimaced, realizing he should give people the benefit of the doubt and not think the worst.

Nina was right. He was jaded.

The coins were not in a book. They were in a plastic zippered bag. But had they been in a collector's book when they'd gone missing? Could this man be the rightful owner?

"If the coins are mine, I'm sure I can prove it to your satisfaction," Hector continued. "I have receipts for some, but not all. I might be old, but my mind is still sharp. I was sure I hadn't misplaced the book. I didn't want to believe it had been stolen. Didn't want to believe he—"

The man cut himself off.

Mateo waited, his heartbeat kicking up a notch.

He heard a tapping sound come through the phone. Subtle, spaced out, but definitely a tapping noise.

"Are you still there, Hector? You said *he*?" Mateo prompted. Who was Hector referring to? "Do you know who the thief is?"

Hector let out a weary sigh. "I have my suspicions, but I don't want to say. Not just yet. On the off chance the collection in your possession isn't mine, I don't want to throw the young'un under the bus."

The young one? Could he be talking about Tucker, who was in his early twenties? To a man Hector's age, that would be plenty young.

"When can we meet?" Mateo asked.

"Other than visiting my wife, I don't have a whole lot going on these days. You tell me when works for you. Although, I'd appreciate it if you'd come to me. I have a bit of trouble getting around. I don't much like going to public places anymore. Not unless it's church or Golden Acres."

"What's your address?" Mateo asked.

The older man rattled it off. "Can you come now?"

"I can be there shortly."

"I'll be waiting."

The line disconnected.

"I sure do hope you have information," Mateo muttered.

"Who has information?" Nina gave him a hopeful look. "Do you have a lead?"

"Maybe." Mateo didn't want to be too confident. "Do you know Hector Gomez? His wife—"

"Maria. Yes, I know them. They're a lovely couple. Maria is a resident of Golden Acres. She has early stage dementia, and had gotten into the habit of wandering away from home. Hector has a bad leg, from a farming accident in his youth if I recall, and walks with a cane. He wasn't able to keep up with her, especially once she started slipping out of the house. He visits daily."

That was right. He had mentioned he had difficulty getting around.

Ah, Mateo thought, perhaps that's what the tapping sound had been. A cane hitting the ground in slow, measured footsteps. Yes, now that he thought about, he was sure that's what it had been.

"He heard about our visit and believes the coins belong to him. He asked if I'd come by."

"I'm going with you."

Mateo's lips quirked. "I didn't doubt it."

He hadn't planned on leaving her behind.

She shook her head. "I can't believe this person stole from Hector, too. He's the nicest man. Oh, what am I saying? They're all lovely people. We need to find out who has done this to them and put a stop to it." Her eyes widened. "Wait. You said something about him having information? What does he know?"

"I'm not sure. He wouldn't discuss anything over the phone." Mateo didn't want to admit

Hector had hinted at knowing who had stolen from him. He would wait until they had the facts.

Using his phone, he confirmed that Hector had given him the correct address. Next, he shot off a text to Lainie. He wasn't going to take any unnecessary risks and had promised his chief he'd let someone know their whereabouts at all times.

Nina decided to leave Coco behind. While usually well-behaved, she knew Hector wasn't steady on his feet. She did not want to risk Coco accidentally tripping him up.

After a short drive to the opposite end of town, they pulled up to a worn-down house that was surrounded by trees. The grass hadn't been mowed recently and Mateo thought maybe that was something he could take care of as soon as he had the chance. It had to be a difficult task for a man who relied on a cane.

"This is the place," Mateo said. "Looks like it could use a bit of TLC."

Nina gave him a warm smile. "When this case wraps, I'm game if you are."

"Absolutely."

They carefully made their way up the rickety steps. Mateo noticed a board was loose and knew that couldn't be safe for a gentleman who had difficulty walking. Yes, a fix-up day was in order.

When they reached the front door, it was open a crack.

"Mateo?" Nina whispered and pointed at the opening.

"Help me...please..." The words came from inside the house.

Mateo and Nina looked at each other in surprise.

"I've fallen," the wobbly voice said.

Nina lurched forward, shoving the door wide before he could stop her. He lunged after her, spotting a frail-looking, gray-haired man on the floor. His back was to them and he was motionless.

Mateo always tried to be vigilant but some things were impossible to plan for. There was no way he could have guessed that a giant weighted net, a fishing net most likely, would be rigged to fall over the top of them the moment they shoved the door open and crossed the threshold. He tried to pull his weapon, but he felt instantly, hopelessly, tangled. The more they moved, the more entangled they became.

"Stop, be still," he ordered. "Only one of us should move at a time."

"Okay," Nina said, her voice breathlessly afraid yet trusting.

A man stepped from behind the door.

He didn't wear a mask. Did that mean he was confident that this time his prey would not get away?

The man was *not* Tucker Holden.

Nina gasped. "Conrad Greene."

"Oh, squirm and fight all you want." Conrad's voice was harsh and taunting. "It's not going to matter one bit."

"He's one of the cooks at Golden Acres," Nina blurted out. "Conrad, what did you do to Hector?"

Mateo lunged for the man and instantly felt the jab of a needle into his arm. Suddenly it seemed as if his veins were full of ice. He wasn't sure if it was the substance now flowing through him or if it was his fear coursing through his body.

"What have you done?" He ground out the words even as he tried to maneuver himself in front of Nina, to no avail. They were hopelessly tangled with every movement making their situation more dire. The syringe came toward her and Mateo growled in frustration.

"You ruined my fun, now I'm going to ruin yours. Permanently."

Nina let out a yelp when he injected her.

Hector Gomez, the real Hector, not the man who made the phone call, who was sprawled out on the floor, let out a miserable moan that Mateo barely registered as his mind became increasingly fuzzier. At least the man was alive.

"Please," Nina said. "You've stolen. But—"

Mateo didn't hear the rest of her sentence as he felt himself lose his fragile hold on consciousness. Tangled in the net, he toppled to the floor, only vaguely aware that he pulled Nina down with him.

The world went black and there was nothing he could do to fight it.

Then he blinked into bright sunshine what felt like an instant later. Only, it was clear time had passed. The rumble of tires on gravel filled his ears, and he realized he was in a moving vehicle. He blinked again, trying to gather his senses as the attack at Hector's house came crashing back through his mind.

Nina!

He twisted and saw her sleeping beside him.

No. Not sleeping. She'd been knocked out as well.

Though his mind was still hazy, reality seemed to settle in quickly. They were in the back of a small SUV. Was this Nina's vehicle? It had black leather seats, just like Nina's. Rock music flowed through the speakers.

It was easy to piece together what had happened. After the perp had knocked him and Nina out, he'd loaded them into her vehicle. Now they were headed…where? Perhaps the bigger question was what did the man have planned for them?

Absolutely nothing good. That was a certainty.

Whatever he had schemed, Mateo intended to foil it. He was awake and becoming more cognizant by the moment. Still, he didn't have a plan and he desperately needed one.

Please, God, help us out of this.

This time, the prayer didn't even surprise him.

Forgive me, Father, for distancing myself from You. I come to You humbly, in my time of desperate need. Not just for myself but for Nina. Please, help me to help her.

How? How could he possibly help Nina

when his hands and feet were bound? He felt helpless but he refused to feel defeated.

He was a long way from defeated.

Nina moaned and her eyes fluttered open. She blinked then looked startled. Her eyes locked onto his and her face showed instant relief. He wished he could reach out to comfort her, hold her in his arms as he had the day at the river. That wasn't possible. Not yet anyway.

Shh. He whispered the word. It was to their advantage if Conrad thought they were still out cold.

She nodded in understanding, raised her hands to her face and scowled at the clothes-line rope that bound her wrists. Anger flitted across her face.

He strained against his own bindings. Wrists and ankles, both trussed tight.

Nina's gaze cut away from her wrists and landed on a fleece blanket.

The back of the Trailblazer was small, leaving almost no room to maneuver, but Nina suddenly seemed to be on a mission. She squirmed closer to the blanket, reached out and tugged. It slid away, leaving an emergency tote uncovered.

What was this? Nina's vehicular version of her fanny pack?

Though her hands were bound, she was able to flip the latch on the box. She tipped it over and supplies spilled out. Emergency food, a foldable shovel, tow strap, bungee cord, work gloves, flashlight.

Jackknife.

The contents had spilled with a clatter and Mateo cringed and held his breath. But the thumping beat of the music had drowned out the sound.

She gave him a triumphant look.

Gravel still crunched beneath the tires.

A new song spilled through the speakers. The man up front began to sing along, his voice frustratingly melodic.

How could he sing at a time like this?

Mateo decided to just be grateful for the extra noise.

He sent up a thank You to God, a constant loop of his sincerest gratitude. He also prayed that Hector Gomez was okay. The sight of the man lying on the floor kept circling through his mind. Had he been hurt? Or had he been drugged the way Nina and Mateo had? As soon as they got out of this predicament, Mateo would send help for the man.

It took some maneuvering, since his fingers

were at an awkward angle, but he managed to open the blade of the knife Nina had rustled up. He glanced at her. Her eyes were huge, hopeful.

Once the knife was open, he realized, with his wrists bound, he couldn't twist the blade edge in the right direction, not while having a good enough grip to cut through the rope.

Nina nudged his foot with hers. When he glanced at her, she held out her wrists to him and lifted her eyebrows in question.

He nodded then reached awkwardly toward her.

The vehicle was bumping and jostling along now, apparently going down a rutted dirt road. He tried to hold the knife steady as he moved it toward Nina. With all the jostling, he was afraid of cutting her, but he had to assume their time was running out. He had no idea how long they'd been in the vehicle unconscious.

Together, they were able to position the blade so that it would have a clear cut against the rope. He gave a jerk with his hands and her rope fell free. She quickly untangled the dangling remnants from her wrists. Just as hastily, she cut him free. Their ankles came next.

It was an odd sensation, lying there. Free. But not free.

He quickly played his options through his mind. He could catapult himself over the seat, attack the guy. But what kind of road were they on? Lots of roads in this area were winding, edging along steep inclines. Or what if there was an oncoming vehicle and they swerved into the wrong lane?

He couldn't take the chance.

"Now what?" Nina's voice, almost inaudible, floated next to his ear, nearly drowned out by the music and Conrad's singing.

His voice was equally quiet. "Now we wait."

He flexed his hands to get the blood flowing.

Then he gripped the knife, hating the idea of using it, but grateful for the protection it would provide.

Chapter Thirteen

Nina fought down the terror that had enveloped her since the moment she'd opened her eyes. She concentrated on her breathing, calming her heart, and reminded herself she was not alone. Mateo was there.

And she knew God was watching over them.

There was no doubt in her mind that it was God who'd blinded the attacker's eye to the blanket and the gear in the back of the SUV. It was God who'd helped her and Mateo cut their bindings free.

He had brought them this far, she had to trust that He would bring them the rest of the way to safety.

It was difficult to wrap her mind around the fact that Conrad Greene wanted to kill them. She barely knew the man, had only seen him in passing at Golden Acres. He'd always had his head down, always seemed to fade into the background. She realized that would make it awfully easy for him to lurk and linger…and listen.

As much as she hated inaction, she understood why Mateo had said they needed to wait.

Ambushing the guy, though that was her first thought, could have disastrous consequences. What if he shot them the moment he realized they were awake? What if Mateo startled him and he swerved into oncoming traffic? Better to hold tight, knowing they had the element of surprise. They were awake. They were free.

Mateo was armed.

The vehicle began to slow…and Nina's heart began to race.

She felt Mateo stiffen beside her.

He took her hand in his, the grip firm and secure. Nina squeezed back, hoping he understood what his presence meant to her.

Too afraid to speak, she could only guess at what he planned to do. Because it's what she would do, had she been the one in possession of the knife. She'd wait until they parked, until their attacker opened the back end, and then she'd strike the unsuspecting criminal.

They slowed, then slowed some more. From this angle, all she could see was lovely clear blue sky and treetops.

They were somewhere secluded then, judging by the thickness of the foliage.

Not a surprise at all.

The unmistakable *click-click-click* of a blinker kicked in. Then they turned left.

What was Conrad's plan? Pull them from the SUV? Shoot them? Bury them in the middle of nowhere? If he killed them, would anyone ever find them? The thought of her parents going through the heartbreak of losing another child filled her with anger and sorrow.

Nina shuddered and blood seemed to pound through her veins, making every heartbeat echo in her ears. She didn't want to die. Not today. She had too much living to do.

She would tell Mateo that she loved him, whether he liked it or not. Because she did and she needed for him to know that.

The vehicle came to a halt.

She backed up against the side of the rear hold, trying to give Mateo room to maneuver as the driver's-side door creaked open. He scooted himself into place, ready to attack the instant the back of the SUV opened.

Any minute now.

Please, God...

She prepared herself for the moment they were faced with Conrad.

Only...

Suddenly the engine revved.

The vehicle leapt forward.

They were moving.

And then... Nina had the distinct feeling they were airborne.

She let out a shriek as she jerked upright in unison with Mateo.

What was happening? This was not right.

There was no one in the driver's seat and a wide blue expanse of water was racing their way.

"Hold on!" Mateo latched onto the seatback, and she did the same, though it did little to hold them in place. When the vehicle hit the water, the impact sent her flying upward. She smacked her head on the ceiling of the SUV. Blood filled her mouth as she realized she'd bitten her tongue.

That was the least of her concerns because it took only a moment to realize that water was seeping in. She glanced around, spotted Conrad on the embankment above as the SUV wobbled then began to fill faster. Conrad turned and walked away, likely satisfied his dastardly deed had had the desired effect.

He had sent them over an embankment, into a lake, thinking they were still tied up and unconscious in the back end. There was no way to open the hatch from the inside.

"We're going under," she moaned.

"Not if I can help it. Get up front." Mateo scrambled over the seat and Nina followed. "We're sinking, but not fast. The engine is still running though it won't be for long."

She heard the desperation in Mateo's tone and wasn't sure why the engine mattered at this point. It was then she noticed the board wedged against the gas pedal, but that's not what Mateo was after. He reached the driver's-side door and began buzzing the windows down.

The engine sputtered…died…and the windows stopped. Dead.

"We need to get out before water starts gushing in." He pointed at the passenger's-side window, down most of the way but not completely. As was the driver's side. "We need to do this carefully but quickly. It's important to balance our weight so we don't flip and roll."

Nina's heart hammered. Flipping and rolling while they were trapped inside with water gushing in would be deadly.

"How do we do this?"

She listened as Mateo shot out his plan rapid-fire. They each needed to slide through one of the open windows. He warned her that if water began gushing in, and the vehicle sank, they would be suctioned down with it.

Nina understood. The two of them moved as quickly as the unsteadily bobbing vehicle would allow until they were each perched in a window.

Mateo's worried gaze fastened on Nina's. "Can you swim?"

"Like a fish." Her wobbly voice betrayed her terror, despite her attempt at levity. The endless hours at the lake as a child, with her loving family, had turned her into a powerful swimmer. Still, she was terrified. Swimming was one thing. Escaping a sinking vehicle was quite another.

What if they went under?

Nina didn't even know where they were. From the little she had seen, she hadn't been able to make out their location. How would anyone ever find them? They would have no idea where to look. She and Mateo had been unconscious for how long? Several minutes? Several hours? She had no way of knowing.

They could be half a state away from Mulberry Creek, so far from home that no one would ever know where to search. They may never be discovered in this watery grave.

Would anyone ever tie Conrad to their deaths? Would he get away with this?

That angered her almost more than anything.

All these thoughts flittered through her mind in a matter of seconds. Then the vehicle jolted. She hoped they weren't going to die, but if they did, she needed Mateo to know how she felt.

"Mateo, I—"

It jolted again. She gasped in horror.

"Go!" he shouted.

Nina shoved out of the vehicle, pushing up with her legs, catapulting herself through the window. In an instant, she was in the open water, swimming away from her Trailblazer. Away from Mateo. It took her only an instant to realize that he had not shoved free of the vehicle at the same time she had.

She stopped, treading water, desperately watching as the Trailblazer rolled then sank.

"Mateo?" His name passed her lips in a choked whisper. An urgent plea.

Please, God…where is he?

★ ★ ★

Mateo had waited a few moments too long before trying to shove himself from the vehicle. He had needed to know that Nina was free first before trying his own escape, because he was terrified that if he moved too soon, it would throw off the vehicle balance and drag her under.

Now, as he kicked desperately, he realized the opposite had happened. The SUV had gone off balance when Nina's weight no longer helped it to stay even. *His* side had dipped and water had gushed in the window, causing him to flip before he'd had a chance to flee.

He was dragged down, pulled into the murky depths of this unfamiliar lake.

The giant breath he'd taken seared against his lungs. The water felt tumultuous around him. His heart cried out for Nina. He didn't know if she was safe. He couldn't help her because he could barely help himself.

He felt topsy-turvy. His body heavy with his drenched clothes. He didn't know which way was up and panic began to set in.

No!

Please, God… Please help me…

The sense of peace that surrounded him in

that moment was like being held by an old friend…or perhaps, more accurately, a loving Father.

He stilled himself, his lungs burning painfully now. Then he remembered something he'd been told at one of the many police force trainings he'd been to. Slowly, he blew out the breath that he'd sucked in before going under. He watched as the air bubbles seemed to float to his feet. He knew then that he'd gotten turned around. What he'd thought was up was down. With a few strokes, he managed to turn himself. He blew out the rest of his breath, fully orienting himself now. The bubbles floated upward and he began to stroke with every ounce of strength he had left.

His head broke the surface and he gasped for air.

He felt as if he weighed a million pounds with his wet clothes. Keeping his head above water was an effort. Yet he thrashed around, desperately looking for Nina.

"Mateo!"

He whirled in the water and spotted her some distance away.

Never could he remember such an intense feeling of relief.

He loved this woman. There was no denying it and he no longer wanted to try. He thought there was a good chance she loved him, too. He wanted more than anything to find out. And he would, as soon as they were free.

"Mateo," Nina said again as she glided toward him in the water. She wore a look of relief so pure, so intense, it made his heart ache.

"You scared me to death. I saw you go down and you took forever to come back up."

"I'm okay." He nodded at the land. "But we need to get out of the water." The heaviness of his clothes continued to weigh him down, and he knew Nina must have the same struggle, so they needed to get to safety while they still had the energy.

Silently, they moved toward the wood-covered shoreline. Not where the vehicle had gone over, because they would never make it up the embankment, but a bit to the north where the ground evened out. Every stroke was a struggle. Fortunately, they weren't very far from it. Relief filled him when his shoe hit the lake bottom. He found his footing quickly. He turned to Nina and held out a hand. She reached for him and he tugged her to him, her body easily gliding through the water.

"We made it." Her voice was weary. She found her footing. "Mateo?"

"Yes?" His heart hammered, partly from exertion, partly with relief.

She placed her hands on his cheeks and kissed him. Her movement was so quick, so unexpected, that he didn't even have time to respond before she stepped away.

"Let's get out of here," she said. "We don't know where Conrad is. He could be lurking."

"Right." He should've thought of that. And would've if her kiss hadn't chased every bit of common sense right out of his head. But he was thinking now, and she was right. "Let's move."

They trudged through the muck, through the weeds, and clambered onto the steep shoreline.

Mateo didn't want to say it, but he feared that Conrad was watching.

Stalking them.

He wouldn't have been surprised if bullets started flying.

None did.

He and Nina quickly moved into the thickest part of the trees before stopping to catch their breath. Trying to gather his bearings, Mateo studied their surroundings.

"This lake isn't familiar to me," he said.

"Where do you think Conrad went?" Nina's gaze scoured the forest. "I caught a glimpse of him walking away."

"I think he assumed he sent us to a watery grave and that he's in the clear." Mateo paused a beat. "Since we don't know that for a fact, I'm going to play it safe and presume the worst. We need to proceed as if he's lurking in these woods."

Nina nodded and, in silent agreement, they moved without saying another word. Cold, wet, and exhausted, they trudged through the woods, trying to step soundlessly despite their fatigue. They hadn't gone far before Mateo spotted a cabin through the trees.

He knew Nina caught sight of it at the same time because she stopped and gripped his arm, holding him in place. "Do you think they have a phone?"

"There's only one way to find out." They trudged forward until they hit the edge of the tree line. Mateo studied what he could see of the property. It was a small cabin, overlooking the lake. The lawn had been mowed, but not recently, making him wonder if it was a vacation property rather than a permanent residence. There wasn't a garage, only a small garden shed, and he didn't see a vehicle in the driveway. He turned to Nina. "Stay here. I'm going to get a better look."

Nina looked like she wanted to argue. Instead, she bit her lip and nodded.

Mateo crept onward quickly, feeling as though he was being watched, but wondering if it was just paranoia after all that had happened. He glanced over his shoulder, startled for a moment that he didn't see Nina, then caught a glimpse of her as she peered out from behind a large tree.

In seconds, he was trying the doorknob of the cabin. It was locked, which was not a surprise. He peered in through the window mounted in the top half of the front door. The door led into a small kitchen.

His heart leapt.

Hanging on the far wall was a phone. A landline, cord and all, was within his view.

"Don't move."

The words sent a sizzle of adrenaline down Mateo's spine, even before he felt the tip of a gun being pressed into his side.

"Conrad Greene," Mateo grated out.

"What is it going to take to get rid of you?" Conrad growled. "You should have died in the house explosion. You were supposed to be dead after the rollover. You should have drowned in the lake. Yet, here you are. Where's Nina?"

Mateo forced a tremble into his voice. "She went down with the vehicle. I tried to save her. I couldn't get her out."

"Put your hands up and turn around slowly," Conrad said. "I want to look into your eyes when you die."

Mateo turned, heart hammering, wondering how he was ever going to get out of this. His eyes widened and he had his answer. The moment he turned, he saw that Nina had sneaked up on them. She held a thick, stubby limb over her shoulder. Before Mateo could even process what was happening, she swung the limb at Conrad's head. The dog-bitten hand that held the gun flew up in the air. Mateo grabbed it and easily tugged the weapon from his injured fingers. Nina struck Conrad again, forcefully hitting him in the back.

He went down with a thud, hitting the ground hard.

"Stay where you are." Mateo's voice was cold. He leveled the gun at Conrad with one hand while managing to worm his way out of his belt with the other. He held it out to Nina. "Care to tie him up?"

"I'd be honored." She took the belt from Mateo and wrapped it around Conrad's wrists over and over, eventually tying the ends together, tugging hard to be sure there was no way for him to wiggle free.

Conrad squirmed into a sitting position and glared daggers at them. "What is it with you two? Why can't I get rid of you?"

"Why are you trying so hard to get rid of us?" Nina demanded. "We never did a thing to you!"

"You ruined everything." Hatred oozed from Conrad's tone. "You should have just minded your own business. It never would've come to this if you would've just left me alone."

"You killed Gloria and Chester." Mateo tossed the accusation out there.

Conrad blinked at him in surprise, clearly caught off guard, just as Mateo had hoped. "The elderly have accidents all the time."

"You became adept at sneaking into houses of the elderly with ease." Mateo forced admiration into his tone.

Conrad smirked. "Mostly, they can't hear so

well. They go to bed early. I've found they aren't usually handy with gadgets like door cams and security systems. I go in quick, get out quick."

"What happened with Gloria?" Nina asked. "Did you kill that dear woman?"

"I didn't really kill her." Conrad scowled at her. "She fell. I was sure no one was home. Turns out she was puttering around down in the cellar. She scared me as bad as I scared her." His tone implied he expected a modicum of sympathy for this. "When she saw me, she was on the top step. Guess I shocked the daylights out of her. She tumbled backward and that was that." He shrugged. "That old Mr. Crenshaw, he came out of nowhere, looking for a drink of water. Saw me going for his coffee can, the one I'd heard him tell his brother he stores his cash in. I knew he'd call the cops so—" he grimaced "—I guess we had a bit of a tussle. He hit his head. No one questioned when Gloria fell. I figured no one would question when old Crenshaw fell. I was right."

"Why bury the valuables?" Mateo asked.

Conrad scowled. "I don't appreciate how nosy you are. I'm not going to answer that."

"Golden Acres is the connection," Nina said. "You work in the kitchen. You don't really chat people up, but I'm sure it's easy enough to drift around the place, overhearing conversations." She didn't wait for a reply. "Gloria and Chester both visited the Senior Center, but that was a coincidence."

He shrugged. "It bought me some time when I heard cops were looking into someone else. That Senior Center volunteer."

"Tucker Holden," Nina supplied.

"All of your victims had ties to Golden Acres," Mateo said.

"No point in denying that." Conrad shrugged. "Chester came to visit his brother almost daily. They'd reminisce about the tough old days. Living through the Great Depression. Chester let it slip that he still didn't trust banks. I happened to be delivering a meal tray to his brother. He also had this Rolex that his highfalutin son gave him. Yammered about it all the time. I figured at his age, he didn't need it. The watch, or the cash. And his son sure didn't, so what difference did it make if I took it? Gloria yammered on and on to her friend about the collections she had. Rose Medallion china, Carnival glass, an antique doll collection, which I did not touch."

Apparently, he'd only stolen the sterling silver.

"And the others?" Nina demanded.

Conrad shrugged. "Yeah, so I took a few belongings. There was still plenty left for their families to fight over. But what about me? I got nothing. My whole life I've been cheated out of what I deserve, what should be mine. My parents have nothing and that's exactly what they've passed down to me. *Nothing.* Joined the army but didn't get the promotion I wanted. My superior officer said I had an attitude and didn't take direction well. Had a good job out in the oil fields but they let me go because some guys wouldn't stop picking fights with me. My wife took off with another guy. Nothing ever goes my way!" he growled. "I was just evening the playing field a bit."

He spoke with such audacity. As if the world owed him. As if these elderly people, who had likely worked hard their entire lives, owed *him.* Conrad's utter lack of remorse left Mateo feeling equal parts revulsion and anger.

"The people I took from were old. They had no use for those things. Or, at least, they wouldn't soon."

Mateo did not feel it was even worth mentioning the obvious, that Conrad had no right to the items. Most of these people had family who would inherit the keepsakes.

"How did we end up *here*?" Nina held her hands up, motioning to the cabin.

He sneered. "Those old people do like to talk. Heard Mildred saying that it was a shame her son didn't use the family cabin very often, but that he was too lazy to clear it out to sell it. It was just sitting empty. At first, I thought maybe I could use it as a hideout, if things got to squirrely back in Mulberry Creek. Came out here to see it for myself. That's when I noticed that it had a nice, clear overlook of the lake."

Mateo noticed now what he hadn't noticed before. Tire tracks through the tall grass. This is where he'd launched the Trailblazer from. From where they stood, they had a lovely view of the lake, but they were looking at it from a slight elevation.

"You were going to drown us in the lake, then what? Just live in the cabin overlooking our graves?" Nina demanded.

"Hardly." Conrad shot her a condescending look. "As soon as I scoped out this place and ironed out my plan, I stored a motorcycle in the shed. After I ditched your bodies, I was going to ride back to Mulberry Creek and no one would be the wiser. But when I was fidgeting around, trying to get it started, I spotted this guy through the window." He looked at them in disgust. "That tranquilizer was supposed to last longer than it did. But I ended up splitting it three ways. Hadn't planned on using it on Hector. Was just going to ensure he took a fall down his front steps, but decided that might be one fall too many. Instead, I was able to sneak up behind him. He never saw me coming. At his age, I figured he'd wake up groggy, con-fused, and none the wiser."

"You impersonated him." Mateo scrubbed a hand through his hair. He felt so gullible.

"Why, yes, yes I did." Conrad's voice mim-icked an older man's. "You were so hungry for information it worked."

"Nina, I think it's time you made a phone call." Mateo stepped toward the door and, using the butt of Conrad's gun, he smashed a hole in the windowpane, knowing he would replace it later. From there, it was easy to reach inside and turn the lock. This was an emergency and he was sure Mildred would understand their need for a break-in.

"I'll gladly make that call," Nina said. "It's time we put this nightmare behind us."

Chapter Fourteen

Mateo gripped the steering wheel of the rental vehicle he was using until his insurance claim was settled and he could buy something new. The driveway leading into Big Sky Ranch was long and winding. For once, it was nice to be heading there with good news.

His body ached and he was tired. Deep, down-to-his-bones tired, but in a good way. This case was wrapping up. Nina's ordeal was over. She was safe. He was no longer tasked with protecting her. At least, not in a professional way.

A frisson of hope washed over him.

Could he have a future with Nina?

He knew he was getting ahead of himself, but the thought of spending the rest of his life with her filled him with joy. She was the brightest ray of sunshine, bursting through the dark, dreary abyss he had been so lost in.

She had made him feel things he hadn't felt in years. Hope. Joy. Love.

Most important of all, he felt his faith growing, stirring, strengthening by the day. She had lost a loved one and she had become strong and courageous, not in spite of it, but because of it.

Nina was young, yes, but he was embarrassed that he had called her naïve. If anyone was naïve, it was him. He'd been unreasonable in his way of thinking. Closed-minded. And she had opened up his mind to all that he'd been missing.

The depth of her faith had reawakened his own.

Thank You, Lord, for bringing us through this ordeal. Thank You for helping me to catch Nina's attacker. Most of all, thank You for loving me and guiding me even when I was too stubborn to admit I still needed You.

He did need God. He needed Nina, too. Finally, he was ready to admit it.

As he rounded the last bend in the gravel drive, he slowed. Nina had asked him to come for dinner. She had warned it would be a large family affair.

He parked near the barn, out of the way of the two children who were playing some type of game in the yard. Mateo glanced around at Nina's loud, boisterous family as he exited the vehicle and strode toward the main ranch house. It had been so long since he'd been at a gathering like this.

Nina's father, James, and Eric, her oldest brother, were on the deck, grilling burgers. Her mother, Julia, and sisters-in-law, Cassie and Holly, were placing tablecloths on picnic tables. Seth, Nina's other brother, was setting up a game of cornhole for Wyatt and Chloe.

It made him miss his family, his parents and sister Mara. He promised himself he'd visit them soon.

Maybe, if the future played out the way he prayed it would, he'd bring Nina along for the visit.

Nina came out of the front door carrying a pitcher of lemonade. Her face lit up brighter than sunshine after a storm. "Mateo!"

She hurried down the steps and placed the beverage on the table before rushing over to him. Clasping his hand in hers, she beamed at him. "I'm so glad you decided to join us. I wasn't sure if you would."

"I thought your family would like an update on Conrad." His gaze darted around. Her entire family seemed to have stopped what they were doing and were watching the two of them with curious smiles on their faces.

Nina arched a brow at him. "I hope that's not the only reason you stopped by."

It wasn't. He had missed her. In the last twenty-four hours, while he had wrapped up this case and she had gone back to her family, he'd realized he couldn't live without her. Absolutely did not want to even try.

With her loving family nosily looking on, he decided this was not the ideal time to pour out his heart to her. That could come later.

"Do you have an update on Hector?" Nina asked.

He wasn't surprised that she would want to know. After their rescue yesterday, emergency services had been dispatched to Hector Gomez's house and care had been rendered. "He spent the night in the hospital, but should be able to go home today. His son is coming to stay with him for a few days to be sure he's doing okay."

Nina's tension visibly eased at the news.

"Mateo, so nice to see you." Julia walked up to him and pulled him into a hug. "We're so happy you could make it."

"Thank you for inviting me."

Julia's eyes sparkled. "Of course. After all you've done for us, not just with Nina, but Eric and Seth as well, you're practically family."

The sentiment caused a lump to form in his throat. Family. He realized now how much he had longed for family. Not just his parents and sister, but a family to spend each day with, to call his own.

"Mom—" Nina placed a hand on her arm, a clear distraction technique "—is there anything else in the house you'd like me to get?"

Julia shook her head as Cassie and Holly approached. "Not yet, but I do believe that we would all like an update. Mateo, do you have any news for us?"

"I do."

Seth quickly got the kids settled in with their game, then the adults gathered on the deck where James could keep watch of the grill.

All eyes were on Mateo.

"We've done a little digging into Conrad Greene's past. Seems he has a problem with anger management. He's had a hard time keeping a job over the years. After interviewing him, he blames his troubles on just about everyone and everything other than himself." Ma-

teo's eyes met Nina's. "It seems he felt he was
entitled to the items he stole, high-value goods."

"That scoundrel." Julia scowled. "Stealing
from the elderly."

"*Murdering* the elderly," Holly added.

Mateo held up his hand. "He claims he didn't
kill Gloria. He's backtracking on admitting to
shoving Chester, but we have surveillance video
proving he was there that night. We'll be able
to build a good case. We're getting more information by the day."

"That's why he went after Nina." Cassie eyed
the baby monitor that rested on the deck rail-
ing. One of the twins whimpered then hushed
again. "He knew she may be able to connect
the items she found to the people they were
stolen from. And from there, he was justifiably
concerned the suspicious deaths would come
to light."

"Did he tell you why he buried the box in
the park of all places?" Nina asked.

"No, but I interviewed his sister and she
gave me some valuable insight. The two aren't
close, according to her, but she does try to stay
in touch with him. She visited Conrad a few
weeks ago and accidentally came across his stash
of goods. When she questioned him on them,

he claimed he'd purchased everything. Said he'd started visiting flea markets and pawn shops and was hoping to make a profit on the goods."

Mateo shook his head. "She didn't believe him, but had no way to prove it. Regardless, she believes he buried them in the park to keep them from her. Said he wouldn't have gotten a safe-deposit box because banks have security cameras. He rents a trailer house and doesn't have any property of his own. Her hunch is that he was going to continue acquiring the valuables for as long as he could. Probably until he lost his current job. Then he'd take off for somewhere far from here and cash everything in."

"Far away where no one would be looking for it," Cassie said.

"Conrad's been pretty tight-lipped, but I have to say her hunch sounds pretty solid to me." Mateo met Nina's gaze for a moment. "His sister said he has a habit of jumping from one job to another. Taking off long stretches of time in between. Months. One time, more than a year. He's worked in nursing homes on and off for a decade."

He saw Cassie's eyes widen and knew her private investigator brain had kicked in. "The elderly are easy targets, sadly. Do you think this is a pattern? Are you going to look into his past employers? See if there are any other suspicious deaths? Or signs of theft?"

"Yes to all of the above." Mateo nodded gravely. "We do have reason to believe this is a pattern. The theft at least. Whether there are other suspicious deaths…well, we'll look into that, too."

"What happens now?" James asked.

"Now, at a minimum, he's being charged with theft and attempted murder." Mateo's voice hardened as he thought of how the man had almost killed Nina, and him, when he'd blown up her house. "Once the investigation into the other two deaths is wrapped up, we'll know if we can add two more charges."

Truth be told, he thought by the time this was over, the charges against Conrad Greene might be as long as the man's arm. They had obtained the surveillance video from Golden Acres. While the cameras hadn't picked up Conrad bribing Coco with food, they were able to verify that he'd been working there that day.

"Regardless," Holly said, "he'll be locked up. Hopefully, for a very long time."

"We all thank you," Eric said, "for a job well

done. It couldn't have been easy watching out for this rug rat—" he reached over and ruffled Nina's hair "—but you did good."

She laughed and ducked out from under him, effectively lightening the mood after such a grim discussion.

A wail burst through the baby monitor.

Eric winced then spun, calling over his shoulder. "I better get her before she wakes her brother. I'll be right back." He disappeared into the house.

"The burgers will be done soon," Julia said. "Ladies, should we grab the food?"

The trio of women followed Julia into the house. A moment later, they traipsed out carrying bowls and platters to the side-by-side picnic tables.

Mateo found himself alone with Nina's father.

He pulled in a breath, stealing himself. He'd wanted this exact opportunity, a moment alone with James, but now that he had it, he was as nervous as a teenager.

"Mr. Montgomery?"

The man turned to him. "Something on your mind, Mateo?"

"Yes, sir."

James's brow arched. "Sir? I think we're on a first-name basis after all of this. Call me James."

Mateo nodded. "I will. I have a question for you."

Nina's father placed the metal spatula on the side of the grill and turned his attention to Mateo. "Ask away."

"I really admire your daughter. She's smart, funny, empathetic, and so full of enthusiasm for life."

James chuckled. "I think you nailed that description."

"I would like your permission to date her."

"I was hoping you were going to ask that." James grinned. "Considering how starry-eyed you make her, I wouldn't dare tell you no." His grin faded. "In all seriousness, I admire you, Mateo. You have a tough job and you do it well. You took good care of my girl. I've known you for over a year now. I think you're one of the most genuine, trustworthy men I know. I can't think of anyone I'd rather see my daughter with. It would be a blessing to see you two together. Hopefully, for the long haul."

James's words were so heartfelt, so firmly spoken, that Mateo felt the weight of them down to his marrow.

"Your blessing means a lot to me." He cleared his throat and forced a smile. "Hopefully, Nina shares your sentiment."

"Only one way to find out." James nodded toward the yard where Nina was chasing after Chloe and Wyatt. "Go talk to her. I think now's as good a time as any."

"I'll do that. Thank you, James."

"Pleasure's all mine."

Mateo descended the steps, his eyes on Nina as she caught Chloe, pulled the beanbag from her hand and began tickling her. Wyatt crashed into them and beanbags went flying as the trio laughed uproariously.

"Mateo, wait up!"

He pivoted as Cassie hustled to catch up to him. She wore a wry smile. "Have a minute?"

A quick glance at Nina confirmed she was still busy with her niece and nephew. It wouldn't hurt anything to wait a while longer before talking to her. "Sure. What's up? Have a case you want to consult on?"

It wasn't an unreasonable guess. He and Cassie had bounced ideas and information off each other in the past.

"Not exactly." Cassie's smile slipped and she was all business now. "You know, Detective, I heard a rumor that you might be in the market for a new job."

He narrowed his eyes at her. "Maybe. What of it?"

"I happen to have an offer for you." Cassie grew serious. "Ever since I helped Eric with the case involving Wyatt's mom, I've been getting more cases thrown my way than I can handle. I have emails coming in daily. You know my specialty is reuniting family members."

He nodded. He knew Cassie had become a private investigator after a long search had led to her birth mother. She had wanted to help others who were in similar situations reunite with long-lost relatives. She was very good at her job.

"Some of the other stuff—" she wrinkled her nose "—I'm not really interested in. I've had some inquiries about cold cases, tracking down swindling business partners, and there's always requests to catch cheating spouses. You get the idea."

"Right." He knew Cassie liked the feel-good cases. And she had every right to pick and choose the cases she was willing to dive into. "That heavier stuff is not really your thing."

"No." She looked at him hopefully. "But I'm thinking it might be yours. Now that we have the twins, I want to cut my workload down, but the requests are coming in faster than ever before. Have you thought of becoming a private investigator? You could choose the cases you're interested in, set your own hours. You can work as much or as little as you choose, but, trust me, I have plenty of potential clients that could keep us both busy."

Set his own hours? Choose how heavy his workload would be? Decide whose case he'd like to dive into?

He had become a detective because he'd felt it was his calling to help people. But after more than a decade in law enforcement, he was ready for something new. There were other ways to help people. Cassie was proof of that.

Mateo leaned toward her. "I'm interested. Tell me more."

Nina watched Mateo and Cassie from a distance. Curiosity nipped at her, but she wanted to respect their privacy. Maybe Cassie was asking Mateo for help on one of her cases. She knew they consulted with each other on occasion. She also knew Cassie had her hands full with work right now. Her sister-in-law had commented that the requests were piling up and she couldn't keep up with them all. While she was proud of Cassie for building such a successful business, Nina knew it stressed her out to not be able to help everyone.

She took the cover off the potato salad as her mother came out of the house with a platter of buns.

Her dad took that as his cue and started piling burgers onto plates.

Mateo and Cassie wrapped up their conversation when Eric came out of the house with Ethan in his arms. Matilda must still be sleeping, though Nina doubted the parents would get a reprieve for long.

She saw Mateo glance at the child in Eric's arms, his face lighting in a smile. Nina had wondered if it would be hard for him to be around the twins, but judging by the look on his face, the baby brought him joy.

Once he helped James carry the platters of burgers to the table, they all sat.

After James said grace, the table filled with lively conversation. Nina enjoyed watching Mateo interact with everyone she loved the most. Yet she was anxious to have him all too herself.

When the meal was over, everyone began to help with clearing the picnic tables.

Her mother pulled her aside. "You've had a tough week. Why don't you and Mateo take a walk?"

Nina was about to protest because it was the polite thing to do. Before she could, Julia gave her a wink and a nudge.

"Go."

Nina didn't need to be told a third time. While her family moved around, she sidled up to Mateo as he was about to grab the empty burger platter. She reached for his hand, lacing her fingers with his.

He gave her a startled look.

"Let's go for a walk."

"The tables aren't cleared," he said. "Shouldn't we—"

"*Go*," Julia said as she walked past them.

"Don't want to argue with my momma, now, do you?" Nina grinned at him.

He grinned back and shook his head. "I sure don't."

She led him toward the trail in the woods. It seemed the obvious place to head because she didn't want to stand in the yard with her family gawking at them. As it was, Nina was sure she could feel their curious gazes burning into their backs. No way was she going to look over her shoulder to find out.

"I hope my big noisy family isn't too much for you."

He smiled and shook his head as they reached the path. "After the week we've had, I think your big noisy family is just what I need."

"Water balloon fight!" Wyatt yelled, his voice carrying through the trees.

Chloe let out a shriek of laughter then Seth yelled, "Run! Run as fast as you can!"

Mateo chuckled. "Sounds like we got out of there just in time." His expression turned wistful. "I miss that. Kids' laughter. There's just something so special about it."

"Yeah, there is." Nina gave his hand a squeeze. She hoped one day he would share stories of his boys with her, but thought maybe it was too soon for that. In time, though, she prayed she and Mateo would have the sort of relationship where they shared everything.

They walked in silence for a while. She stopped once they were halfway down the trail that led between her parents' home and Eric's. The thick foliage kept them from prying eyes. Right now, Nina wanted Mateo all to herself.

It was time they had the talk she'd promised herself they would have if they survived.

God had given them another chance at life. Nina was going to embrace every single day.

Mateo chuckled as he glanced around. "I'm pretty sure this is the exact spot I caught up to you the night you crept out of the house. I still can't believe you were going to take off without telling me."

"Honestly, I'm so glad you caught me," Nina said. "The past week has been such a whirlwind. I'm so grateful I had you by my side. You protected me, took care of me, and trusted me to be a part of the investigation."

"I don't know that I could've stopped you."

She laughed at that. "True." Then she grew serious. "I was going to say something to you while the SUV was going under."

"I remember." He shot her a curious look but said nothing more.

"I love you." Her words were matter-of-fact. "There. I said it. You can't make me take it back."

He chuckled. "Do you really think I'd make you take it back?"

"I thought you might. Or I thought you would remind me again that we're too different.

That you're told old. Maybe tell me one more time that you've become too jaded because of your job." She narrowed her eyes at him. "So, are you going to tell me any of those things?"

"Nope." His eyes sparkled and he flashed her a heart-stopping grin. "I've had a lot of time to think about how wrong I was."

Had he actually admitted he was wrong? Wrong about why they couldn't have a relationship? Her heart leapt with hope and her eyebrows shot up in surprise.

"You see, you've been good for me. You reminded me that I have a lot of life left. I don't need to be a grumpy workaholic. You've reawakened my faith, and I believe that God led you to me, maybe for that exact reason."

Nina felt tears prickle at the backs of her eyes. She blinked hard to hold them at bay.

"In such a short time, you've changed my life in the best way possible. You've made me want to be a better person. A happier person. For the first time in years, I want to open myself up to love again. Maybe," he spoke softly, "even have a family again someday."

"What exactly are you saying?" She wanted to be sure, completely positive, that they were on the same page.

"You need me to spell it out for you?"

She nodded. "Yes, I do."

"I love you, too, Nina."

"I was really hoping you would say that."

He cupped her face in his hands, looked into her eyes, her heart, her soul. With a seriousness that could leave no doubt, he made a promise. "I love you. Now. And forever."

He kissed her then. Not a searing kiss, but the sort of kiss that filled her heart to bursting. It shook her down to her soul, lifted her hopes and dreams to the heavens. She had never known a love so deep, so strong, so full of promise.

"You know what, Mateo?" Her voice was a breathy whisper, full of emotion, but sure. "You're going to marry me someday."

"You think so?" His tone held a gentle teasing.

"Maybe not anytime soon," she admitted.

He winked. "True. We have a lot of courting to do."

"Careful, you're sounding like an old man," she teased.

He looked serious. "Our age difference doesn't bother you?"

"Not at all. It's nine years, Mateo. That's nothing. Certainly not enough to keep me away from you."

"I'm glad to hear it. Because I do believe you are right, someday you'll be my wife."

"All in God's timing."

He smiled. "Yes, in God's timing."

Nina put all her faith, all of her trust, in that. The Lord had watched over her, brought Mateo to her, and gifted her with the love of her life. She would continue to trust in His perfect will.

Epilogue

Nina had grown up going to Mulberry Creek State Park. It was one of her favorite places. She was not about to let anyone, not let any experience, keep her from going there. In fact, she and Mateo had visited the park several times over the past year.

With Conrad Greene behind bars for the rest of his life, she had nothing to fear. He had been convicted of the murders of both Gloria Hanson and Chester Crenshaw. Though his past had been thoroughly investigated, no other suspicious deaths had come to light, while his thievery had proved to be ongoing for nearly a decade.

The items in the lockbox had been returned to their owners, including those that had been discovered after Conrad's arrest.

While her pictures would never hang on the wall of an art gallery, she found that she really

did love photography. She'd gotten much better over the past year. Mateo often accompanied
her, taking responsibility for Coco and her leash
so Nina's hands were free for photos.

She wasn't taking photos today, though.
Today they were there for a picnic. It had become one of their favorite weekend pastimes.
They both had stressful yet rewarding jobs.
Finding balance was crucial and their picnics
had become the perfect way to offset what had
often been a trying week.

Mateo had resigned from the Mulberry
Creek PD because he'd been looking for a fresh
start. He'd gone to work with Cassie, where he
found it satisfying to choose his own cases, set
his own hours. To date, he'd located a runaway
teen, tracked down a small-scale jewel thief, and
had helped Cassie with the footwork involved
in reuniting several adoptees with the biological
families they'd been searching for. Not to mention dozens of smaller cases that still provided
him with a sense of accomplishment.

Nina held Coco's leash while Mateo carried
the picnic basket. They reached their favorite
spot by the river. It was a beautiful, glorious
spring day. Nina had heard that the new eaglets

had hatched last week. Maybe later they'd wander that way to take a peek.

Mateo set the basket down then flipped the lid open. He pulled out the lightweight blanket that rested on top. He spread it and they had a place to sit.

Coco plunked down on the edge of the blanket. She had bonded with Mateo over the past year, too. He'd finally admitted to Nina that he thought there really was something to those special puppy powers of hers. He'd opened up to Nina about his boys, often while Coco was nestled halfway on his lap. Nina's heart had nearly broken listening to Mateo share the deepest depths of his grief. But now was the time to heal, to start anew, while never forgetting the love he'd had for his sons.

"Can you believe it's been over a year since the day Conrad chased us through the park?" Nina asked.

Mateo arched an eyebrow at her. "Hush now. We don't want to ruin today with thoughts of that man."

"Oh, I know." Nina took a seat on the blanket. "Yet, if not for him, if not for that day, you and I wouldn't be together right now. God truly does work all things together for good."

"That he does." Mateo sat beside Nina and, for just a moment, they enjoyed the gentle sound of the creek burbling and the leaves rustling. "This year has been one of the best of my life. You helped me turn from being a jaded detective to a man who looks forward to each and every day. You helped me to rediscover my faith. Because of you, I've been able to talk about my boys again, to remember them without feeling as if my heart is being torn from my chest."

Nina reached over and took his hand.

"I love you, Nina. I'm so blessed to have you—and Coco—in my life."

Nina's heart felt full to bursting. "I'm pretty sure I fell in love with you the moment you offered my starving dog your granola bar. I *liked* you before then. Admired you. Thought you were awfully nice to look at." She winked. "But when you gave Coco the only food you had…" She pressed her hand to her heart. "You won me over."

"With a granola bar."

"Yes."

He chuckled.

"It's more than that," she continued. "I love that you want to help others." Mateo had joined her church and, together, they spearheaded the TLC Program, a group of volunteers who helped members of their community with projects like lawn mowing, grocery shopping, and small repairs. Parents were encouraged to volunteer with their children, and Mateo's passion for this gave Nina a glimpse of the sort of father he'd been. Of the sort of father he would, hopefully, be again in the future. "Your kindness and compassion inspire me every day."

She loved this man so much she could hardly bear it.

"Will you marry me?" Nina blurted. "Because I simply don't think I can live without you. I don't want to live without you."

His eyes widened and he stared at her in surprise.

She was suddenly reminded of that long-ago day when Jimmy had held up his hand for a high-five and Mateo had nearly left him hanging. Only now she was the one left hanging, and her heart dipped as silence filled the air.

Then he chuckled.

Her brow furrowed. "That wasn't exactly the response I was hoping for."

Mateo's eyes sparkled and oh, how she loved to see him smile.

"Your exuberance is one of the things that drew me to you," he said. "Even if you are stealing my thunder, so to speak."

"Stealing your—"

She was unable to finish that thought because Mateo had reached into the picnic basket. Instead of pulling out a sandwich, as she was half expecting, he pulled out a small black-velvet box.

Her heart leapt and she bit her lip. It took a moment for her to tear her eyes from the box and look into Mateo's deep brown eyes again.

"Nina," he said, his tone a contradictory mix of seriousness and amusement, "I had this romantic day planned explicitly for the sake of asking you to be my wife." He opened the box and a breathtaking princess-cut solitaire rested inside. "Will you marry me?"

"Yes!" Tears of joy filled her eyes and she threw her arms around Mateo. "Nothing would make me happier."

Coco yipped her agreement, sensing their excitement and not caring what it was about, as long as her humans were happy.

He squeezed her and Nina melted into his arms, thanking the Lord that Mateo had come into her life.

"Want to try out the ring?" He whispered the words into her ear.

She laughed and pulled away from him. Mateo took the ring from the box and carefully slid it onto her finger. It was a perfect fit, thanks to some guidance from her sister-in-law Cassie, his work partner, who was the only person who knew what he'd planned for the day.

"It's beautiful," she said. "And I think our life together will be beautiful as well."

"How soon are we going to start this life together?"

Nina's hand grazed Coco's back. "We don't have to rush. If you think it would be better to take our time."

"I'm not getting any younger, you know."

She laughed over what had now become a private joke between them. "Then why wait?"

"I see no reason," Mateo said, "no reason at all. I cannot wait to stand before God, our families and our friends, and make you my wife."

He leaned over and kissed her then, a silent promise of their future.

★ ★ ★ ★ ★

A NOTE TO ALL READERS

From October releases Mills & Boon will be
making some changes to the series formats
and pricing.

What will be different about the series books?

In response to recent reader feedback, we are
increasing the size of our paperbacks to bigger
books with better quality paper, making for a better
reading experience.

What will be the new price of Mills & Boon?

Over the past four years we have seen significant
increases in the cost of producing our books. As a
result, in order to continue to provide customers
with a quality reading experience, the price of
our books will increase to RRP $10.99 for Modern
singles and RRP $19.99 for 2-in-1s from Medical,
Intrigue, Romantic Suspense, Historical
and Western.

For futher information regarding format
changes and pricing, please visit our website
millsandboon.com.au.

Romantic Suspense

Danger. Passion. Drama.

Available Next Month

Colton Undercover Jennifer D. Bokal
Second-Chance Bodyguard Patricia Sargeant

Cold Case Kidnapping Kimberly Van Meter
Escape To The Bayou Amber Leigh Williams

LOVE INSPIRED

Search And Detect Terri Reed
Sniffing Out Justice Carol J. Post

Larger Print

LOVE INSPIRED

Undercover Escape Valerie Hansen
Hunted For The Holidays Deena Alexander

Larger Print

LOVE INSPIRED

Witness Protection Ambush Jenna Night
A Lethal Truth Alexis Morgan

Larger Print

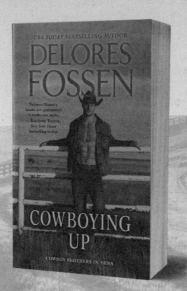

Keep reading for an excerpt of a new title
from the Inrigue series,
K-9 DEFENDER by Julie Miller

Prologue

Two Years Ago...

"You'll always be a stupid country girl!"

Mollie Di Salvo couldn't brace for the next blow when it came. She was still woozy from the hands that had squeezed around her neck until she'd nearly passed out and collapsed to the kitchen floor. She couldn't pull her legs up fast enough and curl into a ball. She swore she heard a rib snap when Augie kicked her in the stomach.

She'd always thought anger was a fiery emotion. But as she squinted through her swollen eyelid at the eyes of her husband, she knew that anger was ice-cold.

This was the worst beating yet.

All because she'd served her granny's biscuits at the dinner party with Augie's parents, the Brewers and Mr. Hess and his date. Delicious, yes. But poor folks and country bumpkins ate biscuits. Augie was embarrassed to see them on his table. Embarrassed that the investment bankers he worked with might think he was a poor country bumpkin, too, with no sense about handling their clients' money.

Embarrassed by her.

Was she trying to sabotage this business deal? A faux pas at this level on Kansas City's social registry could cost him and his company millions of dollars.

Or something like that. To be honest, once she'd drifted away from consciousness, she hadn't heard much of his tirade.

Now all she knew was pain.

Mollie's lungs burned and her throat throbbed as she fought to catch a deep breath. She watched as Augie knelt beside her and clasped her chin in a cruel grip, surely leaving bruises, forcing her to face him. "I'm going out." His spittle sprayed her cheek. "The staff has gone home for the night, so clean up this mess. And don't wait up for me."

She watched the polished black Italian oxfords on his feet, making sure that they were walking away from her and heading out the side door into the garage. She heard men's unintelligible voices, a car door slam, and then Augie's latest fancy sports car revving up and driving away.

Mollie pushed herself up to a sitting position and leaned back against the oven. Breathing in through her nose and out through her mouth, she mentally assessed her injuries. There'd be bruises and swelling, yes—maybe even a cracked rib. But she could survive without a trip to the ER, without telling lies to the doctor and nurses, without explaining why it wasn't safe for her to talk to the police. She just needed to catch a deep breath.

She reached beneath the neckline of her dress to clutch the engraved silver locket she always wore. To her it was more beautiful than the obnoxiously large sapphire and diamond ring on her left hand. The wedding and engagement rings were all about Augie and showing off that he was wealthy and generous. But her locket was the real prize. It had been a gift from Granny. The one link left to her past when she'd been happy and the world was full of possibilities. She'd been so naive.

She had no more illusions of love. Her Cinderella story had ended just over a year ago, only five months into her marriage. The first slap that Thanksgiving night after an endless extravaganza at his parents' estate with his entire family and many of their important friends still rang through her memory. She was an introvert by nature, and the days of prepping and late-into-the-night dining, drinking, and partying had left her physically and emotionally exhausted. When they got home, Augie wanted to celebrate their successful evening. He informed her he was horny and ready for sex. She'd kissed him, explained how tired she was and promised that, after a little rest, she'd give him a very good morning.

He'd slapped her, the move so sudden she would have thought she'd imagined it if not for the heat rapidly replacing the shocked nerves on her cheek. No one said no to August Di Salvo, especially not his low-class hick of a wife. She should be grateful for every little thing he did for her. Augie took the sex he wanted that night, and Mollie knew her dream life had irrevocably changed into a nightmare.

Between the family attorney and his parents' influence, her report to the police the next day had mysteriously disappeared. And the one after that had been pleaded down to a public disturbance and dismissed with a fine.

So, she'd stopped calling the police. She stopped sharing a bedroom with her husband. And she stopped feeling hope.

Now, thankfully, Augie got most of his sex from the string of affairs he had. But Mollie didn't care that he was cheating on her.

She didn't have emotions anymore.

She drew in another painful breath. That wasn't exactly true.

She had fear.

Fear was her constant companion. If Augie wasn't with her, then she knew one of his friends or beefy bodyguards or even someone from the office or their home staff was watching her. The beautiful trophy wife who straightened her hair and dyed it blond because her husband didn't think her natural dark curls looked sophisticated. Who wore heels that pinched her feet because he thought they made her look sexy. Who'd married a man because she'd believed the Di Salvo family taking her in, and Augie supporting her through the worst time of her life, meant they loved her.

How could a smart woman be so foolish? Her loneliness and despair had led to some disastrous choices.

Her granny must be turning over in her grave to see how frightened and abused she had become. She'd grown up without parents, thanks to a rainy-night highway accident when she was four. But she'd been raised with love and enough food to eat, and she'd been taught a solid work ethic and some old-fashioned common sense by her grandmother, Lucy Belle Crane. She was the girl who'd overcome the poor circumstances of her Ozarks upbringing to earn scholarships and work her way through college at the University of Missouri. She had a degree in math education, a year in the classroom under her belt, and a semester's worth of classes toward her Master's degree.

Yet here she was, huddled on the kitchen floor of August Di Salvo's big, beautiful house, afraid to stand her ground with Augie, afraid to call the police, afraid to ask anyone for help, afraid to pursue a teaching job or further her education, afraid to leave, afraid to stay. Afraid. Afraid. Afraid.

Feeling an imagined warmth radiating from the locket in her hand, she pressed a kiss to the silver oval and dropped it inside the front of her dress. Then she braced one hand on the oven behind her and reached up to grasp the granite countertop on the island across from her.

The door to the garage swung open. Mollie gasped in fear and plopped down on her butt. The movement jarred her sore ribs, and she grabbed her side, biting down on a moan of pain and bracing herself for another round of degrading words and hard blows from her husband.

Only, she didn't recognize the man in the black uniform suit and tie who wandered into the kitchen, surveyed the entire area, then rushed to her side when he saw her on the cold tile floor.

He reached for her with a big, scarred hand. "Let me help you."

"No, I…" But he was already pulling her to

her feet. He wound a sturdy arm around her waist and led her around the island, where he pulled out a stool and helped her to sit.

"Looks like you took a pretty good blow to the head." His gaze darted to the placement of her hand above her waist. "Did you hit your side, too? Do you want me to call 9-1-1? Or I could drive you to the hospital myself."

"No. I'll be fine. I'm just—" the well-rehearsed word tasted like bile on her tongue "—clumsy."

She smiled until she saw his gaze linger on the marks she knew would be visible on her neck. "You didn't fall."

The man was too observant for his own good. The others had been trained to look the other way. Mollie realized she was still holding on to his hand, where it rested on the countertop. She popped her grip open and turned away to pull her long golden hair off her cheek and tuck it behind her ear. "You're new here."

Although he frowned at the cool wall of diversion and denial she was erecting between them, he thankfully retreated a step to give her the distance she needed to pull herself together. "I'm Mr. Di Salvo's new driver. He took the convertible out himself, said he didn't need me tonight. But I'm on shift until midnight. It's kind of chilly just sitting out in the garage waiting to work. I was told I could come into the house to get some hot coffee."

"Of course. Everything you need is right here. Regular, decaf. Cream, sugar." Moving slowly, but with a sense of purpose, she climbed off the stool and showed him the coffee bar tucked in beside the refrigerator at the end of the row of cabinets. Ever the consummate hostess, she opened the cabinet above the coffee makers, but winced when she reached for the mug above her.

He was at her side in an instant, grasping the mug and pulling it down for her. "Ma'am, you don't have to wait on me. Can I at least make you an ice pack for that eye? I do have first aid training."

Ignoring his concern, or perhaps taking advantage of it by continuing this conversation at all, she asked for the smallest of favors. "Would you pull down another mug for me?"

"Sure."

When he set the mug in front of her, she poured herself some decaf coffee and cradled its heat between her trembling hands. She scooted off to the side, leaning lightly against the counter. "Please. Help yourself."

"Thanks." He poured himself a mug, fully loaded with a shot of cream.

While he fixed his drink and took a couple of sips, Mollie felt curious enough to make note of his looks. He wasn't as tall as or movie star handsome as Augie, but then, *tall*, *dark*, *and handsome* wasn't necessarily attractive in her opinion. Not anymore.

Her would-be rescuer had brown hair and golden-brown eyes that made her think of a tiger. Despite the breadth of his shoulders beneath his black suit jacket, and the unflattering buzz cut of hair that emphasized the sharp angles of his face, the man had kind eyes. Kindness was such a rarity in her small world that the softness of his amber eyes woke a desire in her that she hadn't felt for a long time now. The desire to step outside herself and do something for someone else—the way she might once have helped a friend in need—the way no one had helped her for more than a year now. "Let me give you some advice, Mr...?"

"Uh, Rostovich." Had he hesitated to share his name? "Joel Rostovich."

"Listen, Joel Rostovich. Get out. Get out of this house. Leave your job. Get away from this family as fast as you can."

He set down his coffee at her dismissal. "You need an ice pack or a raw steak for that eye. If you won't let me drive you to the ER or a police station, at least let me make sure you get to your room safely, and I'll bring you an ibuprofen." He started to pull out a business card. "If you change your mind, you can call—"

"And if you won't get out, then stay away from me. Don't talk to me unless you have orders to. Don't smile. And sure as hell, don't you be nice to me again." She tucked the card into the pocket of his jacket and rested her hand against his chest in a silent thanks for his humanity and compassion. Then she turned and slowly made her way out of the kitchen. "It'll be safer for you that way."

Subscribe and fall in love with a Mills & Boon series today!

You'll be among the first to read stories delivered to your door monthly and enjoy great savings.

WE SIMPLY LOVE ROMANCE